LOVERBOY

LOVERBOY

THE COMPANY #2

SARINA BOWEN

TUXBURY PUBLISHING LLC

1

GUNNAR

"EXCUSE ME, sir. I'm here to pick you up."

I squint at the blond kid who's approached me near the baggage carousel. He's holding one of those signs that drivers use to help their passengers identify them. Instead of my name, the sign bears a silhouette of a skeleton key, and nothing else.

That's The Company logo. And as further proof of his identity, the blond kid tugs aside the V-neck of his T-shirt to show me that he wears the same key inked on his skin.

I have one, too. In fact, I was the second person to ever get the team tattoo, just moments after Max Bayer—my college roommate and now boss—got his.

Even so, I won't get into a car with anyone unless I am certain the situation is legit. I've spent the past four years running our West Coast operation, so there are a bunch of New York-based agents I've never met.

But when I glance at my watch, there's a new text from Max: *I sent a kid to pick your grumpy ass up. The name is Duff. You're welcome.*

"What's your name, kid?" I grunt.

"Duff, sir." He takes the handle of my suitcase right out of my hand. "Shall we go?"

"Thanks, Duff. What's your specialty?" I ask, because everyone in The Company has a specialty.

1

"Precision driving and high-speed ops."

"Sweet," I say as we head for the doors. "Maybe you can take me for a spin on the track before I head back to San Jose."

"It would be my pleasure," he says, holding the door. "How was your flight?"

"Fine. First class makes things bearable." Although I'm not sure why I'm here. Max called me to New York for a short-term assignment, but he didn't provide details. All he'd said was: *it has to be you.*

Now, I like field work as much as the next guy. It keeps me sharp. But the lack of detail from Max is troublesome. And now he's sent an obsequious man-child to carry my luggage and drive me around? There's only one logical explanation.

This assignment must be horrific.

"I'm parked right over here," Duff says, rolling my suitcase toward a gleaming sedan. "Make yourself comfortable. If you're hungry, I've brought a meatball sub from 'Wichcraft and a glass of fresh squeezed orange juice."

My grip freezes on the handle of the passenger door. "You brought me my favorite sandwich?"

"Yessir."

"Jesus fucking Christ."

"Is there a problem?" The kid looks alarmed.

"Absolutely. You *know* Max, right?"

"Of course I do."

"Right. So he took the time to send you in search of my favorite sandwich and my favorite beverage? Does he do that for everyone he asks to take an assignment?"

"Uh, I'm still kinda new here," Duff says carefully.

"The answer is no. He doesn't do that. Exactly what am I walking into, young Duff?"

He gets into the car, then hands me the bag from the deli without meeting my eyes.

I buckle in, and the radio comes on when he starts the car. The first thing I hear is the windbag of a mayor giving a press conference. *Lovely.* I hit the power button on the stereo and settle the car into silence. Then I open the deli bag.

Even if I have my suspicions, I'm not willing to let a perfectly good sandwich go to waste. So I take the first bite as he navigates to the Triboro Bridge. "God, this is good. Do you know what it is?"

"The sandwich?" Duff asks, eyes on the road.

"No, the assignment."

The kid looks uncomfortable. "I'm not at liberty to say."

"Oh fuck. Come on, kid. You're going to make me walk in there cold? Let me know what I'm up against."

"He made me promise I wouldn't tell. You wouldn't want to get me fired, would you? I have student loans."

"Likely story," I grumble. "This better not involve crawling through a drainpipe. I have done that kind of *Shawshank Redemption* thing once for Max and never again."

Duff visibly shudders. "It's nothing like that."

"Will I need a wetsuit? Or hazmat gear?"

"No! But that's the last question I'm answering."

I stew on that as we reach the FDR. "This juice is really good, damn it. But if you let it slip that Max squeezed the oranges himself, I will have to dive out of this moving vehicle just to save myself."

Duff barks out a laugh. "Keep your seatbelt on. The juice is from the deli. You're making a BFD for nothing. It's a cushy assignment."

"Likely story." Why would Max insist I fly to New York to take a cushy assignment? Like I'm not busy enough making both of us rich in California? And he knows I hate New York. "You'd better not be lying, kid. Do you know what my specialty is?"

"No?"

"Information extraction."

"Seriously?"

"You are new, aren't you? I'm just fucking with you. My specialty is covert ops and surveillance equipment. You still don't want to fuck with me. I could rig your toilet paper roll to blast your farts over a sound system in Times Square."

He laughs again. "I've been warned."

"How is Max, anyway? I haven't seen him in a few months."

"Intense," is the first word out of the kid's mouth.

Eh. That doesn't tell me much, because Max is always intense. "How's the vibe around the office?"

The kid is quiet for a moment. "My great-grandfather used to tell me stories about what England was like during World War II. And it's like that. Everyone is hunkered down, trying to get by with too few personnel. We're rationing our time off."

"I see." It's not a bad analogy. The Company is at war in a manner of speaking. Our high-tech clients are all locked in battle with a common, invisible enemy. A ring of shady tech manufacturers has been trying to infiltrate Silicon Valley. Max is trying to shut it down on behalf of our clients, and also on behalf of civilization.

"Morale is pretty good even so," Duff adds. "Because we're on top of our game, and our clients are happy to have us. It's not a thankless job, you know?"

"I do know that, kid. I absolutely know."

o—🔑

Fifteen minutes later I'm handing my driver's license across the reception desk at The Company. The young woman on duty glances at my ID. "Welcome back to the New York office, Mr. Scott! Your security clearance is still active, even though it's been a while."

"Seven months," I mutter. I hate New York. It reminds me too much of being a young, stupid kid. So I don't come to town very often.

"Max is waiting for you in his apartment."

"Where nobody can hear me scream? Awesome." She and Duff both laugh, but I'm not really kidding. I press my hand to the sensor on the turnstile that allows me to pass through to the elevators. And then I do the same on a panel that summons the only elevator with access to Max's living space on the penthouse floor. "Thanks for the food and the juice, Duff," I say as I step inside the car.

"Anytime."

The elevator begins its smooth ascent toward the private living quarters of Max Bayer. His father started this company many years ago as an ordinary security firm. Meanwhile, Max and I graduated from Columbia together and then went off to D.C. to become top ranking intelligence officers together.

It worked. Mostly. But after some years went by, we both wanted out, for different reasons. Max left because an operation he was running went sour. Lives were lost, including someone very special to Max. He felt a lot of guilt. Not that he ever talks about it. Max is a vault.

But after he left, the place wasn't the same. I was tired of risking my life for a bureaucracy that didn't seem to care about me. Nothing can make a guy jaded faster than upholding dubious government secrets.

"Join me," Max had said at the time. "I'm going to reinvent private security for the internet age."

It was a lofty statement, but that's Max for you. Besides, he has a way of delivering on his lofty statements. And although I'm not half the genius Max is, I was one of about three people in the world he actually trusted. So—in spite of the New York location—it was an easy decision.

Now, as I let myself into Max's magnificent lair, I have to wonder what I've gotten myself into. There's a decanter of single malt sitting on the table. There's a glass waiting for me, too, with one of those giant ice cubes—the kind that melt slowly, preserving the hundred-dollar shot of whiskey you pour over it.

"What's the occasion?" I ask. "Thanks for the ride and the sand-wich. But you can imagine that I'm deeply suspicious." I look around the vast room, trying to spot him.

My eyes come to rest on a pair of Max-shaped legs. That's all I can see of him. They're standing on an upholstered chair that prob-ably cost the GDP of a small nation. The rest of him is inside a large air-conditioning unit that's mounted through the old brick wall of his converted factory building.

"Moment," he says.

I wait.

There's a small *bang*. Like the sound of a .22 firing. In the company of another man, that might be alarming. But Max calmly steps down a moment later, removes a pair of headphones and begins to disassemble a Ruger rifle and return it to its case. "Hey, Gunn. Great to see you."

"What were you doing with that thing? Capping pigeons?"

"Nah, I don't mind pigeons. But I do mind that the City of New

York has decided to install a surveillance camera on my corner. That's not good for business."

"So you just—" I make a finger rifle and pop him one.

"It's very efficient," he says, carrying the gun to a safe on the wall and locking it away.

"You don't think you'll get caught?"

"Nah. The butt of the rifle is too small to see in the air conditioner grate. I checked the view first with a drone."

Of course he did.

"Great to see you, man. Let's drink scotch."

"What's it gonna cost me? When you start spoiling me, I get nervous."

He frowns. "What do you mean?"

"You invited your brother Eric over for tacos. Then you shipped his ass to Hawaii. Now he has a baby and he's engaged to be married."

Max scratches his chin. "We're not having tacos. You've got nothing to fear." He picks up the decanter and uncaps it. "The job I have planned for you is a piece of cake. In fact, there are literally cakes involved."

"Hmm," I say, because that does sound better than crawling through a sewage tunnel. But I'm too smart to feel any relief. "Get to the point."

"First let me catch you up on a few developments. Xian Smith is in New York."

"Interesting." We've been trying to prove that Smith is manufacturing compromised processors in Asia for placement into American devices. It's not easy to stay ahead of the cyber security war. Max is one of the few industry leaders who's realized that hardware is the new frontier of cybercrime. Instead of hacking into networks, Xian Smith is taking a different tack: hack the modem before it's out of the box.

It could work, too. Americans love their electronics, and they love to buy them cheaply. Most of our gadgets are manufactured overseas. Smith and his cohort—we still need to know who he's working with—are underbidding honest manufacturers of smart speakers, modems, and servers. Smith sells the cheap components at a loss, and then slightly reengineers them, inserting spy chips to activate later.

Max works day and night to keep our clients' products clean. But it isn't easy, because the smorgasbord of "smart" devices keeps expanding. The people crave their phones, their smart thermostats, and their smart speakers.

If Max and I don't shut down this ring of savvy information pirates, millions of devices will be used to spy on unsuspecting users. Whoever controls the spy chips can reap our secrets and sell them off to the highest bidder. Blackmail. Industrial espionage. Military secrets. If your toaster or your cable modem is spying on you, nothing is safe.

"Smith has been here in town for three weeks already, with no signs of leaving," Max adds.

"That's a long stay for him. There's more business in California. He hasn't tried to strike a new deal with our friend Alex, right?"

Max shakes his head. "But only because Alex is using our tech to scan each motherboard for design flaws or changes. She put him on notice."

"Which means we still don't have the proof we need." I lift my glass of scotch, and inhale the nutty, caramel scent of it.

"Not yet," Max admits. "Alex's products are safe. But Smith has many other clients, any one of whom might be installing his compromised hardware. So I'm picking my way through his client list."

"And how are you doing that?"

"Tireless surveillance. And guess what? I've just picked up a new client. He manufactures motherboards designed for onboard car navigation systems. And some of them are compromised."

"Damn," I say slowly. "Car companies outsource their dashboard technology. And people don't watch what they say in the car. If you had access to that ..."

"Exactly. And guess who made these faulty motherboards? Mr. Smith."

"Fine. Well done. But how does that involve me?" I sip the scotch slowly because I need to stay sharp. Last time I let him get me drunk, I lost five grand at backgammon.

"So—on the one hand—we have Smith in town for an unusual

stretch of time. That's strange enough. But simultaneously there's some really interesting chatter happening in a dark web hacker forum. Did you read about those three hackers who were poisoned?"

"Of course I did. I've never been so grossed out by a news story about hackers." I have to fight off a shudder just thinking about it. Three men on two continents have been killed with a toxin resembling nerve gas. They died sitting at their desks—or writhing on the floor beside their desk chairs.

"Someone has been bragging about those murders. He calls himself The Plumber, and he keeps dropping details that aren't available in the news." Max eyes me over the rim of his scotch glass. "And here's the part that's going to make you think I'm crazy."

"Am I? Try me."

"The Plumber is here in New York, and Xian Smith is here in New York."

"Could be a coincidence," I point out. New York is a big city.

"I'm not done. The third part of this coincidence is that a certain arms dealer has left Turkey. One of our old friends from Langley told me that they think *he's* in New York."

"*Oh.*" I set down my glass. "And I take it you don't mean just *any* arms dealer from Turkey?"

Slowly, he shakes his head.

"Well, shit." We sit in silence a moment while I take this in. I can only name one man on the planet that Max wants to kill. There's an arms dealer known as Aga who murdered some of the members of Max's team.

Including the woman Max thought he'd spend his life with.

"I think Aga is in New York," Max says quietly. "And I think he's given up shoulder-launched missiles in favor of cybercrime."

"Max! What the—?"

"I *know* it's a big leap. I know, okay? You don't have to tell me. But whomever is talking about those killings says that they all died with a red ribbon in their hands. The newspapers don't have that detail."

For a moment I just stare at him. "I'll admit that's creepy. But there are a lot of ribbons in the world. It might be a coincidence. Or a copycat. Those hackers who died were in three different countries."

"I know." He sips his whiskey. "But the chatter is all coming from a New York source. The Plumber posts this stuff from three different places in lower Manhattan."

"Wait, what?" This story is getting weirder by the minute. "Who posts sensitive crap in dark web groups and leaves a *trail?*"

"I've been asking myself that same question. Maybe it's a competitor who wants to expose him. Or maybe someone is scared. The Plumber moves around. He does his posting on public Wi-Fi in busy coffee shops. He wants people to know what the murderer is doing, without exposing himself. And I need you to find him for me."

"Ah," I say, because at last we've arrived at my part of this bargain. "You want me to find The Plumber, so you and he can have a little chat."

"Bingo." Max sips his scotch.

"Okay. Sure. I'll look for your informant. But I don't know what you're going to do if you find him."

"Just talk," Max says. "So long as he's willing."

Yikes. "Be careful, Max. Make sure you're in the right frame of mind here. I know Aga is important to you. But you're pretty important to the rest of us. So I need you to take care."

He tilts his head to the side and studies me. "Thank you, Gunn. I appreciate it. I know you think I'm tilting at windmills. But I need to explore this."

"Sure. Where should I start?"

"You'll begin tomorrow morning at about nine-thirty, after the morning coffee rush has passed."

"So I can get a table at one of the establishments your sloppy hacker likes?"

"Not quite." He slides a photo toward me on the coffee table. It's a storefront called Posy's Pie Shop.

My spine tingles. "Interesting name." There must be a lot of women in New York named Posy, though. Thousands, probably.

"Isn't it? Note the *Help Wanted* sign in the window. They pay fifteen bucks an hour. They're desperate for a barista."

I let out a bark of laughter. "You can't be serious! I don't even drink coffee. They'll never hire me."

"Think about how easy it will be to watch the customers from behind the counter, Gunn. You'll have an excuse to stare at everyone who comes through the door. The hacker posts half his stuff from this one location."

"They'll never hire me! And it's shitty to take a job for two weeks and then bail."

He shrugs. "She'll find someone else."

"She?" My spine tingles again. *Posy's*. It's probably just a coincidence.

Max reaches into the folder and passes me another photograph of a beautiful woman. She's handing a plate across the counter to a customer. And smiling. That smile always made me stupid. I wanted her so badly.

But all I got was a single kiss. And then a whole lot of trouble.

I let out a groan and toss the picture back to Max. "No. You can't be serious."

He puts the photo away. Then he just sits back and watches me.

"You really think I'm going to apply for a job at *her* bakery? That's stupid."

Max waits.

"I can't do that. She hates me. And given the way things ended, the feeling is mutual."

Max sips his scotch.

"She does *not* want to see my ugly mug every day. And she does not need an incompetent barista. I mean—I'm sure I could figure out how to make coffee. How hard could it be? But that's not the point. I don't need to stand around in a bakery for hours on end just to follow up on this stupid lead you're getting from some dark web forum. Even if the perp knows too much about …" I swallow. "A string of murders." Grizzly, horrible murders.

A violent criminal is using Posy Paxton's shop to boast about killing people? *Shit*. Posy isn't equipped for that. She's about as fierce as a kitten.

I let out a sigh of resignation.

Max watches me take all this in. "I knew you'd see it my way. You cared for this girl."

"Did not," I lie. "Fine. What if I did? I was young and stupid."

It was fifteen years ago, for God's sake. I worked at Paxton's—

her family's swanky uptown restaurant—as a bartender. Posy turned up the summer before my senior year of college. It was the first time in my life I ever felt lightning-struck by a girl. She had bright, intelligent eyes. And her quick smile did unexpected things to my body. Every time she walked into the room, my heart rate sped up, and my skin felt too hot.

It didn't even matter to me that she was a horrible bartender. Every time she smiled at me, I forgave her incompetence. Hell, I think I liked it. Because Posy needed a lot of help from me to do the job. I taught her a lot, even though we were competing for the bar manager's job.

I wasn't that worried, though, because I'd been working my way up the Paxton's ladder since I was sixteen. I knew ten times more than she did. I used to tease her about it, too. But even as my mouth was saying, *you call that a margarita?* my heart was saying, *will you please get into my bed?*

She felt it too. At the end of the summer we shared the most outrageous kiss. Afterward, I walked on air, feeling like a game show contestant who'd just won a new car.

Until the next day, when she got me fired.

Posy turned out to be the same kind of unforgiving rich kid I'd spent my teenage years avoiding. And I guess I'm still bitter, because I think I'd rather crawl through a sewage pipe than work for her shop.

"Here's an idea," I say to Max. "I don't have to work there. I can just loiter."

"At your former rival's place of business. Because that's not creepy at all." Max smiles slowly.

Fuck.

2

POSY

"DID YOU SET THE OVEN TIMER?" I ask Ginny, who's filling in as my kitchen assistant.

My sister rolls her eyes. "Uh huh. Forty-two minutes. Just like you told me *three times*."

"Excellent," I say calmly. I love my sister. I would do anything for Ginny and her five-year-old son. But neither of us is thrilled with this situation. My shop is desperate for labor, and Ginny is strapped for cash. So we need each other.

Unfortunately, last week she burned two full racks of pastry. Margins are tight enough around here without throwing away sixty bucks worth of ingredients and two hours of my labor.

Since it's two o'clock, I've been baking for ten hours already. I've made a hundred breakfast pastries, a hundred meat pies, and thirty full-sized pies for the shop. I'm dead on my feet, and closing time is still two hours away.

Opening a cafe is a lot of hard work and risk-taking. I knew it would be. I've had a lifetime of watching how the restaurant industry operates. I opened Posy's Pie Shop with eyes wide open. Newly divorced, and burnt out on my desk job, I needed a new challenge.

And boy, did I find one. I'm already doing a booming business. The place is packed for most of our business hours. My lower-Manhattan clientele is willing to pay six dollars for a slice of my gourmet fruit pie, or nine bucks for a lunchtime meat pie. We sell out nearly every day.

But my costs are high, too. Gourmet ingredients cost a fortune. And I have trouble hiring enough help. I had a terrific staff in place before Lily—my assistant baker—fell in love with Keisha—my barista. It was all well and good until they decided to ditch city life to work on a billionaire's yacht. I lost two terrific employees in one day.

That was a month ago, and I've been struggling ever since. In the first place, I think of Posy's Pie Shop like a family. So losing Lily and Keisha hurt. Since then, I've already hired and fired three people. That hurt, too, since it felt like firing family members.

But one of them was stealing from me and two were chronically late. That's family for you.

"Where's Jerry?" I ask Ginny, who's measuring out flour for tomorrow's first batch of pastry.

"Out back," she says. "Vaping, probably."

"No, I'm not!" Jerry's voice pipes up from just outside the screen door. "I'm reading comics on my tablet!"

Jerry never lies to me. "Jerry, honey, it's time to clean the kitchen. You can read comics after four, okay?"

"Okay, Posy!" The backdoor bangs open and Jerry appears, all smiles. He has Down syndrome, and I employ him through a program that matches men and women with special challenges to businesses that can hire them. He comes in every day at one o'clock to restock things like napkins and cups, and to wash dishes.

He is the nicest guy you will ever meet, and it was a lucky day when I agreed to give him a try in my shop. He is, however, prone to distraction. Not a single day goes by that he doesn't wander away from a sink full of dishes just to catch up on comics.

That's just the cost of doing business with Jerry. Everyone is flawed in his own way, right? Just like in a real family.

"Posy!" calls Teagan from the counter out front.

Crap. "Is it time for you to leave?" I call out.

Teagan is a baker, too. She makes the world-class donuts I buy wholesale to supplement my early morning offerings. But because I'm in such dire need of help, and because Teagan has expensive taste in shoes, I've talked her into working the counter for me a few hours a day, too, on a temporary basis.

"I'm leaving in fifteen," Teagan calls. "But there's somebody here about your barista job."

"Wait, really?" I drop the metal mixing bowl I'd been holding and grab the nearest towel to wipe off my hands. "Don't let her leave! I'll be right there! *Ginny*," I bark. "Listen for the oven timer."

"Yes, master," she says. Ignoring the sarcasm, I dash through the kitchen door, hope in my heart.

I make it as far as the cash register, and then pull up short. There's someone standing by the counter, all right. But it isn't a woman, like I expected. It's a man. His back is to me, because he's reading the menu that's chalked onto my gold-framed board at the front. So I don't quite have the whole picture yet.

But some people make a big impression even from the back, and this gentleman is one of them. The first thing I notice is his confident posture. Straight spine. Shoulders back. Like he's ready to take on the world.

And, fine, there's also his spectacular ass. I don't usually look at asses, but this one is seriously muscular. The fabric of his slim-cut jeans is strained by sculpted thighs and that perfect butt.

The top half of him is just as promising. His T-shirt clings in all the right places to a sturdy set of gym-sculpted back muscles and impressive biceps. His hair is blond, and lighter at the ends, as if he's spent the last few months on a beach somewhere. And as he turns a rugged chin in my direction, I brace myself. It's bad form to drool on job applicants, right?

Then I finally get a look at this man's face. Those piercing green eyes and two days' worth of scruff are handsome enough to turn heads. As a matter of fact, he used to turn mine. Because I *know* this face, even if I haven't seen it for fifteen years. I guess I shouldn't be surprised that Gunnar Scott is still drop-dead gorgeous.

Oh my goodness, cry my hormones. *We were not prepared for this reunion!*

I look down at myself. Smudgy apron. *Check*. Flour on my T-shirt. *Check*. Old jeans and ragged sneakers. *Check and check*.

That just figures, because Gunnar Scott is *that* guy—the one who taught me how forceful desire can feel. The first man who ever turned me into the human embodiment of a hormone rush just by entering a room.

But we were rivals. We spent an entire summer trying to outdo each other at Paxton's Bar and Bistro. We both wanted a job that was rightfully mine. But my asshole father made me compete for it anyway.

Once upon a time, my dad inherited Paxton's from his father, who inherited it from *his* father. I wanted so badly to prove that I could continue the family tradition. I busted my ass that summer, trying to impress my father and earn that promotion.

But Gunnar Scott was a fierce competitor. He even used flattery as a distraction technique. It worked, too. I lost my head whenever he turned those cool green eyes on me. All he had to do was say, "Nice job with the lemon wedges," and I'd melt like butter. I lived for watching him move around the bar with casual confidence, mixing drinks and chatting up the regulars. Or when he sliced limes, and the muscles bulged in his forearms ...

Yeah, it never took much to distract me. And maybe nothing has changed, because Gunnar's startling presence has gummed up my brain. Instead of behaving like a confident business owner, I'm just staring at him like a stunned rabbit.

"Posy," he says in a rich voice that sounds way too familiar. "Nice to see you again."

I gulp. *Nice* is a strange choice of words. We were never very nice to each other. I covered up my raging crush with a chilly demeanor. Or I tried to, anyway. And he was the overconfident macho man who assumed he knew everything there was to know about bartending. Naturally, I argued with everything he said.

And whenever he changed tactics—to flirting with me instead of defeating me—it always turned me into a blabbering idiot. "Are you here for pie?" I blurt suddenly.

Oh dear! My hormones pipe up again. *We're thirty-four years old, and it's still happening.*

"No, I'm not, although I hear the pie is excellent." His smile is silky. It's the smile that used to get the women sitting at the bar to throw down bigger tips. I used to think of it as his loverboy smile.

"I'm here for the barista job." He puts a folder on the counter. "I filled out your application."

Holy cannoli. "What? No way. You couldn't possibly be a *barista.*" The man was a straight-A student at Columbia. And he was ruthless. I would have assumed he was running a company. Or a small country.

"What are you saying?" His smile fades fast. "Are you questioning my career choice? Is there something *wrong* with working as a barista?"

"No. No. Nope," I say quickly, as self-preservation kicks in. There's no need to offend the rest of my staff. But it just doesn't add up. Gunnar had big plans for himself. He put himself through college, double majoring in political science and applied math.

I don't know why I remember his majors, damn it. It's not like I care.

"Do you have a job opening or not?" he asks, frowning.

"She totally has an opening!" Teagan says loudly. She's leaning against the counter, like a plant bending toward the sun. "She needs it *bad.*"

Gunnar's loverboy smile returns. Of course it does—now that he has an audience.

And I have the unhelpful urge to smack Teagan. Women always lose their minds for Gunnar. At least until they get to know him. Then they can't decide whether to kiss him or choke him.

Or maybe that's just me. "Do you have, uh, references?" I ask, still trying to get my head around this strange turn of events.

"Sure. I've got one." He flips the folder open to his application, where he's listed *Joe's Cafe,* which is apparently in Venice Beach, California. "Joe is waiting for your call," Gunnar says. "I told him I was applying for jobs on the East Coast."

"You've moved back here?" I ask, stupidly. Because of course he is. I need to get a grip on the hormone rush that this maddening man always gives me. You'd think I'd have grown out of it. But nope! The hormones of a divorced, lonely woman are apparently easy prey. Is it hot in here?

"I've been on the West Coast for several years. It's been a while since I lived in New York," Gunnar is saying. "Thought I'd give it another try. Are you going to consider my application?" Those pale green eyes bore into me.

No, is my first reaction. And my second one, too. I do not need to turn into a quivering mass of uncertainty every day. I used to bicker with Gunnar as a way of keeping my game face on. We used to prank each other, too. But I don't have the energy for any of that at this stage of my life.

"Posy," he says in that hunky voice of his. "I know we didn't always get along, but I'm a hard worker. I won't screw this up."

Get out of my brain. "Look," I sigh. "How about you come in for a couple days on a trial basis? But you can't get up to any of your old tricks. If you replace all the sugar dispensers with salt, I may not be responsible for my actions."

He snorts. "I wouldn't have done that if you didn't make all my drinks wrong for an entire shift. The Shirley Temple with olives was my personal favorite."

Teagan gasps, and then giggles. "Posy, really?"

"It was a different lifetime," I say quickly, as my neck begins to heat. "Just kids' pranks."

"Totally," he says, aiming one of those loverboy smiles at me.

I look down at his application again, just to avoid that dangerous smile. "This work history is a little thin, Gunn. What have you been doing with the rest of your time?"

"This and that." He shrugs, and since I'm not looking him in the eye, I can only see his abs tighten.

And, wow. That's a seriously impressive body he has. I'll bet he spent the last decade at the gym. But now here he is, in my shop of all places? The coincidence is just strange. "Are you applying to other coffee shops?"

"Of course. I applied at Starbucks first, because they're known for their excellent benefits. But it's an online application. I might as well throw my resume down a well, right?" He sighs. "Besides, the coffee at Starbucks is not top quality. I'd rather work someplace that really cares about the product, you know?" He shrugs again, and I catalog the lift of his impressive shoulders. "And I'm right over on Sullivan Street. So it wasn't hard to find this place—and there was a *Help Wanted* sign right in the window! Actually—"

He turns and strides over to the window on those long, muscular legs. He plucks the sign off the glass and balls it up right in front of me. Like it's a done deal. But I haven't actually hired him yet! The *balls* on this man. I'm speechless.

He isn't, unfortunately. "Why don't you show me around? I'm at your disposal." Then he takes my wadded-up sign and tosses it right into the recycling bin. It lands dead center like a perfect three-pointer at Madison Square Garden.

Teagan sighs happily. "Welcome aboard, Gunnar," she says.

"Teagan!" I squeak at my employee. "That's *my* decision, don't you think?"

"Of course it is," Gunnar says, leaning that rocking body against my counter. "But she won't be wrong. I'm here to impress you. Just like old times."

I let out a growl of displeasure. Gunnar Scott is too confident for his own good. And suddenly it's easy to remember how you can lust after someone and also fight with them all the time. His confidence always annoyed me because I didn't have enough of my own. And it irks me that women melt like butter at everything he says.

Although there was one fateful moment when I melted like butter, too. It was just a single kiss. But *what* a kiss.

"Well. I've got to run," Teagan says, untying her apron. "You can start by introducing Gunnar to Lola." That's the name of our finicky old espresso machine.

"Now?" I ask stupidly.

"You know you need the help behind the counter, Posy. I don't have any more hours to give you." She drops her apron on a hook, giving Gunnar a flirty smile. Then she ducks into the back for her pocketbook.

None of this is okay with me. But I'm so desperate to hire help, that I already know I'll give Gunnar a try. I can't afford not to.

"Right." I sigh. "Gunnar, let me introduce you to Lola."

"Your espresso machine is a woman?"

"She's too beautiful to be a man." I place a hand on Lola's red enamel curves. "And that's handy, in this case. Because we both know how much attention you like to give females. Now let's get started."

3

GUNNAR

"COOL, COOL," I say, waving a hand in the direction of the espresso machine. "Show me all your moves. You always liked things to be done in a very particular way."

My voice is flip, but I can hardly believe that I'm sliding behind the counter with Posy Paxton. It's like sliding back in time. Posy always was a perfectionist. She liked order and precision, which made it difficult to teach her to tend bar. She liked to count out the correct number of ice cubes for each glass. She used to measure every single ingredient with the care of a pharmacist, which slowed her down.

It was cute, but really fucking inefficient. "Show me exactly how you like the espresso to be made. Don't leave out any details, because I know how your mind works."

When I glance up, though, the look in her eye practically knocks me on my ass. It's a look that asks a hundred questions. Like, *what are you doing here?* And, *how much am I going to regret this?*

I can't tell her the first thing. It's none of her business. And whether I quit this job, or she fires me, her regrets are sure to pile up fast. But that's not a problem I can solve. My job is to find a killer and then get the hell out of her coffee shop.

But standing this close to her affects me more than I'd like to admit. Sometimes, after a long absence, people tell each other *you haven't changed a bit*. But Posy has. Her features have softened. She

19

looks more womanly than the angular, skinny girl she was at nineteen. But some things haven't changed at all. Her posture is straight and perfect, as if she's squaring for a fight. And her eyes are still so bright that I feel like she can see right through me.

I'd forgotten how it feels to have a moment of her complete attention. I used to crave it. I spent entire shifts behind the bar trying to get the prettiest girl on the Upper East Side to laugh at my jokes. Whenever she turned to me with a smile, it felt like I'd won a prize.

It wasn't mutual, though. Not really. And I'd better not forget it.

It won't be easy to stop staring at her, though. Not with all that ancient history churning around in my gut. And not with Posy looking *scrumptious*, even in a flour-covered apron. She's wearing one of those sleeveless T-shirts that seem designed to focus a man's attention on the expanse of skin on a woman's smooth arms. And then there are those tight jeans she's wearing …

"Okay," she says, clearing her throat. "Let's begin." The frosty sound of her voice brings me back to reality. It doesn't matter how appealing she is, or how much I used to enjoy sparring with her. I'm going to have to call her "boss" now. That's going to chafe worse than a sweaty pair of briefs after a ten-mile run. This woman kissed me, and then she got me fired from a job I'd taught her.

I guess I'm not over that, either. *Thanks, Max. Great assignment.*

Arms folded, I gird my loins and wait for Posy to explain the espresso machine.

"This is a fully manual machine," she says, laying a hand on its red enamel side. "Italian, of course."

"Of course," I repeat. The Paxton family only settles for the very best. They throw away the things that don't meet their standards.

Like me, apparently.

"Have you used a fully manual machine before?" she asks.

"No," I say quickly. "At Joe's we used, uh, something more automatic."

Posy rolls her eyes, which tells me that I've just admitted to the barista equivalent of being unable to drive a stick shift. But the joke is still on her. Because there is no Joe's Cafe at all. In my line of work, you have to be an excellent liar or you die. I don't even feel guilty about it.

"So, talk to me like I've never touched an espresso machine before." *Because I haven't.* "I'll learn best if I can hear you describe everything in the master's own words."

Her spine straightens a little bit, and I give myself a silent high five. Praise will turn Posy into putty in my hands. The twenty-one-year-old version of me hadn't learned this lesson yet. That kid had a lot going for him, sure, but I can't say I was ever any good at standing back and letting Posy be the expert, even if it was her family's restaurant.

She'd never even held down a job before that summer, which bugged me to no end. Whereas I'd been working my way up the ranks at Paxton's since I turned sixteen. I started as a dishwasher and mop guy. I brought the garbage into the alley, no matter how smelly and gross. I scraped the food off the plates and made them sparkle again.

It literally took me years to work my way up to the best-paid job in the room: bartender. And then Posy walked in one day like the Park Avenue princess that she was, and was handed an equivalent job to mine. And sure—she was a fast learner. But she was also full of ideas and opinions, some of them brilliant, many of them naïve. It drove me bonkers.

To be fair, part of what drove me bonkers was her trim body and perky breasts. Not only did I have to work with the boss's opinionated daughter, I had to navigate her fresh, flowery scent and her delicious cleavage.

I spent that entire summer vacillating between fascination, annoyance, and lust, sometimes experiencing all three at the same time. It's not a comfortable way to live.

"Naturally, we grind as we go, for the freshest experience," Posy says now.

"*Grind* as we go." I repeat. "Got it." And then I give her a wink. An actual wink, like a sleazy asshole. The same thing happened when I was twenty-one, damn it. I turned into a slightly louder, more obnoxious version of myself whenever she walked into the room.

She flips the largest switch. As the machine roars to life, I start to count. *One Mississippi. Two Mississippi. Three Mississippi.* Then she flips it off again.

Three seconds. Fine. A monkey could learn this.

Next, Posy grabs the handle of one of those espresso thingies and holds the basket part under the chute. She uses her thumb to swish a lever back and forth three times, as a tidy pile of coffee grounds fills the little cup, making a rounded shape. Like a breast.

Three seconds on the grinder. Three swishes of the lever. Make a coffee titty. Got it.

She grabs a round little tool and uses it to press the grinds down flat. "Lola is a little fussy about the fill," she tells me. "Too little and the water runs through too fast. Too much, and she squirts out the sides. The trick is to fill her up nice and tight, right up to the *lip*."

I try to hold it back, but it's no use. A laugh escapes from my chest.

"What?" she demands.

"Never mind," I say quickly.

"Seriously?" Posy's eyes narrow. "You're thirty-five years old, and you still hear sexual innuendo everywhere?"

"Thirty-six. And it's just the way I'm made. Carry on."

Teagan—the girl who's supposed to be leaving—snickers.

"Don't you have somewhere to be?" Posy demands of her.

"Yeah. But it's more fun watching him learn to make espresso drinks." She gives me a wink. "Maybe we'll work together next week."

"Hope so," I say cheerfully. Because that will mean that Posy hasn't fired me yet.

Although I think she'd like to. Her eyes turn to slits as Teagan and I engage in some low-key flirting before the woman finally heads out the door.

"Can you pay attention to what we're doing, Loverboy?" Posy asks, and the question is full of vinegar.

"I was already paying attention," I promise. "I haven't missed a thing. Let's see you put it into—" I gesture vaguely toward the machine. "—The thinger dinger."

"The *thinger dinger*?" She gives me a sideways glance.

"At Joe's Cafe we always joked around," I say smoothly.

Posy sighs. Then she glides toward the espresso machine, lifting one smooth arm to fit the filter arm into one of the espresso machine's ports.

The assignment is a cupcake, Duff had told me. I'm starting to see why. The Italian coffee machine is beautiful, and so is the woman using it. It's her confidence that always used to turn me on. I like the way she manhandles the part into place.

Is barista porn a thing? I'll have to check it out tonight on pornhub. I could learn a few tricks and get off at the same time.

Two birds, one stone.

Posy flips the switch, and the machine hums as espresso begins to fill the cup. "Our standard pour for a latte or a cappuccino is two ounces. Every drink is a double."

"Two ounces. Sure. That's how we did things at Joe's."

A few seconds later she flips off the machine, plucks the cup off the ledge and hands it to me.

"Beautiful." I peer into the cup, taking care to note the depth of the coffee in the cup.

"Aren't you going to taste it?" She asks when I hand it back.

God, no. "It smells great," I say, and I guess that's true. The scent of coffee is so much better than the taste. "I was waiting until after you fizzle the milk."

"Fizzle. What do they teach baristas in California?" She grabs a little metal jug and shows it to me. "We use about a nine ounce pour for a latte." She grabs a gallon of milk out of a reach-in fridge below the bar. Then she tips it into a metal jug with the practiced ease of someone who does this a lot.

"Nine ounces," I repeat. "Don't you want to measure those out one at a time?"

"What? That would take forev—" she stops abruptly and levels me with a glare. "Very funny. But I've learned a few things in the last fifteen years, Gunnar."

"Me too, gorgeous. Maybe I can show you sometime." The ridiculous words just fall out of my mouth before I can stop them. "I meant behind the bar. Carry on. I'm ready for the swirly milk part."

She gives me another dubious look and continues the job.

Then things start to happen faster than I can absorb. "Purge the steamer arm." She turns a knob and the machine makes a loud squawk. "And go." She twists something, and the arm begins to hiss and shriek. Posy holds the jug in a way that makes it hard for me to see. But mere seconds later she shuts it off, wipes it with a towel, somehow makes it hiss again, then whacks the jug on the counter twice.

And all the while she's speaking a string of coffee lingo. She says something about foam and temperature and "polishing" the milk.

"You could do a heart or a fern, whatever design you have nailed," she says inexplicably. She's pouring the milk and twisting the cup and talking a blue streak. "And *voila.*"

I look down at the cup she's handed me. "That's a fucking rose," I say, shocked.

"It's my signature design."

"A rose. In *milk.*" It's got layers of white petals, stretching toward a coffee sky.

"The guy who taught me espresso drinks was a great artist. But like I said, it's fine if you can only manage a heart, or a tulip. Everyone starts somewhere."

"Cool," I say.

I'm so fucked.

The bell on the door jingles, and three women walk in, approaching the counter. "Hi! Wow—are you the new guy?" one of them asks, smiling.

"I am," I announce, hoping that I already have the job.

"Well, this is exciting," one of the women says.

Posy grumbles something under her breath. It sounds like *help me, Jesus.*

"Could I please have a mint tea for here, and a slice of the Dutch apple?" She bats her eyelashes at me.

"You handle the drinks," Posy grunts. "We'll go over the cash register and pricing in a minute."

"Of course. One mint tea, coming right up. Where's, uh, the hot water?"

Posy blinks at me, and I know right away that I've asked a stupid question. Then she points to a random switch on the espresso machine.

It says "water" above it. Live and learn. "Right. I knew that."

Posy shoots me a disbelieving look. Then she grabs a spatula and cuts a gorgeous apple pie with slightly more violence than is strictly necessary.

I find the mint tea bags on a shelf on the bar back and serve up the woman's beverage with a smile and a wink. Her cheeks flush in appreciation. "What can I get you?" I ask her friends.

And that's when the wheels come off. This woman wants a "skinny mocha." I have no idea what that is. I look around helplessly for a second, hoping the information just falls into place.

With a low growl, Posy plunks a bottle down in front of me. *Chocolate syrup.* Oh, okay. Then Posy's eyes flip toward the espresso grinder. So I realize the chocolate is going into her coffee.

So I put some chocolate into a cup, and then grind three seconds worth of coffee. But when I dispense it, my coffee titty is misshapen. So the tamper thinger can't make a nice, flat surface, either. This means I'm struggling to put the shot into the espresso machine. I practically wrench my arm off getting it in there.

This is Max's fault, I remind myself. It's a mismatch of skills. I could put together an entire room full of weaponry without so much as a hiccup. But I don't know shit about coffee. I'm going to write that up in my letter of resignation, probably.

To Max. Not Posy.

When I flip the switch on the espresso machine, the first thing I see are coffee grounds dribbling over the side. That can't be good. But luckily, coffee follows. Maybe nobody will notice.

And now the chocolate has changed the volume measurement, so I can't tell how much is two ounces. So I flip it off at will, and then swirl the contents of the cup and flex my pecs at the same time.

The woman across the counter lets out a little sigh of happiness. There's more than one way to please a customer. I take the opportunity to flex my biceps when I take the milk out of the fridge. And then—while the milk frother thingie makes a horrible squealing noise —I address my customer. "That scarf really brings out your eyes."

"This old thing?" she says with a toss of her hair.

When I shut off the frother, Posy is making a gagging sound. The milk in the jug is peppered by giant bubbles instead of smooth foam, unfortunately. But I pour it over the coffee in two blobs. I don't even try to make a design. It looks like ... Huh. It looks like a butt. Go figure.

Even so, I pass it to the customer with a big smile. "Enjoy!"

"Thank you so much," she says, pushing a bill into the tip jar.

"You have a nice day! Who's next?"

Another woman steps forward. She's really interesting looking, too, with dark hair and giant brown eyes that look familiar to me. She's wearing an artistic kimono-style top and about a million bracelets on her smooth wrists. "Posy, hello! How *are* you?"

"Great, thanks," Posy says in an uncharacteristic clipped voice. "What can Gunnar pour for you? The usual?"

"Not exactly," she says with a broad smile. "I'd like a *decaf* latte, half two percent, half skim, sugar-free peppermint, iced, no foam. I'm off caffeine for a while. And a ginger cookie, please."

Oh man. I'm trying to play back that order in my head when I see the blood drain from Posy's face.

Huh. She must know that I'm about to fuck this up. "Could you repeat that, please?"

"Of course!" Her smile grows even wider. "I'd like—"

"I got it," Posy snarls. Then she puts her hands on my ribcage and actually steers me out of the way. "Ginger cookie," she says between clenched teeth.

"Well, okay." I fetch a plate with a single cookie on it, then use the extra time to compliment our customer on her blouse. "That bright color really suits you. I love it."

Posy's smile is menacing as she makes the drink and then cashes out the woman, who thanks her and floats over to claim a table. "What the hell was that?" she hisses when they're out of earshot. "It wasn't that complicated an order. But you didn't even wipe off the basket rim. Or purge the steam arm. And what was that milk design supposed to be? It looked like an ass."

"Some people really like asses," I hiss. "Especially mine. I was giving that woman something to remember me by. But I can up my game, Posy. I'm just a little rusty."

"Rusty," she spits, her blue eyes flashing. "What you are is *clueless*. Why are you even here?"

Irritation rips through me, and I want to tell Posy Paxton where she can put her attitude. It's just coffee, for fuck's sake. It doesn't matter.

But then I remember what does matter. I scan the cafe, where at least two people have laptops open. Someone who has evidence of murder has been using this space to boast about killing people.

And I know what I have to do.

"Posy," I say in a low voice. I force myself to meet her gaze. Her cheeks are flushed with anger, and her eyes are bright. "I need this job. It's, uh …" Yup, this is going to hurt me. "I need it bad, okay? Can you give me a chance?"

Her expression softens. "Well, um, I don't know. You aren't a very good barista. I have a friend who owns a bar. Maybe he —"

Uh oh. "Please? It's for my father. He's recovering from surgery. I need work, and you need a barista. Let me brush up on my skills tomorrow. I'll come in here on Monday knowing what a slim chocolate fizz is. Or whatever that lady ordered."

"*Gunn.*" She rolls her eyes. "It's not that easy. This is a *luxury* cafe. We have to uphold certain standards."

Now I want to roll my eyes, too. The Paxtons are so full of themselves. "Give me one more try. One single shift. That's all I ask."

She sighs. "Fine. *One.* But only because I really need the extra hands on Monday. If it doesn't go well, you should really apply for some bartending jobs. Something tells me that alcohol is more your speed. Do you even drink coffee?"

"On special occasions," I lie. "Thank you for this chance. It means a lot to me." Just to keep her off balance, I lean in and give her a quick hug.

"You're, uh, welcome." She shivers. "I don't know how you're going to become a barista in forty hours. But I'll see you Monday before seven a.m."

"Seven?" I whine. That's four a.m. California time.

"*Seven,*" she barks. "And don't be late."

"Yes *ma'am.*" I give her a salute. Then I pull out my phone and take a photo of the espresso machine. And another one of the whole cafe.

I'd better find this murderer fast. Because I'm going to have a single shift to do it.

After kissing Posy's (delectable) ass for just a few minutes more, I get the heck out of there. As soon as I hit Mercer Street, I walk a block and then dial Max.

"Talk to me," he says.

"Max, we're fucked."

"Why? She hired someone else?"

"No. But I can't do this job. I can't fake it."

"Dude," Max says sternly. "You broke into a drug kingpin's safe with nothing but a cell phone and a set of screwdrivers. You hacked into a Russian mobster's bank account on a first-generation iPod. Don't even try to tell me you can't figure out how to work an espresso machine."

I groan so loudly that a passing hipster's rescue pug lets out a yip of surprise. "It's not just the mechanics. I could probably figure that out. It's the pretentious coffee vocabulary. I've got, like, thirty-six hours to learn how to be a smug asshole?"

"Don't trash talk coffee culture," Max grumbles. "Some of my best friends are espresso products. Take the evening to rest up, and then get your butt into the office at 0900. I'm going to fix this."

"What if we rented a room in the building across the street?" I suggest, looking up at the row of old brick facades. "I could stake the place out the old-fashioned way."

"We're trying this my way first," Max thunders. "I'll see you in the morning."

Then he hangs up on me.

4

POSY

"I ... WILL ... CATS ... IT," my five-year-old nephew slowly reads from a book in my lap. Then he squirms on the sofa beside me.

"What's that third word?" I ask. "Sound it out. What sound does 'ch' say?"

"Catch," he says slowly. "I will *catch* it."

"Excellent," I praise him as I turn the page.

This is a typical evening for me—helping Aaron practice reading, while my sister shoots us worried glances from her seat at our kitchen table. And since I wake up so early, my bedtime is barely later than my five-year-old nephew's.

Aaron slides his pajama-covered rear down the sofa, kicks the coffee table, then wiggles himself into a vertical position again. Reading is whole body work, apparently.

I take a sip of my wine while he slowly reads all five words from the next page.

The tutoring is a favor I offered to my sister after my father's latest crack about Aaron's reading skills during one of our rare visits to his mansion. My father is a celebrated restauranteur, as well as a successful businessman.

He's also an evil shithead. It took me more than twenty years to realize that, and an additional decade to stop caring what he thinks of my life choices. But I'm finally free of him.

Mostly free, anyway. Ginny and I still struggle sometimes,

although with different sets of daddy issues. Ginny is severely dyslexic, and our father never missed a chance to make her feel stupid. She spent her teen years acting out, trying to prove to him that she couldn't be controlled.

I took the opposite strategy—spending lots of energy trying to please that man so he'd notice me and love me. It didn't work. But it did start me down the path of a career I hated, and also led me to marry the wrong man.

My ex and I have been apart for a year now. My father refers to my divorce as my "greatest failure." As if my life were a string of them. I graduated magna cum laude from Columbia University! I was a VP at a Fortune 500 company!

None of that matters to him. He sees me as a divorcée and a failed banker. It was actually daddy's red-faced sermon over my divorce that served as a final wakeup call. Instead of comforting me, he told me I'd thrown away the only good man who'd ever bother with me.

That was the day that I finally saw our father-daughter relationship clearly, and it was a real wakeup call. I'd spent my entire life trying to impress men who were not worth the trouble.

So I started to make some changes. I mostly cut my father out of my life. If it weren't for Aaron and Ginny, I'd never show my face in his home again.

That wasn't my only act of bravery, either. I also quit my dull job, cutting out another thing in my life that made me feel small. Then I opened my pie shop on the ground floor of this building— the one asset I retained after my divorce. The second and third floors were already rented out when I inherited the building. The vacant apartment—spanning the fourth and fifth floors with two big bedrooms and a roof terrace—I kept for me, my sister, and her child.

We're a strange little family of three. Ginny is an artist and a yoga instructor. She also works in my pie shop when Aaron is at school.

As for me, I rarely leave the corner of Prince and Mercer Streets. I get up too early, work too much, and see too little of the sky. But I make all my own choices. And I make excellent pies.

"THE END!" Aaron shouts. Then he slams the book closed.

"That was great. One more?" I ask.

"Nope." He flings the book onto the coffee table. "Maybe I could have five minutes on your phone for reading super well."

"No way," my sister says, jumping out of her kitchen chair. "Head down those stairs, mister. It's bedtime."

Aaron slides off the couch without arguing. But then he says, "That's a big glass of wine, Aunt Posy."

Ginny snickers. "It is, isn't it?"

"Spell big," I demand of my nephew.

"B-I-G," he rattles off. "'Night."

"'Night, kiddo." I peck him on the cheek as he heads off toward the circular staircase that leads down to the lower floor of our quirky pad.

While my sister is putting her son to bed, I make a nice dent in what is admittedly a very large glass of wine.

Ginny reappears as I'm taking a particularly big gulp. I've practically got my entire head in the glass when she plops down beside me. "Rough day?"

"You could say that."

"We've *got* to get you some more help."

"Well, what if I told you a guy came in today to apply for the barista job?"

"Really?" She lets out a whispered shriek. If we sound like we're having too much fun, Aaron will climb the stairs and demand to know what's going on. "That's *great!*"

"Yes and no. I'm not sure he'll work out. In the first place, I suspect he's a terrible barista."

"Uh oh. Can't you train him? Are you going to give him a try?" My sister's eyes are full of hope. She's given me as many hours in the kitchen as she can. But I need to hire at least two more people, and we both know it.

"I'll give him one shift to sink or swim." I shrug, like it's not that interesting to me. But I'm a liar. "I knew this guy in college. He was a good bartender, but that doesn't mean he can make an espresso that's up to my standards."

"Well, they *are* very high standards."

"For a *reason.*" I squeak. But I have a reputation for being very particular. I'm a little sensitive about it.

31

"Who is he, anyway? Do I know him?"

"I doubt it. He worked at Paxton's that same summer I started on staff."

"Wait." Ginny holds up a hand. "You mean Gunnar?"

"Do you know him?" My voice cracks for no good reason.

"Never met the guy. But back then you could never shut up about him."

"What? That's not true." I feel a flush creep up my neck.

"Like hell it isn't. You had a *lot* to say about Gunnar."

"None of it good," I argue. "He was a huge, arrogant pain in my ass. He drove me crazy. Every time I'd make a suggestion about the bar, he'd make the opposite one."

"I'll bet he's super attractive." My sister gives me a smirk. "He is, isn't he?"

"Maybe. Why does that matter?"

"Honestly, that summer you never stopped talking about how much he drove you crazy. I just assumed you had a thing for him."

"I didn't," I sigh. "Okay, I did. I used to feel a little sweaty every time he even glanced at me. Anyone would. He's the kind of hot that *knows* he's hot. He's got this irritating smile. I call it the loverboy smile. He uses it as a weapon."

"The *horror*," Ginny says, grinning. "Which flavor of hot are we talking about anyway?"

"Abercrombie model hot," I grumble. "Tousled blond hair, strong arms, legendary butt." Just thinking about him makes me agitated.

"Did you ever ..." She clears her throat suggestively.

"No way," I say a little too quickly. "He, uh, propositioned me a couple of times, though."

My sister blinks. "And you turned him down?"

"Of course I turned him down! I was nineteen. And ..." I sigh.

"A virgin," my sister finishes. "I forgot about that."

Ginny and I weren't very close during those years. She was busy getting drunk, getting tattoos, and saying yes to the men who propositioned her. I was busy trying to be her polar opposite. We were both fighting our father's war, but not as allies. We know better now.

"It was a strange time," I admit. "Spalding had just shown up in my life. And Daddy liked him a lot. He couldn't shut up about Spalding."

"Is that why you chose him?" She winces.

"He seemed safer." I swivel on the couch, squirming under the weight of this conversation. "He *was* safer, I guess. He wasn't always asking me for sex."

"He was too busy gelling his hair," Ginny says wryly.

My ex is vain, it's true. But that wasn't our real problem as a couple. We were just wrong for each other. I knew it, too. Even when I was nineteen years old, looking across the bar at Spalding's preppy good looks, I didn't feel the pull. There was none of the achy heat that I felt whenever Gunnar Scott placed a hand on my elbow to reach past me for the grenadine or the olives.

I was afraid of that feeling—that frisson of danger Gunnar gave me. But Spalding seemed more manageable. Easier to control. Whereas Gunnar made sexy offhand suggestions about how we might spend time together, Spalding took a different tack. He'd sit at the bar, order a martini and then politely ask me out.

"You and I would make a good couple," he'd said. "We'd be the envy of the Upper East Side." He'd said it so easily—as if our pairing was something the world needed.

Even at nineteen—and I was a naïve nineteen—I'd understood that Spalding was a spoiled firstborn son. He had a way about him, as if life was one big gourmet menu he could order from. As if the world owed him praise, and also a cookie.

I didn't mind as much as I should have, though, because I was the cookie he wanted.

Even so, I was a busy girl—too caught up in the day-to-day work at the bar to bother with college boys, no matter how hot or charming. I turned both Gunnar and Spalding down, inadvertently playing coy while I worked my butt off. Who could date when she got off work at two a.m.?

And who would I even choose? The dangerous boy whose dirty insinuations were probably just mocking me? Or the smooth-talking rich kid who wanted to impress me with a three-hundred-dollar dinner at Per Se?

In the end I didn't have to choose. Gunnar kissed me just once, proving beyond any reasonable doubt that I couldn't possibly handle myself with him, even if I could summon the courage to try. But then he disappeared and never came back.

And the next time Spalding asked me out, I finally told him yes.

After long moments of silence, I find myself staring into my wine glass while my sister watches me cautiously. "Psst. Posy!" She whispers. "Where did you go?"

"No place good," I grumble.

"Tell me about Gunnar. Why do you think he won't last a day in your shop?"

My shrug is listless. "I don't know how coffee works in California, but he seemed incapable of operating Lola. Maybe he's so hot the clients didn't notice that their drinks were wrong."

"Maybe," my sister says dreamily. "I think I might have to swing by on Monday before work and test out his wares. Are you calling dibs on this guy?"

"Dibs? No way," I squeak. "And neither are you."

She lets out an evil laugh. "But why not? I could break my dry spell. You don't care, right?" She pokes me in the elbow and I let out a growl. "Oh wait. Maybe you do!"

"That ship has sailed," I grumble. "A smarter girl would have slept with the hot bartender and with Spalding, too. But I was so rigid in my thinking. I wanted to do things in the right order."

"But there was no right order," Ginny agrees softly.

"No, there wasn't. I was so young. I should have kissed all the boys and had all the sex. I might have realized that Spalding wasn't the man for me."

"This could be your do-over," Ginny says. "You can still sleep with the hot barista."

"No way. In the first place, he won't be around long enough for that. I can't keep a barista who doesn't know how to make coffee drinks. He probably has a girlfriend now. Or a wife. And it's all a moot point anyway. He wasn't actually serious when he used to hit on me."

"But what if he was? And what if he tried again?" my sister asks. "Then again, you probably wouldn't want to take my sex advice. I have a son with someone who's in prison."

34

"A lovely son," I say, rushing to Aaron's defense. I'd die for my nephew.

"The best kid ever," my sister agrees. "But nobody points at me and says *role model*."

"I do," I insist. "You're brave, Gin. You're a great mom, too. There is nothing wrong with us. Apartment 4/5 is a hundred percent admirable." I take another sip of my rapidly evaporating wine.

My sister kicks her feet into my lap and reclines like a queen on the sofa. "Just promise me one thing."

"What?"

"If the hottie bartender propositions you again, you won't turn him down."

"What? I can't promise that. He won't, by the way. But even if he did, I might not be feeling it."

"Promise me you'll *consider* it," she pushes. "In fact, I want you to think it over when you see him again. Like, pretend that he's going to ask you out. And try to imagine yourself saying yes."

"Whatever for?"

"Because you've only ever been to bed with one man in your life. And then that man treated you like crap. You desperately need to broaden your horizons."

"I object to the word *desperately*," I argue. "And I've dated a little."

"A *very* little," my sister corrects. "Just think it over. I'm the single parent, and I get more action. You could be out there having fun."

"Uh huh." I hide behind my wine glass. "Something else happened today in the shop. Saroya came in."

My sister groans. "*Again?* I just want to know why your ex's new girlfriend has to buy *all* her coffee drinks from you? That is not how a stable person behaves."

I have thought this same thing many times. But it's nice to hear my sister say it, too. "Because I have the best coffee in SoHo?" I give Ginny a weak smile. "But, shit, if I were dating a guy, I'd drink second-tier coffee just to avoid his ex."

"She's obviously a drama llama," Ginny says, indignant. "Or deeply insecure."

"Or both," I add. "And I know I shouldn't let it get to me. She always comes in looking like some kind of bohemian runway model, and I'm covered in flour. No makeup. Circles under my eyes ..."

"Because you work too much," Ginny points out.

"I swear, she's the only person who could make me second guess the way I look." *Don't forget Gunnar*, my hormones point out. *Maybe we should rethink our work attire.* "Anyway, there she is, preening and smiling like she's just any customer who walked in for a latte. And I pushed Gunnar out of the way, which is stupid. I should have let him make her a shitty espresso. Maybe she wouldn't come back, right?"

"That's a solid plan. Hire this guy. Stat." She takes the wine glass out of my hand and steals a sip. "Amirite?"

I give her a wan smile. "Ginny, it was weird today. Saroya ..." I'm almost afraid to say it out loud. Because I'll sound like a nut job. "She asked for decaf."

"Oh." My sister goes very still. "She didn't."

"Yes," I whisper. And now I know I'm not crazy. Ginny is suddenly thinking the same thing that I'm thinking.

"It's just mind games," my sister says. But her dark eyes look worried.

"Maybe," I hedge. "She didn't go into details. She didn't say she was—" I gulp.

My sister flinches. "Maybe she isn't. Like I said—mind games."

"Yeah," I agree quickly. "I just wish she'd play them on someone else."

"She will," Ginny says forcefully. "A woman like that needs multiple victims to fuel her ego."

"Let's hope she's a poor multitasker." I yawn. "I have to call Gunnar's reference before I can go to bed."

"Night," my sister says, swinging off the sofa and standing up. "I'm going to bed, too. Tomorrow I'm playing the role of your hot barista."

"So hot," I say, fanning myself.

She rolls her eyes and leaves the room, heading for the staircase down to the fourth floor, which Ginny and Aaron share. My bedroom is up here on the fifth floor, where the living room, kitchen and my bathroom are, too.

Strange family. Strange apartment. But it works for us.

With wine coursing through my veins, I locate my phone and dial the 650 area code number that Gunnar left on his application.

It rings twice, then I hear, "This is Joe speaking."

Well, that was easy. "Hi there. Um, I was given your number by someone I interviewed for a job today. He listed your name as a reference."

"All right, miss. Which hooligan was it?"

I think I like Joe. "His name is Gunnar Scott."

"Ah, Gunnar. Took himself off to New York, did he? I'm glad to hear it. He has a sick father who needs looking after."

"Right. Okay." Guilt stabs me right in the breastbone. When I first met Gunnar, he would never have begged for work the way he did today. *I need to work*, he'd said. "The job is for a barista position. Can you verify that he worked at your cafe?"

"Sure did. Good guy. Hard working. Never late. We're not a fancy cafe, mind you. But Gunnar is smart. He can figure out anything if you give him a chance."

Oh man. It's like he's seeing right into my tortured little soul. "I'll keep that in mind. Thank you for your time."

"Have a nice evening, miss."

"You too."

5

POSY

I LIE in bed a half hour later, trying not to think about my ex-husband and his new girlfriend. If she's pregnant, though, that's going to hurt.

A lot.

I married Spalding when I was twenty-two, after two years of dating. He was a couple of years ahead of me at Columbia. He worked in advertising on Madison Avenue. Still does.

We were pretty happy for several years. At least I thought we were. Although our social life was a little dull, since there were a lot of business dinners with advertisers. And Spalding liked vacationing at golf resorts. We lived a nice life.

Then, when we'd been married several years, I was starting to think about leaving my soul-sucking corporate job to have children. Eighteen months ago, I was on the brink of telling Spalding my plans. But then he had a health scare on the ninth hole at Shinnecock, where he'd gone to try to close a deal with a major airline.

He felt chest pains, and he had trouble breathing. They summoned an ambulance and whisked him away to the cardiac care center at a Long Island hospital. I was summoned from my desk at work, rushing to his side.

After two days of tests, it was determined that Spalding had not had a heart attack.

"Panic can masquerade as a coronary event," the specialist told me. "It's very common, and surprisingly scary for the patient. But he was lucky. All he needs is some lifestyle changes to feel better. Therapy wouldn't hurt. Or at least some meditation and stress relief."

Spalding got the message. No—he got religion. He took a leave of absence from work to "get healthy." He joined a gym. He took a retreat to Mexico, where he studied yoga and the Spanish language.

"I am uno con el universe," he wrote to me during his three weeks away, while I toiled at my desk.

It became a very bad time to quit my job, since Spalding had effectively quit his. My plans would have to wait. Meanwhile, Spalding began talking to a life coach. "Your advertising firm sent me," she said the day she knocked on our apartment door. "I can help Spalding recover his health, his wellness, and his positivity."

Her name was Saroya.

I hated her on sight. But she and Spalding became confidantes. He began spouting wellness aphorisms in every conversation. "What you are is where you have been. What you'll be is what you do now." And so on.

The advertising firm paid for weekly sessions with Saroya. But the cost would prove to be greater than I could tally. Spalding's infatuation was like watching a slow train wreck. He began bringing her up in every conversation. He'd ask her opinion on every small decision he made.

One time he called her from our brunch table at a cafe to ask how he should order his eggs.

The only thing he never consulted her about was the thing I most wanted him to plan—his return to work. At that point I was carrying our finances. And Ginny was struggling, so I was funding her, too. I took on extra projects at work, trying to ensure a hefty year-end bonus.

Meanwhile, Spalding spent his days meditating and browsing the shops. He bought richly illustrated coffee table books and handmade Italian sandals, claiming that his new finds helped him "walk the path of happiness."

Until—finally—he called me at work one day. "I've come to a big decision, and I'd like to share it with you. I made a reservation at Per Se."

"Wow, okay," I said. "Can't wait."

I put on a dress and I met him at Thomas Keller's famously expensive restaurant overlooking Central Park. When I got there, he had a bottle of champagne waiting at the table. I settled in for a romantic meal with my dashing husband. Spalding has the sort of genteel face and bearing that makes people turn for a better look. Gleaming dark hair. Crisp shirts. Shiny shoes.

I used to be in awe of Spalding. I used to feel a little stunned that he'd chosen me. And for the first hour that night at Per Se, I still felt lucky. Then, during the fish course, I asked Spalding what he wanted to talk about. I was ninety percent sure he wanted to tell me he was ready to go back to work, or to make a career change. Something I could support. And then I would tell him how much I wanted to scale back and try to have a child.

"Posy, I think we should open our marriage."

"Open it," I'd said with a smile, because I was still thinking about babies. "What do you mean?"

"I think we should see other people. Sexually," he said, smiling back at me.

A small piece of skate became briefly lodged in my throat as I struggled to swallow. I ended up coughing into my napkin.

Spalding made a prissy face that I saw whenever I did something that wasn't up to his standards. "What?" I gasped. "You mean you want to have sex with—" I didn't finish the sentence, just in case I'd misunderstood.

"With other women," he finished. "And you could do the same, if you chose to. We're missing that spark we used to have. This will be a good way to get it back."

"No it won't," I'd said immediately.

He'd frowned then, as if it had never occurred to him that I wouldn't go along with this. "Posy, you've never tried very hard in bed. You're basically a starfish. I never held it against you, though, because you're good at other things. But at this point in my life, I need to walk the path of joy. This way you'll learn to become adventurous."

"Adventurous? I'm just tired. I work like a dog." It was just sinking in that my husband wasn't going to let this go. This was not a bad dream that I could wake up from. "Are you having an affair?" I'd asked him quietly.

"No!" he said quickly, looking insulted. "That's a nasty question, Posy. I'm trying to save our marriage."

Saroya, I thought suddenly. *This was her idea.* But I wasn't going to say her name aloud. He'd deny it, and I'd sound petty. "No, Spalding. That's not my idea of saving a marriage. And what's your end game? And how will you explain it to our future children?" *Daddy can't tuck you in tonight. He's at his girlfriend's house.*

Yeah? No.

"I'm sorry you feel this way," he'd said primly, adjusting his napkin in his lap. "The root of suffering is attachment, Posy. This is what I need. So you'll have to think it over."

The root of my suffering is you, said a little voice in my head. It was the first time in my marriage when I'd allowed myself to think that.

Taking a deep breath, I'd glanced around the beautiful room, with its twinkling view of nighttime Manhattan beyond the grand windows. "Okay." This was actually happening. I was going to end my marriage in one of New York's most elegant restaurants.

Spalding misunderstood my utterance, though, and his eyes had lit up with victory. "Good girl. Good decision. This might even teach you a few things about how to please a man. You're smart. You might catch on."

My head had snapped back as if I'd been punched. "Catch on?" I'd pushed my chair back suddenly. I had to put some distance between us. There was so much anger rising inside of me that the table couldn't contain it all.

Spalding had clicked his tongue. "I didn't mean right this moment, sweet. Have some more champagne." He'd reached for the bottle in its wine bucket beside the table.

But I'd beat him to it. "Sure. Let's have more." As I hoisted it out of the icy water, I admired the label. Veuve Cliquot was seventy dollars in the liquor store. Probably twice that in the restaurant. And I was paying for it, because I was the only one earning a paycheck.

I couldn't believe Spalding brought me here to wine and dine me on my own dime to ask me if he could sleep with other women. I didn't even recognize him anymore.

Well then. He wouldn't recognize me, either. I'd stood up and leaned over him as he'd raised his champagne flute toward me. But I'd tipped the bottle too far above to hit the glass, thrilling myself as the first of the foamy, golden liquid began to pour from the bottleneck onto his shiny, shiny hair.

Spalding's shriek had made every head in the restaurant swivel towards us. "This is my favorite tie!" he'd sputtered as the last drops rained down on him.

"But attachment is the root of all suffering," I'd said through clenched teeth. "I'm walking the path to joy right out of here."

A waiter had approached with his hands up and open. Like he'd expected me to attack. I'd straightened my spine and handed him the bottle. "Here. This is empty. But don't bring him another bottle. I'm divorcing his cowardly ass and he won't have the money for vintage champagne after tonight."

Then, in the utter silence of the stunned room, I'd lifted my briefcase to my shoulder and left without a backward glance. I'd taken the Subway to Ginny's apartment, where I'd spent the night crying on her sofa.

The following morning I'd gone back to my own apartment at six a.m. Spalding was sitting at the kitchen table, eating peanut butter toast and coffee.

"I don't want an open marriage," I'd told him. "I won't do it. If you make me choose, I'll choose divorce."

"Oh dear. Siddhartha said: If you find no one to support you on the spiritual path, walk alone."

Now it's only me who *walks alone*, though. These days he's walking the path of happiness with Saroya. I called that one. Even if they didn't start up until I'd moved out, it was still a betrayal.

Almost a year later, I'm still angry about it.

And because our divorce was technically my decision, I was forced to buy out Spalding's marital portion of the buildings my grandparents left me. His divorce lawyer was an animal. Spalding had once dipped into inherited money to pay for my MBA, so the judge divided the property I'd eventually inherited. Never mind that I worked like a dog to see him through his so-called medical crisis.

42

And never mind that we were only divorcing so he could boink his life coach.

Even if I'm poorer now, at least I'm free of him. Or I would be, if *she* ever stopped showing up.

I started a pie shop instead of a family. I'm happy with my choice. But if Spalding and Saroya are starting a family, I'm going to need to take up kickboxing, or find some other outlet for my rage. They will raise their bundle of joy next door, in the building he gained by divorcing me.

Ouch. Just ouch. I wonder if Buddha said anything useful about revenge.

I flop around in my bed, trying to get comfortable. Shoving Spalding and his new woman out of my mind isn't easy. And I only manage it when my busy brain flips over to thinking about Gunnar Scott instead.

There's another man who's too attractive for his own good. Although he's handsome in a scruffy way that's different from Spalding's genteel good looks.

My attraction to Gunnar began the very first night we ever worked together. I was—I can admit this now—a terrible bartender at first. I was only nineteen years old, and not a drinker. I had to mix each cocktail with the care of a chemist in the laboratory. One ounce of this, a half ounce of that.

Meanwhile, Gunnar would be just down the bar, pouring liquors I couldn't even pronounce with a flick of his strong wrist.

He made four times as many drinks as I did the first night. I was sweaty and demoralized by two a.m. But Gunnar was sipping a beer and facing the bills in the cash pouch with the finesse of a Las Vegas dealer. "Hey new girl," he'd said between tasks. "You need some help getting up to speed?"

"I'll get there," I'd said defensively.

"Never said you wouldn't." I watched his T-shirt flex over his strong chest. "If you're down, you can come over to my place and I'll give you some ..." His eyes did a slow tour of my breasts. "... special tutoring."

With a gulp, I'd turned away. "If *tutoring* is code for sex, then no thank you."

Gunnar had only laughed. "Can't blame a guy for trying." He'd reached up to grab a thin book off the shelf over the register. "Better take this then, and study it."

I'd taken his copy of *Mixology* and thanked him curtly. By studying that book, I became a more confident bartender. That's when my father hatched his scheme to dangle a promotion in front of both of us at the same time. So Gunnar and I became fierce competitors.

It was so typical of me to fall for my father's scheme. I wanted Daddy's approval so badly that I'd rather go to war with the hot guy in the tight T-shirt than go home to bed with him.

What a waste. I might have had a night of fun with someone who could have taught me to mix a gin fizz and a bloody Mary while naked.

But nope. My misplaced sense of duty and pride forbade me to have fun, or even ask for help.

I close my eyes and picture Gunnar behind my eyelids. He's aged well, damn him. Same scruffy blond hair and hot body. Same loverboy smile. What are the odds that he'll invite me over again? Pretty bad, I'm guessing. If he really needs the barista job, he won't proposition his boss.

Ah well. If he figures out how to make coffee before Monday, I can still watch his muscles flex while he does it.

It will have to be enough.

6

GUNNAR

THE NEXT MORNING I wake up in my SoHo loft. Even before I open my eyes, I hear the sounds of the city. A taxi's beep, and the cooing of a mourning dove on a nearby window ledge. These are the sounds of my childhood, which I spent in a much cheaper neighborhood in Queens.

I don't miss New York. Now that my mother has passed, there's nothing here for me.

Nonetheless, I own a kickass apartment. A few years ago, I bought this place on Sullivan Street as an investment. It's everything I coveted when I was old enough to realize that the patrons of Paxton's Bar and Bistro didn't live in shitty little apartments like I had as a child. My bachelor pad has big windows that let in the sunlight; high ceilings that make each room feel enormous. There's a killer kitchen with a row of leather-topped bar stools.

I swing my legs over the side of the bed and get up to visit the fanciest bathroom I'll ever own. It's a goddamn temple of marble tile and stonework. There's a Japanese soaking tub and heated towel bars. Maybe the heated toilet seat is a little over the top. But hey— this is my kingdom. I get to choose the throne.

After I've had a long drink of New York's finest tap water and a good stretch, I throw some clothes into a backpack. Then I drink a liter of water, don some sweats and leave the building, buying a bagel at a food cart on the corner.

It's a great bagel, too. I guess that's one thing New York does right.

My sweet apartment doesn't have a gym, but The Company does. It's a twenty-minute jog to our corporate headquarters on 18th Street.

The agent behind the desk recognizes me right away. "Gunnar, welcome back to New York!" Her dark eyes light up, and her cheeks flush.

"Thanks, Trina. Great to see you again." I hustle over to the elevator banks and take one downstairs to the gym.

It's a spacious room, but only young Duff is there, doing reps on the squat rack. "Morning," he says, dropping the barbell onto the supports. "How's your cushy assignment going?"

"It blows, but thanks for asking," I mutter, adding plates to the leg press. I have to keep my body ready for action even if Max wants me standing around in a pie shop.

"Hey, I'm spending the week keeping screaming fourteen-year-old girls away from a boy band," Duff says. "Trade you."

I actually consider it. A horde of fourteen-year-old girls sounds easier to withstand than the critical eye of Posy Paxton. "Do you know how to make coffee drinks?"

"Not really. And more to the point, I'm not a surveillance guy."

"So don't tease me," I grumble, catching one foot in my palm, and stretching out my quads. "I'm fragile right now."

"You're gonna bring us a pie, right? I'm partial to cherry and key lime."

"Don't get your hopes up," I grunt between reps. "I'll be fired after my first shift."

"Nah," Duff says. "You hear that?"

"Hear what?" After my tenth rep, I rest the weights and listen. I hear the groan of the freight elevator. "So?"

"That's your training equipment arriving."

"Sorry?"

"Just wait until you go upstairs."

Even though I'm curious, I don't cheat my workout. It takes patience and effort to look this good and stay this fit. At thirty-six, I can't afford to let my body slide.

Not until after I shower and dress do I step into the elevator for a ride to the sixth floor. That's where our offices are—Max's, Carl's, and mine, although I rarely use it. There's also a conference room and a kitchen. But the vast majority of the big space is given over to a our open-plan proofing ground, where we build and test new tools and gadgets.

When the elevator doors part, I see the usual work table. But it's not covered with laser devices or spy gear. Instead, I see a bright red Italian espresso machine. The same model that Posy has in her pie shop. "What the …?"

Max paces toward me, hands in his pockets, face grim. "You've got twenty-two hours to nail this mission, Gunn. You can do this."

"Dude. There's got to be another way. How about I take up a position on the roof across the street—"

Max cuts me off with a slice of his hand through the air. Then he points at a guy wearing a plaid shirt and a beanie. The man is standing with his hands in a prayer position, and his eyes are closed. "Meet your trainer. He just flew in from Portland."

"Portland … Maine?"

"Portland, Oregon," Max corrects. "Hipster capital of the world. Rico won the 2018 Barista World Championship. Rico, your trainee is here."

The man opens his eyes. "Moment. I'm meditating." His eyes flutter closed, but he speaks anyway. "Coffee is a life force. I'm tapping into the soul of my dark master."

"Oh brother." I hope Max isn't paying this guy too much.

"We're on a deadline, my man," Max says. "You've got twelve hours to turn this guy into a world class barista."

His eyes fly open again and he drops his hands. "I'm just fucking with you. People have weird ideas about Portland." He lifts a hand to the beanie and whips it off, revealing a buzz cut tight enough for the Marine Corps. "Okay. Let's pull some motherfucking shots."

"You'll do nicely," Max says. "Rico, this is Gunnar. He's smart, and he's good with his hands. He can build an explosive device out of household cleaners and ten dollars' worth of hardware store items. He can hack into your phone, your car, and your bank accounts. But none of that matters now. Only the coffee. It's life or death."

"That's laying it on a little thick," I grumble.

"Coffee *is* life or death," Rico says. "So get over here and let me see you pull your first shot."

"One moment." I drag Max aside, whether he likes it or not. "How much is this costing us?"

Max shrugs. "Just a charter flight, the machine rental, a hotel room, and his fee for one day. It could be worse."

That's easily fifteen grand. The flight alone could be ten. "You must *really* want to get to the bottom of this mystery that nobody has asked you to solve."

"So what if I do?" He crosses his arms. "Your annual profit-sharing bonus is not in any danger, Gunn. It's not like you to give me a hard time about this. This Posy chick must be a real ball-buster. Who knew Gunnar was afraid of a pastry chef?"

I growl, because Posy has got nothing to do with it.

Okay, she has a little to do with it. But still. "Max, this is border-line psycho. This hacker you're chasing might not lead you where you think he will. Meanwhile, we have paying clients we could be servicing."

"My gut says the murders are part of something big," he says quietly. "And if I'm right, many of our clients are in danger. As is the entire information economy."

This shuts me up for a moment, because security work has its own breed of logic. It's the only job in which you hope that *everything* you do is unnecessary.

Although it often isn't, because the world is a scary place. And hunches are not to be ignored. Especially Max's.

"Fine," I grunt, shooting a glance toward the drill sergeant who's going to teach me to be a barista. "But my next assignment better be something where I get to hack into something or shoot at something."

Max snorts. "You're looking at this the wrong way, Gunn. Think of the look on Posy's face tomorrow when you walk in there and make cup after cup of award-worthy espresso. When she realizes she won't have the satisfaction of firing you."

"Hmm," I say, because the idea does have a certain amount of appeal. "Okay. But you still owe me."

"I know it." He gives me a little push toward the coffee machine.

"Let's go, recruit!" the trainer says, rubbing his hands together. "Jump right in and make your first shot."

"Sure," I say, holding in a sigh, rounding the bar to flip the switch on the grinder. I count to three Mississippis and turn it off, just like Posy does. Then I measure out the first shot of coffee grounds and carry on.

It's all going fine until I'm about to put the tamped-down shot into Lola's twin.

"Whoa, recruit!" Rico barks. "Dude. Always clean off the edge of the portafilter before you load that shot. No excuses. You're not respecting your beans!"

"Huh? Clean the *what?*"

"Port. A. Filter," he enunciates. "That wand in your hand has a name. Don't you have an espresso machine at home? Don't tell me you drink coffee from *pods*." He shudders.

"I don't drink coffee at all."

Rico blinks. And then he blinks again. "Why?"

"Not a fan," I say.

"Fuck me." He throws his hands up. "I don't think I can work under these conditions."

"Listen. I will not have tea drinkers shamed in this office. And just think of your fee, man. You'll be able to afford a lot of fresh ink." The man has more tattoos than New York has hipsters.

He lets out a sigh. "You're right. It's fine. I'll just have to assume a different base of knowledge."

"Exactly. Talk to me like I'm a fifteen-year-old coffee virgin."

"Fine. Let's start over. This is a portafilter." He points at it. "I want you to treat it like you treat your dick—keep it clean and ready for action. Every shot will be pure bliss, if you always wipe the edge before you insert it in the machine."

"Uh, sure." Although I think he took that analogy a little too far.

"Now drop and give me ten push-ups."

"What? I just came from the gym."

He gives me a menacing look. "Fuck if I care. Drop to the floor, recruit. You'll learn. Every mistake requires a punishment."

I hit the deck and bang out ten push-ups. And plot new ways to murder Max. Possibly with a portafilter.

"*Speed ball.*"

"It's …" I know this one. "A cup of regular coffee with a shot of espresso in it."

"*Caffe Freddo.*"

"That's … an iced espresso."

"*Wet.*"

"Uh …" Damn it. "It's how the ladies feel when they meet me."

Rico shakes his head. "Wet means more milk than foam. Drop and give me ten."

I drop to the floor again and bang out another ten push-ups. My arms are quaking because I've done hundreds already.

On the upside, I know a lot about coffee now. And chicks dig big guns, so …

"Is he ready for the big time yet?"

When I stand up, Max is pacing in front of the impromptu coffee bar. "I'm getting there," I tell my impatient partner. "I've already made enough espresso to fuel lower Manhattan."

"You're ready for a test, then," Max says.

"He totally is," Rico agrees. "Bring on the hordes."

"The … who?"

Max pulls his Katt Phone out of his pocket and taps the screen. "Attention Company staff." His voice booms from the loudspeakers mounted on the walls, here and on every other floor. "I've just unlocked the sixth floor to all employees, because we have a special treat for you today. Gunnar Scott wants to show you how excited he is to be back in New York. While supplies last, he'll be pouring specialty coffee drinks for any employee. Come on upstairs and order your favorite. No order is too weird or too complicated!"

Rico snickers.

"Oh my fucking God," I groan. "I was gonna grab a sandwich!" Even as the words leave my mouth, I can see five of my colleagues hustling toward the espresso machine, each hoping to be first in line. "Fuck."

The stairwell door flies open, and eight more people rush towards me.

The first person in line is Shelby, Carl Bayer's executive assistant. "Gunnar, can you really make me a skinny mocha with an extra shot?"

"Of course I can," I promise, grabbing the portafilter and wiping it out carefully so that the drill sergeant of espresso doesn't make me do push-ups in front of my peers. I hit the grinder button, shutting it off at the right time without even counting to three Mississippis.

I never wanted to make coffee. But fuck me, I'm good at it now.

"Gunnar! Can I have a tall latte?" The next person in line is Carl Bayer, Max's father. He runs the personal security side of the business.

"Yessir. And I can make a poodle's face in the goddamn foam." That's another thing Rico taught me. *Let the design flow from your wrist, Gunnar. Tap! Flick! Get that jug closer to the cup!*

"A poodle?" Carl barks. "Make mine a pit bull."

"Yessir."

Meanwhile, the world is burning down. There's a murderer on the loose. Yet here I stand, learning to make pictures with foamy milk.

My stomach growls as I grind yet another shot. And when I look up, the line of Company employees waiting for coffee is so long that it snakes across the giant space, curling around past Max's office door like a cat's tail. I'm going to be here until Christmas.

"Don't be shy!" Max tells the crowd. "Ask him for anything you can think of."

My growl is drowned out by the sound of the espresso machine. There's only one thing I've got going for me right now. A single bright spot on my dark horizon. And that's the look I'll see on Posy's face tomorrow when I start my shift making perfect espresso drinks for her customers.

I'm going to flirt my ass off, too. With the women *and* the men. She hates it when I do that.

I snicker to myself as I clean off the frothing arm with a well-practiced flourish, and hand over another perfect coffee.

"Next!" I bellow, and the crowd cheers.

7

GUNNAR

"HERE YOU GO," I say to the woman at the counter. "A grande, single shot, two pumps caramel, one pump cherry, nonfat extra-hot latte."

"*Thank* you." The woman looks down at her cup, then looks back up at me with hearts in her eyes. "What a beautiful tulip! I don't know if I can stand to drink it."

"Aw, shucks. Your lovely blouse reminds me of tulips." And after that ridiculous order? She'd *better* drink it. I might have to jump over the counter and pour it down her throat. "Enjoy it. Have a great day." I say this loudly for Posy's benefit. I can feel her hovering near the kitchen doorway, just waiting for me to fuck up.

Good luck, sweetheart. You're looking at a guy who just made about fifty complicated espresso drinks without wrecking any of them.

And Posy can't *stand* it. Ever since our very first customer this morning—I made some dude a perfect non-fat cappuccino with a peacock design in the foam, and complimented his eyebrow piercing—she's been watching me with a mixture of amazement, annoyance, and lust.

Okay, that last thing is probably my imagination. But she's practically vibrating with irritation. She was expecting to fire me, I think. But now she can't.

Hell, it's just like old times. After her dad put us in competition, I used to send her all the trickiest drink orders. *Oh, you want a Rum*

53

Martinez? A kiwi daiquiri? That little lady down the bar will help you. Then I'd watch her covertly look it up. She used to carry around that old mixology book and consult it when she thought I wasn't looking. Like a cheater who holds his crib sheet under the desk.

You have to get your kicks where you can. And I'd forgotten how much fun it is to challenge Posy. On slow nights, I'd quiz her *mercilessly.* There was nothing better than watching those devastating cheekbones flush with victory whenever she solved another problem.

I wanted to kiss that look of victory right off her face.

But I was just a dumb kid, spending the whole summer trying to impress a pretty rich girl and her asshole father. Even though the results were fixed from the start.

Spoiler alert: I didn't win either the girl or the manager's job. I never stood a chance.

Two young women enter the shop and approach the counter. I sell them slices of pie and cups of tea. "Just tea?" I ask in artificial outrage. "Where's the challenge in that?"

They smile and bat their long eyelashes. One of them drops a ten-dollar bill into the tip jar.

"Thank you so much," I say, eyeing the tips in that jar. Honestly, I can't even remember how it felt to live off tips. But people do it all the time. I used to be one of them. I don't need the money anymore, though. My stake in The Company is worth over a hundred million dollars.

Meanwhile, I can't forget my true purpose here. Between customers, I slowly wipe the entire width of the coffee counter. Not only does it make me look like a perfect kiss-ass, but it allows the camera pen sticking out of my pocket to get a good look at everyone in the restaurant.

Each time the camera picks up a new customer, the guys in the control room will try—in real time—to match the face with every known facial recognition database.

One particular customer has already piqued my attention. There's an older guy who's been holding court in the corner by the window for two hours already. I can't see his screen, though. It's facing the exposed brick wall on the opposite side of the room.

Meanwhile, he's had two different visitors already, each one taking a seat in front of him for forty minutes at a time. It's like he thinks this place is his office, and that table is his private conference room. At least everyone bought drinks. And one of the guys purchased a thick slice of Chai Swirl Pumpkin pie.

Every slice of pie I cut looks more glorious than the last. Posy might be an irritating trust fund kid with a bossy streak a mile wide, but she bakes a hell of a pie. Each one is a work of art, too. I didn't know you could braid a crust or cut pastry to look like lace. Posy's obsession with detail has finally found its natural outlet.

I'd buy a pie for the guys in the control room, but a whole one costs forty bucks. That's too pricey for an hourly employee to afford, and I can't blow my cover.

"Look, I just don't get it," Posy says suddenly as I scrutinize the customers. When I turn, she's propped against the doorway. She's removed her apron, which means I've got a great view of her curves in the tight top she's wearing. "Why did you screw up the coffee so badly the other day if you actually knew what you were doing?"

"I told you I was rusty," I say mildly. "Spent some time at the University of YouTube this weekend, remembering how to do coffee right."

Her eyes narrow. She doesn't believe me.

Got to give the girl some credit for that, I guess. Her suspicions are very well founded. "You just don't want to see me succeed. You never did back in the day."

She pushes off the wall and stalks forward. "That is *not* true. I always said you were the better bartender. But I was hell bent on being the better bar *manager*. Not that it mattered."

"Not that it mattered," I echo, cackling. "Notice that you're still not ready to let it go."

"You brought it up." She folds her arms, which only emphasizes her breasts. Posy is stacked, and I have eyes and a functioning libido. I'm not really ogling my boss. Not much anyway.

I'm ready to up the ante on our argument when Posy abruptly turns around and disappears into the kitchen.

A moment later I realize why. That same hottie from the other day—the one who wanted a decaf latte—is back again.

Posy doesn't like this woman, and now I'm curious why. "Hello there," I greet her. "Can I make you a *decaf* sugar free peppermint latte, half two percent half skim, iced, no foam?"

Her eyes light up like sparklers. "You remembered! I would *love* one. So long as it's decaf. I can't have regular coffee. It would be bad for the baby."

"Congratulations, and I won't forget," I promise, giving her a cheesy wink. And when I turn around to grind a shot of decaf—which is relegated to Siberia on the wall behind me—I catch a glimpse of Posy out of my peripheral vision. She's in the kitchen, pressed against the wall just out of sight of the counter. Her eyes are closed, and she's braced herself against the wall, as if she needs it for support.

Hmm. That's interesting.

I make this woman's complicated coffee beverage practically on autopilot. I'm really that good at this now. And just as I'm ringing her up, a guy in starched khaki pants and a white linen shirt strides in on shiny penny loafers. "Saroya," he says, approaching the counter. "What's taking so long?"

And I've seen this guy before. His face is familiar, and I'm searching my brain for a reason. His look could best be described as *preppy newscaster*. But I don't think he's actually a face from TV.

"I'll just be another moment," his wife says. "Don't you want a latte, too? I was hoping to share our big news with Posy."

At that, the man's eyes dart toward the kitchen door. "I don't see her. Maybe another time?"

His guilty look is the thing that jogs my memory. "Actually, Posy isn't here at the moment," I say to this man who used to sit at the bar just to flirt with her. What was his name—Skippy? Spiffy? I remember it was something pretentious. "She had an appointment in Midtown," I add, because the look on Posy's face a minute ago tells me that she wishes she really were several miles away.

"Hear that?" the guy says. "Let's get going."

"Thank you for the excellent coffee," Saroya says with a flirty smile.

"Anytime." I give her a panty-dropping smile in return, just to watch her preppy partner scowl. He's eight or nine years older than she is, or I'm the mayor of New York.

As they leave, I glance at my watch. Could this shift last any longer? I clean off the frothing arm one more time.

This job is repetitive as hell. I'd better find that murderer quick.

o—👈

The day is finally drawing to a close by the time Posy finally emerges from the back. And I do a little double take when I notice her red eyes and new makeup job. "Hey," she says.

"Hey," I echo, rinsing out the milk jug. "It's closing time, right?" The last customer left a few minutes ago.

"Right." She clears her throat. "Thank you, Gunn. For …" she makes a vague gesture with her hands toward the door. "If Spalding shows his face again, I'm generally not available."

"Got it," I agree. "*Spalding*. I'd forgotten your ex-boyfriend's name."

"Ex-husband," she says ruefully.

"Oh. Sorry." Yikes. "Was it, uh, a recent breakup?"

"Almost a year now," she says, lifting her chin. "And I'm fine with it. But I don't know why they have to keep coming in here."

"*Well*, Posy. The coffee is top notch. And it just got a little better." I pat myself on the chest.

She rolls her eyes. "I guess your ego hasn't faded in the last fifteen years."

"Nah. If anything, it's gotten bigger. I mean—if you were me, wouldn't you have a big ego?" I wave in the direction of my tight Posy's Pie Shop T-shirt and give her a cheesy grin. It's supposed to be a joke. After all, Posy thinks I'm a barely employed thirty-five year-old barista.

"Maybe I would," she says, blushing.

Huh. I think Posy remembers our big kiss, too.

"Anyway, feel free to let the quality slip if he asks you for coffee. I don't want him in my life."

"It would be against the barista oath to pour an inferior shot," I say sanctimoniously. "But I could be hopelessly rude. That's not against code. And I could definitely spell his name wrong on the cup. I think *Smallthing* has a nice ring to it."

"Omigod." Posy lets out a bark of laughter. "I dare you."

"Consider it done." We're smiling at each other, and I'm startled to realize that I'm flirting with Posy Paxton again. I guess old habits are hard to break. "I'm happy to offend the man with the shiniest penny loafers in Manhattan. Although we might lose his wife's business. She's worth a few hundred bucks of peppermint syrup alone."

"I wish they'd both lose my address." Posy's smile fades. "You know who misses Spalding, though?"

"The Gucci store?" I try.

"My father," Posy grumbles. "He's a big fan. He says that losing Spalding was my greatest failure. As if there's a long string of those to choose from. I graduated magna cum laude from Columbia, but all my father sees is a failed marriage."

"Ouch." Posy's dad is a giant tool, and I could never understand why she worked so hard to please him. Still, I can't resist teasing her. "Magna cum laude, huh? I graduated summa."

"You did?" she scowls. "Of course you did."

"Nah, I'm just fucking with you." I snap the towel close to her hip and then laugh. "But you totally believed me. And it bothered you, didn't it? Admit it."

"It did." She puts her hands up to her face and shakes her head. "Just ignore me. This is what a midlife crisis looks like—a divorce, a career change, and a kitschy pie shop."

Her vulnerability surprises me. And I glance around the pie shop, looking at it with fresh eyes. It's a beautiful space, with golden lighting, warm wood floors, and creamy white wainscoting that gives off farmhouse vibes. There's a shelf that runs all the way across the far wall, and it's decorated with a collection of pristine ceramic farm animals. And each wooden table has a pair of chairs in matching colors.

It's like I'm standing inside Posy's chipper, ambitious mind. "I like it," I say slowly. "And as for midlife crises, I've seen worse. My uncle Pat bought a vintage Camaro and grew some scary sideburns and an unfortunate mustache."

"Thank God it hasn't come to that." Posy turns toward the kitchen door. "Hey Jerry! It's time for your big moment."

"Awesome!" comes a shout from the back. A moment later, the

special needs kid who washes dishes comes flying out. He rushes over to the door and flips the sign from OPEN to CLOSED. "Done!"

"Good work," she says. "You can take off your apron and go home, okay?"

"Okay Posy." He reaches back and fumbles with the strings.

"Hey, Jerry?" I say, reaching for the tip jar. "There was a lady in here who left a tip for you."

His mouth opens in surprise. "The tips in the jar aren't for me."

"I know," I say, because I realize I can't make a habit of this, or the other baristas will have to pony up as well. "But she did it especially for you. Just this once." I offer him both of the ten dollar bills I received today.

He takes the money with wide eyes. "Thanks, mister."

"Oh, I thanked the lady for you. Don't worry."

"Wow, maybe she'll come back tomorrow!"

"You never know," I say with a shrug. "Could happen."

"Bye, Posy!" he says, marching toward the back.

"See you tomorrow," she calls after him. A minute later we hear a bang as the back door is slammed shut. Then she turns to me with narrowed eyes. "I don't know what's more surprising. The fact that you gave Jerry your money, or the fact that two women left you ten-dollar tips."

"How do you know they were women?" I ask. "Plenty of men appreciate this face, too."

She rolls her eyes as she lifts the tip jar, testing its weight. "Good. Lord. It's just like the old days, Gunnar. Your tip jar was always bulging at the seams."

"I can't believe the boss is checking out my bulge," I say before I think better of it. Oops.

"Gunnar!" she squeaks. "Do you have to make everything into a sex joke?"

"Sorry," I flinch. "Old habits die hard. Hey—am I supposed to count the drawer?" I ask, pointing at the cash register.

"It depends on who's working and how big a hurry I'm in. I think I'll count it and then make the deposit while you finish cleaning up."

"No problem."

She takes the register drawer to the end of the counter and stands there to count up the cash, while I wipe down each of the cafe tables for a final time and invert the chairs on them.

With the broom and the mop that I spotted in back, I clean all the pie crumbs and an errant paper napkin off the floor.

It's funny how natural this feels. I haven't worked a food service job in ages. But there's a comfortable rhythm to it that's familiar. My work in security is very exciting, but no job is ever really finished. Closing up for the night feels like an accomplishment.

"All right," Posy says into our companionable silence. "I need to run over to the bank. I can lock up now or leave you here for ten more minutes. Which is it going to be?"

"Go ahead," I say. "I'll finish up here, and then sit down to check my email. I'm expecting a message from my father's doctor."

Her face creases with concern, and I feel like a jerk. "Of course. Go right ahead. Just don't leave before I get back."

"No problem." I watch her shove the cash pouch into her shoulder bag. "Hey—are you okay to just walk around alone with that?"

She stares at me. "I do this every afternoon. What are you, my self-appointed bodyguard?"

Well, actually ... "Never mind," I force myself to say.

"I took a full self-defense course at the Y, I'll have you know."

"You go ahead, then. Sorry to interfere."

She walks out the door, and I count to ten. Then I get up and walk over to the window, pressing my temple against the glass so I can see her pass down the street. The moment she's disappeared, I grab my jacket off the hook and pull a pouch out of the pocket. There's a small camera inside, the size of a woman's lipstick case.

I carry it over to the wall opposite the coffee bar and start looking for the best place to conceal it. Posy's decor makes my deception pretty easy—the shelf with all the animal statuettes is perfect for this. If I'm careful, I can position it to show me the computer screen of anyone who's sitting at the big table in front.

I flip a small switch on the camera housing and then tuck the device between the legs of a ceramic cow. I use a short stack of pennies to lever the thing into an angle that makes sense to me. And then I sit in the chair.

Tapping the face of my watch a couple of times, I call Max.

"Yo!" my partner in crime says. "What have you got for me?"

"I've got fifteen bucks an hour and some tips," I say drily. "I just activated a remote camera. What can you see?"

"A table, your hands, and a napkin dispenser."

"Fair enough." I get out of the chair and head for the door to the back. A glance at the street tells me Posy isn't back yet. I have no idea how long it takes to make a bank deposit. "Any action on the boards today?"

"There was, but I don't have a report on the locations yet," he says. "Pieter is working on it."

"Please, baby Jesus, let there be a reason I made eight million lattes today."

"Your body cam is still broadcasting," Max says. "If you're on the way to the john, you should shut that off."

I reach up and click off the pen-shaped camera in my shirt pocket. "I'm about to download the log files from Posy's computer onto a thumb drive." Between the front of the house and the kitchen, there's a doorway to the world's smallest office. It's basically a closet with a desk wedged into it. I sit down in Posy's office chair and give the computer mouse a shake.

"This is an ancient PC," I grumble. "We were using machines like this back when *Call of Duty 2* was cool."

"It should be easy to crack, then."

"Yeah." In fact, I don't even reach for the password cracking device in my pocket. First, I'll try my hunch. Humans—ninety seven percent of the time—choose predictable passwords. And the logo image for Posy's Pie Shop is as good a place as any to begin. I type L-e-m-o-n into the password window, and then hesitate. "Max, how do you spell meringue?

"M-E-R"

"I got that part. But then ... I?"

"No, E-N-G-U-E?"

Password failed. "Nope."

"Isn't E the way you get a long A in Spanish?"

61

"Shouldn't this be French?"

"Well, do you mean the Latin dance? Or the white stuff on pie?"

"It's a fucking pie shop, Max." I quickly try it the other way.

"Don't get testy with me, cowboy."

"Kind of in a hurry here," I grumble. But the computer blinks to life. "Jesus, the security here is terrible."

"That makes our job easier. Get the modem log."

"Duh." I pull up a command prompt and type like my ass is on fire. I pop a thumb drive into the machine and start the download I need. "Hopefully we can match up some of your message board action with the time stamp on this thing. I hope it goes back a few weeks."

"Same dude, same. Did you check out the employees' devices?"

"Posy has an iPhone. The kid who washes dishes has a battered iPad. The customers *all* have laptops, though. Some of them camp out for hours."

"Roger."

I glance at the command window and then curse. *Transfer failed.* "Max, gotta jump. I'm having some trouble here."

"What? Dude, we need that—"

"I *know*. Later." I tap my watch, hanging up on him. Then I start tapping on Posy's keyboard like crazy.

Shit.

8

POSY

WHEN I PUSH open the door to the bakery, Gunnar is nowhere in sight. *Damn him!* If he left my shop empty and split, I will kill him with my bare hands.

But then I hear his voice coming from somewhere in back. "Okay. Yes. That works. Got it."

I'm not sure why I tiptoe through my own cafe like some kind of ninja. But what is he doing back there? I ease toward the doorway until I can catch an oblique glimpse of Gunnar. He's sitting in my office chair, leaning back like a king in his throne. "Thank you, sir. Until next week. Goodbye." He leans down and hangs up my phone. Then he glances up, catches me watching him, and his eyes widen. "Hey, sorry. My phone died. I didn't think you'd mind if I used the landline."

"Not at all," I hear myself say. But my heart is thumping. "Make yourself right at home."

His grin tells me that it came out sounding snippy. "Thanks."

My twinge of discomfort is ridiculous, right? Using my phone is no big deal. I've always wanted my employees to feel at home. Gunnar should be no different.

Let's face it, there's not much trouble he could get into in my office anyway. Lord knows there's nothing to steal, except for some pie shop T-shirts and my cache of dreadfully expensive vanilla.

The real risk of dishonest employees is that they'll steal from the till. It happens. I wasn't born yesterday. I'm sure it will happen to me someday. The only way to prevent that is to run every single transaction yourself.

I can't do that, of course. Unless I want to operate a one-woman show and work myself into an early grave. Trust is what makes the world go around. If you don't have any, then you can't ever build something larger than yourself.

The truth is that I choose to trust Gunnar, and all my other employees. It's not because I'm stupid—my own father lies with every breath he takes. I choose it because I want to live in a world where trust is the rule, not the exception.

So I smile at Gunnar and try again. "Did you get that email you were hoping for?"

"Yup," he says easily. "My dad's therapy is going to be covered under his Medicare. That's why I had to make a call and confirm his appointment for next week." He stands up and stretches, and I'm hit with the view of his T-shirt riding up, exposing a set of rippling abs, and the narrow trail of hair that descends from his tight stomach toward ...

I jerk my eyes away.

"Something wrong?" he asks, and I swear there's a twinkle in his eye.

"Nope. No. Nothing," I babble. "I could order you an extra-large. T-shirt, I mean! The large is a little snug. I'll do that tonight." I turn around quickly, trying to stem the flow of words from my mouth. "Time to go, trainee. I have to lock up."

"Yes ma'am." He chuckles. Then I hear the wheels of my desk chair squeak as he pushes it in, flips off the lights and follows me out.

"Is he going to be okay?" I ask, regaining my composure.

"Who?" He follows me into the dining room.

"Your father."

"Oh," he says quickly. "Yeah. Just, uh, a bump in the road."

"Is that why you're back in New York?" I press.

"Exactly. I really can't stand New York, but duty calls."

"I'm sorry that my benefits package kind of sucks." Gunnar

wouldn't qualify for health insurance until he'd worked full time for six months.

"It's really okay," he says smoothly. "Dad is covered by Medicare. And I realize you're running a really small business."

"Not like Paxton's," I say with a sigh. Gunnar makes me think about that place more than I'd like to.

"You know ..." He removes the half apron from around his waist and hangs it on one of the hooks on the wall. "I thought you'd be running that place by now."

"You and me both. The whole reason I went to business school is so that my dad would feel good about passing it on to me someday."

"So what happened?" His big shoulders give a shrug.

"My father happened."

"Oh." Those cool green eyes blink. "Never mind. I didn't mean to pry."

"Eh, everybody knows. He sold it out from under me to a private equity firm. I was literally the last to know. My grandfather had been dead barely a year when he took the first offer and cashed out." I swallow hard.

"I'm sorry, Posy," Gunnar says quietly. "I know you had strong feelings about the place."

"I really did." Paxton's was everything to me. I loved the shiny mahogany bar, the chandeliers in the dining room, and the leaded glass windows. I would have done whatever it took to step into my great grandfather's shoes and run the place someday. Paxton's was founded in 1927, on Madison and Seventy-ninth. It was an Upper East Side fixture, where starlets and politicians gathered to dine and meet and rule the world.

"It's a franchise now," I say in a voice that only quavers slightly. "East Hampton. Las Vegas. Palm Springs. Singapore. Anywhere people are willing to pay twenty-two bucks for a martini. Anywhere you can staple up some mahogany paneling. It's just a name now."

"Ouch. That sucks." Gunnar shoves his hands in his pockets. He's sorry he asked. "What time do you want me tomorrow?"

"Same time. Employees who clock in before seven can help themselves to a slice of pie or a pastry."

"Mmm," he says, his rich voice making that half word sound dirty. "I can't wait."

My hormones rejoice. *We can't wait, either!*

That's when it really hits me. Gunnar is a *good* barista, and he did well today. That means I need him behind that counter tomorrow. And the day after that. And every hour that he's willing to work for me.

I'd better order more than one extra-large T-shirt. And I'd better take a lot of cold showers.

"'Night Posy!" Gunnar gives me a wave and leaves by the front door. And somehow I manage not to check out his ass as he goes.

Nobody said running a business of my own would be easy. I was prepared for the long hours, and the constant flow of unanticipated expenses.

But I wasn't prepared for Gunnar Scott. They didn't teach this at business school. There was no coursework for how to handle that awkward moment when a man who gave you the best kiss of your life walks in to ask for a job.

Let's jump him! my hormones shout.

I won't do it, though. I'll go upstairs and make a healthy dinner and go to sleep at nine like a loser.

And I will *not* dream of Gunnar Scott.

It works. Mostly. After a few days, having Gunnar around every morning starts to seem normal. He's always on time, always wearing a tight T-shirt with a pie stretched across his tasty chest. Even the extra-large shirts prove snug on his biceps.

God, he's handsome. And—it kills me to admit it—he's a godsend. I stop darting into the cafe to check on him, because he doesn't need my help. He has the price list memorized. He can make change before the register gives the total, and his espresso drinks are top notch. He's polite, and the tip jar is stuffed with cash at the end of the day.

He's wonderful, damn it. And that makes me crazy.

I'm not the only one who thinks so, either. Teagan loves him.

When they work together, she spends less time staring at her phone, and more time staring at Gunnar.

Jerry's a big fan, too. And Ginny. And my entire customer base. I could just rename this place *Gunnar Scott's Fan Club, With Coffee and Pie*.

Furthermore, I never realized how small the area behind the counter is. When the shop gets busy and I come out of the kitchen to pitch in, I feel like I'm constantly rubbing up against him. He'll reach over my head for a paper cup off the top of the stack, and I'm able to smell his spicy aftershave. Or I'll reach past him for a clean saucer, and accidentally brush my boob against his arm.

"Sorry," he says one afternoon when I take a half step backward only to find my ass pressed against his crotch.

"No worries," I say in a voice as deep as Lauren Bacall's, as my whole body heats in response. It's been over a year since I touched a man and working so close to him is torture. But I try to cover up my discomfort with a joke. "You know, fifteen years ago you would have turned that into a sexual invitation. I think you're off your game."

"Look," he says, frothing a jug of milk with aplomb, while I try not to stare at his flexing arm muscles. "Believe it or not, I've actually matured since college. These days I know better than to sexually harass the boss."

"I know," I say quickly. "It's just that I'm a little wiser than I was back then, too. I think about that summer and realize what an uptight little wreck I was. These days I'm less of a prude, and better at taking a joke."

"A joke? Here's the thing, Posy—every sleazy invitation I ever issued to you was a hundred percent sincere. They all still stand, by the way. I no longer proposition women at work, but if one propositions me, it's *on*, baby." He flips those killer green eyes up at me and gives me a quick smile before turning away to decorate someone's latte with roses.

Several beats later I remember to close my mouth and put a customer's spinach pasty into the oven for two minutes of warming. But my addled little brain is still stuck on Gunnar. Because unless I'm mistaken, he's just issued me a coy invitation to take him to bed.

And I am shook. Did he really just say that?

Promise me you'll think about it, my sister had begged me when I first told her about Gunnar's employment.

For one blissfully long moment, I do. I allow myself to consider asking him upstairs for a drink the next time Aaron and Ginny are out.

But just as quickly, I realize I won't have the nerve. I can still hear my ex's voice ringing in my head, telling me I'm not adventurous enough. Calling me a *starfish*. I'd die if Gunnar said the same thing.

Fifteen years ago, he kissed me, and I knew he was more than I could handle. And now? It's still true.

The oven timer dings, ending my reverie. And I get back to work.

It's not easy to stop thinking about Gunnar, though, especially since other people seem hell bent on noticing him, too. My sister suddenly has more patience for helping out with the morning counter shift than she used to.

"Lord, he's hot," she says to me in the kitchen on one such morning. "If you're not going to take him to bed, I might."

"Ginny!" I squeak. "Lower your voice."

"He can't hear us, he's flirting with a customer." My sister stacks the last of the ham and cheese tarts onto a serving tray and sighs. "He has beautiful thighs."

"What?" I haven't dwelt on his legs. Not yet, anyway. I can't stop watching his hands. His back. That ass …

"Those thighs. The way they stretch his jeans to the max? It's a good thing he wears a half apron or I'd spend my shifts admiring his package."

"Take a cold shower," I grumble. "We can't boink the employees."

"Just a quickie?" she whines. "It's been a long time for me. But at least my dry spell is about to end."

"It is?"

"I'm going on a date tonight," she winks and hefts the tray, heading for the dining room. "Aaron is with his grandparents and I have plans. Don't wait up."

"Got it," I say lightly. Both my sister and my five-year-old nephew have better social lives than I do. Aaron's father is in prison, but the man's parents drive in from Connecticut to pick up their grandson every two weeks for an overnight visit.

It's only me who'll be at home on the couch on a Friday night, then. Yay.

"The mail is coming!" Jerry says, clapping his hands with glee. "Can I get it, Posy?"

"Of course. Be my guest."

Jerry drops a bowl into the sink with a deafening clatter and bangs open the screen door to greet the mail carrier. "Hi Brenda! Do you have anything for us?"

I wish I had half as much enthusiasm for life as he has. Where can I get some?

A moment later Jerry comes bounding back into the kitchen. "Two envelopes. One of them I had to *sign* for! Brenda said to sign my name even though it's for you."

"Thank you. Well done," I say even as my stomach drops. The only documents I've ever had to sign for were divorce papers.

And sure enough, there's a dreadful logo on this particular envelope, from the Office of Workers Compensation. *Open immediately*, it reads. *Legal filing inside.*

Please, Goddess, let this be a routine filing, I pray as I slit open the envelope.

But the goddess has not heard my prayer. The papers inside constitute an accident report for one Louis Perkins. It actually takes me a beat to remember that this name belongs to a kitchen assistant I'd hired before last month. He worked four shifts and then disappeared without calling to actually quit.

Employees ghost you all the time in restaurant work. But the papers I'm holding are certainly not business as usual. According to his filing, Louis Perkins burned himself removing a ginger and rhubarb pie from my oven.

That's plausible. I burn myself a couple times a week, easy. But according to his statement, Mr. Perkins fainted onto the tile floor, bumping his skull on the worktable and sustaining a head injury that prevents him from working anywhere for the foreseeable future.

69

The following page is a lengthy hospital bill, including a two-thousand-dollar trip via an ambulance to the E.R.

"No way," I breathe.

"What's the matter?" Ginny is back in the kitchen and reaching for the apple crumb pie.

"*Look* at this," I say, panic in my voice. "Is there any way this actually happened?"

"Take a breath, Posy," she says, steering me toward a stool. "Let me see. I remember this guy. Griped all week long before he took off." My sister frowns as she flips through the pages. "Motherfucker. This is a load of absolute crap."

"Is it? What if he fell down and didn't say anything?"

"No way." Ginny snorts. "All he did was complain! Endlessly. We rolled our eyes for a solid week. You were already looking around for a replacement before he even disappeared."

It's true. Louis Perkins hadn't liked the early start of our day, the timing of his lunch break, or the temperature of the kitchen. He was a pain in my ass. To think he'd suffered a grave injury—requiring an ambulance, no less—without my noticing? It was crazy. But here was his sworn statement, claiming he required a long-term payout.

Hot tears filled my eyes. "This is going to double my workers comp insurance!"

"No it won't, because you'll fight it," Ginny says fiercely. "He's just a dumbass who's looking for a free lunch."

"Okay," I say, swiping at my tears. "Like I need another thing to worry about."

"Put it out of your mind right now," Ginny insists. "Let's just get through the lunch rush."

"Right. Okay."

"Hey—Ginny?" Gunnar's low voice wafts into the kitchen, and then his handsome face appears. "Got that apple bourbon pie? I need four slices already."

"I'll be right there!" my sister calls, waving him off. When he disappears, she leans in and gives me a quick one-armed hug. "Don't worry. If you feel stressed, just think of Gunnar's voice saying *apple bourbon*." She makes a small noise of satisfaction. "I think I got pregnant just watching him stack those twenty-five-pound bags of coffee this morning."

"Omigod, stop." I'd been just as impressed, of course. It's just that I won't admit it aloud. "Go already."

"I will. But promise me you'll do something fun tonight instead of brooding about this."

"Promise," I grunt. Then I get up and start making another batch of pie crust.

9

GUNNAR

IT'S FRIDAY NIGHT, and I'm deep in the basement beneath The Company headquarters. We have a sparring ring down here.

The crowd tonight includes me, Max, and a handful of our agents. In spite of the protective gear I'm wearing, I have several new bruises and I'm sweating like a horse at the Kentucky Derby.

But I've missed these Friday evening sparring sessions. While I enjoy my work on the West Coast, it rarely affords me the opportunity to sweep Max's feet out from underneath him and drop him on his ass.

"Well played," Max says from the mats. Then he gets to his feet.

"Point to Gunnar, obviously. Max really should've seen that coming," says Scout, our lead investigator. It's her turn to referee.

Max scowls, and we circle each other again. To say that we're a competitive bunch would be a massive understatement. But Max seems distracted tonight, and I've just taken advantage.

I don't get any more points off him, though, before the timer goes off.

"My turn!" she sings out. "I'm fighting Max. Duff can referee."

"Back-to-back matches?" Duff asks, taking the stopwatch from Scout. "Shouldn't Max get a rest?"

"I don't need a rest," Max says tartly. Scout is barely five foot two. She's also a woman. And Max is slightly more competitive than Genghis Khan.

"What shall we play for?" Scout asks, pulling on her head gear. "How about this—if I win, I can choose what we order for dinner."

"You'll pick Indian again," Max grumbles.

"Then don't lose and you can have whatever you want." Scout checks her gloves, and they face each other at the center of the mat, waiting for Duff's signal. When he tells them to begin, they bow to one another gracefully.

But that's the last civilized moment between them. A few seconds later, Max has already made his first attack. But Scout is fast. She's ten inches shorter, with far less reach. But she's got impeccable instincts and the ability to dart like a hornet away from his first kick.

And his second. And his third.

He circles her to try again, and no one can look away. Every matchup is fun to watch, but Max versus Scout is *fascinating*. They look impossibly mismatched. It's a lie, though.

At least Max is no longer distracted. He knows he can't afford to let down his guard.

Scout dances and weaves. She pretends to lunge for him, but it's a trick. The moment he moves to block, she flits away. Circling. Waiting. Trying his patience.

I understand Max's frustration. It's like trying to swat a fly. It's *right* there, and it's smaller than you are. This ought to be easy.

Spoiler: it's not. Max tries a spirited kick which almost connects with Scout's shoulder. But she executes a gorgeous spinning jump-kick, which lifts her high into the air, putting her bare foot right into Max's face.

The crowd lets out a gasp of appreciation as Max's head snaps backward. His arms shoot out to the sides as he hops awkwardly backward, struggling to stay upright.

It doesn't work. He tumbles onto the mat with a thump and an "*oof*."

"Knockout!" Duff says gleefully. "Sorry boss."

"Oh for fuck's sake," Max says, leaping to his feet. "Best out of three?"

But Scout has already peeled off her protective gear. "Spicy chicken it is!"

Max takes off his headset and sighs. "Good on you. That was the fastest loss I've ever sustained."

"I can probably top that next time." She gives him a blinding smile. "You want that lamb dish that you always order?"

"Sure." He flips open his wallet and pulls out a c-note. "Get whatever Gunnar and Pieter want, too. I need to chat with all of you."

"Will do." Scout reaches into the V-neck of her T-shirt and slips the money into her bra. "Chicken Tikka, Gunn? I'll text Pieter. Meet you upstairs in forty-five?" She leaves the ring looking very pleased with herself.

Max watches her walk away, and then he shakes his head. "Gunn, let's get a beer upstairs before dinner."

"I was going to grab a shower." I gesture toward the locker rooms.

"Use mine. There's something I need to show you."

I grab my gym bag and follow Max to the elevator banks. He puts his hand on the scanner and his private elevator opens up. Then he flips open his messenger bag, extracts a copy of the *Post* and hands it to me.

The front-page story is hard to miss. *Brutal Downtown Murder Appears Linked to Overseas Crimes.* "Oh, shit. Right here in New York. You think this is …?"

"Keep reading."

It only takes me a minute to skim the article. The deceased was a thirty-six year-old computer security expert. His brother sent police to his house when he failed to answer his phone for several days. Officers found his body in his garden-level apartment.

The deceased was clutching a red ribbon.

"Could be a copycat," I grunt. "This red ribbon business is awfully melodramatic."

"But very splashy," Max insists as the elevator doors part into his apartment. "Our perp doesn't want his clues to be missed. He's on a mission."

"With what goal, though?"

"Intimidating anyone who gets close to the hardware hackers."

"Do you know what the dead guy was working on?" I ask.

Max shakes his head.

"But if this murder is linked, your informant should be bragging about it already, right? Did anyone post—"

Max takes the newspaper from me and tosses it onto an antique sideboard against the wall. He drops his bag there, too. "At eleven-sixteen today, a post went up from The Plumber. It was made from the pie shop."

My skin begins to tingle. "Right under my nose? Really? What's on my body cam at eleven-sixteen?"

"Well …" Max lets out a sigh. "The camera shows the hand pie you were eating on your break. Looked like ham and cheese."

"Fuck!" I'm so frustrated that I punch the air. "I was in—"

"The back alley. I saw."

"Damn it! Max, I only took fifteen minutes. How could he possibly have picked that time slot?" I drop my gym bag onto Max's thick Persian carpet in disgust.

"Probably just a coincidence," Max says. "If the perp was trying to avoid you, he would have used someone else's WiFi."

"*Hundreds* of coffees," I moan. "I've made so many lattes that I dream about it at night. And this asshole comes in on my break?"

Max shrugs. "It's rough luck, Gunn. But we'll get him."

"What is he saying, anyway? About the murder?"

"He said that the deceased had a black and white cat who was also poisoned at the scene."

"And …?" I ask.

"I verified it already. My guy at the precinct confirmed the cat's death. But it wasn't in any of the reporting."

"What does The Plumber want, anyway?" I ask Max. "Murderers don't brag about it on the internet. Not the smart ones. This guy is clever enough to pull off a string of unsolved murders. But too dumb not to leave a trail around New York?"

"Two possibilities." Max strokes his chin. "Maybe it's a distraction. One of his goons might be dropping these clues in New York, while he hides somewhere else. But I still think it's an associate of his. Someone who doesn't want to be involved anymore, and is trying to expose him."

"Awfully risky," I grunt.

"Yeah, but so is palling around with a ruthless criminal. I think the bossman is here in New York, and he's ordering these hits to send a disturbing message. And it's working, right? Hackers are pissing themselves all over the place, wondering if they're next."

"Sure. Fine."

"... So there's someone on his team who wants out. Maybe the team is large enough that he can post these tidbits without the boss guessing the mole."

"Still risky."

"True," Max admits. "But there's nobody braver than a man who's got nothing to lose. He sees a way out. He takes it. You and I have some more work to do in that pie shop."

I guess he's right. Max's scenario is pretty loopy. But he and I have seen a lot of crime in the last decade. And some of it was even stranger than this. "Can I have the first shower?"

"Go for it," he says.

An hour later, we're sitting around Max's dining table, eating Indian food and trying to figure out what to try next.

"The Plumber is using a Windows-based laptop," Max says. "The pie shop modem logs were very clear on this."

"A Windows machine. Got it," I say. "There's only like a million of those in New York. No problemo."

"We need more cameras," Pieter says. "Gunnar's body cam can't be everywhere at once. I get a lot of coffee porn. Nice technique with the milk, by the way. That unicorn you did for the old lady was your best yet."

"Thank you," I grumble.

"That other camera you planted allows me a nice view of the computer screens at that front table. But the worst crime I've seen so far over there was the purchase of a really ugly pair of shoes from Zappos."

"What about that older guy?" I ask, tearing a piece of naan bread. "He holds meetings at the table in the afternoon. What's he got on his computer screen?"

"He's not our man." Pieter shakes his head. "He's interviewing candidates for Doctors Without Borders."

"Really?" I snort. Unbelievable. We're both in the business of saving lives, then. I hope he's having better luck than I am. "Anything good from the facial recognition database?"

"Nope." Pieter frowns. "One ex-con bought coffee from you yesterday. Grand theft auto. He's a preacher now, and he lives in Westchester. He wasn't carrying a computer bag, either."

"Yeah, that's not our guy. Let me ask you guys this," I say. "How come you haven't been able to ID the Plumber in the cell phone matrix?"

Max puts down his fork and sits back in his chair. "I honestly don't know, and it's pissing me off. We've spent a lot of man hours trying to find the informant's phone, and we don't have it yet."

"Huh." I shove another piece of chicken into my mouth, trying to think. It should be fairly simple to identify which cell phone has visited each of the coffee shops where The Plumber made his posts. Everyone's cell phone has commercial apps that anonymously track the location of the phone. Any company—including ours—can purchase buckets of this anonymous data to analyze it.

No doubt Max has a couple of quants downstairs right now sifting through cell phone location data for lower Manhattan. All they have to do is find a phone that's been to every location within the right time period. Then they can peer more closely at all the matches, analyzing where else those coffee drinkers go. It's baby stuff.

"Anonymized" cell phone data is a stalker's dream. "Do you have too many leads?" I guess. "Is it a problem to sort them all?"

"Nope." Max shakes his head. "Not a single phone passed by all three cafes on the right days. Unless my guys are just fucking this up. They're looking for a flaw in the algorithm, but I'm getting frustrated."

"Must be intentional," I muse. "The Plumber could really be more than one person. If three different people posted those messages, you could never find this perp."

"Or maybe it's one guy, and he's smart, and leaves his phone at home. Whoever is leading me around by the nose is doing a pretty good job of it."

"Come on, buddy," I urge my old friend. "Figure it out. I'm getting fat from eating pie every day."

Scout leans forward in her chair. "How's the product, anyway?"

"It's *so* good," I moan. "I already did the math on this—I'll have to run an extra seven miles a week just to burn off half the calories."

My friends all laugh.

"Every assignment has its own special risks," Max says.

"You're telling me. She makes this gingered mango cream pie that tastes like it ought to be illegal."

Pieter shakes his head. "I'm wearing a bulletproof vest to work this week. And your biggest fear is getting too fat for your jeans? How much of your paycheck are you spending on pie, anyway?"

"Plenty of it."

"And you call yourself a man of self-control," Scout teases.

"*You* try walking a mile in my shoes. The pie maker is a hottie who makes me drool, too. But she's immune to my charms. And I still have to call her boss and do everything she says."

My friends howl.

"And then I have to look at those pastries all day. And it smells like *heaven* in there. At least I'm earning tips."

"Where do they put the tips?" Pieter asks. "In your G-string?"

"In a *jar*, asshole, because this is a classy operation. And—hey—when our clients bail on us because Max has devoted all our man hours to tracking a murderer, at least I can earn a living as a barista."

"Now that you mention it," Max says, sipping his beer. "I think I'm entitled to a cut of your tip jar. After all, I'm responsible for your coffee career taking off."

"Nah. It's not the coffee they're tipping on. It's the *charm*, baby. And I didn't get that from you."

"I don't know," Scout says with a teasing glint in her eye. "If you're so charming, how does the lady boss resist you?"

"He's wondered that for fifteen years," Max says. "He had a whole summer to charm her into his bed, and he couldn't do it."

"Oh, buddy," Pieter says, laughing. "Crash and burn. She's a pretty one, too. Maybe I'll ask her out."

"You will not!" I grunt, and everyone grins at my reaction. "Don't underestimate me. She wants me. It's on."

Pieter laughs, like he thinks I'm joking. But I'm not. Posy used to watch me to make sure I didn't screw up. But now she watches me for fun. I swear sometimes her eyes are stapled to my backside.

"*Gunn*." Max's forehead furrows. "Can't you wait to seduce her until after this is over?"

"I suppose. Although Posy and I are like a steam valve with too much pressure on it. Someone's got to hit the release valve soon, or I may explode. Besides—when I quit this job, she'll be pissed at me."

"Because you're no longer in her bed?" Scout guesses. "The ego on you!"

"Well, sure. All the ladies miss me when I'm gone. But she'll be trying to replace me behind the counter. And I'm getting the feeling it's harder to replace a barista than a lover."

My friends burst out laughing again, and even Max snorts into his scotch glass. "Just don't get yourself fired until we find our man."

"I can't be fired. It's a tight labor market for people who can draw animals in foam."

My friends are wiping their eyes now.

"Nevertheless," Max says, changing the topic. "I'll need most of you for a quick job sometime in the next ten days."

"Oh yeah?" I perk right up at the sound of that. It's been a while since Max and I ran a mission together. "What are we getting up to?"

"Remember when I told you that Xian Smith was in town for a nice long time?"

"Of course. He's still around, right?" This whole crazy pie shop mission is tied up in Smith's potential guilt. If Max says he's lost track of Xian Smith, I'm going to seriously question my life choices.

"Well, he left town for a few days. But now he's back."

"Where'd he go?"

Max shakes his head. "He's not hackable, and our guys lost him at the security checkpoint at JFK. So it could have been anywhere. But now I have a device in his hotel room."

Whoa. "Seriously? How the hell did you pull that off?" An operative like Smith knows how to sweep his hotel room for bugs.

"Get this—" My old friend pushes his plate away. "He checked out of his room at the Soho Luxe."

"You mean when he went out of town?"

A slow grin spreads across Max's face. "That's right. Even crime lords don't like to overpay at a hotel."

"Maybe he didn't know if he was coming back," I point out.

"Maybe." Max's grin turns smug. "But I had a hunch. And since he always stays in the same suite, I planted the device while he was gone. It's a dead-end camera."

"*Oh*." Now I understand Max's trickery. If the camera isn't broadcasting a signal, Smith would have a lot more trouble detecting it in his room. "So you'll have to recover it soon."

"Sure. It will run out of juice in about ..." He looks at his smart watch. "Eight days. You and me and Scout will go in there and pick it up while he's out at a meeting. Even if he's monitoring his room, we'll be history by the time he gets back."

"Okay." That op sounds like fun. Except for one problem. "Just remember—I work seven to four most days. And don't fuck with my lunch break."

Max snickers. "I wouldn't dare."

10

GUNNAR

AT NINE, after my friends and I have finished both our dinner and our meeting, I take a car back down to SoHo. I get out on Spring Street and consider my next move. Tomorrow is my day off from the pie shop, so I don't have to go to bed at ten o'clock tonight like a loser.

Across the street is The Alley Cocktail Lounge, where I can see a TV through the window. There's a baseball game on the screen. The Mets are playing tonight, barely ten miles away from here.

The sight of the baseball diamond on the green glare of the screen puts an unwelcome tug in the center of my chest. As a kid, I used to watch the Mets with my dad. Back when life was simpler. It wasn't ever simple, but I didn't know that. I was just a little boy who sat beside his father on our living room couch in Queens. We don't speak to each other anymore, and I've been avoiding New York baseball for a long time because it reminds me of him.

But I wonder how the Mets are doing tonight.

My feet are moving before I even realize it. Taking care not to get run over by a taxi, I cross the street and head into the bar.

"Gunn!" calls Jerome, the bartender. "Long time no see! Where've you been, man? Sit down and have a beer." He puts a coaster down in front of the only empty bar stool.

"It's been months, right?" I pull out the stool, and just as I'm sliding onto it, I happen to glance at the woman on the next bar stool.

81

Her head is down because she's reading a book. But I'd know the graceful line of her neck anywhere.

Posy Paxton is reading a novel in the middle of a crowded bar on a Friday night, a half-drunk dirty Martini in front of her.

The baseball game is immediately forgotten. So is Jerome, for that matter. Because Posy is wearing one of those tops with a neckline that's wider than necessary. It's slid down on one side, revealing one smooth, tantalizing shoulder. There's a frown of concentration on her kissable face. And the cherry on this libido sundae is the way her wavy hair is loosely collected by a ribbon that looks like it would slide out if I gave it just the barest of tugs. My hand tingles with the urge to do exactly that.

I don't, of course. But *Christ*. Normally I don't ogle every woman like she's my own personal dessert buffet. But this one always stopped me in my tracks. And since she doesn't look up from that book, there's no one to stop my gaze from sliding all over her body.

Get a grip, Scott. I clear my throat, preparing to say hello. She turns the page of her book, oblivious. "Posy Paxton," I say, my voice full of gravel. "You really know how to party."

If I'd expected her to startle, I'm disappointed. "Don't judge," she says calmly. "This book and I are in the best relationship of my life. This book listens when I talk. This book will never stand me up."

"Does it put the toilet seat down, too?" I chuckle at my own joke. "But wait—did you get stood up tonight? That's hard to imagine."

"Is it?" She finally looks up at me. "One year ago tonight, my husband asked me to open our marriage. The ink is barely dry on our divorce. And now he's having a baby with a professional lifestyle guru who's barely legal to drink."

"Lifestyle guru? That's a *job*?"

"Seriously?" Posy gives me a glare. "That's what shocks you about this whole situation?"

"Well, yeah. Because I'm pretty hard to shock when it comes to the shitty things men will do. Your guy blowing up his life just so he can stick it in a sweet young thing who gives his ego a BJ every day? Sorry, honey. That's just not shocking. Men have been pulling that since the dawn of time."

"Glad to hear it," Posy says between gritted teeth.

"—But making money telling other people how to live? Now that's a trick."

"I suppose you're right." She sighs. "But I don't have to like her."

"True," I agree. "And it's not like she needs to make a ton of cash. Not if she's got your ex supporting her."

Posy glances back down at the page, as if the idea embarrasses her. "I heard he went back to work. Babies are expensive." Her voice drops so low I can tell she doesn't want to discuss it.

"What are you reading, anyway?"

She puts her palm over the page. "This isn't an open relationship. Sorry."

I snort. The verbal tug of war with Posy is as familiar as breathing. "Show me," I demand.

"I don't think I will." She lifts her martini glass and downs the dregs.

"Please?"

"Nope."

I'm considering my options when the guy on the other side of Posy turns to face us. He's got a barbell through one eyebrow, and he's wearing a baseball cap that says *Gay AF*. "You know what's funny? The guy on the cover of the book looks sort of like you. Big shoulders. Kind of hot and bossy." Then he gives me a big smile to go along with the compliment.

"*Really?*" I ask. "Could this be true? You'd better show me."

"Nope."

"I can't see my twin? What if we were separated at birth?"

"He looks nothing like you," she says to the page.

"Let me be the judge," Jerome pipes up. "I'm kinda dying of curiosity back here."

Posy groans. "Oh, for fuck's sake." The sound of the f-word coming out of her pouty mouth makes my body tighten in three or four different ways. She lets out a long-suffering sigh and lifts the cover toward Jerome.

I crane my neck so I can see the front of Posy's book. And I see a bare-chested man with long flowing hair and very tight pants. Not baseball-player tight, but more like knight-in-shining-armor tight. "Interesting," I say.

"Don't judge," Posy reminds me.

"I wasn't. Honestly, if you were sitting here reading Nabokov on a Friday night, *then* I'm totally gonna judge. Can I buy you a drink?"

She closes the book and puts it onto the bar, face down. "Sure. Thank you."

"Jerome?" I call. Could you make us two of your rhubarb Collinses?"

Posy's eyes widen. "I don't get to choose my own drink?"

"Sure. You can order any drink you want. But I spent the last ten days watching you put together all kinds of crazy flavor combinations in that pie shop. Who knew that pears and cardamom went together? So I thought you'd like to try Jerome's specialty."

"How do you know I haven't already tried it?" she asks.

Jerome snickers behind the bar. "She's got you, old man. Just fold your cards now. Posy—what can I get you to drink?"

"I'll have the rhubarb Collins, please. I've heard it's wonderful." She gives him a smile, and everyone laughs. At me. Including the eyebrow-barbell guy.

"Two rhubarb Collinses is coming up," Jerome says.

"Make it three," I say. "One for that guy." I point at the guy on Posy's left. "I might as well buy drinks for people who appreciate me."

His face lights up. "Thanks, dude."

"Sorry I gate-crashed your date with the guy in breeches." I elbow Posy, because I'm a pain in the ass. "I bet he's bossier than I am."

Posy rests her slim fingers on the back cover. "You'd be right. But guess what? A bossy man is only fun in the pages of a book."

"Are you sure? Have you tested this theory? People say I'm pretty fun."

If I'm not mistaken, there's a flush on her cheeks. "Which people?"

"Well, female people." I give her a hot smile. "Clothing optional."

Posy gulps.

"Drink up, friends." Jerome slides three drinks onto the bar in front of us. The salmon-colored liquid is served over ice, with a jaunty lemon wheel on the lip.

"Damn that's pretty," our new friend says from under his baseball cap. "Cheers, guys. To pink drinks and baseball." We all lift our glasses and touch them together. "Now if only the Mets could strike this motherfucker out."

As I take a sip, I glance up at the TV for the first time since sitting down. The score is tied. But I don't care as much as I usually would.

Posy is much more diverting than baseball. I don't know why I'm drawn to her. I've never really understood it. We were downright hostile to each other back in the day. And then—at the bitter end— her dad made me angrier than I'd ever been in my life. And now I have to call her *boss* and literally fetch coffee all fricking day.

Even all these years later, she still gets under my skin. There's something about her energy that resonates with me. She's driven and focused. She doesn't suffer fools. Those are traits that we have in common.

But Posy has a warmth that underlies her troubled soul. As if she is doing everything she can to avoid becoming a cynical bastard like me. I see it when she puts an extra cookie in an old man's bakery bag. And every time she speaks kindly to Jerry even when he's forgotten to do something basic—like closing the backdoor.

She's like the nicer, chick version of me. And she's sneaking looks at me over the rim of her glass.

I feel my pulse accelerate. Is tonight the night it finally happens? And why not? We're two adults with no obligations. Why shouldn't we?

Posy catches me watching her, and looks away, her cheeks burning.

"What are you thinking so hard about over there?" I press. *Say it, I beg. Ask me to come home with you.*

I wonder if she has the nerve.

11

POSY

GUNNAR WAITS FOR MY ANSWER, watching me with hungry eyes. I take another sip of tart, fruity goodness and feel a rare looseness in my limbs, as if I'm limber enough to mold myself into the kind of woman who knows how to handle this moment. The possibility of Gunnar and me in bed stretched itself out around us.

He's waiting for me to say something. Except that I've forgotten the question, let alone the answer. He gives me a smile, like he can read my thoughts. And then he lets me off the hook by glancing up at the TV screen to check the score. "Tell me," he says. "Where did you go just now?"

"Nowhere," I say quickly, chickening out. I take another deep gulp of my drink. I haven't had quite enough alcohol to nonchalantly ask Gunnar to come home with me tonight. I want to, though. Really. A lot. He's just the right kind of playboy to get me out of my rut. It won't mean anything to him. He won't have any expectations.

And neither will I, of course. We have nothing in common.

Although lately I find myself appreciating Gunnar for much more than his very fine ass. Who could resist a guy who comes to work on time every day, and makes fabulous coffee for eight hours without complaint?

The old Gunnar would have teased me mercilessly and hidden the sugar cubes when he went on break. The new Gunnar keeps his head down and saves my overworked butt during every shift.

Sure, he still flirts mercilessly with the customers. But nobody is perfect. And I'm just jealous. I'd rather have those pale eyes trained on me.

They were, too, only a moment ago. But I blew it already. He was waiting for me to give him the green light, and I chickened out.

That's a theme with me.

Earlier, I'd spotted him even before he came into the bar. I watched him get out of that cab and then check the time. I saw him look toward the pub, weighing his choices.

My heart had thumped along with only one word. *Please*.

Fine—not my heart. It was other parts of me who were doing all the begging. Silently, of course. Speaking up seems impossible right now. What if he laughs in my face? Or—this might even be worse—what if he says yes? And then we get naked and I can't satisfy him?

You're not very adventurous, Spalding said. *You're not very good in bed.*

My ex is the only person I've ever been naked with. And thanks to him, I'm afraid to try again with someone else. If another man tells me I'm no fun, I don't know how I'd come back from that.

On the other hand, if I don't get out of this rut, then Spalding wins. Maybe I sound melodramatic, but I don't want to die before I experience terrific sex.

It's really no surprise that my drink disappears quickly.

"Look, you don't have to tell me what's on your mind," Gunnar muses, and I realize I've been silent for some time. "But something has you deep in thought."

"Rhubarb," I blurt. "It's, uh, something I've used in springtime pies. But, um, I wonder if I could do better than strawberry rhubarb —that's been done, you know?"

His smile widens. "Is that an occupational hazard? You can't eat or drink anything without reconfiguring it in your mind?"

"Yep." I wave at the bartender. "Another round of these if you wouldn't mind."

"Are you trying to get me drunk?" Gunnar asks. "Please say yes."

My pulse picks up, because it's hard to miss the innuendo there. But I dodge the question, because I've never been brave. "As if two cocktails and a beer would put you under my spell."

"Oh, I'm easy," Gunnar says, giving me an intentionally sleazy wink. "Besides, your pies have already made me slow and agreeable. That key lime and Thai basil pie was amazing. That stuff is dangerous."

"You like my key lime and Thai basil?" I ask, hearing pleasure in my own voice. It never gets old when people tell you how much they like the product. "And I guess it figures that you'd be one of *those*."

"One of what?"

"You have an adventurous palate." I prop an elbow on the bar and try to explain. "People fall into two distinct groups. There're the ones who *always* order the weird flavors. And the Dutch apple pie crew, who always stick to the basics. They don't cross over. It's something I've been thinking about a lot lately."

Thanks to Spalding. He basically accused me of being a Dutch apple pie in bed. The whole reason I'm reading my sister's romance novels is to try to learn what the other flavors are like.

"Huh," Gunnar says. "So, you can just guess which other pies I've tried?"

"Sure, I can. Did you try the pine nut and salted honey?"

"Oh, hell yes."

My smile grows wide. "How about the matcha green tea tart?"

"Well," he shakes his head, "I gotta say I haven't quite gone there yet. But I did enjoy the vinegar date pie."

"Ah! And the ginger mango cream, right?" I press.

"Yeah. Does that make me predictable?"

"A little bit," I say, enjoying myself immensely. "Have you started doing that thing where you try to guess each customer's guilty pleasure?"

He laughs. "Get out of my head. It's my new favorite game."

"How's your accuracy?"

"Pretty bad. I started off trying to use clothing as a clue. I expected somebody wearing a navy blue suit and boring shoes to order the apple crumble. But that theory bombed. And then I tried to assume that people in workout clothes wouldn't pick something sugary. But they totally do."

"You have to look deep inside their souls," I tease. "If you look at the shell of a person, you'll never get their pie order right. In fact, you have to look at their auras."

He snorts. "What color is my aura?"

"Indigo, like tattoo ink. But with a streak of red because you're contrary."

He narrows his eyes. "You're just fucking with me now."

"Maybe I am."

"Okay, lady. But I have an issue with something you said earlier."

"What?"

"*Guilty pleasures.*" He lays a hand over my wrist. "I don't believe in those. I don't think pleasure should make you feel guilty."

"Oh." He's barely touching me, but goosebumps run up my arm anyway. Now would be a great time to make a joke and diffuse all the tension I'm suddenly feeling. But I feel too tongue-tied to pull it off.

Gunnar removes his hand, which is a disappointment. But the next thing he says stuns me back into goosebump territory. "You know, I always had it bad for you."

"You … what?" I ask stupidly.

"Back when we were tending bar, I had a big crush on you. And sometimes I thought you were on the same page. I usually have good instincts about these things. But not that time. You ended up with Mr. Pretty Boy Preppy instead."

My heart is thumping wildly now, and I take a sip of my cocktail to steady my nerves. The truth is that I don't really trust this little revelation. We used to annoy each other, for one thing. But maybe that didn't matter to Gunnar's libido. He was a horny college boy. He probably had it bad for all the girls.

Still. "What if I'm the one who has terrible instincts? Did you ever think of that? And did you miss the part where I divorced Mr. Preppy?"

"Mmm," he says thoughtfully. "I suppose that might explain a few things."

"You're the one who left, anyway."

His eyes narrow. "Do you really think if I'd stuck around, things would have turned out differently? I spent three months giving you the fuck-me eyes, Paxton. But you didn't take me up on it."

Oh mother of God. His gaze is turning hot, and I think it might incinerate me. And then I remember why we never hooked up in the first place. "You were more than I could handle. At nineteen,"

I add hastily. As if anything has really changed. I'm not a blushing virgin anymore, but Gunnar still makes me feel outmatched.

"Excuses, excuses." He clicks his tongue. "I think a girl who can put together a bacon, cherry, and onion tart knows how to take a walk on the wild side. You give yourself away with the sexy cooking."

"Seriously?" This strikes me as so ridiculous that I accidentally snort when I laugh. "Pie-making is something that grandmas do. Not a week goes by without a customer asking—'Oh, *you're* Posy? I was picturing someone elderly.'"

Gunnar grins, and his eyes crinkle at the edges. "Those are the Dutch apple eaters, I bet. Us adventurous types are able to taste the truth. Tell me this—what's the strangest, sexiest pie you make?"

"The Spicy Mexican Dark Chocolate Tart," I say without hesitation. "I use three different chili peppers."

"*What?*" He makes an exaggerated movement, pretending to fall off his bar stool. "Chili peppers and dark chocolate?" His eyes get a happy glaze to them. Honestly, he looks a little turned on by this idea.

"Well, yeah. I love it, but it's not for everyone." And now I've found my opening. "I made some tarts the other day, because Ginny likes them. There's one in my refrigerator at home. It's yours if you want to try it."

"Right now?" he says slowly.

Gulp. "Sure. Why not?"

I've never seen a guy pay a check so fast. Gunnar has us out of there about five seconds later, after dropping some cash on the bar and sliding off his stool. "Let's go then."

That's how I find myself walking down Spring Street shoulder to shoulder with Gunnar.

And I'm not ready. Are we really doing this? Have I misread the situation? Maybe Gunnar really just likes dark chocolate and chili peppers. If I'm not careful, I could make a big fool of myself.

"You're doing it again," he says as we stop for the traffic light at Wooster Street.

"Doing what?"

"Thinking too hard. That's how you spoil your own fun."

"It is?"

"Absolutely. It's the same thing I tried to teach you about bartending back in the day—sometimes you just have to trust your instincts instead of measuring everything to the quarter ounce."

"That does sound familiar." It used to drive Gunnar crazy when the bar was four deep with thirsty people and I'd be meticulously measuring each drink's ingredients.

He'd tried to teach me to mix a drink by feel. But I was too timid to tip the gin bottle over the ice and just let it fly. I knew I'd end up with different proportions in every glass. "That wasn't my fault, though," I say as we watch the taxis stream past us. "I wasn't even legal to drink. I'd never tasted ninety percent of those cocktails."

"And yet you wanted to *manage* the bar." Gunnar chuckles.

"My *family's* bar," I argue, the familiar irritation rising up inside me. My great-grandfather had stood behind that very bar pouring drinks. Paxton's was my legacy. "I had your recipe book to help me."

"Yes, you did," he says with a smile. "But sometimes in life you have to go off recipe."

"I can do that," I protest. "Sometimes."

"Uh huh," he says. "Then show me. Go off recipe right now."

His smile is teasing me, and I'm not sure that I like it. "I don't even know what you mean."

"Here, let me give you a demonstration." Then the jerk leans in and kisses me without warning. As if kissing at a street corner was a perfectly ordinary thing to do.

But I'm not prepared for the multisensory assault known as a kiss from Gunnar Scott. Soft lips glide over mine, before firming into a slow press. The scrape of stubble gives me goosebumps. And the tilt of his head makes me sigh.

Fifteen years have passed, but my body lights up, anyway. Nothing has changed at all between us. He's still the overconfident playboy who's busily deepening our kiss with an expert's attention to pressure and pleasure. And I'm still the confused but hopeful girl who doesn't quite know how to handle a sudden wave of yearning right here on a SoHo street corner.

Raising a hand to his shirt, I try to steady myself against the erotic assault on my central nervous system. But that only makes things worse, because my palm meets the steely heat of his chest. I can't help but lean in, asking for more. He tastes like gin and naughty thoughts.

Then his hand clasps the center of my back, reeling me in. And now I'm completely over my head, unable to process two miracles at the same time: his tongue sliding into my mouth, and his hard body pressed against mine.

He leans in, moving faster now, turning the kiss into a seductive dance. I lose track of the car horns and the people walking past us to the next bar. I'm so completely in the moment that I forget to hold onto my sister's book. It drops to the sidewalk with a loud smack.

The mood is broken. I jerk backwards, blinking from the sudden shock of headlights in the intersection, as well as my own confusion.

Gunnar chuckles. He leans down to snatch the book off the sidewalk. Still frozen in place, I don't take it from his hand. I'm reeling with the terrible knowledge that Gunnar's street corner kiss was one of the top two sexual experiences of my life.

And the other one? His kiss fifteen years ago.

"Come on, Paxton," he says, slipping a hand into mine. "Let's get you home. I've got big plans for you."

Wowzers. I don't know how many cycles the traffic light went through while I was lip-locked to Gunnar. But now it invites us to cross.

With my palm pressed to Gunnar's we cross the street. I'm afraid to speak, because whatever I find to say will sound like begging. Because I need more of those kisses. I need *everything*. I'm not nineteen anymore. There's no reason for me to hold back.

Except nerves, of course. If Gunnar Scott looks me in the eye and tells me I'm no fun in bed, I'll die of embarrassment.

"Still thinking too hard, Paxton," he says. "What did we just talk about?"

"You don't *know* that," I sputter. But I am so busted. "It could be *anything*. It could be seventeen ways to remove your clothing. With my teeth."

"I rest my case," he says, stroking my palm with one naughty thumb. "That sounds overly complicated. I only need one or two ways to rip off your clothes. Three at most," he says.

"At most?" I echo weakly. Because now I'm picturing Gunnar's hands on my body. And I like that picture. A lot.

"And I probably won't use my teeth, because I'm not a patient man tonight." He turns his head to let his eyes wander down my body. I feel his gaze like a physical touch.

"Impatient. Got it," I babble. I've never had the kind of hasty sex that requires hurling clothing in all directions. That sounds exciting, plus it will leave less time for me to feel self-conscious.

We stop at one more street corner. My building is already in view across the way. "So, just to be clear, I'm coming upstairs for a really sinful—" he smiles at me "—dessert?"

Gulp. "I see what you did there."

"Well?" His eyes darken, and his thumb takes another slow sweep of my palm. Shivers climb up my arm and zing everywhere inside me. "What's it going to be?"

Pie and then dirty, dirty sex! my hormones shout.

I would have said this aloud, or some version of it. But I don't get a chance. Because the next thing I hear is the unmistakable sound of a plate glass window breaking.

12

GUNNAR

OUT OF THE corner of my eye, I see the shimmer of the pie shop window as it crashes violently toward the ground.

"Shit." I clasp Posy's hand in mine and tug her diagonally across the street at a brisk clip. En route, I try to work out what just happened. The front door of the pie shop is still shut, with the store's metal security gate still lowered into place. I can see the padlock shining from here.

So whoever broke the window did so from *inside* the building.

Abruptly I change course, heading for the narrow alleyway that runs between two neighboring buildings on this block.

"Stay here," I bark. Then I drop Posy's hand and run down the alley toward the back.

Posy—who never did listen to me—lets out a squeak of protest. And as I run, I can hear her following me. But there's no time to argue the point. Even before I reach the back of the building, someone streaks past me on foot. I step on the gas and give it my all, arriving in the alley seconds later.

But there's nobody in sight. A quick scan of the brick façades around me reveals a multitude of escape options. The guy could have escaped over any number of fences and fire escapes. I look at each one in turn, trying to spot him. But no luck. "Fuck," I curse as Posy arrives beside me. I grab her hand, because she's obviously not that good at listening to my instructions, and I tow her toward the back door of the pie shop. Sure enough, it's standing open, the door swinging gently on its hinges.

"Is someone still inside?" she gasps.

"Stay here. Call 911. Don't come in, no matter what."

Her eyes wide, she takes a step back. Then she pulls out her phone.

I wait until I'm sure she's dialing, and then I hop up onto the back stoop where Jerry likes to sit and read his comics. Then I press on, stepping carefully into the kitchen.

It's a mess. Someone has trashed the place. There are mixing bowls on the floor, and an overturned sack of flour near the reach-in refrigerator.

There's nobody here, though. So I move through the kitchen, which echoes with the quality of silence that makes me pretty sure I'm alone. Posy's tiny office has been trashed as well. The computer is lying on the floor, the screen broken. A file drawer has been ripped from its cabinet and tossed onto the ground.

But my heart doesn't really drop until I step through into the cafe area. There's glass everywhere. Not only is the front window broken, so is the display case. There are shards of glass in the pristine pies that were waiting for their chance in the refrigerator case. Only the antique cash register is unscathed. It's solid steel, though. Hard to manhandle.

The drawer is still shut, too. Posy makes a bank deposit every night, so there probably wasn't much in the register, anyway. But this is still a disaster. I feel sick just looking at the mess.

"Gunnar?" she squeaks from somewhere behind me. I quickly retrace my steps and go back outside. When I step into view, she gives me a quick look of relief. "I didn't hear from you and—"

"Hey, it's fine, I'm fine. But there's no easy way to put this, someone has trashed your place."

"Is it bad?" she asks in a quiet voice.

There's no point in trying to sugarcoat it. "It's bad."

"Oh," she says quietly. Her hands come together, clasped in worry. "I don't, uh, this has never happened to me before. What did they want? What could be missing?"

"I really don't know." Breaking and entering a restaurant after hours isn't very practical. Thieves look for things like computer equipment and technology. They only care about cash value. The pie shop doesn't have anything like that. "I honestly have no idea what they wanted. Your cash register seems intact. But the front window has been trashed, and the display case is broken."

She flinches. "The police are on their way. They said to meet them out front." She moves to join me on the stoop and cut through the store.

"Let's walk around outside," I suggest. "The police will want to get a look before we touch anything." Besides, I really don't want her to see this devastation. Not that I can help it. Whether I delay her or not, Posy is going to be horrified by the full extent of the damage. And nothing I can say will make it better.

But Posy takes the hand that I offer, allowing me to lead her around toward the front of the building. I'd hoped to see a cruiser approaching already.

But instead I see Posy's ex-husband—Spalding—and his new girlfriend. They're both standing on the sidewalk, staring at the glass all over the sidewalk. Isn't it strange that they'd turn up right now? Spalding wears an impeccable tuxedo, though, and shiny shoes. Saroya wears a ballgown and heels.

So it wasn't either one of them that I just chased in the alley. Still. "What are you two doing here right now?" I bark.

Spalding's head snaps in my direction, and his eyes narrow. "Who wants to know? Posy—what the hell? Who is *he?*" Spalding demands with a sneer. "And what happened to your window?"

"Back off. I'll ask the questions," I rumble, forgetting that I'm supposed to be the barista in this situation. "Where are you coming from right now?"

"The *opera,*" Spalding sniffs. "Not that it's any of your business. Posy—we've got to call the police. Did you ever install those security cameras I told you about? This could have all been prevented if you had better security."

Her eyes widen with dismay. "Fuck you, Spalding. Like you give a damn what happens to me."

"Of course I do!" He looks surprised that she'd even say such a thing. He reaches out and grabs the metal lattice that's supposed to protect Posy's window from harm. Then he shakes it. "How'd the window break with this thing in the way?"

Without even thinking I reach over and grab his arm, removing it forcefully from the grate. "Stop it, dumbass. Is there any reason you'd want to tamper with a crime scene before the police arrive?"

"What—?" he sputters. "Unhand me! Are the police even on their way?"

"Yes, and so are you," I say, shooing the ex away with a hopeful gesture. "Move along now. We've got this under control."

"Doesn't look like it," Spalding barks.

"Really?" I take a step toward him, and my body language is a hundred percent menacing. "The lady doesn't want your help. Leave now. Before I remove you myself."

"Come on, honey," Saroya says, her eyes as wide as saucers. "Let's go upstairs. The hot barista is clearly deranged."

They actually back away slowly, as if I'm a grenade that might suddenly blow. Then Spalding pulls a set of keys out of his pocket and opens the door to the building right next door to Posy's. I watch, stunned, as they go inside together.

When I spin around again, Posy is holding her head in her hands and surveying the damage.

"Posy, sweetheart," I say as gently as possible. "Does your ex-husband *live right next door?*" This changes everything. My head is suddenly more full of conspiracy theories than Max's. Spalding could be using Posy's WiFi all day long in the privacy of his own apartment.

Exes are always trouble. Every investigator knows this on a gut level.

"Yes," she says, her voice dull. "Right next door. Although I might see less of them now that you've scared them away. Thanks for that."

"My pleasure. Who puts sugar-free peppermint in their coffee, anyway? It's so obvious there's something wrong with her."

Posy gives me a weak smile just as a police cruiser pulls up and parks in front of a hydrant. "Oh man," a uniformed officer says, climbing out. "That looks bad. Are you the business owner?" he asks me.

I put two hands on Posy's shoulders. "This is the boss," I tell him. "I'm just the barista."

"Sorry for your troubles, miss."

"Thank you," Posy says. "What would you like to see first?"

For the next ninety minutes the cops look around and take Posy's report. When she finally sees the full extent of her trashed interior, her eyes get shiny and red.

Oh, man. I gotta catch whoever did this, just to make that fucker pay. I must be going soft. I'm not usually the kind of guy who's moved by tears.

Turning away, I step carefully toward the far wall of the cafe, noting that the ceramic cow and my tiny camera are still right where I left them.

It was so dark in here, though. The footage is probably going to be useless. Still, it's worth a shot.

"Hey," I say to Posy, as soon as the patrolman walks away from her. "I have some friends who own a security company. Can I call them for you? They'll come over and board up that window first thing in the morning. You can't wait too long. If we have rain, it's going to blow right in through that security grate and mess up these wooden floors."

"Well ..." Posy kicks at a shard of glass with her shoe. "Only if they're not too expensive."

"Yeah, uh, pretty reasonable." In truth, many of The Company's clients pay us a million a year. But Posy will be getting the Gunnar Scott discount.

I pull out my phone and connect to our main dispatch number. "Go ahead, Gunnar," an agent barks into my ear.

If this were an emergency, I'd reply with my location and my backup needs. But it isn't, so I stay in character. "Good evening. We've had a bit of trouble at a storefront on Mercer and Prince. I was hoping you could help us board up a plate glass window that's just been shattered. Of course there's some urgency to it."

"Interesting," the agent says into my ear. "Okay, sure. I'll find someone to get down there. Tonight?"

"Tomorrow morning would be optimal," I say in my super polite voice. "The security grate will keep people out until then."

"If you say so, dude. What time?"

"How does eight o'clock sound?" I ask Posy.

She shrugs listlessly. It's probably just dawning on her that she can't open tomorrow. Her customers will start turning up at seven a.m. to find a storefront straight out of a war zone.

If this were my business, I'd be making that sad face, too.

13

POSY

IT TAKES eighty-seven years for the police to poke around my ruined shop. And all my strength to keep from crumpling onto a cafe chair and sobbing. It's not just the money, either. Although I'm terrified to know what it will cost to fix the window, the display case, and to buy a new computer. But those are just things. Objects are replaceable. I know this.

Even so, I feel violated. Who would vandalize my shop and break glass into my lemon meringue? Who has such animosity toward me that they could do this? It makes no sense. As I told the cops, the most valuable thing in the place is Lola. And she's too heavy to steal.

Nothing makes any sense. I feel shaky and lost.

And then a sudden, loud bang makes me startle.

"Sorry!" a cop calls from the back. "Knocked a broom over!"

And now I'm shaking. My nerves are shot.

"We're finished here, miss," Officer Tomkins says at long last. "The police report will be filed by noon tomorrow, and you can forward that to your insurance company. If you think of anything of value that was taken, you'll be sure to give us a call by ten a.m.?"

"Yes," I say dully. "Thank you."

Gunnar is standing by the metal security grate, examining the dent that was made when the vandal's brick flew through the glass and then stretched it. "This gate may not retract properly unless it's repaired," he says.

I can't even think about that right now. I'm too heartsick to process another problem. "Can I deal with it tomorrow?"

He turns to study me. "Of course you can. I'll ask my security guy to take a look at it when he shows up with the boards."

"Thank you," I say again. And then I yawn.

"Lock up, then," Gunnar says, beckoning me toward the door. "You look like you're about to topple over."

"I'll be okay," I say grumpily.

"I don't know, Paxton," he crosses his arms across his impeccable chest. "You jumped about a foot when that broom toppled over."

"Anyone would!" I stomp toward the door. Even though I've already swept the floor, tiny shards of glass still crunch underfoot, and it just makes me want to howl. I've poured every waking hour into this place for the last ten months.

"Come on." Gunnar gives me a sad smile and holds the door open for me.

Grumpy, I turn my back on him and lock up. As if locking up even matters. The damage is already done.

"Is your sister home?" Gunnar asks as I turn and switch keys, fumbling now for the one that will open the adjacent door—the one that leads to the upstairs apartments.

"No," I say, my voice hollow. "She's out tonight, which is why I was going to—" *invite you over*. I'm too embarrassed to finish the sentence. It seems impossible that Gunnar kissed me on the street corner just a couple of hours ago.

I can't believe I expected a fantasy tonight. Instead, I got a disaster.

Gunnar has been nothing but helpful and generous, though. But it's just like fifteen years ago, when I was flailing behind the bar as he quietly solved all the problems and cleaned up the messes. I used to hate how incompetent Gunnar made me feel at my own family's place of business.

I'm a hot mess once again.

Gunnar clicks his tongue, the way you'd soothe an irritated horse. "Go upstairs, Posy. Get some sleep. Everything will seem less bleak in the morning."

"Will it?" I can only pray that he's right. The lock clicks, and I swing my front door open. Since the pie shop occupies most of the ground floor, the narrow vestibule holds only our mailboxes, the basement door, and a flight of dimly lit stairs stretching upward toward the second floor.

It's perfectly quiet here; I don't hear footsteps or voices. But the familiar staircase still intimidates me. Somewhere nearby, there's a stranger who wants to do me harm. As I glance up into the stillness, it occurs to me to wonder if he's lurking somewhere nearby. Maybe he climbed the fire escape to wait for me alone in my darkened apartment.

Turning slowly around again, I find Gunnar right there where I left him. It's late, and he probably wants to get home. But he's watching me patiently.

"I still owe you a slice of chocolate pie," I blurt out. "I mean—that was kind of a ruse before. But, um, I still have the pie even if the night is kind of wrecked ..." I 'm rambling like a lunatic. But the truth is that I'd rather appear even helpless and unstable than go upstairs alone right now.

"Are you offering me a piece of dark chocolate pie?" Gunnar asks, lifting his too-handsome chin. "Then I accept. Any chance you'd have a glass of milk to go with it? When it's late, I like a glass of milk."

"Yes," I say quickly. "No problem."

"Perfect. Shall we?" He walks right past me and starts up the stairs with a confident step.

Feeling a little ridiculous, I close the door and follow him. "The main entrance to my apartment is all the way up on five," I say as his long legs eat up the stairs. "But there's also a door on four. My place has two levels."

"Okay," he says calmly, marching up the stairs. "Why don't we stop on four, and I'll take a peek inside?"

I feel a wave of pure relief.

Gunnar checks every room thoroughly—first Ginny and Aaron's space, and then upstairs, too.

Having Gunnar step into my bedroom should have been exciting. But here we are, with him checking my closet for intruders while I wring my hands.

"Hey now," he says. "There's nobody here. Except for these guys." He points at a stack of my sister's books on my bedside table.

My cheeks heat as he lifts the first one and studies the cover. There's nothing embarrassing about reading romance novels. Unless you're me, and you're binging on them to try to learn to be a more passionate lover.

"I really don't see the resemblance between me and this guy," Gunnar says, tossing the book on the bed.

"Oh." I glance down and realize that the model on the cover is the same one as on the book I'd been reading in the bar. "I didn't notice that they were the same. The, uh, hockey padding threw me off."

"This modeling gig must pay well, right? Maybe I should try it out for extra cash. I know a guy who used to play hockey. He could lend me the gear." Gunnar picks up the next book, and then the next one. He's trying to distract me from the night's horrors. "These guys are all different. Except this one—" he tosses a book on the bed "—is the hockey player's brother."

"What?" I pick it up and squint at the shirtless model. "I don't see the resemblance. They don't even have the same hair color. Besides, it would be unusual for a hockey player to have a rock star for a brother."

Gunnar snorts. "I'm really good with faces. Bet you five bucks they're related."

"How will we know?"

Gunnar reaches over and flips on my bedside lamp. Then he sits down on the edge of the bed like he owns the place. "It probably says so in here." He flips a few pages and stops on the copyright notice. "Cover model Alex Olsen. And this one …" He lifts the other book and does the same thing. "Blaine *Olsen!*" He lets out a whoop of victory. "Read it and weep, honey." He hands me the book.

"I'll be damned," I say, checking to make sure he's not putting me on. "I guess I owe you five bucks."

"And a slice of chocolate pie." Gunnar gets up off my bed and trots toward the kitchen. "With milk," he says over his shoulder.

I follow him to the kitchen, as if it were completely normal to have midnight snacks with my barista after a two-hour chat with the cops. "Whipped cream on top, or no?"

"No sane man ever says no to whipped cream," he says. "Bring it on."

If I weren't so exhausted, I would think he was hitting on me again. I cut him a decadent slice and squirt some whipped cream on top. Then I pour him a tall glass of milk and sit him down on the sofa to eat it.

"I'm winning at life," he says, cutting a large bite with the fork. "Why don't you get ready for bed while I eat this? I can wait on your sofa until your sister gets home."

"That won't be for hours," I tell him. "You can go. I, uh, already ruined your evening. And tomorrow is your day off."

As soon as I say this, I realize that there's no way I can open the shop in the morning. To my embarrassment, hot tears begin to fill my eyes.

"Oh boy," Gunnar says, diving for a napkin and handing it to me. "None of that, now."

"I'm just so mad," I grind out. "Someone has it in for me. What did I ever do to them?" I blot my tears furiously.

Gunner sets down his fork, looking worried. "I really don't know, Posy. The break-in is weird. But there's nothing more you can do about it tonight."

"I know," I gulp. "And I'll be fine."

Still, I think he's afraid to leave me alone. After I put on my PJs, and he washes his plate in the sink, he shuts out the lights in the kitchen and living room. I expect him to leave, but that's not what happens. Instead, he sits down on one end of the L-shaped couch. "I'll sit a while, unless you'd rather I go," he says. "You seem nervous."

"That's kind of you," I say, feeling awkward. Although he's right. I can't just toddle off to bed, though. So I sit down on the other end of the sectional. It ought to be weird sitting alone with Gunnar in the dark. But it's the least weird thing that's happened tonight.

"I can't believe your ex and his new piece live next door," Gunnar says eventually. "How did *that* happen?"

"He owns that building now," I yawn. "The judge gave it to him in my divorce."

"A whole *building?*" Gunnar sputters.

"Well, not outright. He has a mortgage. But Spalding put me through business school about ten years ago."

"Still. Ouch. What kind of man takes his wife's property in a divorce?"

"His kind," I grumble. "These buildings belonged to my great-grandparents—the ones who started Paxton's. My grandmother was born in this apartment. And she taught me to make pies in that kitchen." I point into my darkened kitchen. "She left Ginny and me the two buildings when she died five years ago. Ginny sold her share to me, in order to finish her degree. So I had to take out a loan. I didn't want to sell any property. But then came my divorce. And I had to choose."

"You let the other building go."

"I did," I confirm, staring up at my darkened ceiling. "All the memories are in this one, anyway. It's fine." But I'm really sick of talking about myself now. I'd rather pry information out of Gunnar. "Where did you go, anyway?" I ask suddenly.

"When? Tonight?"

"No." I lift my feet onto the sofa and rest my head against a throw pillow. "Fifteen years ago, when you quit the bar before Labor Day?"

"Quit?" Gunnar sits up suddenly. "I never quit anything."

"But you disappeared. Right after you—" *kissed me.* I clear my throat. "I got the bar manager's job by default, because you weren't there to kick my ass. Why did you go?"

For a long beat, he just stares at me. "Your father canned me, Posy. I assumed you knew that."

"*What?*" I lift my head off the cushion and squint at him. "He told me you quit and left him high and dry."

Gunnar flinches, like he's been slapped. "Seriously? He said that?"

"Yes. He said that exactly."

Another long moment ticks by, with Gunnar's handsome mouth set into a grim line. Then he groans. "That is *not* what happened. Your father is a bigger asshole than I knew."

"Why would he fire you, anyway? Even if he was trying to keep the manager's job in the family, we were still shorthanded behind the bar."

Gunnar gets up and does a slow circuit of the darkened room. "Do you remember what happened the last night I worked there?"

How could we forget? my hormones cry. *That kiss was everything!*

"I'm not sure what you mean." I clear my throat.

Even in the dark, I can see Gunnar look down and smile. "Aw, you don't remember the kiss? What a blow to my ego."

"Oh, I remember," I admit. Like it was yesterday. His hands in my hair. His hard body pressing against mine. I don't actually remember how it started. We'd been arguing viciously, and the next minute we were kissing. It was glorious.

He stops by the window and looks outside, where the streetlights are shining down on Mercer Street. It's never really dark in New York. "Well, when I came in for work the next day, he called me into his office. He said that you'd complained to him about me. That I'd been very inappropriate with you."

"*What?*" I gasp. "I would *never* have said that."

"But I was," he says darkly. "He wasn't wrong."

"Oh, please. It's not inappropriate if I—" Oh my. I'm going to have to finish that sentence. "—If I enjoyed it."

He shrugs, as if it doesn't matter. "Sometimes people aren't sure what they want. I thought you might have changed your mind later."

"Not hardly," I say emphatically. "And I'm not the kind to go tattling to Daddy. He doesn't listen when I talk anyway. God forbid I had an actual problem that needed solving."

He's still staring out the window, like Mercer Street at midnight is the most fascinating thing he's ever seen. "He made it your fault, too. What a turd."

"I'm sorry, Gunn. I don't know how that happened." My memory of that night is a little sketchy. Not because I've forgotten that kiss, but because it had scrambled my brain. One minute we were shouting at each other over some little bartending dispute. And the next minute we were kissing. It was like a sudden clap of thunder.

We only stopped when my father called my name. But he wasn't in the doorway. He'd been farther off.

"He must have seen us," Gunnar says, as if he's following my memory at the same speed. "Or maybe someone else ratted us out. But he made it very clear that I was a lowlife kid from the boroughs who should have known better than to touch his daughter."

"What an asshole." I thought I was done learning all the ways my father could be an asshole. But I guess there was no end to it. "He lied to me, too. He told me that he'd planned to give you the bar manager's job, but since you quit, he had to give it to me instead."

"Jesus fucking Christ," Gunnar snarls. "He fired me, telling me it was your fault. And then he tells you that you're his second choice? Who does that?"

"Him, obviously. And the funny thing? I could have sworn he liked you more than he liked me." Showing love wasn't my dad's style.

"Not true. He handed me my last check and told me never to come back. And not to file for unemployment or he'd tell the cops I stole from him."

"What?" I yelp. "That's horrible!" My dad is an animal. He really is. "Although I'm not surprised. He's done worse to his own family."

"Like what?"

"Like cutting off Ginny when she got pregnant. And ..." I guess I don't really need to unload *all* our ugliest secrets tonight. "He's not a nice man. And I spent a lot of time trying to please him. I keep telling myself that I won't do it anymore. But do you know what I thought about tonight while I was watching the policemen poke around?"

"No idea."

"I thought, I hope my father doesn't hear about this. He'll think I can't handle my own business."

"We all do that." He sits down on his end of the couch again, his feet up on the coffee table. "The stuff our fathers do to us is hard to forget. Some people never get over it."

"Therapists have to make their money somehow," I say with a yawn.

He chuckles quietly. "I guess so."

We sit in a comfortable silence for a few more minutes, until I realize something strange. "You still wanted the barista job."

"Sorry?" he asks, yawning.

"You thought I got you fired from Paxton's. And you still wanted to work for me. Why? That makes no sense."

He's quiet for a long moment. "A job is a job," he says eventually. "And fifteen years is a long time to nurse a grudge."

"Is it?" I ask. I'm pretty sure my grudge against my father has another decade to go. At least.

Eight hours later, I open my eyes to find sunlight streaming into my bedroom windows. I'm lying on top of my covers, and I'm covered by the blanket that usually lives on the back of the couch.

And someone is moving around in my living room. I'm not frightened, though, because that someone stubs her foot on the corner of the coffee table, and the curse she makes definitely belongs to Ginny.

I sit up, groggy, trying to remember how last night ended. But I can't quite remember anything that happened after my late-night confessional with Gunnar on the sofa.

He must have carried me to bed and covered me with a blanket.

Oh wow, my hormones say. *That's romantic.*

And also embarrassing.

"Hey—are you okay?" My sister appears in the doorway to my bedroom. "I can't believe someone trashed the pie shop! You should have called me!" She puts her hands on her hips and glares at me.

"You were having a fun date, and I didn't want to ruin it. You probably wouldn't have even checked your phone. One of us should be having sex." I cover my face with my hands. "I tried, Ginny. I almost managed it. But before we even got across the street, the vandal shattered the window."

"Oh, honey!" Ginny bounds into the room and plops onto the bed. "Really? You picked up a guy? That's—" Ginny's eyes go wide. "Omigod. Was it Gunnar?"

"Yes," I sigh, feeling embarrassed all over again. "I invited him home for spicy chocolate pie and sex. Instead, all he got was a long conversation with the cops. And the pie, I guess. Eventually."

"Whoa ..." Ginny sits on the edge of the bed. "This is more

shocking than the break-in, Posy. You really went for it? That's bold! How did you put it to him ..." she wiggles her eyebrows "... so that he'd *put it* to you?"

"Actually, I was kind of a chicken," I grumble. "I used the pie as an excuse to invite him over. But my intentions were clear."

"Were they?" She gives me a once-over. "Maybe they weren't clear enough, or you could have gotten some after the whole crime scene thing."

"I was too upset." I sit up a little. "And too tired. What time is it?"

"Nine," she says.

"NINE?" I throw off the blanket. "I have to get downstairs. Gunnar asked some kind of security company to stop by and board up the window."

"Oh, they're just about done," Ginny says with a wave of her hand. "Although it isn't boarded up. They found a glass company that works Saturdays. They're putting the finishing touches on it. And Gunnar had them give your security grate an upgrade."

"Gunnar did what?" I wrestle my PJ shirt off and lunge for my bra. "I can't afford an upgrade." I'm about to spend my day throwing away pie, cleaning up debris and basically starting over.

"You can't afford to get broken into again, though," my sister says, examining her nails. "Aren't you going to ask about *my* night?"

"How was your night?" I ask, jumping into a pair of jeans. "Just tell me the G-rated parts."

"There weren't any G-rated parts," she says with a grin. "This guy had all the moves. I'm going to be thinking about it for a month."

"Aren't you going to see him again?"

She shrugs. "I hope so, but you never know. He seems a little flighty. A little full of himself. He'll probably find someone with fewer obligations to bang. Kind of hard to blame him. But at least I got one great night. It could be months before I get another. But that's okay, I can store it up. I'm like a sex camel."

"A sex ..." I decide not to pursue that idea any further. "Good for you." Let's face it—I really don't understand my sister. We've always had completely different approaches to life. She has a very fulfilling sex life, though, and she's not afraid to pursue it. Note to self.

I dash for the bathroom to quickly brush my teeth and hair before I have to come face to face with the hottest man I almost-but-not-quite had sex with.

14

GUNNAR

IT'S no accident that I let Posy sleep in while my crew fixed up the pie shop. By the time she appears in tight jeans and a T-shirt that says BAKE right across her delectable chest, there's a new window installed on the shop, and a sturdier lock on the back door. The floor has been swept clean, and the display case has been repaired.

Except for the pies themselves—which my guys were sad to throw away—the place looks completely untouched by last night's crime.

Some of our fixes aren't visible to the eye, though. There are six brand new cameras hidden around the cafe. They're top-of-the-line devices, and so well camouflaged that nobody will ever find them. Nothing that happens in this space will go undetected by the team at The Company headquarters.

I feel terribly guilty about this, even though Posy's shop is now safer than Fort Knox. She wouldn't appreciate the deception. Hopefully it will be over soon, and she'll never have to know.

On the bright side, she appreciates the cleanup job I've supervised. As soon as her eyes sweep the room, taking everything in, she squeals with happiness. "Oh my god! Gunnar! This is amazing. I can't believe how much better it looks in here. I'm terrified to see the bill. *Truly* terrified. But I'm still super impressed." She turns slowly in a circle, her mouth open. "My god—I can reopen tomorrow. Even if the insurance company stiffs me, at least I won't be closed more than a day."

"They won't," I say quickly. "I took pictures before they fixed the window."

At that, Posy *smiles*. And it's not just a little smile, it takes over her whole face. And I feel that smile everywhere, because I put it there. As soon as I get the chance, I'm going to make her smile again, for entirely different reasons.

I still want my night with her. How many times can a guy get interrupted? You know that saying—the third time's a charm? It better be true.

"You guys," she says, clapping her hands together. "I can't offer you pie, because it was all ruined. But does anyone want a coffee drink? And the cookies in the fridge will still be good."

"Oh hell yes," says Duff, who's masquerading as a handyman today. He's wearing a zip-up jumpsuit and everything. "Who's the barista around here, anyway?"

Fucking Duff.

"Well, it's this guy," Posy says, jerking a thumb toward me. "But he's done enough already. I'll make you a drink. What do you like?" She walks over and flips on Lola.

"Anything you're making," Duff says, then he follows her over to the counter and leans against it, admiring Posy. And I have the strangest urge to punch him. It's weird, because I'm not the jealous kind.

Huh. I must just be exhausted after that long night on Posy's sofa. I laid awake for hours, trying to decide whether Posy's break-in was related to Max's case.

And now Max is blowing up my texts, wanting to discuss it with me.

I need a nap, I tell him. *Let's talk this afternoon.*

2pm, he fires back. *The Harkness Club.*

Ugh. *Fine*, I reply. *See you at 2.*

The damn club has a dress code. So after my nap and a shower, I put on a nice shirt and head uptown to the richly paneled game room at the club, where Max is an honorary member.

Carl Bayer — Max's dad — attended Harkness College, and joined the club upon graduation. When he started up his private security firm in the nineties, the club immediately employed his services.

Max and I went to Columbia, though, not Harkness. We should be ineligible for club membership. But then, five years ago, Max and I uncovered an embezzlement scheme at the club. Upon recovering a hundred thousand dollars of mishandled funds, the club offered us both free memberships for life. "We're better off with you two permanently on the premises," the president had said with a chuckle.

I declined, because I can't stand stuffy rich people. But Max accepted. And once in a while I find myself sliding into a leather wing backed chair in front of Max. "Did you order lunch?" I ask him. "Because I'm totally putting a bowl of that lobster bisque on your tab."

"Order two," he says, unfazed. "And the duck confit salad."

I flag down one of the obsequious middle-aged waiters, who's wearing a tuxedo at one o'clock on a Saturday afternoon. Poor guy. The reason I worked my ass off in college was so I wouldn't end up serving drinks to rich assholes my whole life. I place my order, adding, "We'd like a basket of those warm cheddar crackers, please."

"Certainly, sir."

"Good call on the warm cheddar crackers," Max says, sinking back into his chair.

"They're the best thing about the Harkness Club," I say grumpily.

Max ignores the dig and opens up one of the club's beautifully inlaid wooden backgammon boards. "Let's have a little game before the food arrives."

"I knew you'd find a way to make me pay for lunch." Max always wins at backgammon, and I can't resist betting against him. Just one time I'd like to clean his clock. So I keep betting.

We roll the dice to see who starts, and Max comes out on top. Of course he does. "Talk to me," he says while rolling for his first move.

"I spent all night thinking about the break-in, and I still don't understand it."

"Same, same," Max says, collecting his dice. "All we know about our perp is that he likes to use bakery WiFi for all his propaganda needs. Was Posy's modem knocked out last night?"

"The computer was trashed, but the modem was only unplugged. I plugged it back in this morning. It's fully functional right now."

"Hmm. That's a lot of hassle for just unplugging a modem. Although the connection log was destroyed, right? That might have been the goal."

I'm not convinced. "They didn't take the hard drive from the machine. If you really wanted to cover your tracks, you'd grab it."

Max doesn't say anything for a while, and I can't tell if he's thinking about the break-in or just concentrating on humiliating me at backgammon. "Maybe the break-in is unrelated," he finally says.

"It's certainly possible. Maybe even probable. And I've been hoping to poke holes in your grand conspiracy all week. The problem is that the break-in makes no sense on any level. There was nothing of value to steal. The vandal didn't spend much time looking through her files, either. It was a straight-up toss and run job."

"Does Posy have enemies?"

I snort. "Posy doesn't make enemies. She makes pie."

"Disgruntled former employee?" he tries.

"Maybe." I shrug. "She got hit with a workers comp claim that she said was bogus. She and her sister were freaking out about it yesterday. But she hasn't even had a chance to respond to that."

"Then we're missing something," Max says. "We began this adventure thinking that Posy's Pie Shop had nothing more to do with the crimes than a convenient WiFi connection. And maybe that's still true. But now you're going to have to dig into the business to be sure."

I look down to see that Max has rolled another double. Fucking backgammon. He always wins. Even the waiter who's brought us our cheddar crackers winces.

This game might cost me two hundred bucks. We'll settle up later, of course, since the Harkness Club doesn't permit gambling. Or even phones. It's a haven from technology in the middle of the city. And the members of this joint pay tens of thousands of dollars a year to strip themselves of their phones in this room.

Rich men are weird. I realize I'm one of them now. But I don't have to act like it.

I bite into a cracker. It's salty and cheesy perfection. *Posy would like these*, I think. I should tell her about them.

But no, I can't. Because baristas don't lunch at the Harkness Club. It's out of character with the role I'm playing at the pie shop.

The truth is I'm bone tired of lying to Posy. My line of work requires lying. It doesn't usually bother me, because I'm working hard to keep bad guys away from good guys. And I'm telling small lies in search of greater truths.

I lost my room key.

The manager sent me to ask you a few questions.

I'm here to fix your computer.

This time it's different. I knew Posy before my days as an operative, so she has a reasonable expectation of hearing the truth from me. I feel closer to her than I expected to. And lying to her feels like a violation.

Installing those cameras in her shop this morning made me feel squicky. And now I'm going to do a deep dive into her private life, too? Although I can't really see an alternative.

"Posy is recently divorced," I tell Max. "Her ex might have a grudge, although I don't see how. He walked away with a nice settlement."

Max glances up at me. "I thought they didn't have children?"

"They don't."

My friend makes a face. "No able-bodied man should ask his ex-wife to support him."

"Preach. He has a younger girlfriend, too. She looks familiar, but I can't put my finger on it."

"Really? You're so good with faces."

"I know. She reminds me of someone, but I'm not sure who."

"Add her to the list," Max says. "I'll handle their finances. You look into everyone's past."

"Sure. With regard to finances, I'd always assumed that Posy was very well funded. Her daddy made a wad selling the family restaurant to a private equity firm. But now I'm not so sure about her bottom line. She's probably real estate rich but cash poor. The price of a new plate-glass window seems heavy on her mind."

"Hmm." Max tents his fingers. "I'll look into it later. Someone in her life may be caught up in this drama."

"It's possible," I concede.

"You know what this means, right? You have to stay sharp where she's concerned."

"Yeah, that's starting to sink in." I need to find The Plumber and figure out who's trying to wreck the pie shop. And I can't let myself be distracted by the pretty lady in the kitchen. It's not good for my concentration, and it's not fair to her, either.

The waiter approaches with a tray, and Max is forced to set our backgammon game aside to make room for our lunch. "I suppose I can finish you off later."

"You know it." I place my napkin in my lap. "Let's eat some stuffy rich dude food first. This lobster bisque is barking my name."

Max gives me a funny smile and picks up his spoon.

○━┱

We never do finish that backgammon game, though. Instead, we head upstairs to the club's library—where computers are permitted—and sit down to spend some quality time looking up all the details of Posy's life.

First I focus on her father. Nothing much to see there. He sold his grandparents' restaurant and cashed out. He owns a penthouse apartment on the Upper East Side and a home in Southampton.

Posy's mother lives in Paris with her new boyfriend. They don't look very interesting, either.

Then I look for dirt on Spalding Whittmer Jr. and Saroya. Usually you can't get anywhere if you don't have a last name, but Saroya is an unusual enough name that I find her right away. She used to be a real estate broker in Brooklyn. Her picture is still on their web page.

Meanwhile, Max is digging into Posy's finances. "You were right. Your rich girl isn't a rich girl anymore," he says when he finds Posy's mortgage documents. "She's increased her debt load *twice*."

Looking over his shoulder, it's pretty hard to deny it. Posy borrowed money to buy out her sister a few years ago. And then she increased her burden again when she had to sign over the adjacent building to her ex.

"Her divorce lawyer should be disbarred," I whisper. She lost a big chunk of her inheritance to her asshole ex. "I think she's supporting her sister, too."

"Really? Why?"

I shrug. "Seems like daddy disowned Ginny when she had a kid with a criminal."

"What kind of criminal?"

I jot down a note to figure that out.

"Still," Max muses. "Posy could sell that building and walk away with some cash in her pocket."

"She doesn't want to. It's the one part of her old life that she wants to save. Her ex is having a kid with his new piece. Posy practically sets herself on fire every time they walk into the place." I feel a spark of anger just mentioning them. Usually I don't get all emotional over a background check. But her ex is *such* a tool.

Besides, I used to think Posy was spoiled. If I'm honest, I disliked her for it. She hadn't worked a real job before that summer at the bar. And she never had the crushing student loan debt that I did. Everything seemed so easy for her.

I'm starting to realize it's not.

"Posy's business is drowning?" Max asks.

"Struggling against the current, anyway. It isn't easy to run a small business in that expensive neighborhood. Her taxes are high. She needs a new roof, and the bricks need repointing. The place is worth millions, but only on paper."

"Messy," Max says.

"Yep." But Posy shows up with a smile every morning at five to make pies and pastries for other people. She's inspiring, damn it.

"Do you think the ex-husband could be dirty?" Max asks. "Maybe he has a Windows laptop and an unfortunate connection to the Turkish mafia."

"I'll check him out. But he seems too clueless to be secretly dropping secrets on the dark web. His new woman, though ..." I trail off, trying to decide what to say about her. "She's different. Icy. Pushing her own agenda. She spends a lot of time in the pie shop. Almost like she's flaunting it. I'm looking at her, too."

"Cool," Max says. "You never know."

I go back to my work, spending a few minutes on Saroya. For a young person, she's had a string of jobs, including the real estate gig. Before that, she managed a car wash in the Far Rockaways. Then the trail goes dark.

"This was a good start," Max says, logging off his computer. "But I reserved a racquetball court for us at three-fifteen."

"I have my gym bag, but I didn't bring my racquet."

"You can use my extra one. And if I win, you can pretend that was the reason."

I roll my eyes, but then I follow him to the elevator anyway. We're pretty well matched at racquetball, although Max enjoys it more than I do. In college, he was always dragging me off to learn what we both called "rich kid sports." Like golf, which I detest. And racquetball, which I tolerate.

But I was never as interested. "Why don't we throw a frisbee around, and leave squash to the prep school kids?" I'd asked one afternoon when we were sweating in a dank basement court somewhere underneath Columbia.

"Because I like to beat people at their own games," Max had said, tossing the ball in the air and catching it. "And so do you, tough kid. We're going to work on your New York accent, too."

"*Nevuh*," I'd replied, letting that Queens accent rip.

But life had other plans for my accent. After college, Max and I went to work together for a branch of government intelligence that I am still not allowed to talk about. And spies don't speak with big fat New York accents. So I learned really fast to tamp it down.

Max leads the way to the posh locker rooms downstairs. I toss my gym bag on a bench and dig through it for a pair of shorts. That's when I happen to overhear a conversation on the opposite side of the bank of lockers that divide the room.

"Run down the city council meeting agenda for me?" asks a very familiar voice. And I freeze in place.

"It's going to be a long one," comes the answer. "At least four committees will take the floor."

"God damn it, I don't have time to sit there for three hours," grumbles another man. And their voices are getting louder.

Without even thinking, I duck into one of the private changing rooms off to the side. And I linger in there, swapping my khakis for a pair of athletic shorts, while the other men leave the locker room.

Max gives me a frown when I finally step out. "Are you allergic to city officials? Got a string of parking tickets I should know about?"

"Nah, I'm good," I grumble. "Let's go smash a very bouncy ball all over the walls."

But now I have a brand new reason to avoid the Harkness Club.

15
———
POSY

AFTER ONE DAY CLOSED, I'm back in business feeding the hungry
people of SoHo.

Although the break-in has taught me to be afraid. Each morning
is an exercise in bravery as I unlock my shop in the predawn darkness, always scared of what I'll find.

But so far, I've always found the new copper lock on the back
door intact. And inside, my shop is as tidy as ever. When I flip on all
the lights, I see that the sturdy new security grate is still there,
protecting my shiny new plate glass window.

That's when relief sets in. And the feelings of gratitude.

In truth, my shop looks *better* than it did two weeks ago. I needed
a decal for my new window, so I chose a better design. Pedestrians
on Mercer Street now walk past a cute drawing of a steaming lemon
meringue pie, with vintage hand lettering that offers: *Pies! Savory
Pastries! Life-giving Espresso Drinks!*

I also took this opportunity to repaint the battered legs of the tall
pine table in the middle of the room. I chose a can of paint in a cheery
pea-green color and did two coats after closing one night. The bright
color seemed risky as I brushed it on, but now it looks cheerful and
adorable.

Who knew my cafe needed an act of criminal violence to spruce it
up a little? And even though I'm a little terrified to think about the

bills coming in, at least I was only shut down for a single day. It could have been so much worse.

And this edgy feeling I have will pass, right? The first two hours of the day—when I'm alone in the kitchen making pastry—is the scary part. But eventually, employees start showing up. Gunnar's knock is the first one. And he always follows up by calling out to me, so that I can identify his voice before I open the metal door.

"Morning," he says as he steps past me, filling the space with his muscular body and a scent so manly that his shaving soap must be seventy-five percent testosterone. "Everything okay here last night?"

"Yes, just fine," I reply in a voice that's hoarse from both silence and sexual tension.

That's the other problem I've had since the night of the break-in. My feelings about Gunnar have gone from irritation and attraction to gratitude and full-on lust. My body will never forget those kisses I got before we were interrupted. And my stupid little heart will never forget the way that Gunnar took care to keep me and my shop safe that night.

But these feelings are apparently one-sided. Gunnar doesn't spare me more than a glance as he heads for the apron rack, tying a fresh one around his waist. Then he washes his hands at the sink. "Need a coffee before the hoards descend?"

"That would be wonderful, thank you," I say in a voice that's too breathy. I clear my throat and try again. "By the way, I still haven't gotten a bill for the new window and the grate."

"Oh, I'm sure you will," he says. "Companies like to get paid." He dries his hands on a paper towel before disappearing toward the cafe. And I catch myself staring at his backside as he walks through the door, wondering how it would feel to lie beneath that strong body.

Given the choice, I would like to thank Gunnar for all he's done for me. And my preferred method of thanking him would be to invite him upstairs, strip off his Posy's Pie Shop T-shirt, and lick him everywhere.

Every time we're in the same room—six days a week—I feel lit up and hungry inside. Every time he catches my eye, I feel a tingle. Every time I hear him laughing with Teagan behind the counter, I ache. Those kisses he gave me last Friday night were magic. And I'm still feeling their lingering effects.

So potent is my attraction to Gunnar that I'm almost willing to break through the ever-present fear of rejection and do something about it. Almost. The trouble is that I do not live alone. Nights without Ginny and Aaron are about as rare as a lunar eclipse. So I couldn't invite Gunnar over without feeling super awkward about it.

Ginny disagrees, of course. "Better get on that," Ginny whispers occasionally in the pie shop kitchen. "Before a customer asks him out first. Or Teagan."

"Teagan has a live-in boyfriend," I always snap in reply.

Still. Every time Ginny mentions him, my eyes take an involuntary journey toward the counter, where Gunnar is inevitably lifting a twenty-five-pound bag of coffee with his Hercules arms to refill the grinder. Or making someone laugh.

My yearning feels bottomless, and I don't know how to handle it. I've never had much experience with lust. I met Spalding at nineteen, so I never learned to navigate a single girl's hookup.

And at thirty-four I don't know how to remake myself as a sexy, confident lady about town. These days, my version of sexy attire is taking off my hairnet and putting on a clean T-shirt.

I could get dolled up and make the first move, maybe by inviting Gunnar out for dinner somewhere. In the unlikely event that he said yes, I'd have to drop hints all evening about how many people there are at my house, until Gunnar finally says, "Let's go back to my place."

Honestly, that all sounds trickier than the three-layer pumpkin, chocolate and cinnamon pie with a braided crust I made once. And that's why ten days have slipped by without me doing anything about my raging attraction to Gunnar.

Besides, Gunnar may have forgotten about me. He hasn't kissed me again, maybe because I'm just too much trouble. But I think he still wants to. Yesterday I could swear his eyes were pinned to my backside while I loaded fresh pastries into the breakfast case. And when I awkwardly lifted my apron over my head at lunchtime, his gaze took in every curve of my chest. Twice.

Yet he hasn't uttered a word about our lost night together. He hasn't suggested a rematch, or even caught me in a compromising position against the walk-in refrigerator door for a stolen kiss.

These are my thoughts as Gunnar reappears ten minutes later holding steaming cups for both of us. I watch the muscles in his arm flex as he hands mine over.

"Thank you," I squeak, hoping that he can't read minds. "What's in your mug, anyway?" I blurt out. My curiosity about him knows no boundaries.

"Mint tea," he says, sipping from it. "I don't do well on caffeine."

"There's always decaf coffee," I point out. "Do you even drink coffee?"

He shrugs mysteriously. "Pleading the fifth amendment, here."

"Like it matters," I tease. "Your tip jar is always overflowing. I know you're a good barista, even if you're secretly a fraud."

I could swear that something flickers past his eyes when I say this. But it's gone a half-second later. "You can be good at making something without enjoying it yourself. I'm sure you prefer some pies over others."

"Not true!" I cry. "I love all my babies equally. Every slice is a delight to the senses."

"I'll bet," he says slowly, his gaze making a slow trip down my body. "You need anything more from me before I open up?"

Yes! Ravish me. "Just take these quiches for the front case, thanks." I hand him the tray and hold back another hungry sigh. I can honestly say that I've never felt this kind of overwhelming attraction before in my life. But it's worse than that. I *like* Gunnar Scott. I like his company as much as I like the way he fills out his jeans. And when he sticks a fork into a pie I've made, and then moans, I want to sit on his lap and feed him bite after bite.

But not today. There's work to do. I'm forced to put aside my libido and bake the heck out of a dozen different recipes. I barely catch a breath until the afternoon, when the mailman arrives at the back door.

The stack of mail includes a bill from a company that uses a skeleton key as its logo. But this is weird—there's no name listed. It's an invoice for one plate glass widow, installed, plus a new security grate with electronic controls, installed. I brace myself to look at the total owed.

It says $507.52.

Wait, what? I read the whole page again. But there's no mention of a payment plan, or another bill forthcoming. Just the total, barely five hundred bucks.

For a moment I'm giddy. But then I realize it would be immoral to simply pay this and pretend that someone in their billing department hasn't misplaced a decimal point.

"Gunnar," I say, walking abruptly into the cafe. "I have a problem."

"Do you now?" he asks, looking up from the jug of milk he's frothing. He moves it slowly in a circular motion under the frothing arm, and I feel myself getting a little hot just watching the slow, grinding motion.

Jesus, Posy. Get a grip. My cheeks turn pink. "There's something wrong with my bill from your friends at the security company."

He looks up. "Really? What's the matter?"

"It's too low. By a lot." I hold up the page to show him.

He squints at the number. "Eh. I told them you had a long history in the restaurant business. Maybe they know your dad or something."

"But that's not right," I sputter. "My father has nothing to do with this place. He's never even been inside."

Gunnar doesn't even flinch. He's busy pouring milk onto a latte, the foam forming the shape of a cat's face. "Here you go, Lina," he says to a customer. "The kitty of the day has one floppy ear."

"You're so talented," the customer gushes. "Thank you, Gunnar!" She shoves a five-dollar bill into the tip jar.

"Aw, shucks," he says. "You have a nice day, now." He waves as she walks away, then eventually turns to where I'm standing here, fuming. "Chill, Posy. So they gave you a price break, maybe. It's nothing to get upset about. This is exactly why I don't drink caffeine. It makes people ragey. Is it time for my lunch break yet?" He pats his impeccable abs. "A growing boy needs to eat."

"No," I say, agitated. "I need another thirty minutes before I can cover for you."

"All right. Don't be a stranger." He gives me a maddeningly sexy smile.

I spin around and storm back into the kitchen, my body pinging with hormones and confusion. Who are Gunnar's friends, anyway, that they could practically give me a new window? "Who does that?" I ask my empty kitchen, because Ginny is outside on her phone, and Jerry has snuck off to read comics.

The only answer I get is the ding of the oven timer. So I get back to work.

16

GUNNAR

YOU DO A WOMAN A FAVOR, and she only gets agitated. Ah well. I tried.

There's a short break between customers, so I wipe down the counter, hoping Posy won't make too big a deal over the low bill we sent her.

The night of the break-in, we basically turned this place into a security fortress. Cameras capture everything in high resolution from every angle, 24/7. It's awfully invasive. But I need to know if The Plumber is connected to Posy's business or family. And I need to know soon.

I don't feel great about it, though, because it isn't even working. We still don't have a suspect. There must be something I'm missing. "Hey, Teagan," I try during a rare lull behind the counter. "How'd you get into making donuts, anyway?"

She looks up from the phone that's always glued to her hand. "Everybody likes donuts. It's a recession-proof business."

"Sure. But not everyone makes them."

She stashes the phone. "Well, it's kind of a personal story. My family went to Hawaii when I was seven. It was the only really big trip I can remember us taking together."

Bingo. You should always ask a small question first. If I'd asked Teagan about her family, it would have sounded suspicious. But asking about donuts got her talking anyway.

"We got these Portuguese donuts at a shop on Oahu, and they were still warm. We ate them on the beach, and I rinsed my fingers in the ocean. It was the best thing I'd ever eaten, and twenty years later it still seems magical."

"That's a nice story," I say. "And you haven't been back there?"

She shakes her head. "I always wanted to go. But my parents were killed in an accident a few years later. I went to culinary school, and I worked for some fancy restaurants. But I didn't like those jobs. Famous chefs are all assholes. So now I work for myself. I make the donuts for a few customers, and I work here for extra cash. I'll never be rich, but it's a good life."

"Sure is," I agree mildly. The bell on the door jingles, and another customer walks in. To my surprise, it's Saroya. She's wearing a sequined sweater, bright red lipstick, and a somewhat sheepish expression.

Interesting.

"Hello there, Gunnar," she says, blinking rapidly. "I was hoping you might have a decaf sugar-free nonfat peppermint iced latte with my name on it."

I paste on a smile. "Of course, madame." I'm as friendly as possible, although it is just a little weird that last time we saw each other, I called her boyfriend an asshole, and then she said that I was "obviously deranged." Honestly, I didn't expect to see her set foot in this place again. And I was perfectly okay with that.

On the other hand, I'm told that I am a truly great barista and pregnant women are well known for their cravings. "Would you like that for here or to go?"

"For here, please."

I grab a glass from the clean stack and get busy making her disgusting drink. People are weird. Her especially. While I'm making the coffee, I take surreptitious glances at her. Saroya is very busy examining the cafe and eyeballing the clientele. She's studying the pie shop like there will be a quiz later.

I can't help but wonder why she's so obsessed with this place. I guess it's possible to become fixated on your boyfriend's ex, especially if they were together for a long time. That's the only reason I can think of why a woman might spend a lot of time in her partner's ex-wife's cafe. Maybe she's jealous of Posy for some reason. Maybe there's tension at home. Maybe Saroya has some reason to think that Spalding isn't over Posy.

And maybe he isn't, because Posy is amazing.

"That will be four-fifty, please. Anything to go with it?"

Saroya turns toward the counter again, taking in the pies on offer, examining them with that slightly judgmental squint that's weirdly familiar. "No thank you." She passes me a five-dollar bill.

I can't figure out who she reminds me of, and it's going to bug me. "You know," I say as I'm making change, "the first time I made you a latte, I thought you looked really familiar to me. Have we met before?" I pass her two quarters.

Her eyes narrow immediately. "No, of course not. I'd never seen you before in my life." Then she picks up the cup of coffee and walks quickly away from me, without even putting that change in the tip jar. And without the usual amount of flirting. So that's weird. She takes a seat across the room, her back to me.

Posy emerges from the kitchen. "Hey, Gunnar, you can take that break now. I'm all set." Her eyes dip, as if she's embarrassed for snapping at me.

"Yeah, thanks," I say slowly. "Heads up, though, about table number four."

Posy's eyes dart over to where Saroya is seated, sipping her drink and flipping through a magazine. "Oh. Seriously? Thanks for the warning."

"You want me to stick around?"

She shakes her head. "Nah. Go on. I can handle her."

I go back into the kitchen and help myself to a sausage hand pie that's cooling on the rack. I grab my laptop, too, and go outside to sit on the back step. I eat the pie one-handed while I do a little Google searching. Saroya's social media is locked down, including the lists of her friends. But then I find an old Twitter account called @Realtor-Saroya. She hasn't touched it in years.

But your past always catches up to you, doesn't it? As I skim past a list of old apartment listings, I find that in 2016, Saroya retweeted a bunch of things about the Rockaways Cheerleading bake sale. That rabbit hole leads me to a high school in the farthest reaches of Brooklyn, and its cheer team.

Apparently cheerleaders take a lot of photographs, because there are a million. She's only identified as Saroya D. But that's enough. I find photos of her in a million poses.

Yet it's a plain old selfie that finally gives me the information I need. Saroya D. is pictured holding a trophy and standing beside a woman who could only be her mother. Their eyes are different, but their smiles are a perfect match. They have the same nose, and the same dark, gleaming hair.

But what's more—I've *met* Saroya's mother. The moment I see her face, a name pops into my mind. *Anna*. It only takes me a moment longer to recall where I met Anna. At Paxton's Bistro. She worked as a hostess during my first year there, when I was just the errand boy who took leaking bags of garbage out back and tossed them into the dumpster.

I never had a real conversation with Anna the hostess. She was always up in the front of house and I was always in back. But I remember that she was fearsome, and the servers were all a little afraid of her.

And Saroya is her daughter? That's another link to Posy. A huge coincidence. Unless it's not a coincidence at all …

I stare at the old picture until my eyes are practically cross. As if sheer willpower could make the women in the photo animate and tell me exactly what I need to know.

"Gunnar?"

I whirl around at the sound of Posy's voice, slamming the laptop shut in a hurry. "Yes?"

"Are you ever coming back from break? Or are you too busy looking at photos of cheerleaders to make coffee again?"

Shit. "Just reading something about a charity bake sale that my friend sent to me." I stand up and dust crumbs off my apron. "Sorry to dilly dally."

Posy gives me another dubious look. "No problem," she says stiffly, before turning to go back inside.

Shit ∫hit ∫hit. I don't think she had a good enough look at my laptop to pick out Saroya and her mom. There were at least five photos on the screen. "Everything okay?" I ask as I follow her through the kitchen and into the cafe. "Except for my tardiness, of course."

She stops behind the counter, which thankfully has no line in front of it. She crosses her arms, one hip cocked against the bar. "I'm fine," she says, her eyes flashing.

There isn't a lot of extra space back here, but lately it feels even smaller. She smells like lemon zest and vanilla extract. I never realized that baking scents were an aphrodisiac, but there you have it. And I'd like to get even closer to her. And naked, too.

But I will resist. The case I'm working keeps getting more complicated instead of less, so I can't go there. "Did she say anything?" I ask, dragging my foggy brain back to the problem at hand.

"Who?" Posy whispers, her eyes a little glazed and her cheeks a little flushed. I'm not the only one who feels it.

"Your nemesis at table four," I say softly, jerking my chin toward the chair where Saroya had sat less than an hour ago.

"Oh. No," Posy says quickly. "She left without a word to me."

"Well that's good, I guess." I pick up a rag and wipe the bar, even though it's already clean. "Just curious. How did she and your pencil dick of an ex meet, anyway?"

Posy snorts before clamping a hand over her mouth. "She's a wellness coach."

"You mentioned that, I think. And he was in the market for wellness?"

"Our health insurance company sent her after Spalding's health scare."

"Oh." I turn that over in my mind and come up blank. "Something happened to him?"

"Well ..." She frowns. "Eighteen months ago he had a panic attack. But he thought it was his heart. And then he didn't go to work afterwards, just in case. My husband's company sent her to shoehorn him out of his convalescence."

"Okay?" I wait for more.

She shrugs. "The more I talk about it, the weirder it sounds. Spalding had some kind of midlife crisis. I don't know if he's really that easily frightened, or if he just relished the attention and the time off. If I'd known then what I know now, I would have walked away from him sooner. Instead, I spent a lot of time worrying about him while he was busy meditating with his future child bride." She rolls her eyes. "I should have hired a P.I. to figure out if he was cheating on me. I should have fought harder to keep my net worth out of the red. But I hate confrontation almost as much as I hate liars. So here we are."

Three women walk through the door of the pie shop, interrupting this revealing little conversation. And when I turn to greet them, Posy disappears.

But later that night, I take another hard look at Saroya. Her wellness website was registered a year and a half ago, which means that she would have turned up on Spalding's doorstep almost the moment she opened for business.

That's weird, right?

I write an email to Max and his hacker minions, asking them to take a look at her bank accounts. And what they find is that Saroya was cashing checks last year from a restaurant—the Coconut Grill on Third Avenue. But not from any corporations.

And earlier today, I demonstrated that Saroya had prior knowledge of Posy's family. Her mother worked for Mr. Paxton long enough for all the waiters to be a little afraid of her.

By the time I shut off my computer at the late hour of ten-thirty, I have more questions than answers. What the hell is Saroya after? And what does it have to do with the Paxtons?

I don't have the first clue. But she's the only pie shop insider who's getting more interesting instead of less.

What's your game, Saroya D? And where is it headed?

17

POSY

THE LOW REPAIR bill still troubles me. But I write out a check anyway and tuck it into my purse.

I sure hope my father's connection to the restaurant industry didn't have anything to do with the low total. Gunnar doesn't understand how important it is to me to succeed without the influence of Peter Paxton III. My dad is toxic. He taught me to doubt myself.

And I'm still good at it. A whole week passes before I gather the courage to invite Gunnar out to dinner. I choose Friday for this moment of bravery, because Saturday is Gunnar's day off. If I go down in flames, I'll have thirty-six hours to avoid him before we come face to face again.

Thirty-six hours won't be nearly enough, will it? Maybe this is a terrible idea.

I worry about it all day. But suddenly it's closing time, and Gunnar has already counted the drawer, cleaned the bar, and is tipping all the chairs upside down onto the tables.

I'm about to lose my chance.

Meanwhile, I fuss with the flavored syrups, taking inventory of every flavor. But I'm so nervous that I count the coconut syrup three times. And then I overfill the raspberry syrup until it leaks all over my hand when I try to replace the pump.

"Shit," I whisper, just as Gunnar also says something from

directly behind me. "What?" I yelp, whirling around, startled. And then I collide with his hard chest.

Gunnar looks down at the front of his Posy's Pie Shop T-shirt, where raspberry syrup is smeared in a glossy, dripping blob.

Now I'm mortified. "Omigod, I'm sorry. What were you saying, anyway?"

"I said, *careful, I'm right behind you.*" He lifts his pale green eyes to mine and shakes his head. "At least it's quitting time."

"You can't leave like that. Come back to my office a second," I urge, pointing with sticky hands toward the back. "I'll grab you a fresh T-shirt for the walk home." I flip on the sink and plunge my sticky hands under the water. "I keep a couple of extras for emergencies."

"It's not far," he says with a shrug. "I don't really care."

"You look like you're starring in a b-grade slasher film," I point out. "And you'll smell like a fruit pop."

"You say that like it's a bad thing." He gives me a silly wink, and my achy little heart thumps wildly. Can you still ask a man out after you spill red goo all over his pecs?

"Come on," I say, brushing past him to get to my tiny office. "I'll wash that shirt this weekend, okay? Maybe I can even get the stains out. Take it off."

Yeah baby! my hormones cry. *Take it all off.*

Down, girl.

By the time I get my hands on an extra-large shirt and turn around, Gunnar is standing there in the hallway, shirtless.

Holy shit, my hormones whisper. *We already know about the muscles. But we had no idea about the tattoos.* Gunnar's chest is decorated with an elegant vine that climbs asymmetrically across his ribcage. My gaze traces its stem from one side of his waistline, up his stomach muscles, and finally across his pecs. And in the center of it, there's an old fashioned key looped into the tendrils.

It's beautiful.

"Had your fill, yet?" Gunnar asks quietly. "Can I put the shirt on now?"

Oh dear. I'm suddenly conscious of my open jaw, where my

tongue is practically hanging out. I thrust the shirt at Gunnar. "Sorry. Here you go. Can you have dinner with me tonight?" I blurt.

Oh, crap, my hormones say. *That's our bad. Sorry about the awkward timing.*

Gunnar's hands freeze in the midst of pushing through the arm holes of the shirt. When his face reappears through the neck hole, it's wearing a wince. "Hell, Posy. I can't. I'm sorry. It's not that I don't want to."

"I'm sure you're busy, no big deal," I rattle off.

"There's something I have to do tonight. A favor for a friend."

"Yup. Of course you do." I want to die now.

"Look," he rests one powerful arm against the door frame. "It would be a bad idea anyway. Not that it isn't tempting. Because we wouldn't stop at dinner."

I gulp.

"You're the boss. And I'm just a bad bet."

We love bad bets! my hormones shriek.

"I understand," I say. Then I pull myself up to my full height and make my face as impassive as possible. "Have a lovely day off. I'll see you on Sunday, okay? Rest up for the brunch crowd."

"Right," he says, tilting his head to study me with those pale green eyes. "You have a great Friday night."

I give him a wave, because it's either that or admit that my Friday night is going to be pretty lonely. Gunnar steps out of view. I hear him gather his backpack and his jacket and let himself out the door.

I just stand there for a minute, breathing. And I remind myself that this was good practice. In the unlikely event that I meet another man who's even half as appealing as Gunnar, I'll do better next time.

Then I go out front and lock up, pulling down the security gate — the one that Gunnar found for me, damn it. He's a better man than I ever guessed. He's a great employee. But he doesn't want me. Maybe he can sense that I'm not that much fun. That I don't know how to walk the naked path of joy. Maybe he could tell just from a few kisses.

Or maybe I'm being a psycho right now and beating myself up over nothing. The man has plans, and he doesn't want to bang his boss.

I double check the locks on the front and back doors. Then I order myself to go upstairs and plan a little fun for tonight, no matter what. Except Ginny and Aaron are at a kindergartener's birthday pizza party, so my two sidekicks are unavailable.

Since I refuse to sit home alone, I change into a short skirt, grab a book, and then take myself out to the same bar where I ran into Gunnar two weeks ago. I sip another of Jerome's special cocktails and try not to think about a certain hot barista with a tattooed chest.

Maybe it's my lucky night, because there's another guy down the bar who's eyeing me as I read. He's attractive in a very ordinary way. As I turn the pages of my book, I try to imagine flirting with him.

But, nope. It doesn't take. The book turns out to be more appealing than flirting with a stranger. This one is about a football player who's in love with the coach's daughter. And when they have shower sex, I forget all about the guy down the bar. By the time the scene is over, I've finished my second cocktail, and I need a cold shower myself.

And it's only eight-thirty.

I close the book and take a deep, calming breath. I should get home. Maybe Ginny and I can watch a movie together after Aaron goes to sleep. I tip the bartender and slide off my bar stool.

Just as I'm walking toward the door, I see someone emerge from the building across the street. I stop short when I realize it's Gunnar. And he's wearing a tuxedo.

Holy hell. My hormones are already in a weakened state, and the sight of Gunnar in a bow tie and a well-tailored black tux makes me go a little weak in the knees. He stops on the sidewalk, checking his smart watch. It's a big, fancy gadget that he often glances at during the workday.

His bow tie is slightly askew. The look is very devil-may-care. Very Brad-Pitt-on-the-way-to-the-Oscars. He looks fabulous, but I still have the urge to go over there and straighten his tie, just so I can touch him.

I wouldn't stop there, though. I'd probably untie it instead. And then the buttons of his shirt would beckon, and I'd undress him just so I could see that tattoo again. Those vines that I would like to trace with my tongue. And—

Wait.

Hold on.

That key on his chest. I've seen it before.

I'm still standing inside the bar, staring out the door like a weirdo. But I dig the bill out of my purse anyway. And there it is, right on the invoice. The same key, facing the same way.

It could be a coincidence. Old keys are very pretty. But that doesn't stop me from opening the door and stepping out onto Spring Street anyway, determined to ask Gunnar to tell me more about the security company that fixed my window.

But Gunnar is already walking away. I trail after him with my eyes until his sun-tipped hair turns the corner onto Thompson Street.

Later, I won't be able to explain why I did what I did. For no good reason, my feet turn east in hot pursuit. It's a nice night, and there are a lot of people on the sidewalk, ambling around SoHo. I dodge them from time to time, hanging back, watching Gunnar walk farther downtown. He crosses Broome and then Grand, then slows as he approaches the Soho Luxe hotel.

As I watch, he gazes up at the building. Is that where he's headed? There's a lovely bar on the roof, although Gunnar is a bit overdressed. He looks more like a maître d' than a party-hopping hipster.

He turns sharply before he reaches the main entrance, though. He's ducked into the alley, where the loading dock is. That's a strange way to approach one of the hippest downtown spots. Why doesn't he just go into the front door like anyone else?

A man comes out of the shadows to hand him something. This guy is blonder than Gunnar, and he's pinning something to Gunnar's suit. A name tag, I think. Then he hands him a clipboard, too.

Now hold on. That blond guy is familiar, too. I remember making a latte for him. I've made coffee and pie for half of lower Manhattan at this point. But *this* latte was just two weeks ago, on the morning Gunnar's friends fixed my plate glass window. The guy—Duff—was one of the work crew.

What the hell is happening here?

Gunnar lifts his head and glances around, and I have to dive behind a kiosk to avoid him seeing me.

But what the fuck? *A favor for a friend*, is how Gunnar described his evening plans. But who are these friends? And why is Gunnar dressed in a penguin suit?

He nods at Duff, checks his big watch one more time, then enters the hotel through the side door.

Since Duff is still standing there, I can't follow. So I head in the opposite direction, right through the front door. And as I take in the busy lobby, I spot Gunnar again. He's waiting for an elevator.

I hop behind a potted boxwood that's been clipped into the shape of a lollipop, and I watch Gunnar's tuxedo pants and his shiny shoes until they disappear into the elevator car.

After a count of five I scurry over there and watch the numbers light up as the elevator car ascends. I assume he's headed to the bar on the roof, but the elevator stops on the sixteenth floor. After a lingering pause there, it returns to the lobby. Empty.

Naturally I hop in and press the button for sixteen. Because that's what a needy, suspicious, half-insane pie baker does.

The doors slide closed, and the car begins to travel upward. Gunnar has some explaining to do.

18

GUNNAR

IT'S quiet on the sixteenth floor, where all the best suites are located. I'm loitering in an alcove near the service elevator, trying to impersonate a bored husband waiting for his wife to emerge for their night out.

A few yards away, Scout pushes a housekeeping cart toward the largest suite in the hotel. We don't make eye contact.

I'm here to guard Scout from two threats: the first is the hotel security staff. Scout is impersonating a housekeeper and breaking into a suite. Hopefully whomever is manning the security cameras right now is too lazy to squint at the video feed and ID her as a stranger.

The second threat is the ruthless international criminal Xian Smith. Not only do we know he's involved in a ring of industrial espionage, we also suspect he ordered a hit on a Thai manufacturer of motherboards this past fall. He's a dangerous man who has killed to get what he wants.

Tonight, though, Xian Smith is attending the Met Gala. Max watched him get into a limo just before Duff, Scout, and I converged on the hotel.

"Scout's in," Max murmurs into my earpiece. He's watching Scout's body cam from a van parked across the street. He can also see the elevators and the hallway, thanks to the stick-on cameras that Scout and I deployed on our way up here.

There's nothing to do right now but wait. So I do my best impression of a bored guy. I take out my phone and pretend to flip through my messages.

Inside the hotel suite, Scout can't just grab the camera that Max planted there and run. Smith probably has his own spyware set up in that room. So Scout has to spend a moment or two changing the towels and plumping the pillows. When Xian Smith realizes his room has been entered, we want him to think it was a routine evening turn-down service.

"Fuck," Max breathes into my ear. "What is Posy Paxton doing here?"

"What?" I whisper into my watch. "Where?"

"Sixteenth floor. She just emerged from the elevator and turned down the hall. Away from you."

"Fuck," I curse.

"She followed you here?" Max guesses.

"No idea." Why would she, though? "Should I go get her?"

"Stay put," Max says. "If she makes it all the way down to you, then you can grab her."

That sounds simple enough, but I'm no longer as relaxed as I was a few minutes ago. If Posy makes a scene, and hotel security comes running ...

"Jesus Christ," Max breathes. "He's back. Xian Smith is in the elevator. Don't move."

Now I know what it means when people say *I went cold inside.* Even as I tap a button on my watch that lets Max know I understand, I feel an icy chill slide down my body. Scout, Xian Smith, and Posy are all about to converge on the sixteenth floor?

Disaster.

"Fuck!" Max barks. "He made the elevator cam. It's gone dark. Scout, *get out of there.*"

My heart drops. And then it drops again when Max keeps talking.

"Gunnar, stand by to grab Posy. She's coming back in your direction. And—mother of God."

All my blood stops circulating when I hear Posy's voice. "Excuse me. Have you seen a guy in a tuxedo pass this way?"

"Lo siento. No hablo Inglés," Scout replies. *I don't speak English*.

I reach out and ring for the service elevator, trying to do the math on how to get both women onto it in the next five seconds.

But it's already too late. All my blood stops circulating when I hear Smith say, "Step away from my room. No staff is allowed in there."

"Stay put, Gunn," Max whispers harshly. "Let Scout try to talk her way out of there."

"No hablo Inglés," Scout repeats. "Quieres hablar con el jefe?" *Do you want to speak to the manager?*

"Fuck you," Smith says in an ice-cold voice. "I don't know what you're trying to pull." There's a loud crash, and then Posy screams.

In a flash I'm in that hallway, my eyes locked on Posy. She's standing there with her hands over her mouth, in the classic posture of shock. And she is way too close to an angry, violent crime lord.

Smith has upended Scout's pilfered laundry cart in a fit of rage. And Scout is backing slowly away, in perfect imitation of a frightened maid.

"Gunnar!" Posy squeaks, which is really inconvenient, since my manager's name tag says *Fred*. "There you are!" Her big eyes look up at me, frightened.

My impulse is to go to her, shield her with my body, and evacuate her from the premises. And maybe from the entire city. But I can't. I've got to fix this mess. "Just a minute, ma'am," I bark in her direction. "It's only been five minutes since you asked me for those towels." I whirl on Scout. "The towels were for *her*. This room is not to be entered. *No puede entrar!*"

"What did she steal?" Xian Smith says, kicking around the contents of the laundry cart. "You're not as slick as you think you are."

No kidding. "Sir," I say in my most obsequious voice. "I'm sure nothing was stolen. It's a simple misunderstanding. I'll deal with her." When I glance up again, Scout has already vanished. She's probably in the service elevator, or dashing down the back stairs. Which means I've only got Posy to worry about now. "I'll make sure this doesn't happen again. And let me send someone to clean this up right away."

Smith is still digging through the laundry, trying to figure out if this was truly a hotel mix-up or exactly what he suspects it to be—an invasion of his private space for the purpose of espionage.

"Come with me, please," I bark at Posy, my tone so cold that the temperature in the hallway declines by ten degrees. We've got to get out of here before hotel security arrives and exposes me for the fraud I am.

And here I thought tonight's job would be quick and easy.

Trying to appear purposeful and unhurried, I step away from Smith and beckon to Posy, without looking at her. She's a smart woman, so she says nothing. The fire stairs are closer than the elevator, so I push open the door and usher her through.

The last thing I do before leaving is to glance back at Smith. He looks up at me, rage burning in his eyes. I snap the door closed behind me. "Go," I say. "Quick, now."

We dash down the stairs, but there are a lot of them.

"What just happened?" Posy hisses after a couple of floors.

"Later," I grunt. "Come on. Hustle." I doubt that Smith will try to confront us in the lobby. A smart spy would check all his security feeds first.

But you never know.

She falls silent, possibly because it's hard work running down fifteen flights of stairs. Meanwhile, I tally up tonight's collateral damage. Smith knows my name now. Or at least part of it. And he's seen Scout's face, as well as Posy's. I feel sick about that. Smith knew better than to come at us on the hotel property. He's a familiar face at this hotel, and their security is watching.

But tomorrow is a different story.

We make it all the way down without incident, catching up to Scout on the final flight. When Scout grabs the maid's pinafore and throws it down onto the stairs, I hear Posy gasp. And when I turn to look at her, Posy is a picture of pink-cheeked adrenaline and wide-eyed confusion.

"Come on," I say gently. "There's a van outside. Stay right beside me."

"I've got your six," Scout says, lining up behind Posy.

I open the stairwell door a crack. And as I do, a couple in evening wear brushes past us, heading up the stairs. They obviously didn't want to wait for the elevator, and they don't spare us a glance.

Smith is nowhere in my field of vision, so I beckon to the women, straighten my spine, and stride into the lobby like a man who's not in a rush.

Out of the corner of my eye, I see Scout touch Posy casually on the elbow. "Have you had the margaritas here? They're excellent."

Posy's face doesn't play along. Her expression wonders what planet she's landed on, and when she can grab the first shuttle off.

And I don't blame her one bit.

19

POSY

ON AN ORDINARY NIGHT, I would never climb into a windowless van with a strange woman who's just impersonated a hotel maid, and who is now babbling at me about margaritas.

Then again, this is not an ordinary night. Gunnar's urgency is contagious. He practically frog marches me into the vehicle while my confused little brain tries and fails to keep up with current events.

That's how I find myself sliding onto the leather bench seat of the strangest van I've ever seen. In the corner—behind the driver—there are two panels of monitors. I recognize the video feed from the hallway where only a few moments ago I felt both terrified and deeply confused.

There's a chair in front of this setup, bolted to the floor. And as soon as Gunnar climbs onto the seat beside me and slams the door, a dark-haired man swivels around in this strange chair to scowl at us.

He's familiar, too. He's a friend of Gunnar's, but I haven't seen him for fifteen years. He used to come into Paxton's once in a while when Gunnar was working. What was his name? Matt? No, *Max*.

Remembering his name gives me a sense of victory, but it's fleeting. I still don't understand anything that happened tonight. "Who are you?" I demand as the van shoots forward. The motion makes my body slide against Gunnar's.

Nobody answers except for my hormones. *Ooh, we like the feel of Gunnar! Especially when we're scared.*

"What is happening?" I demand.

Again, I get no answer. Instead, Gunnar grabs a seatbelt and straps me in, the way I used to do for Aaron before he was old enough to do it for himself. Gunnar's jaw is so tense that I worry that it might crack.

"Who was that man upstairs?" I try as the van takes a corner and accelerates.

Gunnar's arm comes around me to hold me steady as the driver does a few more quick maneuvers.

"Did you get it?" Max asks the maid who obviously isn't a maid. His eyes have the intensity of lasers.

"Of *course* I got it." She's the only one who looks the least bit relaxed. In fact, she reaches for an apple that's braced in the cup holder and takes a bite.

"Don't tease me."

"Fine," she says, reaching into her bra and pulling out a device, which she hands to him.

"You are a fucking goddess," Max says, staring at the object in his hand. "Where's the spent battery?"

She takes another bite of the apple, then wiggles a hand into the pocket of her skirt. A moment later she's handing off a gray unit the size of a cell phone, a cord protruding from one end.

"Good work, as always." Then he turns to look at Gunnar, and the two men seem to lock attitudes at the same time they lock eyes. "You, on the other hand, have some explaining to do."

"Oh, bite me," Gunnar grumbles. "This mission was fucked from the start. Maybe you'd like to explain why the perp turned up seven minutes after you told us he was gone?"

"He *was* gone," Max thunders. "I watched him get into the car myself."

"Not gone enough."

Another opinion comes from the driver's seat. "You both fucked up. But I can settle this pissing match. Max was outmaneuvered by a paranoid international criminal. Gunnar was tailed by a piemaker." He swivels around, and I recognize the one called Duff. "No offense, Posy. I'm sure that pie is killer. Not that I'd know, because Gunnar won't share."

And now I've had enough of being confused. "What is *happening?*" I shriek. "Who was that guy? Why were you stalking him? Why impersonate the hotel staff? What is up with this strange van?"

"Stalking isn't really a word we use," Max says, rubbing his chin. "It's so negative."

A high-pitched shriek of frustration erupts from my throat, and the woman holding the apple core glances my way. "Somebody needs a margarita. Max should buy, especially because I can't safely enter the Soho Luxe for the foreseeable future. My name is Scout, by the way. Nice to meet you, Posy."

"Nice to meet you," I say through clenched teeth, because my parents were always big on manners, and old habits die hard.

"Duff, after you're sure nobody is tailing us, could you drop me at home?" Gunnar asks. "I'll talk to Posy."

"Somebody had better talk to Posy!" I holler. "And it better be good."

"Good plan. Be discreet," Max cautions. "Can I ask, Posy, why you were following Gunnar tonight?"

"Because nothing makes any sense!" I howl. "The lowball bill for the window. With the key on it. It's the same key that Gunnar has right here." I place my hand on my sternum.

"Oh, *dude.*" Max scowls at Gunnar. "Reason numero uno for not getting naked on the job."

"You've got the wrong idea," Gunnar argues.

"I spilled raspberry syrup all over him," I clarify.

"Hot damn!" Duff says. "Can you spill some on me, too? I mean —I've tried chocolate sauce in bed. But variety is awful nice."

"But we weren't ..." I realize that my questions still have not been answered, and I try once again to get this conversation back on track. "What is the key?"

"A logo," Duff supplies. "Every company needs a logo. It's extra helpful for us, because we don't tell anyone the company name. Most of us have that tattoo. All the guys I know who work for The Company."

"But Gunnar works for me," I argue. And then I immediately realize that I've missed something big. Maybe Gunnar isn't there for fifteen bucks an hour plus tips. It always seemed weird to me that he turned up in my shop looking for work.

The barista with a single reference who doesn't drink coffee. Who volunteered to work six days a week.

"Gunnar," I say slowly. "Tell me again how you came to be a barista in my shop?"

"It's complicated," he says.

"I HAVE TIME!"

"First stop, Spring Street," Duff says, slowing the van to a crawl. "No tail, but watch yourselves."

"Thanks Duff. Before we go, is everything quiet at the pie shop?" Gunnar asks, removing his seatbelt. Then he reaches over and removes mine, too. "You're getting out here with me."

"SAYS WHO?" I'm prepared to keep howling until I get some answers.

But Max stuns me into silence by pressing a single button on his high-tech console, changing all the images on the monitors behind him. And what I see on those screens makes my eyes widen.

Every camera view is inside my pie shop. There's my counter in the nighttime shadows, the lemon meringue standing tall. And there's a shot of table four, and another of eleven. There's also a view of my front door, and a view of the back.

"What the hell?" I whisper. "Where did those cameras come from?"

"Gunnar will explain," Max says.

"Come on," Gunnar says, putting a hand on my lower back. "Still clear, Duff?"

"Clear."

Gunnar opens the back door and tugs on my hand. "Quickly now."

Numb, but still needing answers, I follow him, hopping down to the pavement.

He puts a firm hand on my back, looks up and down the sidewalk, then pulls me toward his front door.

Sidestepping him, I disengage his hand from my body, even though I like the feel of it. "I'm not going upstairs with you," I say, sounding just like a petulant child.

"I need you to," he says simply. "You're easier to protect up there."

"Protect from what?"

"I'll tell you *all about it* upstairs," he growls, unlocking the front door and holding it open for me.

And I step through. But only out of pure curiosity. "I'm still mad," I say, just for clarification. "I don't like you anymore."

Just keep telling yourself that, my hormones chuckle.

"You shut up," I whisper.

"Sorry?" Gunnar asks, closing the door behind us.

"Not you," I grumble. "I need some more explaining from you."

He sighs. "Yeah, I know. Come on."

Gunnar lives in a small but chic little building—the kind where the elevator opens right into his third-floor apartment. When the doors part, we step into a soaring, open-plan space with a huge living area, white plastered walls, a stone fireplace, a killer kitchen, and double doors opening to a big bedroom in back.

"Jesus, Mary and Joseph," I breathe. "You could never live here on barista money."

"You're right." He takes the tuxedo jacket off and tosses it over the arm of a giant L-shaped couch. It's just like mine, except larger, newer and about ten times more beautiful. The leather looks like butter.

And I feel like the world's biggest idiot. "You lied to me."

"I did," he says, teasing his bowtie apart.

"You really work for Max."

"Exactly." He threads the bow tie through his collar and tosses it onto his jacket. Then he unbuttons the tux shirt collar.

"The barista job. It was all just a ruse. You're *spying* on me!"

"Not on you," he says calmly.

"Is it ... are you with the police?" I squeak.

He shakes his head. "No. Max's company does high-end private security, and some industrial cybertech work. There's a criminal who's been using your pie shop WiFi to brag about a series of murders. You might have seen them in the newspaper. The killer poisoned ..."

"I read about those!" I snap. "Those were scary and disgusting. I don't want anything to do with that."

"I know you don't," he says calmly.

"Why do you keep agreeing WITH EVERYTHING I SAY?" I shout. "It's so fucking irritating!"

"Oh, *I'm* irritating?" he returns. "You act like you're the only one who has ever missed the joke. You tailed me tonight, and I didn't even notice. You, with the stealth skills of a kitten wearing a bell around its neck."

"I CAN BE VERY STEALTHY!" I shriek.

"Obviously." He unbuttons the collar of his shirt, and my eyes dart to his strong neck, and the few blond hairs visible on his upper chest.

Keep going, my hormones beg. They won't shut up even when I'm very angry.

And I'm still very angry. "It's not okay. You can't just spy on someone's pie shop with your spy tools and your sneaky friends. That's my LIFE in there!"

"Look, did it occur to you that I don't want you to lose your life?" he snaps. "That maybe I realize you don't need to be at the dangerous epicenter of someone's grudge against a killer? A menacing person who's made himself very comfortable in your shop, Posy. I only lied so I could figure out who that is."

"Well it's not me!" I squeak.

"I know." He unbuttons that shirt a little further. I watch the ink from his tattoo appear slowly, one sexy button at a time.

The key comes into view, which reminds me of the handsome asshole's duplicity. "This was all a game to you. I'm just an unwitting little cog in your wheel. You're *using* me."

"Hey now," he says, his cool eyes flashing. "I know it's a lot of information. I realize it's a big shock. But try to remember that I also busted my ass for the last three weeks, making coffee eight hours a day. I show up early and I stay until the job is done."

It's all true. But the lie still burns, because ... "I thought we were *friends*," I gasp, knowing how pathetic I sound. But I've always prided myself on drawing my employees close. We depend on each other.

I thought we did, anyway. But I was wrong.

"We *are* friends, damn it," he says. "The pie shop is pretty great, and I care a great deal about what happens there."

"That's bullshit. You're just saying that to make yourself feel better," I argue. And then a brand new and truly *horrible* idea occurs to me. "Wait—was it you? Did you and Max break my window? So you could fix it and put cameras everywhere?

"No! Posy—!"

"You *did!*" I squeak. "You walked me home from the bar at *just* the right time to witness it. How convenient for you to keep me busy that night. Did you follow me to that bar? You did! And then on the way home you—"

My next realization is so awful that I actually choke on my words. Everything that happened between us that night was a lie. The way Gunnar propositioned me, just so he could walk me home. Kisses on the sidewalk, just to distract me. And after the break in, he stayed close by and held my hand while the cops took my statement.

"Omigod," I whisper. "Oh. My. *GOD.* I've been played by yet another man."

"Slow your roll," he thunders. "I have no fucking idea who broke into your shop. But I've just spent the last week trying to figure it out."

"*LIAR!*" Spalding was right. I *am* terrible at sex. I can't even tell real kisses from fake ones. It's utterly humiliating, and fat tears spring from both of my eyes. "You kissed the poor, lonely baker so she wouldn't notice what you were up to."

"Bullshit!" he shouts. And suddenly he's right in front of me, all up in my space. "You've got it backwards. I just spent the last week trying *not* to kiss you, because everything got so complicated. The case is still up in the air, and—"

"The *case*," I spit. "It's all about the case. That's all you ever cared about."

"It's not," he thunders, his face red. He reaches out and grabs the belt loops of my skirt, towing me closer, as if proximity would make his argument more logical. "I'm trying to explain, but you won't listen."

"Because it's bullshit." I whisper at close range. His green eyes are enormous at this distance. "I don't believe anything you say."

"Oh, for fuck's sake. Then believe *this*." That's when the asshole leans in and kisses me. It isn't a bashful kiss, either. He tilts his head and consumes me with firm hungry lips. I'm hit with his clean scent and the heat from all that skin so close to mine. Surprise makes my knees wobble, so I reach out to steady myself.

But my palms land on that hard chest. And—wow—the heat rising off this man makes me crazy. I don't know how it happens, exactly. But the same mouth I used a minute ago to snarl at Gunnar is now kissing him back.

He likes it, too. He hauls me against his hard body, wrapping his arms around me. And now his tongue is in my mouth.

I let out a groan of surprise, because I had no idea it was possible to be so irritated and so turned on at the same time. This frustrating, untrustworthy man is devouring me the way a starving man takes down a fat slice of apple pie.

It's a wonderful, terrible kiss. I know I should stop. But I just don't want to. Not even when my back suddenly hits the wall, where Gunnar's hard body has trapped me. "I've always wanted you," he mutters between kisses.

"Shh!" I order. "Don't talk, for God's sake. You'll ruin it." I thread my fingers into his hair and pull him in for another kiss.

"You don't believe me," he grunts against my mouth, as if this is some kind of surprise.

"Of *course* I don't believe you. Men lie. You, for example, lie to me all day long." As I say this, I'm unbuttoning the rest of his shirt.

A wrinkle appears in the middle of his forehead. Then he kisses me once again, but very slowly. "The only kind of lying I'm doing tonight is the kind where I lie on top of you."

Oh my.

"—And don't say you don't want that. Because then you'll be a liar, too."

That is sadly accurate. "Two wrongs don't make a right," I grumble, shoving the shirt off his shoulders.

"Now who's talking too much?" He dives in for another kiss, and my blood begins to pound. This is madness. I shouldn't let him kiss me. I shouldn't suck on his tongue, making him moan into my mouth. I shouldn't arch my back to push my hungry body closer to his.

No, I should kick him in the shins and storm out of here.

But this Gunnar wants to distract us with once-in-a-lifetime sex, my hormones whine. *We can storm out later, after we see where this goes!*

Which turns out to be straight to every nerve ending I possess. Because Gunnar's kisses are overwhelming. He kisses with his whole body. A firm thigh slides between my legs. A big hand cups my ass as he delves a little more deeply into my mouth. We kiss until my lips are chafed and my nipples ache inside my bra.

"Paxton," he pants between kisses. "We've come to a crossroads."

"What?" I gasp. "Why?"

"Five minutes from now you'll either be on your way home with a polite Company escort. Or naked on my bed with your legs in the air. Which is it going to be?"

NAKED! scream my deepest desires.

Except I'm very bad at sex. And I'm still mad at Gunnar. I pull back another centimeter. As if that could possibly dull the zap and sizzle between us. "You put cameras in my workplace. Is this just your way of trying to slide that by?"

"I want to slide something, that's for sure." He runs his hands down my body, and I nearly purr like a cat. "And I will apologize thoroughly for the subterfuge. But not right this minute. Because I can't think right now. Not with my brain, anyway. So choose, Paxton. Am I calling an agent to drive you home? Or am I removing all your clothing?"

"I haven't decided," I say as he kisses his way down my jaw.

"No? Then why is your hand down my pants?"

Oh, geez. Look at that.

That was all us, my hormones confess. *But isn't this fun?*

"Fine," I say sharply. "I'm in. But now will you stop talking?" Since my hand is already in the neighborhood, I rub my palm down over his erection.

His answering growl thrills me. Then he lifts my hair in his hand, bends his handsome face down, and begins making sweet love to my neck.

It's ... wow. I shiver as his lips and tongue trace a path across my throat. Then his hands reach around to cup my ass, pulling me flush against his hard, hot body. There's no mistaking his intention, or his arousal. And when he lifts his head to kiss me again, I let out a shameless moan.

Who knew I was such a pushover? Each kiss makes me looser and more pliable. Like pastry dough in capable hands.

"Honey," Gunnar rumbles. "Let's get you onto the bed."

"No," I say, because I don't like how easily he's won me over. At least from the neck down.

"Cool, cool," he says between kisses. "Maybe you want to hop up on the counter. Or maybe you're hoping I'll bend you over the couch."

Ungh. Yes, please. Do us on the couch!

"Here's the thing, though," Gunnar pauses while his mouth takes an erotic journey across my collar bone, and my skin erupts in goosebumps. "The condoms are in the bedroom."

"Oh," I gasp. Suddenly his bedroom sounds like a good plan. "Okay."

He doesn't take my hand and lead me in there, however. That's what a gentleman would do. Gunnar bends his knees, hoists me off the floor and tosses me over his bare shoulder. My shoes fall off and land with twin thuds on the floor.

I'm so startled that it takes me a moment to let my shriek of outrage fly. All I can see from this angle is the floor moving, and Gunnar's butt.

It's a spectacular butt. Still, I prefer to travel under my own power. A moment later the ride is over, though. He tosses me onto a giant bed, and I land ungracefully in the center of his comforter.

I glance around at the huge room. It's such a bachelor pad, with nothing on the walls except for a framed poster of the original Matrix movie. One wall, though, is covered from floor to ceiling in bookshelves. And every one of them is full of books.

My heart beats a little faster. I love a man who reads. I *trust* a man who reads. And not just *Golf Digest*, either, like my ex.

When I glance back toward Gunnar, his tuxedo pants are already missing. Then he hooks his thumbs in the waistband of his briefs and pushes them *right* off. The most gorgeous naked man that I have ever seen in my life is stalking toward me, his erection jutting up and out. He means business. He wants me.

Oh boy, my hormones whisper. *It's finally happening. Gunnar Scott is going to do us. Right now.*

20

GUNNAR

I PUT a knee onto the bed, bracing myself on my hands, and take in Posy's expression. Her lips are bitten with my kisses, and the pulse point at her throat flutters wildly. She's a little bit stunned, and a whole lot turned on.

I'm done holding back. She and I have been dancing around each other for way too long.

And I've had it with this whole stupid night. I'm relieved that Posy finally knows the truth.

Hours ago—which seems like another lifetime—she finally got over her hesitation to go slumming with a guy like me. I couldn't believe that she asked me to dinner and I had to say no, for so many reasons.

I've had it with a lot of those reasons, too. My life is seriously complicated. And thanks to me, so is Posy's. Whenever I picture her standing right in front of a violent criminal, I feel cold all over.

But she's safe right now. And I'm going to pretend for an hour or two that everything isn't a goddamn mess. I'm going to reduce the evening to a simple equation that both Posy and I can understand. Her plus me on this bed.

"Paxton," I bark. "You're thinking too hard again."

"No, I'm not," she argues automatically.

"Okay, prove it."

Posy scowls at me. But she never could back down from a dare.

She lifts her top over her head and tosses it away. Then she kicks off her skirt.

I suck in a breath when I see her sitting in the center of my bed in nothing but tiny little lace panties and a black demi bra. "You're trying to kill me, right? That's why you put this on and followed me into a hotel?"

"No!" She makes an irritated noise. "This underwear wasn't for you."

"Uh huh." I straddle her thighs, tilt her chin up toward mine, and kiss her until she whimpers. Slowly, I drag my thumb across the swells of her breasts. "You are spectacular," I whisper. "I was a twenty-one-year-old bartender who used to dream of doing *this*." I lie her back onto the bed and then lower my face between her breasts. I tease the lace cups down until her rosy nipples protrude above the fabric. And then I circle first one and then the other with my tongue.

"Oh boy," she moans. "Unnngh."

I dip and swirl and suck, until she pushes my face away. "What the hell? I'm busy here."

"You've got me all trussed up like a chicken." She reaches behind her body and unhooks the bra, and her breasts bounce free of it. "There. Carry on."

"I don't think I will," I tease, and Posy makes a noise of dismay. "But don't you worry your pretty head about it. I have other work to do here." I work my way up to lavish her mouth with kisses. Then I work my way down again, into the valley of her breasts and then down her tummy.

When I reach those lace panties, I set about kissing every inch of that scrap of fabric. While Posy moans, deep and low. "Gunnar," she pants. "*Ohhhh.*"

The sound of her pleasure makes me ache. I'm so hard. And she's so soft against my mouth. I tongue the lace, teasing her. And when I close my lips over her sweet pussy, Posy sobs my name. "*Please,* Gunnar."

"Soon, honey." I slip one fingertip under the fabric. And my body tightens as I discover how wet she is for me. I glance up into Posy's huge eyes. She's propped herself up on her elbows, her hair spread out on her tits, her cheeks pink.

I've always wanted to shake her loose like this. My gut told me how much fun she would be when she let her hair down. Posy is the kind of girl who makes people work for it. She doesn't trust easily, and she keeps her own council.

It's a privilege to see her like this—hair mussed, lips red. She looks wild. Debauched. And I'm the lucky guy who gets to be here for it.

Slowly, I slide the panties down her legs. Then I look up and check her face. Posy is breathing hard, her eyes heavy with lust. Holding her gaze, I lean down and lick up the center of her. "You taste better than any pie." I place my hand across her mons and use my thumb to gently tease her clit. "Reach into the bedside table, would you?"

"O-okay," she stammers. Then she flops back on the bed and reaches for the drawer.

That's when I drop my head and pleasure her again with my kiss. Posy arches against my tongue and moans loudly.

I love teasing her. Posy is usually so wary and cautious. But not right now. She's a hundred and ten percent invested in her own pleasure. It's so beautiful watching her let go to reach for it. I'm going to make her yell my name.

In a minute.

I back off just at the crucial moment, and Posy lets out a moan of dismay.

"Where's that condom I asked for?" I ask calmly.

Pink-faced and cursing, she sits up, reaches into the drawer, grabs a condom and throws it at me.

With a chuckle, I move to sit up near the headboard, and then I open the packet. I'm so hard it hurts. Posy watches me cover myself, her chest rising and falling with each rapid breath.

"Lie down, honey," I say. "I need you on your back."

She gives me the sort of frown that I always get when I try to boss her around. And then she defies me, swinging a knee over my thighs instead, climbing into my lap.

"Oh I see," I whisper at close range. "Well, you're welcome to ride this bull. But I won't be using the amateur setting for you."

Posy rolls her eyes at my ridiculous taunt. When I smile, she smiles back. Then she kisses me.

And it's quite a kiss, full of heat and yearning. My hands find their way into her hair, and I pull her more tightly to my chest, just to make sure we can't be any closer than we already are.

Oh wait—we can. "Do it, honey. I need you now," I say between kisses. It's not an exaggeration. For fifteen years I've needed this.

I've needed *her*.

And I feel like I'm dreaming when Posy rises up on her knees, trapping my cock beneath her. Our eyes lock as she slowly takes me inside, her tight heat surrounding me inch by luscious inch. When she lowers her ass into my lap, fully seated, her eyelashes flutter. She lets out the most deliciously helpless sound.

For a moment, everything stops. We share a slow breath. Her face is flushed, and her pupils are blown. And my world shrinks down to the small space of my lap, where Posy and I are locked into this most intimate embrace. "You're exquisite," I breathe, my hands cupping her face. I give her a quick kiss, and then I move her hands to my shoulders. "Go on. Don't lose your nerve now."

I'm desperate for it. Fifteen years of hunger surges inside me as Posy rocks forward, clenching her shapely body around my cock. Then she rises up on her knees and sinks down again, before I remember to breathe.

"Fuck," I curse as the sudden friction sparks a jolt of pleasure.

Her eyes widen, and she does it again, setting a quick pace.

"More," I urge. "Don't ever fucking stop." My hands find their way to her hips, and I work her body against mine. Words of praise fall from my lips as she continues to move. *Beautiful. Yes. Goddess.*

I'm blissed out and trouble-free, except for one problem—this will end too soon if I'm not careful. So I move my hands to Posy's breasts, which bounce erotically with every thrust. She gasps when I give her nipples a light pinch.

"Gunnar!" she pants, throwing her head back.

That's a girl. "Don't come yet, honey," I tease, moving my hand down her belly.

She arches her back and moans.

"Not yet, okay?" I manage to work my fingertips between our

bodies, teasing her sweet pussy. "No matter how good it feels, hold on."

But I'm back to my old tricks again. I'm only bluffing. I need to make her cry out in pleasure. I need her to feel what I'm feeling right now.

"Good girl," I whisper.

And that's what tips her over the edge. Posy looks deep into my eyes and shudders helplessly. Her body clenches around me, and I grit my teeth to stave off my own release.

She's beautiful as she comes, moaning and sighing into my mouth, her arms tightening around my chest. I actually have to think about the Yankees vs. the Mets for a second to keep myself in check.

"Oh no," she says as she sinks down onto my cock for the last time, going still. "I-I'm sorry. I'm bad at this."

"*What?* How do you figure?" I kiss her twice. "I haven't had this much fun in years. Maybe ever." I can't stop kissing her as she softens against my body. "Hold onto me."

"Hmm?" she asks, her voice pure bliss.

I roll us over, until she's lying on her back, and I've braced myself on my forearms over her. "You okay?"

"I've never been more okay," she slurs.

"Good." I rock slowly against her. "Kiss me, and I'll take you there again."

"It won't work," she gives her head a shake. "Don't worry about me."

"You're doubting me right now?" I give her that smile she was teasing me about earlier. The full wattage tip-jar smile. "Then I guess I have something to prove."

She rolls her eyes. But I mean business. So I take her mouth in another heated kiss. And I do what I do best. Until she's whimpering and shaking and begging.

This time I don't hold back. With a groan that could wake up lower Manhattan, I release every last ounce of tension in the form of a climax for the record books. And she answers me with a happy shout, as her fingernails dig into my back. "Gunnar!"

Finally sated, I flop down onto the sheet. My body is spent, but my smile might never go away.

We lie there quietly afterward. My satisfaction is deeper than mere sexual release. I can't stop kissing her hair, and I can't stop caressing her soft skin. So many things went wrong tonight.

But so many more went absolutely right.

"I have so many questions," Posy whispers. "But I'm sleepy."

"Tomorrow I'll answer them all," I tell her. "Put your head down right here." I ease her onto my chest. "Rest now, sweetheart."

Her body goes still. And even if nothing has been settled, I feel more at peace than I have in years.

21

POSY

WHEN MY PHONE blares a Green Day tune into the darkness at four-forty-five a.m., I'm confused about several things at once.

Where am I?

Is there really a hard-bodied man stretched against my back?

Why does my body feel so well used?

Then I open my eyes and realize I'm in Gunnar's bedroom, not mine. And it all comes rushing back to me. The hotel. The threatening man on the sixteenth floor. The van. The spying.

The sex.

Whoa. That last thing is almost more unbelievable than the rest.

Gunnar groans beside me. "What time is it?"

"Quarter 'til five." I sit up, slide sleepily off the bed and fetch my bag where I dropped it in Gunnar's living room. I shut off my alarm and then go back into the bedroom. "Can I borrow your shower?"

"Anytime," he mumbles into the pillow.

I slip out of his bed and pad across the cool floorboards toward his bathroom. When I flip on the light, I find the room to be even more impressive than I remember it from my hasty visit here at midnight.

Seriously. What the fuck, Gunnar? I'm still angry about his lies. *I really need this job*, he'd said. It tugged at my heartstrings.

And I hate feeling gullible. Why is it always men who make me feel that way? My father was the first asshole to make me feel like a fool. And then came Spalding.

My track record is terrible. Just introduce me to an asshole. Any asshole. I'll believe him.

So here I stand in Gunnar's bathroom, which would fit right in at the Playboy Mansion. There's a bamboo floor and elegant glass tiles on the walls. Big fluffy towels wait on a gleaming towel bar outside the walk-in shower.

I'm so annoyed. But I'm going to shower like a queen anyway.

After taking care of business, I turn the water on full blast and wait for it to heat up. And then I slip out of the T-shirt Gunnar lent me to sleep in, and step beneath the warm spray.

Oh, this is heaven, even if it belongs to a liar.

He didn't do it for a bad reason, my hormones weigh in.

"Shut up. You don't know," I whisper.

But then I zip my lip, because the bathroom door opens. And Gunnar walks right up to the shower, opens the door and slips inside.

"Morning," he says gruffly. Then he leans down and kisses the juncture of my neck and shoulder.

And I am shook. "Morning," I squeak. "What are you doing out of bed? It's your day off."

"It's never my day off," he says, grabbing the soap. He lathers up his hands and then begins washing my back.

I want to argue, but it feels *really* nice. So nice that I let out a groan as he begins to massage my lower back.

"Too much?" he asks quietly.

"No way. But I don't know why you're up, and I don't know why you're doing that. I can't go back to bed with you. Someone has to make the pies."

His hand pauses on my back. "I know that, Paxton. I just wanted to be near you. Turn around."

Reluctantly, I turn to face him. The water rains down on us as I stare up into his gorgeous eyes.

"I'm coming to work with you this morning," he says.

"Why?"

"Just to make sure you're safe." He picks up a bottle of shampoo, dispenses a blob into his hand, and then begins to rub it through my hair.

Holy moly. His hands are magic. Maybe I have some kind of undiscovered scalp-rubbing kink. It feels so good.

When I close my eyes to keep the soap out of them, it makes the moment seem even more unreal. I'm naked in a fancy shower with Gunnar Scott. Is this real life?

I plant a palm in the center of his chest. His skin is slick and warm. "Mmm," he says, and I feel the vibration under my hand. "Are you sure you can't open late this morning?" Soapy hands take a quick, gratuitous trip down my breasts. And then he kisses my neck.

"Oh, I'm sure," I say quickly. Because if I get into bed with him again, I'm afraid I'll never leave. I tilt my head back to rinse off the shampoo. "Behave yourself."

I hear his chuckle, and when I can see again, Gunnar is already lathering himself up in a businesslike fashion. As if this were a perfectly normal way to start the day.

It could be, my hormones suggest.

But they're wrong. Gunnar is a temporary blip in my life, and I'd better not forget it. I wouldn't even be here right now if it weren't for the mess I'm in. "How much danger am I in, exactly?"

Gunnar closes his eyes to rinse his hair, and I ogle him shamelessly while he can't see me. There's that tattoo again. A work of art, on a work of art. "Probably not much, but I don't want to risk it."

"Who was that guy last night?"

"I'll explain while we walk to work," he says, turning off the water. "Ladies first." He opens the shower door, and points at the towels. "I'd offer you coffee, but I don't have any. I don't even have a coffee machine."

I step out and grab one of the fluffy white towels. "Did you learn to make espresso just to work in my shop?"

"Yup." He ties a towel around his lickable waist. "But if you want that story, you'll have to get it out of Max or Duff. You'll laugh your butt off, I'm sure."

"And when I called that reference for you in California—"

"Just one of Max's agents. Sorry," he says.

That icky feeling comes back—the one that makes me feel certain

I'm doomed to be duped by fast-talking men. "Were you even *in* California? Where did the lies begin?"

He gives my shoulder a squeeze. "I'm in San Jose about three quarters of the time. I hate New York."

"And this apartment?" I ask, leaving the palatial bathroom. Even in the predawn darkness I can tell that Gunnar's place is beautiful. If it's even his. "Where did it come from?"

"It's mine. I bought it. But it's empty most of the time."

"But why?" I ask.

"Well, it's an investment." He walks over to a nice maple dresser and opens a drawer. "And my company is based here. I don't just work for Max. I own a stake in The Company. But that's not really what motivated me to buy this place."

"Then what did?"

"Owning a sweet pad in the city was a bucket list item. I spent the first twenty years of my life getting stomped on by rich New Yorkers. So owning a piece of the pie felt like revenge. But maybe the joke's on me, because the taxes and the condo fees aren't cheap."

"Revenge on who, exactly?" I grab my shirt off Gunnar's bedroom floor and try to shake it out.

"Rich assholes in general." He shrugs, and then removes his towel to step into a pair of boxer briefs. "It's not the most logical thing I've ever done. But this is a great neighborhood."

God, that butt, my hormones sigh. *The most perfect butt in New York City.*

Still.

"I just need four minutes to get dressed and then I'd better scoot off to work," I tell him.

"I'm at your service," he says, looking over his shoulder to give me a slightly dirty wink. But his smile is warm.

I'd better stay far, far away from that smile. It's dangerous in so many ways.

"What's his name?" I ask Gunnar as we walk along the still-darkened Soho street. "The guy on the sixteenth floor. And what did you want from his room?"

"We know him as Xian Smith," Gunnar says. "The tech community knows him as someone who brokers the manufacture of electronic components in China. But Max and I have some theories about his real motives."

"What kind of theories?" I press.

Gunnar chews on his lip. "It's better if you don't know too much about it. But Max is a foremost expert in cybersecurity. And network security is meaningless if your hardware is corrupted. We've spent a lot of time investigating hardware hacks this year."

"Fine. So what was that thing Scout put in her bra?"

"Surveillance hardware. We're trying to figure out who Smith is working with. What he does all day. What his real name might be. All that fun stuff."

"So you hacked him."

"Yup."

"Even though you think hackers are horrible people."

"Some of them," Gunnar counters, nudging my hip. "Don't take his side just yet. He's also responsible for murder in cold blood, as well as a factory fire in China."

"Is he the one who's posting murder messages on my cafe WiFi? He didn't look familiar." I pull out my keys, because we've reached the front door to my building.

"It's not him," Gunnar says with a sigh. "But Max thinks it's related. That's really all I can say. Except for this." Gunnar stops walking as we reach the front door of the pie shop. His gaze makes a quick scan of the empty street, and then he puts his hands on my shoulders. "I will keep you out of it, Posy. It's my problem to solve. I kept you out of the loop because I thought it would be over soon. I wanted you to focus only on pretty pies and coffee drinks. That was a mistake, and I'm sorry. But I will keep all the assholes away from you."

"Okay." I look up into those pale green eyes and see intensity there.

"I'm sorry that any of this ever visited your shop. The murder posts began two weeks before I showed up, though. I didn't walk this through your door, I promise."

"Okay," I croak. "Thank you."

Then I'm stunned when he pulls me into a quick, tight hug. "You can put me to work in your kitchen."

"What? I thought you were just walking me home."

"Well, I'm up now. I don't know crap about making pies, so pick something easy."

"Can you peel apples?" I unlock the metal grate and push the button to raise it up.

"I can try."

"Good enough. I'll take the free labor. Fire up Lola, will you?"

"Yes, boss." He gives me another cheesy wink.

"Hey, Gunnar?" I close the door behind us and check that it's still locked.

"Yeah?" He's already behind the counter, turning on the espresso machine.

"Today you should make another sign for my window—Barista Wanted. You're going to catch this guy, right? And then disappear?"

"That's the plan," he says, checking the beans in the grinder.

"Then I need to hire somebody. Stat. Why'd you throw away my sign if you knew I'd still need it?"

He leans his forearms onto the bar and takes me in. "That was just a bit of swagger. I'm sorry. I'll fix it."

"Thank you," I say. And then I hurry into the kitchen so he can't read on my face how conflicted I am about all of this.

He follows me a few minutes later. "Okay. Where do you keep the apple peeler?"

"It's on that shelf." I point. "That thing with the handle."

"Wait, really?" He reaches for my grandmother's antique apple peeler. "This looks like some kind of torture device."

"If you're an apple, I guess it is. Clamp it to the counter. Let's go, Gunn. I have apple turnovers to bake. Apples are in the fridge."

Since Gunnar is good with his hands—a fact I know all too well now—he figures out the peeler right away. It only takes him ten minutes to peel and core all the apples I'll need today.

"This thing is amazing. I didn't know you could make an apple into a Slinky! Do you have any more? Would it work on a pear? How about a potato?"

"Nope. You're done. Step away from the produce."

"But—"

"Gunnar," I chide. "Clean up all those peels. Now I have a question."

"Hmm?"

"What's the company called? You never say the name."

"Ah. It's a secret. Only the principals know. The employees who own shares."

"But why? Who'd work for a company if they don't even know the name?"

"About two hundred people." Gunnar chuckles.

The more I hear about this place, the more insane it gets. "Tell me the name. I won't spill it."

"Sorry, sweetheart. I can't do that."

Of course he can't. I shouldn't care. He has his life, and I have mine. We're not a couple. There's nothing between us except for a WiFi signal and a night of explosive, toe-curling sex. "Fine. Don't tell me. But I'd still like you to make me a latte."

"Yes, boss. Whatever you say, boss. See how good I am at saying that? It hardly makes me want to vomit at all." He flashes me that wonderful, evil smile. The one that makes women's panties fall right off.

And then he goes to make my coffee.

22

GUNNAR

WHEN I RETURN to the pie shop many hours later, Teagan is working behind the counter. "Hey, Gunn," she says, looking up from her phone. "Isn't it your day off?"

"Just couldn't stay away," I insist, heading over to where Scout is seated at a corner table, posing as a customer.

"Working hard?" I ask, taking the chair opposite her.

"It's a tough assignment," she says from behind the computer monitor. "I mean, sex is nice. But the raspberry vinegar tart I just ate was on a whole other level."

"Raspberry vinegar, huh? I haven't tried that one."

"More for me." She closes the laptop and stows it. "I can go, right?"

"Yeah. As soon as you tell me what you saw here today."

"Not a thing." She crosses her arms, impatient. "This is boring as fuck, Gunnar."

"But that's a *good* thing," I remind her.

"So you say. But it's also why I'm never asked to sit still."

She's right—Max employs her strictly as an investigator. He doesn't ever ask her to be anybody's security detail. I wonder why she's here today, but I can't ask that question now.

"Any news?" she asks me. "I'm dying to know what was on that thing." She's referring, of course, to the camera she recovered from Smith's room last night.

167

"There was some chatter." I pull out my phone, which is a secure device. And I open an app we often use to communicate privately. Using the pad of my finger, I slowly draw a series of letters. Each one disappears a moment after I draw it, but not before Scout can see that I've written R-U-S-S-I-A-N and then T-U-R-K-I-S-H.

Her eyes widen at that last one. "Really? How many languages can one guy know?"

I shrug. But the news is troubling, because it makes Max's hunch look stronger. Smith may be working for the same arms dealer who ruined Max's life ten years ago.

"All right. I'm out of here," she says. "Go talk to your girl."

Your girl. I like the sound of that better than I really should. I spent the whole day thinking pleasant thoughts about Posy. It's been a long time since a woman got under my skin the way she does.

Scout gathers up her stuff. "Later, Gunn. You've already cut into my leisure time."

"Later." I walk away without asking what her idea of leisure is. Bungee jumping, probably. Or knife-throwing. She's an adrenaline junkie.

My leisure time today began at the shop's seven a.m. opening hour, when Duff came in to relieve me. After explaining to Posy that there would be a Company agent on the premises until further notice, I went home and took a two-hour nap, after which I did a quick workout and then had a meeting with Max.

But now that closing time is near, I'm here to escort Posy on her run to the bank, and then wherever else she wants to go.

When I peek into the kitchen, I catch Posy alone. She's bent over her work, braiding three delicate strands of dough together and humming to herself.

I couldn't tell you why I stay silent for a moment, just watching her. But there's an energy to Posy that's always fascinated me. Piemaking isn't a life or death job, but she brings a laser-like focus to everything she does.

It was the same all those years ago behind the bar. I used to roll my eyes every time she'd carefully measure out the liquor for a gin and tonic. But I'm not rolling them anymore. Posy isn't the pampered girl I assumed. She's so much more than that.

She must feel my gaze on her, because she turns suddenly, startled. "Jeez, Gunnar. I didn't hear you come in."

"Sorry," I grunt, stalking across the room towards her.

She bites her lip and looks away. Like she's not sure how to play it. But I know just what to do. I stop in front of her and lean down, giving her a single, soft kiss. "Are you okay? You look tired."

"Can't think of why that might be." Her cheeks go pink as she says it.

Chuckling, I lean in and kiss her again, a good one this time. It's a kiss that remembers all the fun we had last night.

Until the back door bangs open. "Are you *kissing* Posy?" Jerry demands.

"Yes. People do that sometimes."

"You have to ask her first," Jerry insists.

"Right," I agree.

"I didn't hear you ask," Jerry argues.

"He asked very quietly," Posy replies as she puts the heel of her hand in the center of my chest and pushes me away.

"How long until I flip the sign?" Jerry asks, the kiss already forgotten.

Posy glances at the oven clock. "Twenty minutes. You can wash these pie plates out." She carries a stack of dishes over to the sink, and deposits them at his workstation.

"Okay," he says, turning on the water. "I will do it." The water makes a racket against the metal pie plates, and Jerry sings loudly as he works.

Posy takes the pie she'd been finishing and slips it into the oven. "This is for my nephew. He got an A on his spelling test."

"Lucky guy. What flavor is it?"

"Chocolate pecan."

"Can I have a piece?"

She frowns at me. "You think I'd present my nephew with a pie that's missing a slice? What kind of favorite aunt do you think I am?"

"Well ..." I laugh uncomfortably. Then I lean a little closer to keep our conversation private. "Can I buy you dinner? It's either that or I'm spending the night in a car on this block."

Posy's eyes widen. "You mean—for security purposes?"

"Yeah. Sorry." I cross my arms in front of my chest. "It doesn't have to be me, if you don't want it to be. Max would send someone else."

She grabs the table with both hands. "Is it really that bad? You still think that guy might try to track me down?"

"Probably not," I say quickly. "But I'd rather be extra careful until I figure out what the hell is going on. The WiFi murderer. The break-in. I'd like to think that it's not related, but—"

"—You think it is?"

"I think it could be. And I don't want you caught in the middle."

She bites her lip, the same one that I kissed a moment ago. "Okay. How am I going to explain to Ginny and Aaron why you're in my apartment?"

"I can stay in the car. Or get someone else to do it."

"No. If there was really a problem, I'd want it to be ..." She gulps. "You."

"All right," I say, strangely touched by this decision. "If it's easier, I can hang out down here in the cafe until after Aaron goes to bed."

"No, that's silly." She gives her head a shake. "Ginny is making fried chicken and Caesar salad for dinner. You're invited. But—" she clears her throat. "You have to sleep on the couch."

"Of course," I agree immediately. "I wouldn't assume otherwise."

Teagan sticks her head into the kitchen and calls to me. "I gotta dash fifteen minutes early. Gunnar, can you watch the counter?"

"Sure," I call. "I'll be right there!"

Posy waves me toward the cafe, which has nearly emptied out. "I did everything except clean Lola," Teagan says.

"Sure, sure. I can't do that for you on my day off. No problem."

Teagan gives me a secretive smile. "Isn't this the second time I've seen you here on your day off? I'm only giving you a better excuse to stick around and make heart eyes at the boss."

"Thanks, I guess."

She grabs her purse from under the counter. But before she walks away, the door opens to admit two beefy men in cheap suits.

Cops, my brain says immediately. *Interesting.* "Can I help you guys? I was just about to turn off the espresso machine, but you made it just in time."

"Sorry," the bald cop says. "Not here for coffee. Are either of you the manager?"

"No," Teagan says. "Why?"

The second cop pulls out his wallet and shows us his shield. "NYPD special intelligence department. We're tracking a guy who mighta been seen in here. He's bad news."

"What kind of bad news?" Teagan asks.

"Can't really talk about it."

"Huh." I frown appropriately. "Got a picture of him? Between the two of us, we're behind this counter seven days a week."

"That's the problem," the bald guy says. "We don't have one. We're hoping you guys could help us out. If you let us put a camera in here, we could find this guy. The mayor really wants him caught."

Oh, like it hasn't been tried, I privately grumble. And the mayor can bite me. "But how would that work?" I ask aloud. "If you don't know who you're looking for, what good would it do?"

"We know him," his buddy says. "But we need a *picture*. That's the point of the cameras."

Sure, asshole. These guys are looking for the same person I am, for the same reason I am. They're just a little late to the party.

"I gotta run," Teagan says.

"Go on," I agree. "I'll handle this."

She leaves, and my phone starts dancing a jig in my pocket, probably because Max is watching this little exchange. "Let me get the boss for you, okay? I don't have the power to decide these things."

"Okay, man," one of the cops says.

"Hey, Posy?" I call out. Then I walk to the kitchen and stick my head inside. "Boss? Oh great and powerful one? There's some guys here to ask you a question!"

Frowning, Posy comes toward me.

Say no, I mouth.

She blinks. Then she passes me and greets the cops. "Can I help you?"

"Ma'am, are you Posy?" one of them asks.

"I am."

"I thought you'd be older!" he says with a chuckle. "I thought you'd look like my nonna, maybe. She makes pies, too."

Posy turns to give me a look over her shoulder that says, *do you see what I have to put up with?*

I wink, and then pull my phone out of my pocket. Max has been ringing me continuously since the cops walked in. I finally answer it with, "Hey, Mom. What's up?"

"She isn't going to allow the cops to set up in her shop, is she?" he barks.

"Probably not."

"They'll see all our equipment."

"Thanks, Sherlock. I realized that."

"We've got to find our Plumber," Max says. "We've got three days, tops. These guys will come back with a warrant."

"I know, Mama. Drink some prune juice and calm down."

"Find him. He isn't a customer. We're missing something."

Fuck. Fuckity fuck. He's right. But I can't discuss it now. "Talk soon?" I say cheerfully.

"Yeah, go," Max says, hanging up on me.

"It just wouldn't feel right," Posy is saying. "My customers don't expect me to photograph them."

"But you could help us catch a bad guy," the cop argues.

"Bad at what, though?" Posy asks. "You didn't say. Does this have anything to do with my break-in?"

"What break-in?" the bald cop asks.

Posy puts her hands on her hips. "The one I reported earlier this month. Did you guys even look into it?"

They exchange glances. "Tell you what—we'll look into that tonight. We'll come back in a day or two, and maybe you could help us out after you sleep on it. I'll leave my card."

"Thank you," she says stiffly. And they're gone a moment later. "Jerry!" Posy calls. "You can flip the sign."

Jerry comes trundling into the cafe to do his favorite job. And— on a hunch—I go the opposite direction, into the kitchen, where Jerry's iPad is sticking out of his backpack near the door. I grab the tablet, and it's unlocked. He must have been on it only a moment ago. I hurry to see what apps he used today.

And I learn nothing. Jerry likes WebToons and the Marvel website. He got a couple messages from his mother. That's it.

Fuck.

I slip the iPad back into his backpack just before he reenters the room. "I'm goin' home," he says to me, grabbing his stuff, and opening the back door. "See you tomorrow Gunnar."

"Have a nice evening, kid." I lock the door behind him, and then I walk back into the cafe to find Posy leaning on the counter, looking troubled. "You okay?"

"No, not really." She straightens up. "I hate this. I hate having cameras in my place. And now the cops want to do the same thing?" She throws her arms out to the side. "This is crazy. I could say no to all of you. I could turn off the WiFi, right? This could all be someone else's problem."

"Well, sure," I say carefully. "But then he'll just use someone else's."

"I don't even know this is *real*, Gunn," she says. "I've taken your word for the whole thing. I feel like an extra in a Hollywood thriller. I don't know the whole story, I haven't seen the script. I'm just supposed to go where you tell me without asking questions."

"I'm sorry," I say. "I'd be frustrated, too."

My phone buzzes again in my pocket. I pull it out. Max is calling, and there's a text from him on the screen. *Let me speak to her.*

Oh man. I answer the phone and hold it toward Posy. "Max."

"He's watching us argue?" she asks. "That's fucking creepy."

"The cops got his attention," I say. "And you *know* this is real, because suddenly there's a whole lot of people interested in your internet connection."

"Why ME?" Posy shrieks. Then she takes the phone from my hand. "Why me?" she repeats to Max. "Can't someone else be the hero today? I'm tired."

They talk for a couple of minutes. Max is a charming fucker when he wants to be, especially to women. The younger agents call him *ladykiller* behind his back.

Eventually, Posy hands back my phone. "This is madness," she says grumpily.

"I agree. What did you and Max decide?"

"He promised he'd hand over the information he gets to the cops. He said that he was ahead of them already, and that it wouldn't help to let them come in here and hang more cameras if there was a chance they'd find yours."

"All right," I say carefully. I know we're asking a lot. "There aren't many people who are as sharp as Max."

She rolls her eyes at me. "You're only saying that because he can see you right now. Does he read lips?"

I throw my head back and laugh. "I'd say it anyway. Now come on. Let's make your bank deposit. I'm walking with you this time."

"Why?" She stalks over to the cash register and opens the drawer.

"Because we can't afford any more bad luck, okay? Just humor me."

"Fine." She counts out a stack of twenties. "Just as soon as my pie is out of the oven."

"If you want to know the truth, this whole thing is just a ruse so I can get a piece of chocolate pecan later."

"Congratulations, then. I guess it worked." She gives me a glare and returns to counting the drawer.

23

POSY

GUNNAR SCOTT IS SLEEPING on my sofa.

Or at least he will be, if Ginny ever leaves my room.

We all had a very pleasant dinner together. Aaron and Gunnar made equivalent noises of delight over the pie. "Some kids don't like nuts in their food," Aaron had said. "But I think that's silly."

"You're a hundred percent right," Gunnar had said. "I don't know what people have against nuts."

"Were you a picky eater as a child, Gunnar?" Ginny had asked, a sneaky smile on her face.

"Not at all," he'd said, setting his fork on his empty plate. "I've always thought more is more. Pretty much about everything."

Then he'd looked me right in the eye and winked.

"Posy was a picky eater," Ginny said.

"I was not!" I don't know why I'd been so quick to defend myself.

"You didn't eat mussels."

"They're chewy," I'd said while trying not to gag.

"Or oysters. I'll bet Gunnar likes oysters. I wonder if he likes *clams*."

Sometimes sisters are the worst. Mine has no boundaries whatsoever.

"I like food, period," Gunnar had said, watching Aaron eat his slice of pie. "There wasn't always enough."

"Why?" my nephew had asked, raising his head to stare at our guest.

That's when Gunnar seemed to regret that small confidence. "Eh, I don't remember. What's your favorite food, anyway?"

He was really nice to my nephew. But when Ginny took Aaron downstairs to get him ready for bed, I was relieved.

She came back, though, and now she's sitting on my bed, interrogating me. "How long is he going to sleep on our couch?" she asks. "I hope it lasts a week."

"A *week?*" I whisper sharply. "Why?"

"Eye candy," she whispers back. "Why won't you tell me all the details from last night?" She'd tried all morning to get a story out of me, but the pie kitchen isn't very private. I don't want to talk about it, anyway. I'm confused. That man lied to me, and I had wild monkey sex with him anyway.

"Maybe he has supersonic hearing," I say under my breath. "Besides, I don't kiss and tell."

"You should," she argues. "This is big. No more dry spell."

"Shhh!" I hiss. "I can't believe you're focused on my sexual exploits instead of the *reason* that man is on our couch. You seem barely interested that we may be in danger."

Ginny gives me a maddening shrug. "Those hacker murders don't have a thing to do with us. And half the neighborhood uses our WiFi, because I made you spring for the fastest service."

"Sure, sure," I sniff. "A murderer walks among us, and you just want to know if Gunnar has a nice penis."

"Does he?" She presses her hands together in a prayer position.

"God, woman. Go back downstairs and read a dirty book. I don't want it to seem like we're in here gossiping about him."

"But we *are* in here gossiping about him," she points out.

"No. *You're* digging for dirt, and I'm refusing to provide any."

"You owe me," Ginny says, rising from my bed. "I will get this story. Was it amazing?"

I shrug, but my face heats, giving me away.

"I knew it!" she squeaks. "Spalding can go eat a bag of dicks. Who needs him, anyway?"

"Not me. I don't need you right this second, either." I make a shooing motion. "Go on. I need my sleep."

"Ten bucks says you don't get any sleep." She points at the door and wiggles her eyebrows.

"You're the only one keeping me awake," I point out.

"You're no fun. Hey—what's that?" She points to a small device on my bedside table.

"Oh, it's a panic button. It's something Gunnar's company lent me, just in case. If you press it, a herd of badass security guys will come running."

"Do they all look like Gunnar?" Ginny asks. "Maybe I should just —" She reaches for the button.

"Ginny! Don't!"

She cackles, withdrawing her hand. "Why should you have all the fun? Goodnight, Posy."

"'Night."

She finally leaves.

Alone at last, I tuck myself into bed. But Ginny was right, damn it. I don't sleep. What's more, the floors in this old building squeak, and I keep hearing Gunnar walking slowly around my living room. Maybe there's been a development.

I'd better check, right?

Taking care to tie a light robe around my nightgown, I tiptoe into the darkened living room, where Gunnar is seated on my sofa, head bowed.

He looks up the moment I open my door. "Hi, honey," he says. "Am I keeping you awake?"

"A little," I admit. "But not because you're loud."

"You want me to go? I could take a chair out in the hall."

I shake my head. "No way. It's fine. I just wondered if there was a reason you weren't sleeping."

His smile is no less potent in the dark. "Nothing worrisome. Just thinking too much."

"What about?"

He cocks his head and considers me for a second. "Can I ask you a question? The other night, before everything got complicated, why did you ask me out?"

"Oh." Well, crap. I don't really want to admit how attractive he is to me. "Do I need a good reason? We have some chemistry. And I was tired of being that boring person sitting home at night while my ex walks the path of joy with a woman ten years younger than I am."

"Makes sense." He reaches over and strokes my cheek, and I lean into his hand without even realizing it.

"The better question is why you turned me down," I point out.

"Only because my investigation got more complicated than I expected. See, before your break-in—when I thought I was just looking for a stranger in your cafe—I was perfectly happy to bang the hot boss."

I roll my eyes, even though I like the sound of that, and I'm incredibly flattered.

"But after that night, I found myself digging into the details about your divorce and trying to figure out if someone was targeting you specifically. And that's when it got weird. I didn't want to read up on your private life and then pretend to ask you a bunch of questions I already knew the answers to."

This answer isn't what I expected. "So you *do* have some scruples under there somewhere."

"Oh, I have lots of them," he says quietly. "My job might seem strange to you—lying to strangers and sticking my nose in other people's business. But the world is run by people who just take as much as they can, from whomever they want, as often as possible. I try not to be that guy. And I try to protect my clients from those guys."

My heart rate seems to slow down as I listen to these words. But I'm still not sure about him. "You confuse me. I want so badly to believe that you're one of the good guys, or that good guys even exist."

"They exist. But being a good guy isn't always a simple thing to be. Not in my line of work. There are lots of moments when I'm not sure what to do, even though I work for the best guys in the world."

"I'm glad to hear that. But one of the reasons I hired you was that you said you needed the money for your sick dad."

He flinches. "Point taken."

"You didn't need the money at all," I point out. "But a sick dad? That's very manipulative."

Gunnar leans back against my couch and tucks his hands behind his head. "Yeah, and the funny thing is I use that lie all the time. It's my favorite one."

"Your dad isn't sick?"

He's quiet for a long moment. "I honestly wouldn't know. I haven't spoken to him in about twenty-five years."

"Oh. Why not?"

Gunnar's eyes cut over to mine. "It's complicated."

"I'm sure it is," I say quietly. "But why is information such a one-way street with you? You asked me to trust you, and to invite you into my home. You've read everything legally available about the state of my failed marriage and my struggling business."

"Some of it isn't legally available," he murmurs. "And I read it anyway."

"Nice," I say. "I'm so happy to be an open book for you."

Gunnar sighs. "But it's embarrassing to me. You're not the only one on this couch with daddy issues. When I was a kid, I thought it was normal that my dad didn't live with us in our Queens apartment."

"Where did he live?" I ask, not bothering to hide my curiosity.

"I don't actually know. I never went there. He was my dad, and I accepted the whole situation as normal. Some mornings—maybe once a week—I'd wake up, and he was there, drinking coffee at the kitchen table with my mother. It was sporadic, though. There'd be months when we saw a lot of him, and then he'd disappear for a while. My mother said he traveled for work."

"Oh." I swallow hard, picturing a small Gunnar waiting for his daddy to show up again.

"He wasn't very interested in me," Gunnar says quietly. "The only thing we bonded over was baseball. He started showing up in the evenings sometimes, especially during the summer. I didn't care much for baseball before that, but I'd sit beside him on the sofa, and he'd tell me all the players' stats. He'd bring me those cheap packs of base-ball cards, and they became my favorite thing in the world."

I sat very still, listening to this story. It's the only personal thing Gunnar had ever shared about his past.

"He even said: 'we'll go to a game sometime when you're older.' And I think he regretted it immediately, because I started asking him when. Other boys in my neighborhood had been to Shea Stadium with their dads. The bleacher seats were cheap, right? And I was starting to notice that my dad had really nice clothes, and that he brought expensive-looking bottles of wine to our house to drink with my mother. So when my thirteenth birthday was coming—it's in July—I just asked him if he could get tickets. There was a home game that day, too. Against the Colorado Rockies."

I hold my breath, because I don't know where this story is going, but I'm betting it's no place good.

"He said *we'll see*, like parents everywhere." Gunnar chuckles. "But then, three days before my birthday, he turned up with a wrapped gift, telling me to open it on my birthday. So I asked him about the baseball game. And he said—sorry, kid, I'm traveling. I was crushed, because I'd spent the week picturing us in the stadium together, eating hot dogs and popcorn."

I wait, knowing the story isn't over.

"On my birthday I opened the present, it was a new glove with a ball. That seemed like a nice consolation prize to me, because at least it was baseball. And then I sat down to watch the game on TV, even though he wasn't there." Gunnar chuckles bitterly. "Maybe three minutes later I saw his face on the screen. He was sitting in the second row—the power seats—with a hot dog in his hand, and his arm around another boy who looked something like me."

My gasp is full of rage. "What?"

"Yeah." He smiles, but it's sad. "My mother never expected that to happen, I guess. She sort of stuttered through an explanation. She told me he was married to someone else, and he had two other children, and a penthouse somewhere on Park Avenue."

"Oh my *God*. And I thought my father was a dick. You have siblings that you'd never met?"

"Still haven't. They're better off not knowing their father is a tool."

My heart aches to hear it. "What happened the next time he came back?"

"He didn't. I told my mother I hated him, and I didn't want to see him again. It was just something you say in anger, you know? But she must have told him to stay away. And he did—at least as far as I can tell. She struggled after that, and I felt kinda bad. But she never complained. She died the year before I met you, so I never heard the whole story—the version you'd tell your adult kid when he was ready."

I lean back against the sofa, stunned. "I'm sorry, Gunnar. And you haven't seen him since?"

"Nope." He shakes his head. "And I never did make it to a game at Shea Stadium before they tore it down. That's my strange little tale, Posy Paxton. Now you know. Our fathers have a few tricks in common."

"You figured it out well before I did, though. I spent two decades of my life trying to please mine."

"We both tried to please him, if memory serves." Gunnar reaches over and gives my elbow a squeeze.

Sitting here on the sofa in the dark apparently makes both of us feel confessional. "You know, right after I got the bar manager's job, I walked in on my father making out with one of the waitresses."

"*Really.* I wish I could say I was surprised."

"Well I was. But there they were. She was that blond—a few years older than I was. A Parson's student, I think?"

"Greta?" Gunnar guesses. "Was that her name? Or Gretchen? I think I saw them together once, too. There was a lot of giggling, and then she came out of his office. I wondered."

"You never said anything," I grumble. It was a terrible shock seeing my father lip-locked to a college girl. He and my mother never seemed to have a very happy marriage. And they divorced a few years later. But the flagrance of my father's actions had stunned me.

"What was I supposed to say? I was a college kid, too, paying his way through school on tips. You don't critique the company the boss keeps. I didn't even have proof."

He's right, of course. "You understood him before I did. And I lived with the man for two decades. Maybe that's the biggest differ-

ence between you and me—wits and cynicism. Your job acknowl-
edges the underbelly of humanity. Mine assumes that everything is
fixable with a slice of very expensive pie. I guess it's no shock that
you're more successful." I kick the edge of the coffee table in frustration, and all I get is a pain in my toe.

"Hey now, don't do that." He reaches down and grabs my feet,
pulling both of them into his lap. "In the first place, you run the most
successful pie shop in SoHo."

"The *only* pie shop in SoHo."

He smiles. "That's not the point. Your optimism is the thing I like
best about you. There's a bar with your family's name on it—you
decide to figure out how to run the place, with no help from the man
who's supposed to pass it down to you."

"I had help from you, though," I point out.

"So what?" He shrugs. "You got in there and rolled up your
sleeves. You measured gin by the half ounce, and invented a song to
help you remember all the ingredients in a *Harvey Wallbanger*. Even
when you were irritating, you were really pretty cute. And that's
because of your upbeat attitude. We can't all be cynical grouches."

"Vodka, Galliano and orange juice. Plus a dash of self-right-
eousness and incompetence. I was an irritating rookie, wasn't I?"

"Occasionally."

"You told me I should wear V-necks, and my tips would improve.
Instead of thanking you for the advice, I gave you a lecture about
feminism."

"I deserved it. That was just gratuitous on my part," he says with
a grin. His strong hands begin to massage the arch of my foot, his
thumb lovingly stroking my skin.

"Omigod," I moan, and then slap a hand in front of my mouth.
There's a chance my sister is still awake, reading one of her favorite
dirty books and listening for signs of mischief upstairs.

Gunnar snickers, and then switches feet. I basically melt back
onto my sofa and try not to moan like a porn star. I spend a lot of
time on my feet, and they're often achy at the end of the day. Nobody
has given me a foot rub since …

Ever. I have literally never had a foot rub like this. Gunnar works his hand up my ankle and then back down again, stroking the muscles, smoothing the skin. And how did I not know how sensitive the bottoms of my feet were? The longer the massage goes on, the looser I feel.

And, fine. I'm turned on. All it takes is a foot rub and I'm ready to strip off my clothes and let him do me on the sofa. The sooner the better.

"What are you thinking about?"

"Nothing," I say quickly. I refuse to admit that Gunnar has turned on my libido as easily as I can turn on the oven broiler.

"Uh huh," he says, as a knowing smirk appears on his face. "Me too. Why don't you come closer and we can do nothing together?"

I don't move, though, because I don't want to seem as eager as I feel. I still have Spalding's critique ringing in my ears.

"You don't trust me," Gunnar says, his thumbs making sweet love to the arch of my foot.

"I'm confused about you," I admit. "But it's not just that. I have an uneasy relationship with—" I drop my voice down so low it's a miracle he can hear me. "—Sex."

"Hmm," he says, switching my right foot for my left. My feet are basically sexual organs now. Are footgasms real? "How did—" he drops his voice the same way I did "—sex do you wrong?"

"It was Spalding who did me wrong," I admit.

"How 'bout I do you right?" Gunnar asks with a grin. "I didn't hear any complaints last night."

"Oh, there weren't any complaints," I whisper. "But last night was a lightning strike. I don't believe it can happen like that again. I'm not —" How to phrase it?

"You're not what? My lightning bolt is ready, baby."

I let out a snort. "I'm not as confident as you. I've been told that I'm not any fun."

His hands go still right in the middle of a glorious instep rubdown. "Come again?"

We'd like to! my hormones shout.

"I'm not fun. I don't have moves. You didn't notice last night, because we were both liquored up on adrenaline. But before last night I'd only slept with one man in my life, and apparently he was just putting up with me all those years. He says I'm …" I swallow hard.

"What?" Gunnar whispers, and his eyes have gone scary.

"A starfish," I whisper.

Gunnar's head jerks back like he's been slapped. "Baby, that's just bogus. I have scratch marks on my back that prove he's a liar. Do you know what kind of man calls his wife a starfish?"

I shake my head slowly.

"A cheating man. A guy who needs his wife to divorce him so he can bang a younger woman. Which he only wants in the first place because he's afraid to get old and die."

Everything goes quiet inside me. I've been needing to hear that for a long time. I mean—Ginny said basically the same thing. But she's my sister. She's always on my side. Gunnar must think I'm okay in bed, or he wouldn't be staring at me right now, his expression full of heat and intensity. "Thank you for saying that."

"It's just the truth." He eases my feet off his lap. Without a word, he crooks his finger at me.

Oooh! My hormones squeal. *Gunnar wants us.*

I'm on all fours without even realizing it. And then I'm crawling toward him.

"Damn," he whispers. "Your ex is the dumbest man on the planet."

If I wasn't already humming with desire, that would have done it.

"Come here, honey. Kiss me." He beckons again. Then he kicks one leg up onto the couch, orienting his body in my direction, waiting with a wicked gleam in his eye.

I have courage running through my veins. So I reach for his fly, pop the button on his pants, and lower the zipper. Without waiting for an invitation, I reach inside his briefs and curl my hand around his erection.

"Oh, fuck yes," Gunnar growls. His hand curls around the length of my hair.

Who knew that being a vixen was so easy? All I have to do is lean down and taste the salty tip of him. Gunnar makes a sound of shock that lights me up inside. I work his briefs down a little bit and pull his cockhead against my tongue, weighing it. Caressing it.

Gunnar braces his hard body against my sofa and yanks his trousers down a few inches, making my job a little easier. "That's a girl," he says in a low voice. "See what you can do now."

So I do. It turns out you can easily forget your insecurities when the object of your pleasure is practically throbbing under your touch. I get busy licking and kissing and sucking with all I've got. Gunnar is loving it, too. You can't fake this level of enthusiasm. Whispered encouragements and dirty curses fall from his lips, until he lets out a grunt and tries to nudge me aside. "That's enough, honey. I'm close."

But I'm a very goal-oriented person. So I hollow out my cheeks and give it to him good. Gunnar makes a deep sound of urgency, so I brace for victory. But instead, I find myself lifted off his dick and onto his shoulder. Somehow he rises from the sofa, holding my waist in one hand and his trousers in the other.

A squeak of terror leaves my throat as I am hoisted into the air. That's twice in two days. I'm not sure it's dignified for a grown woman to be hauled around like this.

Ten seconds later, though, I realize that dignity is overrated. Gunnar has tossed me on the bed, and then ripped off his clothes. He kneels down and pulls the two halves of my bathrobe apart like some kind of sex-starved superhero. He lifts my sleep shirt, dips his head down and finds my breast with his hungry tongue.

"You—" he says, breaking off to torture my other breast. "Are a good time, Posy Paxton. Don't ever let anyone tell you otherwise."

My heart soars to hear it. And then Gunnar recommits himself to pleasuring me, and pretty soon other parts of me are soaring, too.

24

GUNNAR

THE COMPANY IS PERFECTLY capable of watching Posy's building for signs of trouble. There's no practical reason I need to spend more nights in her bed.

But there are plenty of less practical ones.

The next night, I take Posy out for a romantic dinner. When we get back, Ginny and Aaron are already downstairs for the night. So we don't even have to keep up the ruse that I'm sleeping on the couch.

I walk her right into her bedroom and unzip her dress. Let the games begin.

This quickly becomes part of our routine. I work in the pie shop most mornings, leaving Posy's apartment before Aaron is out of bed. After my shift, I take off for a workout or a meeting with Max. But by evening time, I'm back in Apartment 4-5, dining with Posy and sometimes Ginny and Aaron. I'm thirty-six years old, and this is the only moment I can name where my life had so much routine. And I think I like it.

One night I cook my favorite dish for them: fish tacos with lime and cilantro. I even make homemade sangria to go with it.

"Why can't I taste the sangria?" Aaron asks.

"It's a grown-up drink," his mother says, giving me a sideways glance. Ginny was perfectly happy to see me show up here a few nights ago. But with each passing day, she seems less happy to see me.

Posy is the opposite. Even now, as her sister gives me a death glare, Posy smooths the arch of her bare foot over mine. She gives me a soft smile and takes another sip of sangria.

I pick up the pitcher and refill her glass. I'd do anything to get another smile from her. This is new for me—all this domestic tranquility. I like it more than I expected to. "Have another taco," I say, offering her the platter.

"Do you cook for your wife?" Aaron asks suddenly. He takes another taco, too.

"Nope. I don't have one."

"Why not?"

"Some men don't want a wife," Ginny says quickly. "They're not the marrying kind." The look she gives me implies that she's put me firmly in this category.

"Maybe I just never got around to it yet," I argue. She thinks she's got me all figured out. "I travel a lot. My job is hard."

"Your job making coffee?" Aaron asks.

Ginny snickers into her sangria glass.

"I've worked many jobs," I clarify. "I move around a lot. It's very distracting." I can't really explain to him that my job is dangerous. That I need to keep my focus on the work.

"Can we play Go Fish after dinner?" Aaron asks me.

"What about your reading?" Ginny asks.

"I could read to Gunnar," Aaron says. "And *then* play cards."

Yup. Sometimes my job takes many forms. "Sure, pal." I don't mind the little guy's company. He's awfully cute. "But I have to clean up the kitchen first."

"I'll clean up," Posy says. "You cooked."

"I guess that's a yes, kid."

Aaron slides off his chair and runs to get his book. "I hope the men never finish painting your apartment," he says. "I like it when you're here."

Ginny rolls her eyes. "They'll finish all right," she says. "Men always do."

Yeah, I'm not touching that one. It's obvious that Ginny has some baggage. Her boy's father is in prison for passing bad checks. That can't be easy.

I feel like a heel for lying to the child about my presence, but the truth isn't a good option. I don't want to explain why we're taking extra precautions with building security. And I *really* don't want to explain that I never actually use that blanket and pillow we've left each night on Posy's sofa.

Thank goodness the kid's room is a floor below, and Posy's bed doesn't creak. I'd hate to try to think of a passable explanation for all the noises Posy makes when the grown-ups have their bedtime.

Aaron returns with a book and beckons me over to the sofa. And I listen to him read a pointless story about a snail, while Posy smiles at me over the rim of her wine glass.

And Ginny glares.

O──†

Two hours later, I've got Posy mostly naked and whimpering into my mouth as I kiss her senseless. When I break off the kiss, she looks up at me with trusting eyes. Her cheeks are pink and her lips are swollen from my kisses. "Why aren't you naked yet?" she asks, reaching for my fly.

"Because I like to torture you a little bit," I say, leaning down to kiss her neck.

She shoves at my zipper, then tries to push down my trousers. "Off," she says impatiently.

"And people say you aren't fun in bed," I tease her.

"Don't mention *him*," she grumbles. "That's not a turn-on."

"I rest my case," I say, kicking off the pants. "You're always fun, Posy. If a little impatient." I lean down and drag my tongue across her collar bone.

She squirms beneath me, her legs wrapping around mine. She's begging me with her eyes to hurry up.

Naturally, that means I plan to go even slower.

I kiss my way across her chest at a languorous pace. She's still wearing a bra, though, along with some little red panties. So she reaches back to unclasp her bra.

"Hey now," I say, gasping her hands and stopping their business. "We're doing this my way."

"Why's that?"

"Because my way is fun."

She groans. "I'm beginning to wonder whether men and women have the same idea of fun. Your way takes too long."

"Says you." I remove my T-shirt and toss it off the bed. "Let's play a game to work on your patience. Do you have a couple of silk scarves?"

Her eyes widen. "What for?"

"I'd like to restrain you, if you're game."

"Why? Is that ..." She licks her lips. "... Fun?"

I hesitate for a moment, because fun is completely subjective. "It is for some people."

She swallows hard. "There are scarves in the top drawer. Get them."

Again, I hesitate. Because it was never my goal to force Posy to do something that didn't interest her. But now she's watching me with clear, curious eyes. So I stand up and open the top drawer of her dresser, pulling out two silk squares in different colors.

"What have I gotten myself into?" she asks as I kneel once again on the bed.

"Trouble, that's what." It comes out sounding cocky.

"Okay. Teach me," she says, offering her hands. "Where do you want me?"

Anywhere, sweetheart. "How about you grab one of those central rungs on the headboard?"

She lifts her hands over her head and does as I ask. But when I lift one of the scarves up to tie around her wrists, she flinches.

"Sweetheart," I say gently. "There's no earthly reason we have to do this. It's just a game. It's not important."

"I hate the idea of having my hands restrained. It's just ..." She shivers. "I'm sorry, but that isn't fun for me. I have nightmares about having my hands tied behind my back."

"Hey, don't apologize. In fact, sit up for me."

"Why?" She sits up anyway. "Now I've ruined the mood."

"Nah. Pay attention for a second. Instead of restraining you, I'm going to do the opposite. I'll show you how to break out of restraints."

"What?" She laughs. "I thought we were going to do wicked things to each other."

"Oh, we are." I toss the scarves onto the bed. "But I know lots of tricks, Paxton. The things I learned at spy school are fun in a different way. And if this is a trigger for you, I can teach you how to defeat it. Let's pretend someone is going to zip tie your hands together."

Posy shivers again. "That literally figures into my nightmares."

"Then don't ever get arrested by the NYPD. But if you do, here's how to get out of a zip tie. The first method is to brace your hands into fists. Try it. Show me."

Posy brings her hands together, making two fists.

"Yes, but brace them end to end. Like this." I arrange her fists in the right way, and then draw a gentle finger across her wrists. "See this? Believe it or not, you're creating just enough extra space that afterward you can make prayer hands ..." I rotate her palms together. "... And you could wriggle one hand out."

"Good to know," Posy says with a smile.

"Now, if the cops notice your setup and make you place your hands in a tighter position, you still have two more options. You can wear away the plastic on a rough surface, like a brick. Or you can tighten the zip tie with your teeth." I mime this action. "Then pull 'em tight and—" I whack my wrists against my knee. "Split them apart."

Posy leans forward and kisses my chest with soft lips. "Have you ever had to do that on a mission?"

"Oh, sure. I once had to do it twice in one day."

"Is it wrong that I find this topic very hot and manly?" She trails across my pecs with her wicked mouth.

"Not at all. Feel free to express your enthusiasm for my—" I clear my throat suggestively. "Manhood." I wind my hand in her hair and guide her head toward my cock.

"Mmm." She tortures me with little licks and kisses down my abs. Then she nuzzles my cock.

"Yes, baby. Do it," I pant as she finally takes me into her tight, wet mouth.

I'm in heaven. And is it terrible for me to hope that the Pie Shop perp is never found?

When it's time to go back to California, I'm not going to want to go.

25

POSY

I MAKE sure to give Gunnar a dose of his own medicine. I tease him mercilessly with my tongue and my hands.

My ex's complaints still weigh on me. I don't know if that will ever go away. So I put everything I've got into pleasuring Gunnar, until his breath comes in desperate gusts, and his powerful thighs clench with need.

And then I abruptly stop.

"Hey," Gunnar rasps. "What's the hold up?"

"Hey, being a tease is your idea of fun. I'm just learning from the master."

He groans. "You always were a good student, Paxton. Fine, fine. On your back. It's time for your next lesson in fun."

That sounds okay to me, and I lie back on the bed. Gunnar's eyes travel over my lingerie, and I feel the weight of his gaze like a physical force. He's awakened the sensual part of my personality, and I hadn't even known it was sleeping.

"Try this for me—reach up and hold onto the headboard slats," Gunnar says. "And don't let go. I'm asking you to restrain *yourself*, if you can."

"All right," I agree. "Do your worst."

He stretches out between my legs, his mouth dropping lazy kisses near my navel. There's nothing better than the sight of his powerful shoulders bunching as he teases me with soft kisses and scruffy cheeks.

His hair looks so soft, and I have the urge to run my fingers through it. But I leave my hands where he's ordered me to put them. And he was right. This *is* fun.

Then Gunnar picks up one of the abandoned scarves, and I wait to see what he'll do. First, he holds it up and drags just the corner across my belly. The touch of cool silk is so light that I get goosebumps immediately. "You're giving me chills."

"Yeah?" he says, dragging it across my skin again. "Well, you're giving me some big ideas. Let's try one more thing." He lifts the scarf and gently covers my eyes with it. "Can I tie this?"

"Sure, as long as my hands are free." I'm happy to give one of his ideas the green light, even if I feel silly as he ties the silk behind my head.

"If you change your mind, just knock it out of the way, baby," he says.

"Got it." The silk blocks my view of his rugged face, which is a crying shame.

But then Gunnar kisses me suddenly.

Oh.

Oooh.

Ohhhh.

Wow. So that's why blindfolds are fun. I can't see his approach, so each kiss is a surprise. I find myself arching off the bed, hungry for more. But I don't let go of the bed to reach for him.

"Good girl," he whispers, and the sound is unpredictably close. His breath in my ear gives me chills. All my senses are dialed up to eleven. All I can do is lie still and experience this.

And what an experience it is. I receive another kiss, but it's over before I'm ready. His mouth wanders sweetly down my neck, and my goosebumps redouble. I toss my head to the side to give him better access. But I can't predict where that tongue will land next.

It's thrilling.

Gunnar goes on to pleasure me in random, delightfully unexpected places. One nipple gets a kiss. Then my hip bone. The other nipple is sucked suddenly but firmly into his mouth, which makes me gasp.

"So sexy," he whispers, smoothing his hands down my body, as if I'm a fine object he's inspecting. I can feel his gaze on my nakedness, but I can't see it. My body has become his plaything, and it feels extra dirty in all the best ways.

I arch my back, putting myself on display for him. I've never felt so wanton in my entire life. Or so beautiful.

My ex was dead wrong. I'm a whole lot of fun, and I'm about to be even funner. Because Gunnar chooses that moment to brusquely grasp my legs and part them, his big hands repositioning me for his pleasure. A series of light kisses lands at my inner thigh, climbing toward bliss. I feel the heat of his breath just shy of where I need his mouth. And then …

Nothing. Gunnar waits, without touching me. I let out a huff of frustration and hear his answering chuckle. My thigh muscles clench. The expectation I feel is almost unbearable.

He clicks his tongue with a soothing sound. Then a roughened palm sweeps up my leg, and one thumb strokes me casually right where I need him.

With a moan and a roll of my hips, I seek more contact with his naughty hand. He strokes me sweetly, making soothing sounds. It's lovely, but it's not enough. And when his tongue finally flattens between my legs I cry out in happiness.

This is a revelation. Good sex has nothing to do with technique, does it? It's all about desire and connection.

I have *so* much desire for Gunnar Scott. And miracles must be real, because he has so much desire for me. Every shocking little thing he does makes me moan—every lick and kiss and sneaky puff of air against my sensitive flesh. (Fine—maybe technique matters a tiny bit, because who knew I wanted someone to blow on me right there?)

Then, just when I'm feeling so desperate I could scream, and more than ready to rip off this blindfold, he abruptly fills me with his cock. The motion is so firm and sudden that my breath stalls in my chest and every muscle in my body tightens around him.

"Fuuuuck," he says on a gasp. "So good. Every time." The

mattress depresses under his weight as he plants his hands on either side of me and finds his rhythm.

I can't speak, because I'm overwhelmed by the multifaceted assault on my senses. But now we're in perfect sync. I can't see a thing, but this time his kiss doesn't surprise me. I'm ready for the sensual slide of his tongue into my mouth and the friction of his heated skin against my aching breasts.

We strain together. It's fast and rough and a little bit wild. I'm still hanging on to the bed, but not because Gunnar told me to. It's a matter of bracing myself so I'm not pounded into the headboard.

And just when I think I can't take any more, the blindfold is swept away. The most beautiful man I've ever seen is looking down at me with heat and yearning in his green eyes. And that's it for me. All my own yearning comes to a rapid, heated crest, and I let out a cry of happiness as I shatter into a hundred pieces.

Gunnar lets out a guttural moan and thrusts his hips a few more times, slowing down with each one. And then he shudders mightily and makes a sound of deep satisfaction.

I'll never get tired of that sound. Years from now, when he's long gone, I'll still hear it in my dirtiest dreams.

26

GUNNAR

IT ALWAYS ENDS LIKE THIS—WITH me flattened on the bed, half on top of Posy, my brain left behind somewhere in a neighboring zip code. I've made it my personal mission to prove to her that she's fun in bed. But that meant proving it to myself, too.

There's no denying how much I care for her. I never wanted to live in New York, but it's hard to think about leaving right now.

But that's just the endorphins talking, right?

I'm really not sure anymore.

"Gunn. You're heavy."

"Sorry, baby." I move to the side and then pull her into my arms. I cooked for her tonight, and then I blew both our minds in bed. It was the perfect day. But even perfect days end.

I close my eyes and wish it weren't so.

o—🔑

Every morning Posy's alarm goes off at an ungodly hour. I always find myself wrapped around her body, her curves in my hands, her rump tucked against me. Even though I don't start work as early as she does, I wake up just to spend a couple of minutes admiring up close all the things I used to admire from afar. The slope of her nose. The softness of her skin.

"I have to get up," she inevitably says.

"What if you didn't, just this once?" I always reply.

"Owning a business is like owning a dog," she tells me. "If you don't get up and deal with it, there will only be a big mess later."

"That's why they invented dog walkers," I point out. "Hire somebody besides Ginny to work in the kitchen. Then we can spend the morning in bed one of these days." I run my hand up her leg and under her nightgown just to incentivize her.

"Hiring people is really difficult," she says, nudging my hand away. She sits up, swinging her legs over the side of the bed. "I couldn't get good help in the kitchen for what I pay myself."

"How much do you pay yourself?" I ask. "Whatever it is, I think you should give yourself a raise. You deserve it for having the willpower to get out of a bed that I'm naked in."

She turns her chin and gives me the first smile of the day. "Your ego is already awake, I see."

"Not just my ego." I push the sheet down and show her my boner. It never goes away these days. And I've noticed that Posy enjoys looking at it.

She licks her lips, and I feel a moment of hope. But then she stands up anyway. "Better save that for later. Go back to sleep for another hour and a half, but don't be late for work. Those lattes aren't going to make themselves."

I turn my smile into the pillow. Before she walks away, she leans down to run a soft hand through my hair. And then she gives me a soft kiss goodbye.

Two hours later I'm tiptoeing out of the bedroom, my shoes in hand, when I come face to face with Ginny Paxton. "Heck, lady," I whisper. "You startled me."

"Sneaking out again, are you?" she gives me a stare.

"I always leave before your little boy gets up. If my presence really bothers you, I could bring Posy home to my place."

"That won't actually solve anything," Ginny says, arms crossed, expression steely.

"Look, you used to like me, and now you don't anymore. Is it something I said?" I ask, stepping into my shoes. "Might as well get it off your chest."

"Fine. I need you to be careful with Posy."

"We're very careful," I say through a yawn. "There's another one of my team members outside watching the pie shop right now. We're very good at what we do."

Ginny waves a hand, dismissing my promise. "I don't mean it like that. I'm sure you're the biggest, baddest security dude, and so are all your friends. And you gave her that panic button device, for those rare moments when you're not in her bed. But so what, Gunnar? Whoever's killing hackers on the front page of the *New York Times* isn't interested in Posy anyway."

"That's true. So what's your problem?"

"My problem is what comes next," she says. "You won't stick around when this is done."

"How do you know?" I ask indignantly. Even though it's a fair question.

"Because I just know," Ginny says quietly. "Men say nice things when they want something. I'm used to it, but Posy doesn't have as much practice. That ass she used to be married to made her feel like a piece of crap, too."

"Oh, please," I scoff. "Do you really want to compare me to him?"

She gives me a critical head-to-toe glance. "I'll admit that the packaging is better in your case. And the way my sister looks at you, I know you're way better in the sack."

I've always been good at taking a compliment, but I decide to let this one fly by without acknowledgement.

"How much longer will you be in New York?" she asks. "Days? Weeks?"

"I'm not sure," I hedge.

"Well, after the Posy-watching gig is over, will you be in the neighborhood on a regular basis?"

"That's hard to say."

"Is it? You tell everyone who will listen how much you hate New York."

"Well—"

"Is your job dangerous?" she interrupts.

I don't even try to skirt that one. "Yes, once in a while. But I have a terrific team to back me up."

"Uh huh." Her jaw is tight. I've had easier interviews when I was detained by Chechen rebels at the border. "And when your boss declares victory, are you just going to waltz out of here leaving Posy with no barista?"

"Unfortunately. But we already put a sign in the window, looking for help."

"Oh, well." She sniffs. "As long as you put a sign in the window."

"Hey—the labor shortage is not my doing," I argue. "Before I walked in, she was in the same boat. I've made a metric fuckton of coffee for Posy."

Ginny doesn't care about logic, though. She crosses her arms again and glares. "Just think about what you're doing, Gunnar. She's a thirty-four-year-old woman with a ticking biological clock. Her ex threw her away like a used paper towel. If you're going to break her heart, do it soon."

"Who said anything about broken hearts?" But even as I ask the question, I realize it's entirely possible. I have feelings for Posy. So it's only logical that she may have feelings for me.

Ginny shakes her head sadly. "If you give someone a little taste of perfection, they want more of it. They won't be able to stop thinking about it. She deserves more than you can give. My sister doesn't trust people easily."

"That's because she's smart."

"Oh man." Ginny shakes her head, her expression turning sad. "Then it's worse than I thought."

"What are you talking about?"

"Two deeply cynical people don't have an easy road together. Posy needs a man who thinks that happiness is possible."

"When did I say it wasn't?" I challenge her. This is the strangest conversation I've ever had. "I'm happy."

"Uh huh." Ginny rolls her eyes. "Having fun isn't the same thing as being happy. I learned that lesson the hard way, and I learned it pretty young. Fun is something you're good at. You have an exciting job and adventurous taste in pie. Happiness is a different thing altogether. It's slowing down long enough to let someone else get near you. Think about it."

At that, Ginny turns around and retreats down the stairs to her and Aaron's part of the apartment.

It's a busy morning behind the counter. They all are. Teagan and I sling a lot of coffee and breakfast pastries. The tip jar is rocking, and the donuts are all sold by the time the line dies down.

"Can I step out for a break?" I ask Teagan, who's watching a makeup tutorial on Instagram, like a good Millennial.

"Sure," she grunts.

So I pour myself a cup of tea and head for the back. When I reach the kitchen, I pause at the door.

Posy has her phone pressed to her ear. She's ordering flour in fifty-pound bags. "What's the price for almond flour?" With her free hand, she's weaving the lattice of a beautiful cherry pie.

Just watching her, I feel a jolt of wonder. How is she real? With her quick hands and her bright eyes and that luscious pink mouth arguing with the bakery supply company. She tilts her head, taking a fractional second to admire her work. But then she sees something that isn't perfect, and reaches down again to fix it.

That's Posy. She only holds still when she's asleep. The satisfaction of her warm, spent body in my arms all night is something I've grown to cherish.

She turns her chin, catching me smiling at her. And she returns the smile. I feel something warm and unfamiliar pass between us, and it lands in the center of my chest with a happy thud.

And yet Ginny thinks I'm a bad influence. What the heck does she know, anyway?

I pass Jerry, who's whistling as he washes a baking tray, and carry my tea out the back door.

There stands Saroya, bent over at the waist, her hand reaching for something that's just out of my line of sight. I step out a little further, letting the door bang shut behind me, and Saroya straightens up quickly. "Oh hi," she says a little breathlessly.

"What are you doing?" I ask, my voice less than polite. I step off the stoop and turn around, so I can see whatever's captured her interest.

"There's a broken window," she says, plunging a hand into her pocket. "It looks trashy. You should tell Posy to have it fixed."

Sure enough, there's a broken pane in a small window that's nearly at the level of the sidewalk. The whole thing is maybe twelve inches high, and two feet across, and sectioned into four glass squares. "What's down there, do you think?"

Saroya shrugs. "A cellar? How would I know. But it looks like crap. These old buildings always need something. I keep telling Spalding he should sell and find someplace a little easier to maintain."

"A nice condo, maybe," I suggest. Saroya is the luxury condo type. I'd bet cash money that she wants a doorman with white gloves and gold buttons. And I'm happy to make the suggestion, because it would be easier on Posy if they moved to a different neighborhood.

"Exactly," she says, beaming. "I mean, history is neat, but not if you have to do the maintenance yourself."

"Uh huh." I take a careful sip of my scalding tea. "I'll tell Posy about the window." Although the broken pane isn't a security risk. Only a pigeon could fit through there.

"Thanks, Gunnar." She swishes off down the alley. "See you later for coffee!" She turns toward the street and disappears.

What is your game, lady? The question lingers in my mind. But I haven't found anything else incriminating about her. She doesn't have a fat bank account making overseas wire transfers, or a sudden change of identity. At least not that we can find.

And Max and I are pretty devious.

Speaking of Max, he's had it. This mission was his idea, and now I'm worried that it may be his undoing. All week long, my colleagues have rotated through the coffee bar line, a new one every couple of hours. They ask me for ridiculously complex lattes (like an extra hot half-decaf caramel latte with an extra shot), and then they take a seat in the back corner, watching the customers come and go.

We're watching the whole street, too. But we've got nothing. The Plumber continues to post missives right under our noses. And Max is about to lose his mind. "We're missing something," he keeps saying, and I can't disagree.

And now I have a new voice message from him. I put my earpiece in and listen. "This message is for Gunnar Scott," Max's voice says. "You're at the top of our waiting list at the salon. I can get you in for a cut, color, and blowout at two p.m., if you can leave work early today. Hope to see you then. Kisses!"

That's Max's latest code for *get your ass to the office*. He never tires of inventing new ways to summon me. But the message is clear. I'm needed this afternoon.

So I go inside and beg Teagan to stay until closing today. And I leave right after the lunch rush.

⚷

"This ... wow." It's not my most articulate statement. But we're locked in Max's office and nobody can hear me anyway. I'm looking at a print-out of The Plumber's latest web posts. And shit is getting personal. I feel nauseated as I read what looks like a desperate plea.

To us.

You want answers, but you're not looking in the right place. A dozen security guys who think they're smarter than everyone else. Cops across the street, too. None of it is working.

They're hungry. They will try to show you. I think it's personal. This ends badly unless you find them before they hit you first.

"He's talking about us," Max says flatly.

"Cops across the street?"

"NYPD intelligence set up in a second-floor commercial space across the street. Pieter spotted them last night on his stakeout shift."

I grunt and read the threat again. "We *are* smarter than everyone else. But not smart enough, I guess."

Max rubs his neck. "And we're not immortal."

"The use of *them* is really strange," I remark. "Who talks like that?"

"Someone who's afraid," Max says. "The Plumber is a dissatisfied foot soldier. I think he wants to throw his boss under the bus."

"Yeah," I say slowly. "I'm coming around to seeing it that way.

202

The bragging has evolved, hasn't it? This sounds like a plea more than a boast."

We're both silent for another long moment, until Max suddenly says: "I'm taking you off the pie shop."

"What?" My chin snaps up. "What are you talking about?"

"The Plumber is right—we're looking in the wrong place. And you've outlasted your usefulness there. Unless it's an inside job, you'd have found him already. We have so much other work to do on this investigation. Tomorrow you and I will go over every loose end. Why does he call himself The Plumber, for example? How many plumbers are there in SoHo? There's a lot we could be doing."

"But what about Posy?" I blurt out.

"She'll be well protected." Max puts his elbows on the desk, and his chin in his hands. "I'll keep staff at the shop."

"But she'll be shorthanded."

Max smiles slowly. "Aw. Look who's developed some professional pride behind the coffee bar."

I groan. "Give me forty-eight hours. I have to hire a replacement. What's that site people use to post jobs?" I grab my laptop and flip open the lid.

"No clue," Max says. "But you'd better find it fast. I can't give you two days. Besides." He picks up the print-out and shows it to me again. "If The Plumber actually knows who I am, the best thing you could do for your girl is stay away."

An icy chill climbs up my spine. "We have to find this guy."

"No kidding."

"I've been distracted," I say slowly. "He's right under my nose somewhere."

"Agreed."

"Maybe he's in an upstairs apartment—in Posy's building, or the ones next door. Let's go in there as the gas company, maybe? Or pretend there's a gas main break? Why didn't we do that already?"

"Because it's illegal?" Max gives me a dark look. "You were supposed to find the guy by looking over his shoulder. But I guess it's time to pull the Con-Ed truck and the jumpsuits out of the cellar and knock on some doors. I'll get Pieter on it. You hire a barista, or beg Posy's forgiveness, or both."

"Okay," I say dully. "On it." I pick up my computer and leave Max's office, heading for my own little-used office at the end of the row. Someone keeps it clean and dust free, even though I only visit it a few times a year.

Ginny was right, I realize as I settle in to look at job posting sites. She said I'd flake off and leave Posy hanging. And that's exactly what I'm about to do.

And I don't know why I didn't see that coming.

IT'S during the lunch rush when a brand-new disaster strikes.

"Posy?" Teagan says, sticking her head into the kitchen. "The health department is here for an inspection."

"Okay," I say calmly, but my hands begin to sweat. I glance around the kitchen, hoping they haven't caught me with anything out of the refrigerator.

My eye lands on an open carton of eggs just as the inspector appears in the doorway, a white coat on, and a clipboard in his hand. "Eggs," he says in the voice of an automaton, writing it down quickly, and I feel my heart drop. "To prevent contamination, they must be refrigerated to forty-five degrees."

"But they need to be at room temperature to whip up properly," I argue. "And I'm going to use them all."

"Doesn't matter," the robot says. "The code makes no distinction. Please correct the deficiency."

Biting my tongue, I close the carton and carry the eggs to the reach-in refrigerator. I know better than to argue. But if he'd come just twenty minutes later, all those eggs would be doing laps around the mixer. I'm making meringue today.

This is just a spot of bad luck. I'll lose a few points for the eggs. My last health department inspection was an A-, because there's always some little thing that isn't perfect. But you can't have *two* little things, because then your grade starts slipping. Or—God forbid —three.

So I start praying to St. Gourmet, the patron saint of restauranteurs that the inspector won't find anything else to complain about.

St. Gourmet isn't listening, apparently. Just when I think the inspector is finished, he asks to see the cellar.

"We aren't storing anything down there," I tell him. "It's not convenient enough."

"But it's on your form as a designated storage area," he says in a flat voice. "I am required to look."

Oh, for heaven's sake. "Okay. Let's go."

I lead the man out of the pie shop's front door, and then into my own front door. I unlock the door to the basement, and I descend the stairs carefully. Then I pull the string that illuminates the ugly space with a single bulb. "See? There's nothing down here but mechanicals." There's a giant boiler that heats two buildings at once, and a double electrical box.

"Oh dear," the inspector says, crossing the space.

"Oh dear what?" I demand.

The man points, and I see two dead rats on the floor, near the cellar wall. "Evidence of vermin," the inspector says, checking a box on his clipboard. "And, furthermore, easy access for vermin." He points his pen at the one little window out on the alley.

And there's a hole in one pane. I'm so screwed.

"But we're not using this space!" I squeak. "There's nothing to contaminate!"

It doesn't matter, though. Two minutes later he's gone, leaving me with twenty-eight points against Posy's Pie Shop, which will translate to a C grade.

I'm so screwed.

Back in the kitchen, I feel chastened. I'm great with details, and I've always studied to get an A. The poor inspection feels like a personal failure.

I make two of the world's most beautiful meringue pies, each one with a crust that won't be soggy, a filling that will hit the tongue with a bright burst of sweetened acidity, and a fluffy cloud of toasted meringue on top. But it's a hollow victory. I need someone to give me a hug. Someone who knows I'm better than a C-grade human.

I need Gunnar, damn it. Where is that guy? Teagan tells me he stepped out to run an errand.

Finally—when it's almost closing time—I hear his voice in the cafe. And something lifts inside me. I forget all about the stupid inspection, and I wonder whether he'd like to go out for a sushi dinner tonight.

I wash my hands and check the mirror, just to be sure I don't have blobs of lemon curd on my apron. And then I step out to greet him.

Gunnar has his back to me, just like the first time I saw him in my shop. This time, though, I'm more intimately familiar with the muscular butt in those jeans. And the strength and passion in those hands that he's using to tape a new sign to the front door.

"Hey, Gunn," I say, leaning against the doorframe. "What's with the new sign?"

"Posy." He turns around abruptly. "I didn't see you there." His handsome face is sheepish.

Uh oh, my subconscious says.

I step closer so I can read the sign. ***Barista needed immediately. Signing bonus offered***.

"Signing bonus. What the heck is that all about?"

"I thought it would help. I'll foot the bill for a qualified candidate to get a thousand bucks for agreeing to start right away. What do you think?"

I think I've never gotten angry so quickly in my life. "That's not your call, is it?" I bark.

"Well, no." He winces. "I was trying to solve our problem."

"*Our* problem," I echo. "You mean my problem. The one I have with unreliable men? Is this it for you? Just like that? Poof, and I'm down an employee?"

His sheepish face tells me all I need to know.

"I see. You've had your fun here. Does that mean you were successful with—" I stop myself before asking if he'd identified the

207

killer. He won't be able to say so out loud, not in front of the last two customers who are still enjoying my WiFi connection even though their cups are empty and their pie plates contain nothing but crumbs.

"Just so you know, I'm going to lean on Teagan for some more hours. And I can work tomorrow," he says. "Until noon."

"Until noon." Does he mean *only* tomorrow until noon? Another glance at his guilty face confirms that it's true. "I see." And damn it, I do see. It was always going to happen like this. Why did I not understand that?

"I'm sorry," he says. "I feel terrible about leaving you in the lurch."

"Right." I swallow hard. "Of course you do." Why do I feel so crushed? It's not just the barista job, either. Gunnar means a whole lot more to me than coffee. And now he's done? With me, too?

I shouldn't leap to conclusions. "Listen, what if we got some sushi tonight and did a little brainstorming about the new hire?"

"We'll definitely have that conversation." He frowns. "Tonight isn't good for me, though."

"Oh," I say quietly. "I see."

One of those lingering customers clicks his laptop shut and prepares to depart. Needing something to do with my hands, I hustle over there and take his cup and plate off the table. "Thanks for coming in," I say cheerfully, although I'm dying inside.

Is this really it? I thought Gunnar's time in my shop would telegraph its ending. That there'd be a big moment of clarity when he and Max sorted out their mystery and celebrated its conclusion.

But I guess I'm not privy to that part. Gunnar is going to disappear as quickly as he arrived—from my shop, and from my bed. And it's abundantly clear that I'm going to be far more upset about it than he is.

I carry those dishes swiftly out of the room. "Flip the sign, Jerry!" I call out. "I'll wash these last couple of things."

"Okay, Posy!" He gives me a big smile.

I turn on the water with a blast into the metal sink, and it's loud enough to cover the sound of my unhappy sigh. I hose the coffee dregs out of the cup like it's the most important thing in the world. Then I grab the soapy sponge and scrub.

"I will *not* pine for that man," I say under my breath. "Pining is for losers."

But he's so pretty, my hormones whine. *And we want him around. We might even be falling in love with him.*

I scrub the plate and take deep breaths, so I won't do something stupid. Like cry.

When I shut the water off, Gunnar is standing in the doorway to my tiny office, and he's talking to Teagan, I think. "Come on, now," he says. "I'll walk you out." He's giving her his loverboy smile. And when she steps into view, he puts his arm around her back and leads her toward the front of my shop without a backward glance at me.

He's turned on the charm, hoping to convince Teagan to take a bunch of extra shifts behind the counter. He's trying to assuage his guilt at abandoning me like a used napkin.

I'm going to be eating takeout sushi alone on the sofa tonight, I realize. With the same extra-large glass of cheap white wine I was drinking the night that Gunnar walked back into my life.

How fitting.

"Posy?" Jerry calls from the front. "I know we're closed now, but someone is here to see you!"

Please, God, let it not be another health inspector. "Coming!" I trot out to the front with no small amount of trepidation. What else could go wrong today?

But it's not a health inspector. It's a young woman with dark skin, clear brown eyes, long, elaborate earrings and her hair piled into a jaunty bun on top of her head. "My name is Monique. I'm here about the barista job," she says. "If you're on your way out, I could come back tomorrow morning. But I saw your sign in the window, and I'd love to fill out an application."

I blink back my surprise. "Nice to meet you, Monique. Let me just grab that application. I'd be happy to stick around while you fill it out. The last barista quit, leaving me high and dry. He couldn't even be bothered to give me two weeks' notice." My anger burns brightly as I say these words.

But my foolish gaze looks toward the street anyway. Ready for a glimpse, in case he passes by.

He doesn't, though. So I nip into the office and grab an application, and a good pen. Then I bring it out to the young woman in front. "Here you go! Can I ask if you've worked as a barista before?"

"Oh, totally!" she says, giving me a beautiful smile. "My summer job is at Maxi's Coffee in Peoria, Illinois. Our machine isn't quite as pretty as yours. It's a Cecilware two group. But I'm sure I won't have a problem adapting. I'll make you some test drinks if you want to see me in action."

"Let's do that," I say, stepping behind the counter to flip Lola back on. "What's your availability?"

"Well, Tuesday and Thursday aren't good for me. But I piled all my classes onto those days, so that I could work the other five. NYU is expensive."

Five days of availability, including weekends? I nearly squeal with joy. "I can work with that," I say coolly. After all, Gunnar has turned me into a more cynical person than I used to be. It's quite possible that Monique is some kind of spy. If there's one murder plot afoot in my cafe, there could easily be a second one. Or a third. The world is full of liars with their own twisted agendas.

I watch Monique write her name onto my application in a pleasant, loopy script, her earrings swinging playfully as she writes.

Nope! my subconscious says. *She's a cheerful college student who needs money for beer and books.*

The truth is that I'm just not cut out to see the world the way Gunnar sees it. I'm the kind of girl who expects people to be who they say they are, right up until the moment they let me down.

And I *like* myself this way. If Monique is secretly a caffeine-crazed alien with a secret mission to colonize the Earth, I'm not going to figure it out until her spacecraft touches down in the alley outside. That's just the kind of girl I am.

Monique finishes the application and looks up. "Shall I make you a drink? What will it be?"

"A decaf latte, please. Lola is a little finicky with the tamp. I won't take any points off if it takes you a couple of tries to get it right."

"I'll win her over," Monique says, ducking behind the counter and heading right to the sink to wash her hands.

I'm smitten already.

Humming to herself, Monique grinds a shot of decaf and tamps it expertly, dusting the group head of stray grounds. And she cleans the frothing arm like a pro.

A few short minutes later I'm sipping an excellent latte with a foam bunny on it. "When can you start?" I ask.

"Well, I could come in tomorrow. I need the paycheck. Your, um, flyer in the window says something about a signing bonus."

That was Gunnar's big idea. But I'll be damned if I'm going to take his guilt money. "It's five hundred bucks after your first shift, and another five hundred after your first month."

Her eyes light up. "That's wonderful. I can buy my last two textbooks, and still have money for beer."

"Be here tomorrow before seven," I tell her. "Welcome aboard, Monique."

"Thank you, ma'am."

"Call me Posy," I insist.

The minute she leaves, I text Gunnar. ***Don't bother coming in tomorrow. I found someone else.***

28

GUNNAR

IT'S TEAGAN. I can't believe it. The Plumber is a gum-chewing donut-making Millennial.

A few minutes ago, I burst in on her in Posy's office, where she was tapping madly on her phone. And when I glanced at the screen, instead of Instagram, I saw the ugly black screen of a dark web message board.

We locked eyes. But it only took me a moment to get over my shock. Then I clamped an arm around Teagan and said, "You're walking out of here with me right this second. And you will smile, damn it." And then I grabbed that damn phone and shoved it into my pocket.

I didn't even get a chance to say goodbye to Posy. On our way out, I felt her anger radiating in my direction, as hot as the sun.

It's well deserved, that's for sure. But I don't have time to worry about it right now. Because I've finally found The Plumber. And I've frog-marched her onto the sidewalk and into a taxicab, all while pretending to chat her up. As I walk her toward the cab, past the NYPD's cameras, and whoever else is watching the pie shop, I smile the smile of a dude who's out on a hot date with a younger woman.

"Where are you taking me?" she asks after I give the taxi a destination a few blocks away.

"To my office," I say, clasping her wrist in a tight hold, just so she doesn't get any ideas. "And if you try to make a run for it, you won't get far. My guys are following us right now."

I have so many questions. Who is Teagan, anyway? And who spoofed her phone to make it appear on the WiFi connection as a Windows device?

But I don't ask anything of my hostage, who's trembling visibly as the cab pulls over. I pay him, and then tell Teagan to get into the black Company sedan that Duff has just pulled to a stop behind us.

"Who are you?" she whispers as she slides onto the leather seat behind Duff. The locks click into place, which means Teagan's door won't open now. Duff is no fool, and our cars are the shit.

"I'm the world's best barista," I mumble as I tap my watch and leave Max an encrypted voicemail. *"Bringing you a treat at the office, lover! Your favorite donuts. See you in five minutes."*

"Nice one," Duff says from behind the wheel.

"Thanks," I say, but my mood is pretty sour. How the hell did I not figure this out earlier? Although—to be fair—I've looked over Teagan's shoulder dozens of times only to see Instagram on her phone.

"I want a lawyer," she says.

"Well, I'm not a cop."

"Who are you, then?"

"Good question. It really depends on whether you're guilty of killing hackers. I might be the guy who quietly saves your butt. Or the guy who hands you over to the police. It depends on what you have to say, and if you're smart enough to say it."

"I'm not guilty of anything. But I can't talk to you, or someone could die." Her eyes fill with tears, and I feel instantly terrible. I'm not a fan of intimidating women. But I've just done exactly that.

Teagan—if that's her real name—owes us nothing. She brought a lot of shit to Posy's door, which wasn't nice. But it's possible that she's just a pawn in someone else's evil game. She sure as hell doesn't look menacing.

Duff steers the car into the rear entrance of The Company headquarters, and the garage door is quickly shut behind us.

"Where are we?" she squeaks, pressing her body into the corner of her side of the seat.

"This is my office building," I say calmly. "Nobody is going to hurt you. But you're right—people could die because of what you know. But if you tell us, we can sort it out. Now come upstairs." Duff unlocks the back doors, and I climb out, taking care not to touch Teagan when she also leaves the car. It's not like she can escape. There are two men at the exterior doors. "Would you follow me, please? We have an interview room just down that hallway and up a flight of stairs." I point to a glass door.

Biting her lip, Teagan follows me. Duff is bringing up the rear, but he hangs back, giving her space. I press my palm to the security panel and open the door.

Scout is already waiting on the other side. "Hello there. Do you mind if I pat you down for weapons?" she asks Teagan.

"Uh, no?" Teagan says, looking terrified. "I don't have anything but my phone and my wallet."

Scout—who's two inches shorter than Teagan but deadlier than a bag of rattlesnakes—quickly pats her down. "Thank you for that. Come right this way."

The next hour is very illuminating. From the look of fear on Teagan's face, it's easy to see that our donut maker is in way over her head.

But once Max and Scout sit her down around the conference table with two bags of chips, a selection of cold sodas, and proof that we can tie every one of The Plumber's pie shop posts with video evidence of Teagan on the premises, she caves in faster than a sandcastle at high tide.

"Everything I posted, I did for my boyfriend. He's just a bookkeeper who found himself working for the wrong guys," she says, eyes downcast. "I mean—this one in particular is super scary."

"Super scary how?" Max asks, leaning back in his chair and appearing far more relaxed than I know he really is.

"My boyfriend always found him creepy, and he has a short temper. But his office seemed pretty normal at first."

"What kind of office is it?" I ask.

"It's upstairs at a nightclub. He goes in two times a week to do the club's books. The ledgers are mostly ordinary—alcohol and a big payroll. But they also pass him receipts with dodgy information on them. My boyfriend is supposed to put them down for 'miscellaneous expenses.'"

"Huh," Max says noncommittally. "Nightclubs are often fronts for a whole lot of things. Drugs. Money laundering."

"I wouldn't know," Teagan insists. "Anyway, there are also a bunch of computers up there—more than a nightclub would need. My boyfriend is a bookkeeper by trade, but hacking is his hobby. So he notices powerful computers, you know? And the machine they put him on has a lot of horsepower."

"Interesting," Max says, leaning forward. "What kind of hacking does he do?"

"Breaking into first person shooter games." She shrugs. "He sells cheat codes to sweaty gamers in South Korea."

"Isn't that illegal?" I ask.

"A little bit," Teagan admits. "The game manufacturers are always trying to close the loopholes. But my boyfriend likes the thrill of the chase. It's a cat and mouse game between him and the game manufacturers."

"Okay," Max says. "So how did your hacker boyfriend get you posting murder details on the dark web? Connect the dots for me."

"Well, these guys in the nightclub office are a weird bunch. They won't let him do the books remotely. They won't let him use his own computer, and he has to put his phone in a bowl while he's working there. It's a little paranoid, but not that off base, right? Some people just don't trust the cloud. So he's on one of their rigs, and he starts poking around this PC one day just for fun. Kind of like driving someone else's Ferrari. And someone had left a private message channel open ..." She sighs.

"So he read it," Max guesses.

"Yeah." She heaves a sigh. "He shouldn't have read it. There was some scary shit on there. And he didn't want to be caught reading it. But it worried him. He needed to know if he should even be working for these people. So he ..." She hesitates.

"Mirrored it to another channel?" Max guesses. "To read later?"

"Yep." She swallows hard. "The thread he saw was about some

215

kind of super creepy poison," she says, shivering. "When he read it that night at home, he got kind of freaked out."

"Oh man," Scout says, taking another corn chip from the bag. She's here to play the good cop, I think. In case Teagan needs convincing.

"Yeah, my boyfriend wanted to drop him as a client. When the creepy boss asked to increase his hours, he made an excuse, like he was too busy with his long-time guys. But the scary dude offered to triple his pay and give him even more hours, so he stayed." She hangs her head.

"And that was a mistake?" I offer gently. "Did he hear more things that he shouldn't?"

"Well, it's funny that you put it like that. My boyfriend has almost no hearing." Her eyes tear up again. "He's almost completely deaf. But he's really good at lipreading. And—this happens all the time to people who have a disability—they treat him like he's blind and stupid, too. The younger guys that guard this office, they will say anything in front of him. They talk about who they're going to shake down next. And my boyfriend pretends like he can't understand anything they're saying."

"So he hears a lot," Max says.

"In a manner of speaking, yes. And *then* ..." she takes a big breath. "The first hacker murder hit the newspaper, and they couldn't shut up about it. My boyfriend noticed that they knew more about it than was in the papers. So that freaked him out."

Now we're getting somewhere. "So ..." Max's eyes are as bright as I've ever seen them. "You think these guys are killing hackers for the scary boss?"

"They might be," she says quietly. "But the way they talk, it seemed more like they know the guys who did it. Meanwhile, the messages keep rolling into that mirrored channel. There's talk of obtaining more poison gas. And how to move it from place to place."

"Can you show us the channel?" Max asks.

She shakes her head. "I'm not the hacker."

"So who spoofed your phone to behave like a laptop on WiFi?" I ask, because that's the trick that fooled me.

"My boyfriend. Obviously. He needed me to help get the authorities' attention, but he didn't want anyone to figure out who was ratting them out on a public WiFi. I only post things when he's at work on their machines. We figure they can see his keystrokes. They won't think it's him. Because it isn't."

"Uh huh. But let's back up a second," Max says. "I want to hear more about the scary boss. Have you seen this man? Do you know what he looks like?"

She shakes her head again. "My boyfriend doesn't want him to know I exist. They never ask him about his personal life. But they have his home address, and his social security number. He wants to just disappear, you know? But it's not that easy."

"I understand that," Max says. "Take me through your thinking, then. Why share the details of a crime on a public WiFi? What purpose does that serve?"

"We're just looking for a way out of this mess!" Her eyes burn with fury. "We didn't really know how to point a finger at the boss without giving too much away. We couldn't name the location of the office, because we can't tell if the murderers had actually been there. So we triangulated it instead, with the WiFi locations."

"But there's thousands of people who live and work inside that triangle," Max argues.

"Yeah, I got that. But did you miss the part where I said we don't actually know what we're doing? I make *donuts*, for fuck's sake."

"But your guy is a hacker," I point out.

"Sure, but his big crime is selling cheat codes to teenagers. The only thing he's ever killed is the Gargoyle on level Z of Starmancer."

"He played level Z?" Scout asks, her head popping up. "Whoa."

Max shoots her a look that suggests she really shouldn't change the subject.

"So what's your plan?" Max asks, cracking open a soda. "Empty the contents of your donut account and move to Costa Rica? Hope he can't find you?"

"Something like that. We don't have a real plan. We were just hoping someone would swoop in and take him away in handcuffs."

"But they didn't. So you upped your game, right? You've been posting about a planned killing."

"Yeah. They're pissed off at some guys who are in their way."

"In their way of what?" Max presses.

"Something about selling hardware to a car company. They never said what the hardware was, or if car was really a car, or code for something else."

Well, shit. That sounds like our new client. So Max—and me by extension—are the target now?

Cool, cool. Just another day at The Company.

"... My boyfriend feels so bad," Teagan says tearily. "Someone is going to die if we don't do something."

"Here's a crazy thought," Scout says. "Why didn't you go to the police?"

"Because we stole information off someone else's computer. And we sound like psychos!" Teagan throws her arms in the air. "Picture me going in there and trying to explain a mirror channel to a beat cop. I barely understand what it is myself. They'll make a report, and send me home again, right? These guys have our home address and my boyfriend's social security number. I don't know how to get away from this. And I didn't have a better idea. We were just hoping someone was paying attention. And you were paying attention, right? But I still don't see how you can help me."

"Teagan," Max says, propping his hands behind his head. "I need his name. And I need to meet him. Today."

She makes a face. "I bet you can't help us at all. If you're not the police, you can't protect us."

"I can hide you for a while. My primary business is protecting high net-worth clientele. I employ hundreds of guards, recruited from militaries around the world. I can put you in a safe house in New England for a few days until I can get this guy into the hands of the authorities."

"Why would you, though? And what if they don't catch him?"

"Because I'm the guy who's getting in his way of selling the hardware. And I don't want to die."

"Oh," she says heavily. "He wants you dead, and I'm drinking your soda. Why don't I feel safer right now?"

Scout lets out a snort. "You're really selling this, Max."

Max ignores her. "Look. If your creepy boss is who I think it is, the State Department wants him. If we can prove his location, I'll summon the guys who will take him away in handcuffs."

"And what if it's not the right guy?" she challenges.

"We can find you a backup plan. I have a branch on the West Coast. Worst case scenario—I'll get you new identities and put you up for a month in California. You can find some new clients. I'll be your reference. You can just disappear and start over somewhere new."

I expect her to hate this idea. But she doesn't. "That's really tempting. But what if you don't follow through?"

"You're going to have to trust somebody. Why not me? Now tell me your boyfriend's name."

The guy's name is Geoff Pinter, CPB. Max sends an agent to Geoff and Teagan's apartment, bearing a note from Teagan. And Geoff is a smart enough man to follow him back here.

When the bookkeeper eventually steps into the interview room—after he's patted down and surrenders his phone and smart watch—he and his girlfriend exchange a quick, hard hug, and then a bunch of rapid-fire sign language.

I don't know what they're saying, but it might be: *These people are all a little crazy but they don't seem to want us to die.*

It's the truth, anyway.

They finally sit down, and Max is all business. My friend always manages to broadcast a calm demeanor. But I've known him long enough to sense the excitement radiating off him.

This could be big for Max. He's wanted to catch Aga for more than a decade.

Max attaches a keyboard to a computer projection on a screen that we can all see. Then he passes the keyboard to Geoff, and begins the interview. "Please tell us the boss's name. And what does he look like?"

Geoff begins tapping on the keyboard, while we all look up at the screen to read his answer. *He introduced himself to me as John Smith.*

Of course he did.

The checks I cash say JS Entertainment. He shrugs. *He is older than you. Maybe late forties or fifty. His head is shaved bald. He has an olive skin tone. He usually wears black jeans and a black suit jacket over a white shirt. Once, just jeans and a black T-shirt. He looks like a guy who's taken care of himself. Like he goes to the gym. He had a mustache when I started, but then he shaved it off.*

Max looks directly at Geoff to catch his attention. "Does he have any scars on his face?"

Geoff points at his neck, just to the side of his chin. Then he types, *Right here. A thin scar. And the man's nose has a bump right here.* He taps his own.

Max doesn't say anything for a moment. But I can tell he's struggling to remain calm. "Interesting. I'd like to show you a group of photos and ask if you see him."

Of course.

I flip open the folder I'm holding and pass over the black and white print-out we made before he arrived, with a red marker. There are twelve photos on that page, all of men in the same age bracket as Aga.

Geoff uncaps the marker and—with zero hesitation—circles a photo at the edge of the page. He glances up at Max, then taps the paper twice. *That's him.*

Max goes completely still. And then a slow smile spreads across his face. Max doesn't smile all that often, so the effect is startling. "Okay, Geoff," he says calmly. "Here's what's going to happen next."

The Company headquarters becomes as busy as a hornet's nest in a heatwave. Anyone off duty is recalled to base. It's time for recon, and last-minute intelligence.

I instruct a team of analysts to learn everything we can about the block where Geoff goes to work. Who owns the building? When did the club open? And so on. If Max is going to prove that a notorious arms trafficker is living in Manhattan and running his operation out of a SoHo nightclub, we're going to need to make some connections.

If we're very, very lucky, we can help the feds prove that Aga is guilty of a petty crime, and they can hold him on that while they try to prove his ties to the murders or to old weapons deals.

Geoff's interview continues, too, as we press him to recall anything he can about the finances of the nightclubs, and the shady transactions he was asked to book. Dates. Amounts. Names. Anything he can.

"Why did you call yourself The Plumber?" I finally remember to ask. "What's the significance of that?"

There's an old sign painted on the bricks right across from the nightclub. It says The Plumber in red letters.

"Oh, shit." Another damn clue I could have found if I'd looked.

I am very tired, Geoff writes. *Can we take a break?*

I glance at the clock and note that it's ten o'clock. Oops. "I'm sorry to keep you so late. We can take you home and watch your building, or we can check you into a hotel room."

He and Teagan communicate in sign language for a moment.

"Take us home," Teagan says finally. "But we don't want to be seen getting out of your car."

"No problem," Scout says. "We'll drop you a few blocks away and follow you discreetly. And you'll carry these, to explain where you've been." She opens a folder and removes two playbills from the musical *Hamilton*.

"Okay," Teagan says, fingering the program. "I wish this were real. I wish I were watching a musical instead of trying to catch criminals."

"If we do this right, you can be," I promise her. "Tomorrow you'll make donuts and go to work as usual, okay? And Geoff will go to his regular appointments before coming home for the night. We'll watch both of you from a discreet distance. We'll pick you both up for the op the next morning." That's when he's due back at the nightclub. About thirty-six hours from now.

"Thank you," she says, standing up to go. Then she lifts her chin and looks me right in the eye. "I really need this to work. I'm counting on you."

"Of course," I say smoothly. "Don't worry."

Although there's still plenty to worry about. I need to get this guy. And I need to do it soon.

29

GUNNAR

AFTER TEAGAN and Geoff are escorted home by two of my operatives, I wolf down a wrap sandwich that somebody ordered for me a few hours ago. Then I head upstairs to Max's office, where he's been squirreled away making calls. It's his job to get the right G-men fired up to take Aga out, and he needs to do it fast.

He's not on the phone now, I observe, looking in through his office window. There's a small fleet of empty coffee cups on his desk, and a plate filled with crumbs. He's tapping furiously on his computer keyboard. The screen looks black, though, because his office window is a very special kind of glass. It's bullet-proof, because Max will always have enemies. Furthermore, it blocks certain rays of light, so nobody can read his screens through the window.

I knock on his door. He looks up to see me, then reaches for a button on his desk. I hear the soft click of the door unlocking for me, so I go inside. "Hey man. How's it going?"

"Close the door," he says quickly.

As if I'd forget. I pull it shut with a tight click and take a seat in front of him. "How are you doing?"

"Fine. Why?" He swivels around in his desk chair and studies me.

"Because you're vibrating with excitement," I say with a chuckle. "I've seen calmer six-year-olds on Christmas Eve."

"No idea what you're talking about." He grins.

222

"So. What are you going to do to Aga once you see him?" Max has wanted this man's head on a plate for ten years.

"Me? Nothing. But the State Department will swoop in immediately after I confirm his identity. I knew they'd want him."

"Don't they want to verify it themselves?" I ask.

"They'd rather let me take the risk," Max says drily. "Then they'll arrest him on some flimsy nightclub charge that never gets adjudicated. He'll just disappear. You'll never see his name in the paper. He'll never surface again."

"Yikes."

Max shrugs. "Do you know how many people he's killed? Hundreds, directly. And untold thousands via the weapons he sold in Syria. That man, that *brilliant* man—" he closes his eyes and shakes his head "—he devoted his life to making money off any dangerous device or substance that came his way. He could have built things. He could have led his countrymen forward. He could have taught more brilliant minds to do great things."

"What a waste," I agree, hoping Max will calm down. I should remove all the coffee from the building before his heart explodes. "In thirty-six hours, it could all be over. What will you do if they don't get him?"

"They'll get him." He leans back in his chair and lets out a big breath. "I can't really process it, though. And it isn't really about me."

I suppose that's what he's supposed to say. But we both know it matters a great deal. What must it feel like for Max to be so close to something he's waited ten years to do? To bring down the man who killed the woman he loved.

"How are you doing, anyway?" Max asks me.

"Fine, dude. What do you mean?"

"If you go back to Cali next week, that's pretty much the end of your time with Posy."

"Yeah, thanks for the memo." I give him a sour look. "My head is totally in the game now."

"I know that."

"I'm sorry it took me so long to finger Teagan. I apologize for my distraction."

Max frowns at me. "It was a slick op, Gunn. They disabled the cell service and the GPS in her phone and spoofed it to Windows. Then they re-installed Instagram to fool anyone who was nearby. Top notch tech in the hands of a donut maker."

"Still," I grunt. "I let a woman play me, because I was busy staring at another one. I won't lose focus again."

"Everyone loses focus." Max scratches his chin. "Well, everyone but me. But you're totally into Posy. When were you going to ask me for a permanent assignment in New York?"

"Never."

"What?" He gives me a look like I'm not making sense. "Why not?"

"*Because.*" I know that's a dumb answer. But in my defense, Max asked a really stupid question. "Because I hate New York. And because I'm just like you—married to this job. We're a couple of mercenaries, and we like it that way."

"It wasn't always like that." Max folds his hands behind his head. "I used to have someone. And I would have done anything for her."

"Look how that turned out." As soon as the words are out of my mouth, I regret them. It's not Max's fault that the love of his life was killed by the same terrorist we're trying to pin down with the book-keeper's help.

But Max doesn't even flinch. "I'd do it all again. I mean—I'd happily skip the part where I got the intelligence completely fucking wrong, causing the deaths of at least three people. But there's no parallel universe in which I don't love her. You can save yourself from terrorists, but you can't save yourself from loving the right woman. It doesn't work like that."

"Who are you?" I grunt, and I'm not really joking. Max never talks about her. *Cassie.* I haven't even heard her name in five years.

"Who are *you*," he echoes, "to walk away from someone who loves you? I'm not proud of what happened. But I never walked away from her willingly. Why would you do that if you didn't have to?"

"*Max.* Why are we doing this right now? We're working on the most important operation since ... maybe ever. You're about to get exactly what you want. Let's just get the work done."

He picks up one of his Blackwing pencils and taps the eraser onto the desk. "What I'm getting is a poor substitute for what I really want," he says quietly. "But your life could turn out quite differently."

I don't even know what to say to that. "I'm already thirty-six years old. It's not like I'm going to grow up to be an optimist. You and I see a lot of dark things. We know too much and we take a lot of risks. No woman really wants a piece of that."

"Doesn't she? Did you even ask?" He tosses the pencil onto the desk. "Nobody's life is all sunshine and rainbows. There's the part where you eat your spinach, and when you're done, you get a piece of pie for dessert. You can have both, Gunn."

"I like spinach," is the most intelligent thing I can think of to say.

"Go home and get some sleep. There's more to do tomorrow."

I rise from the chair and leave to do as he says.

Or I try to, anyway. But I don't sleep very well.

The next day is just as busy at work. We meet with some clandestine asshole from the State Department. We give him reams of information, and all he gives us back is a promise to take a hard look at the photos of Aga that Max is promising him.

"That's it?" I grumble when we're back in Max's office. "He didn't even say if they'd arrest him."

"They'll arrest him," Max says, eating another take-out sandwich without even tasting it. "Tomorrow by noon. Now check on Teagan and Geoff, then go home and rest."

By the time I get home to my silent apartment, I have a new voice message from Posy. I spend a few minutes pretending that I'm not in a hurry to listen to it. It's not like I'm going to hear words of love. She's justifiably angry at me. I walked out on her without much explanation. I didn't even say a proper goodbye.

Not to mention that she's shorthanded right now. And all I did about that was put a sign in her window.

Yeah, she's mad at me. And I deserve it.

I pull out my phone. My finger hovers over the playback button for a half second. Up until now, I've been doing a good job of putting Posy out of my mind for a couple of days.

It's really for the best. After all, I promised I'd take care of things. I swore I'd get the assholes out of her shop and out of her hair, so she could go back to concentrating on pie.

But her message on my phone is like a drug. I feel the pull. And my resistance fails as I tap the message and lift the phone to my ear. Because who am I kidding? I even close my eyes so I can listen better to the sound of her sweet voice in my ear. *Hi Gunnar.* She lets out a sigh. Then she goes on.

Look, I want to be mad at you. But I can't stop thinking about you. I don't know where you are right now. And I should probably just leave you alone. But something strange happened, and I couldn't help wondering what you'd think.

Yesterday, I got a visit from the health department, and it was off cycle. I didn't give the timing much thought, because it's always stressful whenever it happens.

This inspector was especially thorough. He wanted to see the basement storage room, which I don't use. But I'm not allowed to say no. And then they found two dead rats down there, below a broken window, so I got a bad grade.

I let out a groan, because I don't like where this story is going.

Today I called the exterminator, because that's what you do even if you already know how they got in. But the guy who showed up said something really weird. The rats in my basement aren't Norway rats—the kind that everybody has in New York. These were pet store rats. Somebody broke the window and put them there.

So that's just freaky. Maybe it happened the night of the break-in, and I just didn't notice. But it has to be intentional. So I called the health department and asked them why they'd come early. And they said there was a complaint of vermin that inspired their early visit.

Posy gets quiet for a second, and I'm not sure if the message has been cut off. But then she speaks again.

Someone is trying to hurt the pie shop, and I don't know why. It's tempting to think that it has to do with whatever criminal you're trying to lock up. But putting rats in my basement and then calling the health inspector is a petty maneuver.

It's my problem to solve. I don't even know why I called. I don't really need you to fight my battles. I have to get used to not having you around.

The customers have to get used to it, too. You wouldn't believe how many people asked for you today. Where's Gunnar? When is he coming back?

This happened last time, too. After you left the bar, people asked about you for months. I tried really hard not to be offended. But you were fun, damn it. It wasn't the same after you left. The only good thing about it was that I could test one of your theories without you noticing. I started wearing low-cut tops to get better tips.

You can probably guess what happened. My tips jumped twenty-eight percent the first night. So then I was even more irritated at you than before.

I smile to myself. And my heart aches just picturing Posy behind that bar trying out her low-cut top. For science.

This is the longest voice message ever, and it's probably going to cut me off soon. So I'll just close by telling you that my new hire is terrific and I don't miss you.

You know I'm lying, right? I do miss you, damn it. But I understand why you're not here, and I'll just get used to it. Stay safe out there.

Bye.

When the message ends, I sit there for a while, holding my phone to my ear like a ninny. But I'm just not ready for it to end—the message, or my time with Posy. It's crazy to think that I'm not going back to the pie shop. It's like leaving a movie in the middle, before you get to see what happens.

I'm invested, damn it. I want to see her again.

But after I waste a few minutes feeling sorry for myself, I realize I've got the perfect excuse to go over to Posy's one more time. I have a bad feeling about how those rats got into her basement. And I might even have a way to prove it.

"Hey, Mark?" I ask the guy who answers The Company switchboard. "I need you to pull some video for me. From a camera on the back door of the pie shop."

"Sure, Gunn," he says. "What am I looking for?"

"Two days ago. About ten in the morning. Maybe ten-thirty. Find the bit where I come out the back door with a cup of tea for my break. Back up immediately from there—grab the footage of a woman who stopped in the alley. I don't know how wide the angle of that backdoor camera reaches, but I think she was up to no good back there. I spotted her when I came outside."

"Sure, sure," Mark says. "I'm on it."

"Thanks, man."

⌐══╼

An hour later, I call Posy back.

"Gunnar," she says, sounding surprised. "I regret leaving a long, pathetic message on your phone."

"I don't regret it," I tell her. "There was nothing pathetic about it. Except for the part about your health department visit. Can I come over? There's something big I want to show you."

"You showed it to me already," Posy says drily. "I'm already a fan. But maybe that wouldn't be wise."

"Wow." I laugh. "Tough crowd here tonight. Can I please stop over?"

"In the first place," Posy says. "Aaron and I are playing a vicious game of Go Fish. It's just the two of us tonight. And in the second place, what's the point? You hate New York. Is that going to change?"

"Well, probably not," I admit. "Although I'm a fan of one part of New York—the part that's wherever you happen to be."

Posy is quiet for a second. "My life is here, Gunnar. Yours isn't. That's just reality."

She sounds so sure. But I'm starting to understand that my solitary lifestyle is a choice, not an inevitability. And I'm finally starting to realize why people settle down with someone special.

Because when you find that special person, it's really hard to walk away.

"Listen, this is important," I beg. The truth is that I could send her the footage and be done with it. But that's not good enough for me. I want to help Posy solve this problem. I want to be there when she needs me. "I just need fifteen minutes of your time."

"Fine," she says with a sigh. "I'm available to talk to you at eight-thirty."

That must be after the kid's bedtime. "Great. I'll be there."

After we hang up, I go outside and visit the bodega on the corner. I buy a dozen roses. They're not as fancy as the flowers at a florist's shop, but it's the best I can do at the moment. It occurs to me that Posy is named after a flower, but nobody ever buys her any.

What does a posy look like anyway? I make a mental note to figure that out. And then I'll hunt some down.

I'm a very stubborn man. Whatever I put my mind to, I can achieve. And impressing Posy is my new goal. I don't really know what a future for Posy and I would look like. But I do know that she and I aren't done. We can't be.

30

POSY

AARON DOESN'T WANT to go to sleep, because he overheard me telling Gunnar to come over.

"I haven't seen Gunnar in dayyyyyys," he complains as I tuck him into bed for the eleventy-billionth time.

"He's not royalty," I grumble. "And he's just popping over to give me something. You're not missing a thing."

"But I liked it when he was here," Aaron says.

Me too, kid. Me too.

Nevertheless, I adjust Aaron's nightlight—which is shaped like a rocket ship—and show myself out.

Then I dash up the stairs and into my bedroom for a five-minute makeover. Just because I've accepted the fact that Gunnar is exiting my life doesn't mean I want to look like a wreck while he does it. I put on a cute little scoop neck top over my jeans. I brush my teeth and my hair and put on some lip gloss.

Then I scrutinize myself in the mirror.

Nice going, that little voice says. *Cute enough to make a point, but not trying too hard, either.*

My phone buzzes with a text. ***I'm downstairs, but I didn't want to hit the buzzer and wake up the kid.***

Gunnar is outside! my hormones shout. But I ignore them, along with that fizz of excitement in my tummy.

I cross the living room and lean on the button that unlocks the front door. My goal is to get rid of him as soon as I can. Then to drink a big glass of lonely girl wine and read a dirty book in bed.

A moment later I open the door to find him standing there with a dozen roses.

Flowers! my hormones shriek. *He loves us!*

If only. "Hi Gunnar. Is this what you wanted to show me?" I ask, taking the bouquet that he's offered.

"Nope. That's just because I miss you." He steps in, closes the door, and gives me a sudden one-armed hug. He drops a kiss to my temple, too.

My hormones light up like horny fireflies on a hot June night.

I step away, carrying the roses to the kitchen, where I grab a vase off the top of the refrigerator and fill it with water. "So what did you want to show me?"

"Yeah! What is it?" yells Aaron from downstairs.

Amused, Gunnar walks over to the top of the stairs, and addresses the kid. "It's just a boring work thing. For the pie shop. I promise you're not missing out."

"Will you play Sorry with me sometime?" my nephew asks.

"Kid, next time I'm in New York, you and I can have a pie shop Sorry date if your mom says it's okay. Now go to sleep."

"Night, Gunnar!" Aaron yells.

"What is this boring pie shop thing?" I ask a few minutes later when we're finally settled on the sofa. I've left a couple feet of distance between us, but the scent of roses is making me a little crazy. I wonder what it would be like to date Gunnar seriously.

Stressful, probably. He has a scary job. And other women would always be throwing themselves at him.

"It's about your rat infestation," Gunnar says, pulling his laptop out of a messenger bag, and setting it on the coffee table. "There are many species of rat, apparently."

"I know that," I say a little too curtly.

"Ah, but I'm not sure you know about *this* kind of rat." He presses a button, bringing a video to life on the screen.

"Is that Saroya?" I ask, leaning forward to watch her stroll into the frame carrying a tool in her right hand. It might be a screwdriver.

She leans over and pokes that thing right through my basement window, making me gasp.

She tucks the tool back into her jacket pocket. Then she leans over again to inspect her work, just as someone's head comes into view at the bakery door.

It's Gunnar's head.

"You saw her!" I blurt. "Oh my God. She planted those rats, right? What did she say she was doing out there?"

"I wish I'd seen the whole thing, honey. But when she showed me the window, she had the balls to complain that it looked trashy. I'm sorry, Posy. I didn't realize what she'd done until I listened to your message."

"How could you?" I can barely wrap my mind around it myself. My breath is coming in fast gasps. "She's out to get me. *Why?* She already got Spalding. Wasn't that her goal?" I feel lightheaded all of a sudden. Nothing makes sense.

"Come here." Gunnar moves closer to me on the sofa and wraps an arm around me.

The brace of his warm, sturdy body calms me down a little. I rest my cheek against his shoulder and take a deeper breath.

"I don't know what her game is. She's not a well person. But you're going to be all right."

"Okay," I say, taking a deep breath against my panic. "But I need to tell her that I'm on to her. And that she can't get away with it."

"That might work," Gunnar says cautiously. "I want to do some more digging, though. There might be a reason she wants to hurt you."

"Besides her being a complete and total psycho bitch?"

"Well, yeah." Gunnar strokes my hair. "I've been looking into her. And I think her mother used to work at Paxton's. Maybe her mother got fired, or something."

"Really?" I gasp. "Is that Saroya's problem?"

"Not sure yet. But I'll find out what I can." He drops a kiss onto my head.

"Thank you," I say, noting my position, which is just a few inches shy of reclining in his lap. I'm supposed to be cutting ties with

Gunnar and looking out for myself. Oops. "Can I have that footage? I'm going to send it to Spalding."

"It's in your email inbox already," Gunnar says.

I extract myself from his embrace and fetch my phone. The email is right there. I save the video to my phone and then write a new email, attaching it. *Spalding, look at this please. It's important.*

Then I tap his number and dial, hoping to leave a voice message.

But the jerk picks up. "Posy! Is something the matter? I thought piemakers went to sleep before now?"

"Usually," I snap. "But tonight I got a very disturbing video off our security system. Spalding, you're not going to like hearing this. But Saroya is trying to interfere with my business. She broke a window, and probably planted vermin on the premises. Then she called the health inspectors—"

"Posy! That's nonsense. Saroya wouldn't—"

"Check your email. I just sent you the proof. And—" my head is practically exploding as I start linking together the possibilities "—she may have been responsible for my break-in, too."

"Posy! This is crazy talk—"

"—Not as crazy as she is. Go check your email." I hang up on him. And then I power my phone all the way down, so he can't call me back.

"Wow," Gunnar says. "Strong move."

It was, and now my hands are shaking. I pace back and forth across the living room rug. "I will not be his doormat any longer. I thought pouring a bottle of vintage champagne over his head in the middle of a fancy restaurant would have gotten him out of my life. But he's still right next door. With his ..." I take a deep breath instead of letting loose with an ugly stream of words. Although Spalding deserves them all.

But Aaron doesn't. And I'd lay odds that he's listening downstairs.

"What's the connection?" I ask. "Between Saroya's mother and the restaurant?"

"All I know is that she used to work there," Gunnar says, standing up beside me, and putting his hands on my shoulders. "But we'll know more soon. And I hate to point this out, but the fact that Saroya is turning out to be a jealous nutter is actually good news."

"How?" I gasp.

"It means that your recent problems are probably unrelated to the criminal that Max is hunting down."

"Oh." I gulp. "I suppose that's a silver lining."

Gunnar pulls me into a hug, and I relax against his broad chest without really meaning to. But it feels so good. His broad hand strokes my back. "I missed you."

"Why?" I scoff. "I'm a wreck. My business is always on the brink of disaster. I get up at five every morning, which isn't all that fun. My ex's girlfriend is trying to sink me. It's just long hours and drama here all the time. You hate my city. And you never wanted to set foot in my shop at all. You don't even like coffee!"

"But I like *you*, in spite of the coffee and the drama. I miss curling up with you after a long day. I miss talking to you on my break."

"You miss the pie," I grumble, not willing to believe it.

"That doesn't make me a bad person," he whispers. "It takes a lot of calories to build all this muscle."

I laugh into his shirt collar. The things he's saying are so seductive to me. I don't really need a man in my life. But I sure want this one, damn it.

"We're not over, you know. This wasn't just a convenient fling."

"Yes, it was," I argue. "It's about to become really inconvenient. You'll see. In a few days you'll be back to your old life, and you'll forget about me."

"Look, I don't have the details figured out yet," he admits. "But I want to try to see you. And if you'd let your guard down for five minutes, you'd want to as well."

Yup, my hormones weigh in. *We're here for this.*

"Tell me we have a chance," he presses. "I probably have to go to California soon. But I want to come back."

"YOU CAN COME BACK!" Aaron yells from downstairs.

Oh boy. "Aaron, get back in that bed. It's late."

"I want to see Gunnar! Are you going to let him come back?"

"Yes!" I yell, just to get rid of him. But who are we kidding? If Gunnar says he wants to see me, I'm not crazy enough to say no.

"Goody," Gunnar says, taking my face in two hands. He leans in, smiling.

His kiss lands softly on my mouth, and it's so wonderful that everything goes dark.

No, wait. Given Gunnar's noise of surprise, I determine that everything really *did* go dark. The power is out.

We break apart, just as a little voice down the stairs says, "Aunt Posy! My nightlight went out!"

"Can you reach your flashlight?" I ask my nephew.

"Sure can," he says. "I'm coming up there."

So much for kisses.

"Does this happen a lot?" Gunnar asks, stroking a thumb across my cheekbone. "Is your electrical on the fritz?"

"Not really," I have to admit. "What if …?" A terrible thought occurs to me. "Saroya did this. Spalding looked at that video and went apeshit on her. And now she's getting even with me."

"Hmm." Gunnar looks thoughtful. I can see his face, because it's never really dark in New York, and light bleeds in through the windows. "How would she get access to the electrical panel?"

"It's a shared space," I whisper. "Spalding has a key to that basement. That's how she planted the rats."

Now here comes Aaron, flashlight in hand, looking for a reason to stay up with the grownups. "I don't want to be alone downstairs. I heard a noise in the hallway."

"You did, huh?" I ask. "What kind of noise."

"A monster, prolly. Can we watch TV until the lights come back on?"

"That's not how power outages work," Gunnar says. "I'm going to go take a look at your electrical box in the basement, okay? Where can I find it, Posy?"

"Oh, you don't have to," I grumble. "I'll do it."

"Hey," he says, catching my hand. "I got this. That's what I've been trying to tell you. I'm around for all of it. The fun, the pie, and also the circuit breakers. You stay put."

Oh my. Gunnar knows just what to say to a girl. "The basement door is just past the mailboxes in the vestibule. Let me grab the key."

I find my purse in the dark and pull out my keychain. "It's this one—on the end."

"Got it," he says, pocketing my keys. "I'll be back in less than ten minutes, okay? If I'm not, I want you to call The Company switchboard and tell them I'm having trouble."

A frisson of fear runs through me, and I cross to where he's standing by the door and lower my voice so Aaron can't hear. He's already playing with my phone on the couch, though. "Be careful," I whisper, putting a hand on Gunnar's chest. "What if she's really cracked?"

"I'll be fine," he says, giving me a quick kiss on the cheek. "Just sit tight for a few minutes and I'll let you know what I find."

I love you. The words are right there, but I gulp them back. It's way too soon.

And anyway, the door is already clicking shut behind him. So I sit beside Aaron on the sofa. "What are you looking at?" I ask him.

"You only have lame games on your phone," he complains. "Maybe we should download a new one."

"Maybe you should go back to bed," I counter. "Your mom could come home any minute and find you up. She'll yell at both of us."

"She won't yell," Aaron argues. "Not *that* much." He starts up a Lego game.

And I let him. Because I'm a softie, and we are in the middle of a power outage.

A minute later, though, I hear a noise on the stairs. "Ginny?" I call, nudging Aaron playfully. "We're up here. Both of us."

But no voice calls out in greeting. I hear heavy footsteps on the stairs. And the hair stands up on the back of my neck. "Ginny?"

The heavy footsteps approach slowly. I grab the phone out of Aaron's hands and fumble for the flashlight setting, then I shine it toward the stairway. A bald man appears there. A *stranger*. Fear freezes me in place. Because he's pointing a gun at us.

"Put down that light," the man says icily. "Do it now."

I drop the phone onto the couch. Then I reach out and shove Aaron to the floor between the coffee table and the sofa. "G-get down."

"Don't move," the man says. And we both freeze. "I won't hurt you if you do exactly as I say." He's arrived at the top of the stairs. And my heart almost fails when I see there's a second man behind him. They both advance slowly. "Whose laptop is that?" the bald man asks. "Your boyfriend's?"

"Y-yes," I stammer. "Take it."

The second man slides forward and grabs it in gloved hands, tucking it into his jacket. He also grabs my phone off the sofa and pockets that.

"You have a land line?" the bald man asks.

"No." I shake my head vigorously.

"Any other phones in the house? The kid have one?"

"No," Aaron says from the floor. I put a hand on his small back, and I notice that we're both shaking.

"Smart watch? Cellular tablet?"

"No. Nothing," gasp.

"Good. Now stand up." I pop up like a jack-in-the-box and do as he asks.

"Good work. Turn around. Hands behind your back. I need to restrain you."

Panic sizzles through me. The idea of my hands tied up makes me want to vomit. But I will hold myself together for Aaron. Slowly, I move my arms. And then I remember the sound of Gunnar's voice telling me what to do. *Brace your fists end to end.*

Quaking, I do it.

The other man advances, and I feel something like a plastic loop tighten around my wrists.

"Sit." I'm maneuvered back onto the sofa. "Now, I want the kid on your lap."

"Come here, sweetie," I say to Aaron, and he wiggles immediately into place, huddling against me.

"Hold still," says the man with the gun, while his silent friend approaches us with a roll of duct tape. "Hands together in front, kid."

Please don't put that on my mouth, I inwardly beg. I'm so afraid right now. I don't know why that's the one thing I don't think I can bear. But somehow it is.

The man stretches out a long length of tape and then wraps it around Aaron's skinny wrists. Then he tapes the two of us together, the tape circling us so many times—around our waists, and then our legs.

It's probably been less than three minutes since they entered the apartment, but it feels like an eternity. I can smell his sweat and his breath and I have never been so scared.

I don't say a word, though. I press my cheek against the back of Aaron's head, and I silently ask for his patience. *I'll get us out of this buddy. I don't know how, but I will.*

Then it happens. The man takes another piece of tape and slaps it over my mouth, ear to ear.

And then he tapes Aaron's.

My nephew whimpers, and big fat tears gather in my eyes, and I blink them away. I can't cry. I can't.

"Listen up," the bald man says, his gun still staring at me with its dark sinister eye. "You don't move. You don't scream. Nobody can hear you anyway, with all these windows closed, and a whole floor between you and the neighbors on three."

I nod, to show I understand how right he is.

"Don't move off that couch until morning. You don't show up in the pie shop tomorrow, and someone will come lookin,' right? You stay silent until then. You understand?"

I nod one more time. I need him to leave before Ginny shows up.

They recede toward the door. "Hurry," the bald man grunts at the other. "He needs you in the basement."

The *basement*. I gag behind the tape. *Gunnar*.

The door closes with a click, and I start moving my mouth right away, fighting the tape. I free my top lip, at least. "Aaron," I whisper. "You can get your mouth open if you try really hard. But we have to help Gunnar. We're going to head for my bedroom."

That's where the panic button is.

"He said not to move!" Aaron says, his mouth already free.

"We're doing this for Gunnar. He needs us."

And so will Ginny, if she happens to come home at just the wrong time.

I inch my butt toward the end of the couch. I'm afraid to lose my balance and fall onto Aaron. I use my knee to force the coffee table a few inches away from us, and it makes a horribly loud creak.

But I don't care. Those men will be halfway to the basement already.

Aiming my torso toward the open rug, I lean forward and rise to my feet. My thighs are screaming because the tape keeps me from straightening up. I start inching along, limping toward the bedroom, Aaron a heavy, destabilizing weight.

"You're strong, Aunt Posy," he says.

I am strong, damn it. Strong enough to get to that panic button. "Work on your hands," I grunt. "Can you get them free?" I wriggle one hand against the other one. I'm not sure there's enough room to get free.

But the panic button is only twenty feet away. Dragging us into the bedroom seems to take forever, but it's probably less than a minute. I can't think about the basement or Gunnar or those men. Just the button. It's on the bedside table. When I get there, I lean heavily against the table and try to figure out how to push it.

"See that button?" I wheeze, still trying to get my hand out of the zip tie. "Let's see who can press it first."

"I can!" Aaron says. "The tape doesn't cover my fingers. Get me closer."

That's when I finally manage to wrench my hand out of the restraints.

Aaron's finger and mine pile onto the button at exactly the same moment.

"It's a tie!" he says happily.

Suddenly, there's a soft red glow in the darkness as the button does its thing. For two seconds, I'm filled with relief.

Then I hear a gunshot. And Aaron bursts into tears.

31

GUNNAR

IT'S pitch dark in the hundred-year-old staircase of Posy's building, so I'm using the flashlight function on my watch to illuminate the shadowy stairs. I ease past the apartments on the third and second floors, listening. But all is quiet.

Meanwhile, my watch is pinging with error messages from the security equipment we installed in the pie shop. *Loss of power Camera One. Loss of power Camera Two,* and so on. If the power is out in the bakery, that means it wasn't just a circuit breaker or two that was flipped.

Someone's cut power to the entire building. I take a second to tap out a message on my watch. ***Power out in Posy's building. I don't like it. Taking a look in the basement.***

I suppose I could wait for backup. But there's a five-year-old kid who needs his nightlight. And It's probably Saroya making trouble with the circuit-breakers.

It gets brighter near the first floor, as the soft glow of the lights from Prince Street filters in through the front window. I haven't heard the front door open or close these past few minutes. And I don't see anyone. Although I can't see the basement door until I've reached the main level.

As I step off the last tread into the vestibule, I turn slowly to face the rear of the building, where the basement door is. But someone is standing there in the shadows.

"Who's there?" I call in a nonthreatening voice.

Two things happen at once. The shadowed person in front of me holds up a high wattage light, blinding me. And the front door wrenches open behind me.

I go for the gun in my waistband holster, getting my hand on the revolver, but I don't shoot, because I haven't identified the threat.

There are moments in everyone's life when split-second decisions will matter. And this is one of them. By the time I turn my head to see who's coming through the door, it's too late. The goon behind me is already attaching his iron hands to my elbows, yanking my arms back into a vice grip. His partner advances toward me with that brutal light held high in the air like a weapon.

It's not Saroya.

I can't raise my arms or move my body. But I *can* angle my hand toward the floor behind me, and fire off a single, deafening round.

The goon behind me screams, and his buddy kicks the gun out of my hand a split second later. I wrench out of his grasp and pinball off the wall to try to break toward the door.

But it's no good. The guy whose foot I shot has not given up. He blocks my path, and his buddy sweeps my feet out from under me. And—worse—the pounding of feet coming down the stairs accompanied by whispered curses tells me the rest of the bad news.

There are four of these guys.

"Don't fucking twitch, or I'll blow off your head right here," pants another large man with a gun as he leaps down the last stairs and into the vestibule. "Your girlfriend will have to clean it up."

I go perfectly still. But I'm rapidly forming several conclusions. First, I fucked up big time. I shouldn't have come here tonight. They were waiting for me. Second—even worse—I never should have left Posy and Aaron alone upstairs.

I push that last thought aside, though, because I can't help Posy until I get out of this jam.

"Get up nice and slow now," the new guy says. "You're going to log into your computer for us."

The fourth guest at this party pulls my laptop out of his jacket and opens the lid. The last time I saw that computer, it was a few feet away from Posy. That was only five minutes ago, though. They couldn't have done much damage upstairs.

"The laptop is biometric," I say carefully. "Once you walk away from me, the machine shuts down." This isn't strictly true, but it could keep me alive. And right now The Company security system alerts should be lighting up more brightly than the Empire State Building.

"Fuck it. We'll just remove the hard drive, then," says the goon-in-chief. "Take him to the basement. We gotta do this quick."

Shit. *My guys better hurry their asses up.*

I'm prodded to my feet and shoved toward the basement door. It's dark down there, and my arms are pinned, making the descent tricky. I reach the bottom and spot a chair and a table waiting. But in my peripheral vision I catch a glimpse of something that makes me cold inside.

One of the goons is pulling on a gas mask. And there's a red ribbon looped over his arm.

I'm hit with so much dread I actually stumble, causing the man holding my arms to yank hard on them. Max says there's nobody braver than a man with nothing to lose.

That's not me anymore. I have everything to lose.

Taking a deep breath, I force myself to walk carefully across the room, taking in my surroundings. The space is lit only by one of the goons' flashlights. But aside from the chair, there's very little down here that I could use as a weapon. I spot that narrow little window Saroya broke—the pane is still damaged.

The men shove me toward the chair.

"Hurry," the boss chides.

As soon as my ass lands on the seat, someone moves behind me and grabs my hands. I make fists, hoping for a zip tie instead of cuffs.

I'm rewarded by the bite of plastic against my skin. Thank fuck. But then someone places a metal canister on the table in front of me. It looks like a miniature oxygen tank.

But there won't be oxygen inside it. I don't know what that substance is, or how fast it can kill me. I only know it won't be pretty.

Now all the goons except the gas mask guy are backing away

from me. This is it. Either I'm going to save myself in a big fucking hurry, or I'm dying in this basement.

I've walked into a trap without even telling Posy that I love her. I missed my fucking chance. But if I survive the next hour, I'm not wasting any more time.

Mr. Gas Mask walks over to the circuit box and flips a switch, probably restoring electricity to the building. A single lightbulb flickers to life over my head. The other men hustle up the stairs.

It's time to make a decision. Am I going to try the stairs, where the goons may be waiting with their guns? Or try the tiny window? I'll only get one chance to get out of here.

Before I make up my mind, things start to happen fast. Mr. Gas Mask walks over and pulls a pin from the canister. I take a deep breath and hold it just as I hear a hiss.

He bolts for the stairs.

"GUNNAR!" shouts someone in the distance.

I hear another gunshot. Followed by more shouting.

The window it is, then. I'm quickly shucking off the zip tie, just as my eyes start to burn. *Holy fuck*. I clamp them closed. I stand up, feel for the chair, and grab it. Raising it blindly into the air, I poke the chair legs in the direction of that window. My lungs are burning, but I hear glass breaking, and I stab at it a few more times, needing to clear as much glass as I can so I can get out of that small space.

It's chaos behind me. I hear muffled shouts from the gas mask guy. Is he trapped down here too?

I drop the chair and risk my eyes for a peek at the window. I've cleared about eighty percent of the glass, and it will have to do. Hopping onto the chair, I tear my palms to shreds at the first touch of the tattered window frame. But I need clean air, and I need it right now.

The gas chokes me anyway, my chest compressing with pain, and I cough and then gag.

Pain tears at my hands, but I ignore it. I've pushed my head through the opening, where I take a gulp of the fresh air.

"GUNNAR!" a voice shouts from somewhere.

"STAY OUT OF THE BASEMENT!" I rasp, my voice shot. I don't know if anyone can hear me.

But then I feel hands clawing at my legs, and an anguished, muffled shout. *The gas mask guy.*

I kick violently, needing another few seconds alone to clear the rest of my body out of this window.

Instead, I hear the loudest gunshot I have ever heard in my life at the same moment that red-hot pain tears through my leg. I gasp, my bloodied hands slipping on the window frame.

There's a tug of war on my body, and so much pain that it ceases to make any sense at all.

Then everything goes black.

Motion. Shouting. Pain.

Posy is speaking to me, but I can't hear her voice. Her eyes are wide and frightened.

Her father puts an arm around her. "Come here, darling, sit down. I'll wait with you." His eyes have an appraising squint that has always annoyed me.

Squinty eyes? That seems important. If only I could remember why.

My father tells me to keep my eye on the catcher. He's calling for a fastball.

My mother smiles.

"I'm waiting right outside," Posy says.

Everything is cold.

32

SCOUT

IT'S BEEN twelve hours since Gunnar was shot in the basement on Prince Street. I can't think too much about it. There's no time for emotion. I have a mission to run.

This morning we're sending Geoff into the nightclub for his book-keeping gig. With Gunnar fighting for his life in the hospital, and Max crazed with worry, and the team short-staffed, the mission falls to me to direct.

Usually, I don't run missions. I'm not a hacker or a techie. My specialty is human nature. If Max needs access to an office or a hotel room, I'm the one he sends inside. No matter how secure the location, a disarming smile from me does the trick. Bending the rules is my superpower.

In the wee hours of the night, though, I broke my own rule.

Max was out of his mind with worry, and raging at the hospital staff. He's never lost a Company operative. And it's breaking him that we might lose Gunnar—his college roommate and dear friend.

We're all upset. But we don't all show it the same way. Max shows his fear by snarling at everyone in his path, including his staff, his friends, and anyone wearing an NYU lab coat.

At the urging of Pieter and Duff, I drove his Triumph over to NYU Medical Center to pick him up from the hospital. Since he doesn't like other people riding his bike, he came outside to give me a piece of his mind.

"What were you thinking?" he'd asked me, standing on the sidewalk looking shredded. "I didn't ask for a lift. And I certainly didn't ask you to ride my bike."

"I was thinking that you're going to be arrested for disturbing the peace in that waiting room if you don't walk away for a few hours. Did you actually *kick* a soda machine? What good is that going to do?"

"They weren't giving me the information," he'd barked.

"Max, get on the fucking bike and go home," I'd begged. "It's two a.m. Get a few hours of sleep and give Gunnar a few hours to recover before you get thrown out of this place."

Gunnar was still in surgery then. The asshole who shot him managed to nick his femoral artery. In spite of Pieter's tourniquet, and Duff's NASCAR driving, Gunnar almost bled to death in the back of the sedan.

He's still unconscious. And the doctors aren't sure yet if they've managed to save his leg.

I'd forced Max's helmet into his hands. "Go home."

"How are you getting back?"

"We both fit on that bike. Or I'll take a cab."

"Get on," he'd snapped.

I rode all the way back to West 18th Street with my arms around Max's angry, sturdy body.

There aren't many people that I trust. But Max is one of them. If I'd been the unlucky person who got shot, I know he'd be kicking vending machines in my hospital waiting room, too.

Back at headquarters, I planned to nab a bunk in the off-duty room and crash. But Max growled at me to come upstairs with him for a drink.

At two a.m. Just the two of us.

That's something we used to do a lot. But we don't anymore. Not for a couple of years.

Max must have forgotten, though. Because he pressed me against the elevator wall and devoured me with angry kisses. I didn't leave his apartment until five in the morning.

I could have said no.

I *should* have said no.

And not because Max is the boss, or because either of us gives a flying fuck about the optics.

The problem is that I give a lot of flying fucks about Max. And sex with him always leaves me feeling raw and vulnerable.

I don't like feeling raw, and I really *hate* feeling vulnerable.

It was a failed mission, anyway. Max is still a wreck this morning as I put the finishing touches on the mission plans in a sixth-floor conference room. "No mistakes. No extra risks," he says curtly.

"Got it," I assure him.

"Nobody goes into that building. But if somebody goes into that building, it's me. You're in the van for this op."

"Max! You're going to the hospital. You're not part of this mission." Forget the sex. Now I just want to punch him for treating me like a child.

"I'm going. Not joking, Scout. Argue again and you can watch from the control room."

Yikes. "Has there been any news?" Has there been some terrible development at the hospital that nobody's telling me?

He shakes his head slowly. "I'm calling in some specialists."

"Great idea."

I've heard this already, though. The Company rumor mill says that Max summoned vascular surgeons from Johns Hopkins and from Harvard. He also summoned a plastic surgeon for the cuts on Gunnar's face, where the broken window glass shredded him. He even summoned the mayor of New York.

Okay, that last thing is probably just gossip.

"Did we get anything off the cameras last night?" Max asks.

"It's a nightclub, Max. There were two hundred people on the cameras. But nobody who looks like our guy."

"How's our bookkeeper this morning?"

"I'm going in to check on him right now. How's Posy doing, by the way?"

He shakes his head. "Not good. She won't leave the hospital."

"You could go and take her place," I try. Lord knows this mission will be less stressful if he leaves me in peace.

Max gives a quick shake of his head, letting me know that I'm out of luck. "I was working on him, you know."

"Working on ... Gunnar?"

Max nods miserably. "I was going to suggest he relocate to New York. God knows who I'd find to run the California office. But he could have had a life here."

"He still *can*," I say firmly. "Stop it already." I give him a little nudge out of my way, and then head into an interview room, where Geoff the bookkeeper is waiting. Pieter has already outfitted him with a tiny camera affixed to the strap on his backpack. "Almost ready?" I ask him.

Geoff shrugs, looking terrified. He knows that two of Aga's men were arrested last night, after our operative shot one of them in the center of his bulletproof vest. But one man escaped. And one man died trying to get out of the basement window after Gunnar.

His gas mask failed. He died by the same chemical weapon he was trying to use on Gunnar.

"Geoff, I'll say this one more time. You don't have to go in there. You still have a choice."

He shakes his head, picking up a dry erase marker and writing on the whiteboard. *The State Department won't relocate me if I don't go through with it.*

"That's probably true," I admit. "But you have other options."

If I don't do this, they go free. And they'll kill me anyway. Let's go, he writes on the board. *I'm tired of being afraid*.

I get up and open the door for him.

O—¶

Duff is behind the wheel, as usual. I'm sitting in the control seat, watching the monitors.

Max is sitting on the bench, grinding his teeth.

On the monitor in front of me I watch Geoff walk up a flight of stairs. The tiny camera is so good that I can see dust motes in the air when he walks past a window.

Come on, I inwardly beg. *Let's see a terrorist in high rez*.

Geoff pushes open a door, then arrives at another one. He presses a buzzer to ask for admittance.

Nothing happens. He presses the button again.

Geoff waits, and I age about three years.

Then he reaches out and tries the doorknob. I see it turn in his hand. I'm holding my breath as he opens the metal door.

It's brighter inside than I'm expecting. Sunlight blazes into the camera, dappling everything with a bright white light. So it takes me a moment to register what I'm seeing.

An empty room. Nothing in it. Nothing on the walls. Nothing on the desks. All the file cabinets are standing open.

Geoff makes a startled noise.

Our terrorist is gone, along with all the evidence that he was ever here.

When I turn to look at Max, his head is in his hands.

33

POSY

I SPEND forty-eight hours at the hospital before Max orders Duff to take me home to rest.

"You don't want to get me in trouble, do you?" Duff asks, batting his eyelashes at me. "Go home and get some sleep, or you're gonna get me fired."

Since I'm asleep on my feet, I succumb to this bit of trickery.

The next morning, though, I get up and shower before heading out to go right back to the hospital.

The blood is gone from the front vestibule of my building. Max's guys swooped in and cleaned it up, along with the broken glass and the lethal poison gas in my basement.

This time I didn't even blink when Max said he'd take care of everything.

Gunnar is in stable condition now. According to the text on my phone, his leg has good vascular flow, which is supposed to be good news. But as I step out onto the street and scan for a taxi, it's not comforting enough.

I need to see him open his eyes, and I need to hear his voice. It's been two and a half days since he was gassed and shot. They don't know yet how else he might have been affected. His lungs. His eyes. His sharp mind. It's all a big question mark.

"Posy!"

Still jumpy from the other night's horrors, I whirl around. But it's only Teagan, sticking her head out of the door of the pie shop. My heart still pounds as I ask, "Is everything okay?"

"Fine," she says. "But I wanted to send you off with some donuts for Gunnar, just in case he's ready to eat today. Here." She holds a bag toward me. "There's a half dozen in here. Plus two very hot lattes, courtesy of the new guy that Max sent in. You can share the other one with whoever's on duty."

"Thank you," I say quietly.

"Text me if there's any news." Teagan is full of remorse. She feels terrible that she brought trouble to my door, and that Gunnar is fighting for his life.

And I'm trying to be civil about the whole thing. "I'll let you know if he wakes up."

"Please. I'll be thinking of both of you." She gives me a wave and disappears inside.

In between raging at the medical staff, Max sat me down and told me as much as he could about Teagan and her boyfriend's troubles. "Geoff is at a safe house now, until I can find him a job on the West Coast, under a different name," he'd told me.

But the terrorist they were hunting has left New York anyway. Max has a source who told him the guy slipped out of a private airport in Pennsylvania. So Teagan and Geoff are probably safe.

At any rate, Teagan insisted on coming in to work to help me keep the pie shop afloat. While Ginny is busy spending all her time with her traumatized child. Poor Aaron is still rattled.

"Aunt Posy is my hero," he keeps telling my sister. "She got her hands out of handcuffs."

We are all struggling. I haven't even set foot in the pie shop either. My new barista is doing the best she can, but I'm still short-handed.

Max is helping with that, too. He flew in a famous barista—some guy from Portland. And he hired a pastry chef from the Culinary Institute of America on 18th Street to fill in for me.

The one person who's surprised me with his attentiveness has been my father. Dad keeps showing up at the hospital to see how I am. He offered to send Aaron to therapy, and he even asked me if I needed any money to hire extra labor for my business.

It's funny, but I never wanted his help with anything before. And I couldn't imagine turning my back on the pie shop. But with Gunnar in the hospital, I just don't care anymore. I'll let my dad and Max handle whatever they're willing to handle, just so I can spend more time with the person who really matters.

Gunnar can't die. Our story isn't over yet.

I stick my hand in the air and hail a taxi. "NYU Medical Center please." I need to see my man.

When I arrive, it takes me a little while to find Gunnar's new hospital room. It's on a special floor for important people—with paneled walls, and a hush that makes it feel more like a hotel than a hospital.

Luckily, I'm already on the list of approved visitors. That's probably Max's doing.

I arrive outside Gunnar's door, which is open. Duff sits quietly in a chair next to the bed. I can't see Gunnar's face, though. He has a bandage on his cheekbone, and another on his jaw. His eyes are wrapped, too. But his chest rises and falls with each deep breath, and the sight of it calms me down.

He's still here. He's still with me. Now he just has to wake up and be okay.

I'm just about to step into the room when my phone starts to ping with a flurry of texts from Spalding, of all people. *Posy, please call me. Saroya has gone missing.*

Oh please. Like I'm supposed to care about that? But the texts keep rolling in.

You were right. She was trying to harm your shop.

And she wasn't pregnant, Posy. She lied about that.

Who lies about that?

I'm beginning to think she's unhinged. It sounds crazy, but I'm beginning to wonder if she even sought me out to break us up. Remember how she just showed up and said she worked for my health insurance company? I just got off the phone with them. They never sent her!!!!

So that's what it looks like when Spalding gets a clue. It looks like four exclamation points.

I don't know what to tell you, I reply. *That sounds deeply suspicious. I can't even guess what she has against me. But this is your problem, not mine. You're the one who decided that sticking your thumb drive into her USB port was more important than our marriage.*

There's no need to be crude, Posy.

I know it's petty. But I take a quick photo of my middle finger and text it to him. Because I really don't see what's wrong with a little crudeness right about now.

Duff laughs, and I look up to see him watching me. "Rough morning?"

I'm just about to answer him, when I catch sight of Gunnar's hand. It's moving! He raises it slowly toward his eyes.

I let out a gasp, and Duff jerks his chin toward his colleague. "Whoa there!" he says, catching Gunnar's hand as it reaches the bandages. "Careful."

"Duff?" Gunnar rasps.

And I'm instantly crying. My eyes spout tears, and it's all I can do to muffle the sob that's escaping from my chest.

"Yeah man," Duff says. "Hang on a sec. Let me find someone who works here."

"Why can't I open my eyes?" Gunnar asks, sounding disoriented.

I cry harder. Silently.

"There's tape and bandages. Don't panic, okay?" Duff strides toward me, and I step back to get out of the way. I take a deep breath and try to calm down. I'm no use to Gunnar as a weepy mess.

But he *spoke*. He's okay!

I cry some more, just because.

A grey-haired nurse has already come running. She bustles into Gunnar's room and lays a firm hand on his arm. "Mr. Scott, you're recovering from a major surgery. Try to hold still, okay? We're paging your doctor."

"So thirsty," he says with a groan.

"Would you like a sip of water? I've got a straw."

"Please," he whispers.

"Careful," she says, angling his head up a few degrees. "If you cough, it will hurt."

He takes a small sip. Then he takes a bigger one, and has trouble swallowing. I hear him cough, and then immediately groan.

"Oh honey," the nurse says. "What did we just talk about? Here's an ice chip." She slips it between his lips when he stops coughing. "And how is your pain?"

"Fine," he grunts around the ice.

"Then I'll go find that doctor, and he'll take a look at your eyes." She hustles out again.

I dig a napkin out of the donut bag and blot my tears away. Duff catches my eye and winks.

"My throat feels terrible," Gunnar rasps. "Like there's ground glass in it."

"Maybe there is," his colleague says.

"What happened?"

"Well, I don't know how much you remember, but you got shot right before I hauled you out of that basement. You woulda bled out right there in the alley if Pieter didn't give you a tourniquet."

"A tourniquet ..." He pauses. "... Upper leg?"

"Yeah," Duff says, his voice husky. "You had a major surgery, and it's gonna add a few seconds to your hundred-meter dash, let me tell you."

He swallows hard. "It's still there, though? The leg?"

"Still there," he says cheerfully. "Although it was touch and go for a while. And Max almost got thrown out of the hospital at one point."

"Why?"

"For yellin' at doctors."

"It was that ugly, huh?"

"Yup!" Duff says. "Your GSW only shredded soft tissue, which was lucky. But it nicked a major artery. So you could have easily bled to death. You remember asking me a few weeks ago to take you for a spin on the racetrack?"

"Uh huh."

"Well, I took you for a real spin through Manhattan. Too bad you don't remember it. I hit eighty miles an hour on Third Avenue."

"Jesus. Did the pedestrians on Third Avenue survive it?"

"Sure! Like steerin' around cones on the raceway! And it worked, didn't it? You're still here."

"Thanks man." He yawns. "How long have I been here?"

"Two and a half days."

"Did anyone else get hurt?"

"The other guy down in that basement didn't make it out. And there was blood in the vestibule. Did you hit someone, or was it yours?"

"I shot at someone's foot while I was trying to evade them."

"You must have hit him. One guy escaped, two were arrested. They shot at Phelps—he was wearing a vest."

Gunnar takes that in. "So the only one who died was the one that was actually supposed to kill me?"

"Yeah man."

"Okay. Now tell me about Posy. They got my laptop from her. Is she—" He hesitates. "Tell me the truth. Is she okay?"

"You can ask her yourself." Duff gets out of the chair. "I'll be out front."

I enter the room at last, my tears mostly dry. There are so many things I want to say to Gunnar, but right this second, I don't know where to start. I set the bakery bag down and then pick up his bandaged hand. "Hi." It comes out rough.

"Hi," He says, closing his fingers around mine. "You okay?"

"I'm fine," I say, but my throat is closing up, so I'm not very convincing. "I've been so worried about you."

"Hey," he says, giving my hand a squeeze. "I'm still here. I don't know about my vision. And it's possible that my ass doesn't look quite as flawless as you're used to."

"Gunnar," I squeak. "You're still perfect."

"I'm sorry, honey," he says. "I'm not even close. And I never should have left you alone that night."

"We're fine. I'm fine. I just need you to get better."

"They got my laptop," he says. "That means they were in your apartment."

"Only for a few minutes," I say, downplaying my terror. "And I have to thank you for teaching me how to get out of zip ties. Never knew that would be so useful."

Gunnar makes a noise of dismay, and the machine that's monitoring his pulse starts beeping faster.

"Hey—I'm sorry. That was supposed to make you laugh. I hit the panic button. One of your guys was upstairs within minutes."

He grips my hand more tightly. "Holy—"

"Hello, Mr. Scott!" booms a new voice coming through the door. "I'm Doctor Warren, and I'm here to check on those eyes. You had some chemical irritation."

Gunnar blows out a breath. "*Chemical irritation* is too polite a term for whatever gas was in that basement with me." He shivers. "How bad is it?"

"Well, let's take a look. We bandaged your eyes to keep them lubricated. Excuse me, please." The doctor addresses me. "Would you like to step outside?"

"She stays," Gunnar says in a firm voice.

"There's a homemade donut in it for you," I say, trying not to seem like a pest. But I'm not leaving this room until they drag me out. Instead, I skirt around the bed, trying to get out of the way. From the other side, I lay my hand on Gunnar's strong wrist.

Then I say a silent prayer. *Please don't be blind.* It won't make me love him any less. But I want Gunnar to have his sight.

It seems to take forever for the doctor to unwind the bandage around Gunnar's head. And I hold my breath as he pulls the gauze away from his eyelids. "Hold on a moment. There's some mucus I can blot away." He dips a cotton ball into something and dabs at Gunnar's eyelids.

I run out of air, and take a gulping breath, and Gunnar squeezes my hand.

"All right," the doctor says. "You'll probably be light sensitive."

Gunnar's beautiful eyes flip open. They're red, and they look irritated. But he turns his chin right away and smiles at me. "Hi, gorgeous."

My own eyes well up immediately.

"Oh baby, don't cry. I'm okay."

"I kn-know," I stammer. "But I was so worried."

The doctor pulls out one of those eye charts and holds it up. "Could you cover one eye and read the third row, please?"

"Z Q R ..." Gunnar does pretty well at this quick-and-dirty eye test.

"You'll still need to make an ophthalmology appointment for a thorough exam after you're released," the doctor cautions.

"Uh huh," Gunnar says. "Thanks." I can almost hear him dismissing the idea. "Thank you." The doctor takes his leave. And then the brave, crazy man in the hospital bed says, "Did you say something about donuts?"

"Yes," I say, swatting at my tears. "Teagan is beside herself with worry."

"She's at work? Is that safe?"

I explain that Geoff is in hiding and that the criminal mastermind Max is hunting has disappeared into the wind.

"Fuck," Gunnar says, relaxing against his pillow. "Max must be in a *state*. Is there a button somewhere to sit me up?"

The nurse comes clucking back in just then. "You want to sit up? It may cause too much pressure on your wound."

"Let's find out," Gunnar insists. "I heard there were donuts."

"You haven't been cleared for solid food," she says, arming herself with a remote control device, and pressing a button that slowly raises Gunnar's head. "You'll start with a clear broth. Maybe a popsicle."

"Did I have gut surgery?"

She shakes her head.

"Then a donut won't kill me. I almost died, nurse. Are you really going to stand between me and a homemade donut?"

"You should be more respectful to the woman who's in charge of bathing you," she says, straightening his pillow. "Here." She angles the swiveling table into place over his lap. "At least have a few more sips of water first. And go slowly, okay? You had a long surgery and respiratory distress. You don't recover from that overnight."

"How long will it take?" he asks. "Tell it to me straight."

"Well ..." She sighs. "Wound care will be important for the first couple of weeks. But then your surgeon will have some strong opinions about the rest. He'll give you a timeframe for when you can put weight on that leg. Two months, maybe? Or longer if you need a second surgery."

"Yikes."

"How's your pain in this position?" she asks, patting his good knee. "Scale of one to ten?"

"A three," he says.

"Let me know if it gets worse." She turns to leave, then stops to look back at him. "And don't you dare get any powdered sugar in those bandages on your palms."

"I'll feed it to him," I offer.

She rolls her eyes. "Lucky man."

"You know it!" Gunnar chuckles as she disappears. "Okay, baby. Hit me with a bite of donut. What's the special today?"

I retrieve the bag and open the box. "She sent you apple cider and ginger cinnamon."

"Let's have both, then." He taps the table with one of his bandaged hands.

As I spread a napkin onto the table and reach into the box, my emotions are bouncing around faster than the bonus level of a pinball game. I feel a rush of joy that I'm here beside him. And a deep, cold fear for what could have happened.

Don't forget about us! my hormones sing. *Gunnar may be temporarily out of commission, but we'll be waaaaaiting!*

Today I recognize this symphony of emotions for what it really is. *Love*. That's the sum of joy and fear and desire all together. It's terrifying. I never meant to fall in love right after leaving a bad marriage. And Gunnar may well decide he's had enough of New York, given the way things turned out.

Love doesn't care, though. Love is hopeful anyway. Love sets out two donuts on the table and gently breaks off a bite-sized piece. And love lifts it to Gunnar's waiting smile.

"Mmm," he says as the ginger falls on his tongue. "Marry me."

I let out a shaky laugh, because I'm overemotional right now. "I'll give Teagan your regards."

"No," he says, licking his lips as I raise the straw to his mouth. "I don't want to marry Teagan, or this donut. Although the donut would be higher up on the list. Someday I'm going to ask you to marry me, Posy. This bachelor is turning over a new leaf."

"*Gunnar,*" I breathe, breaking off another bit of donut. "They must have you hooked up to some pretty great drugs."

He pins me with those cool eyes. "You don't understand. I came over to your apartment to tell you that we weren't over. And I said it was because we were having so much fun. I don't know why I had to be locked into a basement with a weapons-grade poisonous gas to be able to say this. But I love you. And I want us to be together."

GUNNAR LOVES US! my hormones shout.

"Honey ..." I pull one of those coffees Teagan sent me out of the bag and open the lid, because I need coffee for this conversation. "Don't try to plan your life twenty minutes after waking up from your gunshot wound surgery."

"Aw." He reaches out a bandaged hand and catches my cheek. "I promised myself that if I got out of that basement, I'd tell you how I really feel."

"But—"

"But nothing. Sometimes a guy needs to have a reckoning moment to get his priorities in order. Tell you what. I'll get myself back into shape and then ask you again. Looks like I'm not going back to California anytime soon. I'm trapped here with you, baby. Use me." He gives me flirty eyes, and then—my weakness—that loverboy smile.

"Damn you for being hot even when you're in a hospital bed."

Gunnar reaches up to fiddle with his hospital gown, tugging the halves apart a little.

"What are you doing?"

"This part of me doesn't have any holes in it. So I'm using my best assets to convince you." He takes a sniff of the air. "Is that a cappuccino? Who made it?"

"Some guy named Rico that Max flew in to cover the pie shop."

Gunnar lets out a bark of laughter, but it makes him cough. And he doesn't stop until I give him another sip of water. "Rico the barista?" he asks finally. "Lots of tats? Gruff voice?"

"That's the guy."

"He taught me everything I know. I worked my ass off for that guy. You know why? Because I wanted to impress you. I've always wanted that."

"*Gunnar.*" I don't know what to do with that.

"Hey—I have a question. And I need an honest answer."

"Okay?" I'm afraid of what it might be. I take a nice gulp of Rico's excellent cappuccino and prepare myself.

"Tell it to me straight. Is Rico's coffee better than mine? You always seemed to appreciate the lattes I brought you before we opened each day. But a guy needs to make sure his girl isn't faking it."

I choke on the coffee. "Gunnar!"

"Just taste it again and tell me if it's better than mine. Do I have to take more lessons with Rico to convince you I'm serious about you?"

"This is the craziest conversation we've ever had. This coffee is excellent." He frowns, so I hurry to finish my thought. "But it turns out that technique isn't as important as I thought. There's nothing quite like the sight of you—with that loverboy smile—bringing me my first cup of the day. When you used to open up the cafe, and bring me a latte?" I look over my shoulder to make sure we're alone. "I felt it *everywhere*."

Gunnar lights up like he's just won the Stud of the Year contest. "Excellent answer, baby. But I still need to know how I stack up. Let me taste it." He leans forward, asking for a sip.

"Seriously? You hate coffee."

"I haven't eaten in two and a half days, and it smells good. Just try me."

So I hand it over.

34

GUNNAR

TAKING care not to spill it, I take the travel mug from Posy's hands.

My girl is doing her best to keep it together. I can tell she's rattled. And I probably look terrifying, with a hole in my leg and a bandaged face.

But I hold her eyes and tip the cup towards my mouth. It's bad form to spill coffee onto your bare chest when you're trying to woo a girl. As the cup reaches me, I get a hit of that fresh coffee smell. And then the hot liquid washes over my taste buds, treating me to a wash of slightly aromatic acidity that's immediately softened by the creamy milk.

And it's … Wow. "That's delicious!"

"What?" Posy laughs. "Gunnar! You tease."

"No, baby. I love it." Another gulp goes down my throat, and the heat feels wonderful against my aching throat. "I haven't had coffee since college. Maybe I should have given it more of a chance."

"College?" Posy tilts her head to the side. "You don't mean dining hall coffee, do you?"

"Well, sure. But it was free, you know?"

"*Honey.*" Posy gapes at me. "You say you don't like coffee. But your benchmark is that brown pisswater from the college urn? That's like trying Velveeta and deciding you don't like cheese."

"I guess there's still a thing or two I could learn from you. Here." I force myself to hand the cup back. "I don't want to hog it all."

"Oh, don't worry." She bends over and grabs a second cup out of her bag. "They sent me with two. The other one was to share."

I reach down and pick up the donut as best I can with my clumsy, bandaged hands. Then I take a nice bite and wash it down with Rico's cappuccino. "Goddamn, it's good to be alive."

"You never say things like that." Posy says. "It's the drugs. All of a sudden you like coffee, and you're full of crazy ideas. If you tell me you actually like New York, I'm going to ask the nurse to call a psychiatrist."

Aw, my girl still doesn't believe that I'm serious about her. But that's okay, I'm going to convince her. "Come here. Come closer."

"Why?" Posy steps in. "Do you need something?"

"Yeah, this." I lean over, which makes my leg wound move in an uncomfortable way. But fuck it. I kiss her neck anyway. "It's not the drugs, baby. A guy can change his stripes when he realizes what's important."

She wraps an arm around me and holds me tightly. "I need you, crazy man," she whispers.

"I need you, too."

We stay like this a long time. My leg is throbbing, but I don't care. Posy is here. And she brought donuts.

Eventually, though, there's a commotion in the hallway. "Why was I not told when he woke up?" demands an arrogant voice.

Then Max practically skids into the room. He takes one look at me in the bed, and his shoulders relax. No—all of him relaxes. He bends over and grabs his knees, letting out a loud gust of air.

"Huh," I remark. "I guess a few people were worried about me."

"You have no idea," says Carl Bayer, striding in after his son. "Thank you for deigning to regain consciousness today. We were all about ready to sedate Max."

"We sure were!" yells Scout from the hallway. "I have a tranquilizer gun at the ready."

Max stands up, looking affronted. "Haven't lost an employee yet, Gunn. What were you thinking, walking into that trap?"

"Oh, he wasn't," Carl says. "It happens to everyone at one point or another. Love makes you stupid. Doesn't make him a bad person."

"I am sorry, though," I tell both of them. "I should have waited for backup. Hell, I should have waited forty-eight hours to see Posy. It seemed really urgent at the time." I turn and give her a big smile. "Sorry baby. I just really missed you. But I don't think I made the impression I was trying for."

"Oh, Gunnar." She gives me a soft glance in reply. And it's almost worth the gunshot wound.

Okay, it's probably not worth a gunshot wound. But it's still nice.

There's another bossy voice in the hallway now. "Is this where he's been moved? That's a good sign, right?"

"Shit," I whisper. That voice is not a welcome surprise. "Is that ...?"

"The mayor," Posy whispers. "It's the weirdest thing. He keeps showing up to see how you're doing. I don't get it. Maybe he wants to look tough on crime?"

"Max!" I groan. "Seriously?"

"It was me," Carl says quickly.

"You knew?" I watch the door in spite of myself. I'm not interested in seeing that man. Not much, anyway.

"Sure, kid. I do a thorough background check of everyone at the Company. Wasn't even hard."

And there he is, darkening the doorway of my hospital room in a tasteful charcoal suit and a fedora, looking every inch the aristocrat. His eyes snap onto mine, and he looks me up and down. Then he sighs.

You could hear a pin drop in the room. Everyone's staring at him. He glances around at them after a moment, then has the decency to look sheepish. "Hello," he says stiffly. "It's good to see you are on the mend."

"Is it?" I struggle to keep the bitterness out of my voice. "Aren't you glad I didn't need a kidney? That would have been a tough decision, right? And hard to explain to the family."

"Holy hell!" Posy says beside me. "*You're* Gunnar's father? Seriously?" Her voice rises in anger. She's like a steam valve that's breaking under pressure. "You're the asshole who was too selfish to take his own child to a baseball game in Shea Stadium? HE'S STILL NEVER BEEN!"

"Posy," I chuckle. "It's fine. I could buy a ticket if I wanted to go."

"It's *not* fine! I voted for him! TWICE!" she shouts at my father. "Our beloved mayor. What a load of crap you've been spinning."

A uniformed police officer—probably assigned to my father's security detail—pokes his head into the room. "Everything okay in here, sir?"

"Everything is NOT OKAY," Posy yelps.

"I'm fine, Schultz," the mayor says. He takes off his hat in a gesture of defeat, and without it he looks a couple decades older. "My political successes have always been greater than my personal ones. You aren't even my only kid who hates me. Everyone I'm close to gets there eventually. And I know I haven't been a real father to you. But there's still one thing I can teach you."

"What's that?" I ask, because I can't think of a thing. Except for the stats of every Mets player since I gave up watching baseball.

"Don't ignore the people who matter in your life, because you'll miss them when they're gone. You even took a bullet to turn your woman's electricity back on."

"Not intentionally," I mutter.

"I've heard worse reasons. And in my lifetime, I've taken a lot more risks for my constituents than I ever did for my family." He sighs. "I regret that sometimes. And, sure, I'm a little relieved that you don't need a kidney. My organs are probably too pickled with gin at this point to do you any good."

"But what happens when *you* need a kidney?" Posy pipes up. "Did you ever think of that?"

"Good question!" calls Scout from the hallway. "Men never think this shit through."

I want to laugh. But instead I reach out and hook my uninjured pinky around Posy's, just to let her know that her loyalty moves me.

"Guess I'd better hope I never need one," the mayor says. He replaces his hat on his head. "Be well, Son. I'm glad to see you have so many people who've got your back."

"We do, sir," Carl says.

He turns to go. "If you need anything, though, go ahead and call me. I'll answer."

Oh, like that will ever happen. "Thanks," I grunt.

My nurse struts back in just then. "The mayor of New York was here to see you?" Her eyebrows practically disappear into her silver hair. "Aren't we fancy. But now I need everyone to clear out of here. You can have one more minute with your wife before we send you down for a couple of tests."

"I'm not his—" Posy says, but it's too late. The nurse has marched out again.

"Well then. Take care," Carl says.

"Thank you." I lean back against the pillow and take another sip of my new best friend. "This is really invigorating," I say, swirling it around in the travel mug. "Who knew?"

"Literally everyone," Max says. Obviously now that I'm not dead, he's back to being his usual know-it-all self. "I'll be back tonight to check in on you. Got a lead to chase down, first."

"What is it?" I ask, because I can't help myself.

"I heard that Xian Smith was detained at the border. He was in a limo headed to Canada."

"*Really*. That's interesting."

"Only if it's true. See you soon. Duff is stationed right outside, if you need anything." He gives me a wave and slips out the door.

I'm alone again with Posy, which is a nice way to be. "Is there anything I can do for you?" she asks.

"Just come here a minute." I beckon to her. "That's all I ever needed from you."

Smiling, she steps closer.

"I mean, it would be great if you could get me out of here."

"That's going to have to wait," she says, carefully draping an arm around me. "But as soon as they let me, I'll take you home and make a fuss over you."

"Aw, that sounds nice. Will there be pie?"

"There will. And I hate to point this out, but it seems like you're stuck in your least favorite city until you heal up."

"That's okay with me, so long as I can get more of your attention. I'll try not to hate New York as much as I used to."

She kisses me on an unbandaged part of my face. "Well, your disdain for my city makes more sense now. When is the jerk's term up, anyway?"

"At the end of the year." That's when his influence over the city will wane. It's a shame I let his influence over me affect me as much as I did. "Fuck it. I'm asking Max for a permanent transfer to Manhattan. Effective immediately."

Posy lets out a squeak of surprise just as I capture her pretty face between my fingertips and kiss her. Right on the mouth.

35

POSY

Seven Months Later

I'M LATE, damn it. So when I see the elevators at the SoHo Luxe starting to close, I put on a burst of speed. "Hold the elevator," I gasp, skating on my dressy shoes toward the closing gap.

A hand shoots out to stop the progression of the doors.

"Thank you," I gasp as I step over the threshold.

"What floor, miss?" asks the woman. She's wearing a maid's pinafore and carrying a stack of towels.

I'm instantly suspicious. She may be an operative in disguise. I know things.

"Um, rooftop. Thank you," I say, and she presses the button.

We ride up two floors before the doors part and she gets out.

I can't help myself. I press the *door open* button, then stick my head out and watch her walk down the hallway.

She joins two other women in maid's uniforms, hands one of them the towels, and then grabs a vacuum cleaner and heads into an open room.

Okay. She's probably part of the hotel's cleaning staff. But ever since I met Gunnar, I look at life just a little differently. You never know when a guy who looks to be sleeping behind the wheel of his car is really on a stakeout. Or if the elevator's light fixture is secretly reading the texts on your phone.

I don't really know why Gunnar wanted to have dinner here tonight. He only said that it was perfectly safe because Xian Smith hasn't been seen in New York for months, not since the Canadian authorities let him go after only a ten minute detention. "Max was beside himself. He wanted to nail that guy. But we don't have to worry about bumping into him at the SoHo Luxe."

So here I am, stepping out of the elevator at five minutes past seven o'clock on the Friday night before Memorial Day. And the first thing I see is the deepening sky over Manhattan, with a million twinkling lights set against it.

"Wow," I gasp. "Nice view." It's been years since I was up here. Late in my marriage, my life had become a grind. I hadn't even realized it.

But not any longer. With a quick scan of the elegant dining tables, I zero in on the hot guy who's waiting for me in the corner. And then I hustle over there.

Gunnar catches sight of me and rises from his chair.

He's still rehabbing the injured leg. He walks with a limp, and running doesn't work so well just yet. But he works out with a physical therapist twice a week and does upper body work in the gym with his pals at Company headquarters.

But he's shockingly healthy, and awfully upbeat for a man who had two more surgeries after his incident. "You're late, baby," he says. "I thought maybe you were going to stand me up."

"Never," I say, although I know he's just teasing. "The puppet show ran longer than I expected." It was my afternoon to hang out with Aaron because Ginny had an art class. I've scaled back my hours in the pie shop. Originally, my goal was to be there for Gunnar as he healed. I moved into his apartment so he wasn't reliant on a visiting nurse.

It's just that I never left. We're having too much fun together. And I only work at the pie shop five days a week these days, and reasonable hours. The rest of the time I spend with my family or with Gunnar. And sometimes both at once.

"How was your day?" I sit down and drape the napkin over my lap. "Nice table, by the way. You must have given the hostess your best loverboy smile."

"Isn't it though?" He gives me one, too. "My day was just fine. I'm working on a camera that reads sound waves off distant light fixtures."

"Dare I ask why?" Some of the things Gunnar is working on for Max right now are so intricate that I get lost as soon as he tries to explain.

"When you talk, the sound waves you're making wiggle everything around you, even if you can't see it with the naked eye. But we're building a super sensitive video relay that measures these vibrations off a lightbulb—because those are easy to see at a distance. And Max's nerds will write a piece of software that translates the lightbulb's wiggles into an audible recording of the distant conversation."

"Yikes," I say as the waiter approaches.

"Evening, ma'am," he says. "Can I bring you a drink to start?"

"Why yes! Someone told me that you guys make an excellent margarita."

The waiter flashes me his own tip jar smile. "That's absolutely correct. I recommend the Conmemorativo margarita on the rocks. Would you care for salt?"

"Yes please," I say easily. He takes Gunnar's order, too, before walking away.

"He upsold you on the tequila with that smile," Gunnar says, crossing his arms. "You were putty in his hands."

"Does his technique make you jealous?" I whisper.

"Not in the least." He gives me a warm smile. "Thank you for coming out with me tonight."

"You know me. I'm easy." Although, to be honest, I still have a mild case of PTSD from the last time a man made a reservation for an expensive meal and then told me he wanted to *discuss his plans*. "I don't know why you picked this place, though. Did you want to tell me something about the hunt for *you know who*?"

Gunnar shakes his head. "No way. We're here for the magical view of my new favorite city. And for the margaritas."

I beam, because Gunnar isn't really kidding about loving New York. He's thrown himself into some new projects at work, and we've been dining our way across Manhattan.

"There's three things I want to discuss with you."

"Three?"

He reaches across the table and covers my hand with his. "Can I just say upfront that none of them involves opening our relationship? Don't panic, okay?"

"Who's panicking?"

He grins.

"I guess I'm not that good an actor."

"You know why we used to bicker behind the bar?" he asks, squeezing my hand.

"Because you were a slick, overconfident know-it-all?"

"No." Gunnar laughs. "Because we're so much alike. We both like to be in control of every situation. And it freaks us out when we can't be."

"Fair enough. Drop your bombs already. I don't like mysteries."

He reaches into a pocket and pulls out a small envelope. Inside are two tickets. "Check this out. I just received them today." He holds them near the candle flickering on the table, so that I can read the print.

Mets vs. Rockies. July 17th. Mayor's Executive Box Seats.

I gasp. "That's your birthday."

"It is. We're both invited."

"Will he be there?" I have to ask.

"Yes, actually. I asked the same thing."

We both crack up. The mayor has reached out to Gunnar a number of times these last few months. He's asked him to lunch and he even introduced him to his other two grown children. Gunnar said the first meeting was awkward as hell. But now he and his half-brother play pool together every other Thursday at a divey billiards club in Alphabet City. "It turns out that my half-brother doesn't like rich guy games very much either," he's told me. "Go figure."

"Well, that's fun. I'd love to go to the baseball game with you. What else do you want to tell me?"

The waiter turns up again with our drinks, though. And then we order dinner. So it's a few minutes before we're alone again.

"Look," Gunnar says, still holding my hand. "I've been waiting for this."

The sky is a brilliant shade of pink, and all of New York looks like a fairy tale. "It's beautiful. But what does that have to do with—" I catch sight of Gunnar's free hand, and the little velvet box he's holding. "Oh *my*."

"Posy," he says. "I brought you up to this rooftop so you'd know that I've really come around on my feelings about New York. I'm happy to stay here forever, so long as you're by my side. Will you be my wife?" He opens the box with his thumb, and there's a beautiful emerald cut diamond ring inside.

I'm literally speechless. If you'd asked me a year ago whether I'd ever marry again, I would have laughed in your face.

But nobody's laughing now.

"Yes," I gasp. "Wow. I didn't see that coming."

He smiles, removing the ring from the box. "Try this on, then. Let me know what you think. I know you have very strong feelings about the way you like things to be."

"You're just teasing me now," I say with a giggle. "It's beautiful."

"I know you've done this before, though," he hedges. "I don't know what the other one looked like. I stood in that store and worried that I was going to choose something that reminded you of him."

"It's not the same *at all*," I gush. And I mean both the ring and the man. "*Nothing* is the same. I'd be honored to be your wife."

"Lucky me," he says, standing up, leaning over the table and kissing me.

I lean in and kiss him right back. And when we break apart a moment later, the whole restaurant is watching. When Gunnar sits back down, there's some polite applause.

"Thank you, thank you!" Gunnar gives everyone a wave. "We're here all week."

"Stop," I giggle, admiring my hand. "This dinner is even more exciting than I thought it would be."

"That's every day with you, sweetheart," he says. "Especially the days when you bring home pie."

And I kick his good leg under the table.

The food is probably wonderful. I'm not sure I even bother to taste it. I'm too happy.

Gunnar asks me what kind of wedding I want, and I tell him a *small* one. "Planning a wedding is a drag. Planning a honeymoon, though? That's something I can get behind."

"Fair enough. Then that's what I want, too."

It takes me all the way to the dessert course to remember that Gunnar had three things to discuss.

"Okay, yes," he says when I prompt him. "I really don't want to kill the mood. But I also don't want any secrets between us. So I have to tell you that I learned a few new things about Saroya."

"Oh," I say softly. She disappeared the morning after Gunnar's injury, which was also the morning after she and Spalding had a huge fight. Nobody has seen her since, and there were no more strange incidents at the pie shop. But a few months ago, Gunnar asked me if he could look into her some more, and I'd said yes.

"Posy, you're not going to like what I found. It has to do with your dad."

"Oh." I gulp. My dad and I have been getting along better lately, too. "All right. What is it?"

"Saroya's mother didn't come to work at Paxton's until 1998. But in 1996, your father started paying her a monthly check. It came out of an account your father has in Grand Cayman."

"A secret bank account?" I roll my eyes. "Was he hiding money from my mother?"

"Probably."

"Okay. That's not that surprising. But why was he paying …" I think about it for a second. "Oh hell. How old is Saroya?"

"She was born in 1996."

My stomach drops. "Oh my God. You think—" I can't even say it out loud. "She's his …"

Nope. Still can't say it.

"She might be his child," Gunnar says gently. "Though DNA tests weren't as common back then. It isn't a certainty."

"But he paid her," I repeat. "So he thinks she is."

"Yeah, probably," Gunnar says quietly. "The checks stopped after Saroya turned eighteen."

"But she wanted more." My head is spinning. "My dad is rich. She thinks she got a bad deal. And she came after *me?*"

Is there any other way to explain this?

"She's angry. She wants what other people have," Gunnar says simply. "We all do, right? She just hasn't handled it very well."

"I'll say," I snort. "She might be my—" I can't say it.

"Half-sister," Gunnar supplies for me.

"But she didn't tell me that. She still tried to ruin me. It's like a Greek tragedy."

"Euripides would be impressed," he agrees.

"I mean, I feel for the girl on some level. But she got someone to throw a brick through my window."

"Allegedly," Gunnar says with a sad smile.

"No wonder the break-in makes no sense. We never considered revenge or jealousy as a motive. What *is* her motive, anyway?"

"She might need some professional help," he says. "But you'd have to feel very alone in the world to do what she did."

I take in a deep breath and blow it out. "Wow, Gunn. Just wow."

He gets up from his seat, carries his chair around the table, and deposits it next to mine. Then he sits down and pulls me into his arms. We both look out at the city lights, twinkling against the dark sky.

I lean into him and sigh. Saroya may be my half-sister. That's ... startling. And confusing.

But everything is a little less confusing with his arm around me. "I love you," I whisper.

"And I love you," he whispers back. "Sorry to blow up your brain twice in one night."

"I really enjoyed the first one."

He laughs. "I'll always be here to pick up the pieces."

I lift his hand to mine and kiss the back of it. "Thank you, Gunn."

We lapse into a comfortable silence, both of us admiring the night sky, until Gunnar says, "is that a shooting star?"

"No. That's the flight path for JFK."

He kisses me on the temple. "I just had a fun idea."

"What?" I'm not sure I can handle any more surprises tonight.

"Let's get married at Paxton's."

I let out a bark of laughter. "Oh God. Let's! Back to the scene of the crime. I wonder if my dad is still in touch with the management."

"Oh, I'll convince them. Don't you worry, Posy Paxton. I'll show you how it's done. Can I be in charge of the cocktail menu?"

"Hell no," I say before we both crack up with laughter.

THE END